Praise for Laura Lee Guhrke and
the Scandal at the Savoy Series

"The best in historical romance!"
—Julia Quinn, *New York Times* bestselling
author of the Bridgerton series

"Laura Lee Guhrke has a lively style that sizzles."
—Jane Feather, *New York Times* bestselling author

BOOKSHOP CINDERELLA

"Packed with chemistry and fun, this is a fairy-tale treat."
—*Publishers Weekly*, starred review

"It has been a while since Guhrke's last superbly written historical
romance, but her latest artfully constructed literary confection is
well worth the wait. George Bernard Shaw himself would appreciate Guhrke's clever riff on his classic, *Pygmalion*, not to mention her
sprightly prose and sparkling, champagne-fizzy wit."
—*Booklist*, starred review

"A promising start to a cheery new Victorian romance series."
—*Kirkus*

"A great mix of wit and attraction as opposites clash and romance
blooms."
—*Library Journal*

Lady Scandal

ALSO BY LAURA LEE GUHRKE

Bookshop Cinderella

Lady Scandal

LAURA LEE GUHRKE

FOREVER

New York   Boston

Forever
Hachette Book Group
1290 Avenue of the Americas, New York, NY 10104
read-forever.com

First Edition: June 2024

Forever is an imprint of Grand Central Publishing. The Forever name and logo are registered trademarks of Hachette Book Group, Inc.

The publisher is not responsible for websites (or their content) that are not owned by the publisher.

The Hachette Speakers Bureau provides a wide range of authors for speaking events. To find out more, go to hachettespeakersbureau.com or email HachetteSpeakers@hbgusa.com.

Forever books may be purchased in bulk for business, educational, or promotional use. For information, please contact your local bookseller or the Hachette Book Group Special Markets Department at special.markets@hbgusa.com.

Print book interior design by Taylor Navis

Library of Congress Cataloging-in-Publication Data has been applied for.

ISBNs: 978-1-5387-2264-0 (trade paperback), 978-1-5387-2265-7 (ebook)

Printed in the United States of America

LSC-C

Printing 1, 2024

CONTENT WARNING

This book contains references to past miscarriages and suicidal ideation.

1

London, 1898

"I cannot, Madame Comtesse. You ask the impossible."

Declarations of that sort had never bothered Lady Delia Stratham. They rolled off of her like water off a duck's back. "And that surprises you?" she replied, giving the man opposite her a wink. "But, Michel, you know the impossible is my favorite thing."

The lithe young Frenchman on the other side of the worktable did not respond to that bit of raillery the way she'd hoped. Instead of a good-natured laugh, he heaved a sigh. "I tell you it cannot be done."

Despite having heard those exact words from two other members of the hotel staff already this morning with similar results, Delia refused to be deterred. She gave the Savoy's head florist her most winning smile, one that usually disarmed even the most intransigent opponent. "But, darling," she began.

Michel cut her off with an outburst of French so rapid that even Delia, fluent in that language since the age of seven, had a hard time following it. Something about how he was not a miracle worker, nor was he a tennis ball to be batted about, and how he wished that the managers of the Savoy would make up their minds what they wanted. Concluding his tirade with a few choice curses, he seized a pair of pruning shears and a handful of red dogwood twigs from the worktable between them and began lopping off the ends with alarming savagery.

Delia studied him, at a loss on how to proceed. Charm and wit had always been her two greatest talents. They had not only captivated three husbands and garnered Delia an abundance of loyal friends, but had also inspired César Ritz, manager of London's Savoy Hotel, to offer her a job. The famous hotelier's unconventional decision had shocked society, but it had proven to be a godsend for Delia in the wake of her third husband's death, and in the five years since, it had also been a shining success for the hotel.

Today, however, Delia wasn't feeling like much of a success.

First, Escoffier, the hotel's famous head chef, had gone into a flaming rage at her simple inquiry as to why the napkins in the restaurant were no longer being folded into swan shapes. He, too, had unleashed a torrent of angry French at her, rattling off a diatribe against the new regime and their spies—whatever that meant—and declared he could not work amid these constant interrogations. She should, Delia was told, talk to Ritz, and he had nothing more to say. He had then marched off to take the remainder of his anger out on his sous-chef, and a bewildered Delia had tactfully retreated, tabling any questions about the swans for another day.

Then had come Mrs. Bates. Having lost her lady's maid to one of Paris's most renowned houses of haute couture during her recent visit to that city, Delia had asked Mrs. Bates if the hotel could provide her with a maid from the hotel staff until she could hire a new one of her own. The Savoy's head of housekeeping had responded to this seemingly innocuous inquiry by bursting into tears and declaring the "new way" (whatever that was) impossible. Then she had ducked into the nearest washroom and slammed the door in Delia's bewildered face.

And now, here she was again, with another resentful employee on her hands. This time, however, was the most surprising of all. Escoffier, though cerebral and methodical by nature, had sometimes been known to fly off the handle, and Mrs. Bates had always been a dear old curmudgeon who often required a generous amount of buttering up to soothe her injured feelings. But Michel?

She stared at the lithe, mustachioed young man on the other side of the worktable, at a loss how to reply, wondering what on earth had happened during her month in Paris. Like Escoffier, Michel DuPont was brilliantly artistic and usually eager to embrace even Delia's wildest flights of fancy. But also like his fellow Frenchman, Michel was proving uncharacteristically intractable this morning.

Delia took a deep breath and tried again.

"Dearest Michel, I don't understand," she said, also speaking in French, hoping that conversing in his native language would help calm him down a bit. "We went over our designs for the new bouquets before I left town. Early tulips, narcissi, and hyacinths from January to March, lilacs and peonies for April and May, and roses and hydrangeas through the summer. It was all quite fixed, I thought."

The florist stopped attacking the dogwood stems and looked up with a scowl. "Oh, what a difference a few weeks can make."

Delia repressed a sigh at this unhelpful response. "So I'm discovering," she muttered. "But *why*? What's happened in my absence that has you making the new arrangements with all the same blooms we've been seeing since October?"

"They aren't all the same," he muttered, gesturing to the bouquets currently under discussion that were lined up on a shelf behind him, ready to be placed throughout the Savoy's long, elegant foyer. "I put mahonia in with the bay leaves and dogwood. The yellow does make a difference, no?"

"Does it?" She studied the line of bouquets in last season's milk glass vases without enthusiasm. "I'm inclined to doubt. Dearest, you know it's important at this time of year to show our guests that spring is just around the corner, but when I look at these arrangements, I have the impulse to wrap myself in a blanket, sit by a fire, and roast some chestnuts. I know your creative mind, Michel," she added as he groaned. "I know you would never do this if you didn't have a good reason. What's happened while I've been away? It must be something catastrophic," she went on when he didn't reply, "for you are not the only one out of sorts today. So tell me what is going on?"

He paused in his task, looking up. "I'm surprised you don't already know. You usually know everything, *Madame*."

Apparently not. "I arrived back from Paris very late last night," she reminded. "Just what am I supposed to know?"

"No, no," Michel replied at once, shaking his head. "If you do not know, I shall not be the one to inform you. Go to your office and read your correspondence, then you will see."

"And have Madelaine herald my return with a stack of letters that need answering in one hand and her shorthand notebook in the other? I can't, Michel," she added as he opened his mouth to respond. "Truly, I can't. Not before luncheon. And since I'm right here in front of you, why don't you simply tell me why you've changed your mind about the flowers we chose?"

"Very well, if you must know." He flung up his head, shaking back his hair like an angry young thoroughbred. "It is the expense."

Delia blinked, so astonished she couldn't think how to reply. In the five years since Ritz had hired her to work for him at the Savoy, never had she been expected to consider expenses. "I don't understand."

"Forced bulbs are very costly. And the new vases of cut crystal you wanted—they are expensive, too, *Madame*."

Delia couldn't help a laugh. "Well, of course they're expensive, darling! This is the Savoy, after all. We don't do anything on the cheap."

"Not until now."

Delia frowned, growing more confounded by the moment. "What on earth does that mean?"

"During your absence, every department was ordered to submit a budget for the year."

"A budget?" As she repeated the words, Delia thought of Escoffier and Mrs. Bates, and began to get an inkling of what was making everyone so cross today. But what had prompted this notion of budgets? Surely not Ritz. Extravagance was that man's middle name. Michel spoke again, however, before she could inquire.

"Since you were not here, I was asked to make a budget for the flowers. I did, based on what you and I had discussed, and I was immediately told to reduce it by 20 percent." He tossed down the pruning shears with a thud. "Twenty percent? What am I? A worker of miracles?"

"But who would—"

"I explained that the only way I could do what he asked was to buy whatever late blooms the flower sellers had left from their winter inventory."

"And Ritz found that acceptable? I don't believe it. He knows better than anyone the importance of seasonal flowers to the hotel's ambience. He would never expect you to settle for last season's leftovers. Never."

Michel waved his hand impatiently in the air. "It is not Ritz of whom I speak. Ritz has gone to Italy."

"Italy? But when he was leaving Paris, he told me he was coming back to London."

"And he did, but then he left again. Some catastrophe has arisen at the new hotel in Rome. If he were here, perhaps none of this would be happening."

"But what of Echenard? He would never make such a decision, either."

"Echenard does not matter. He has been overruled; you comprehend?"

Delia did not comprehend anything. At this point, she was completely at sea. "But Echenard is Ritz's second-in-command, and I am third. Who could possibly—"

The bell over the front entrance of the shop jangled, interrupting her, and Michel glanced past her, looking through the open doorway of the workroom to see who had entered his domain.

Delia, however, had no intention of allowing him to be diverted from the crisis at hand. "Michel, I don't understand any of this. No one but Ritz or Echenard has the authority to countermand my instructions."

"Someone does, *Madame*," he mumbled, shifting his weight from one foot to the other as he looked at her again. "Now, someone does."

All this ambiguity was beginning to make her as frustrated as everyone else. "Michel, for heaven's sake, stop talking in riddles and tell me what's going on! What prize idiot decided it was a good idea to turn our lovely spring bouquets into winter's last gasp?"

"The prize idiot in question," a deep male voice behind her replied in carefully enunciated, painfully bad French, "would be me."

Delia turned to find a man standing in the doorway of the florist's workroom—a man so attractive, she knew she'd never seen him before. From the moment she had first put on a party dress, pinned up her hair, and danced a waltz with a boy, Delia had noticed and appreciated the members of the sterner sex, especially the attractive ones. Had she ever met this man before, or even met his eyes across a room, she'd have remembered the encounter.

He was exceptionally tall, for one thing—tall enough that he topped her five-foot, eight-inch frame by a good six inches. His wide shoulders filled the doorway, tapering to narrow hips and long legs, making him such an ideal example of the male physique that her thoroughly feminine heart skipped a beat.

Her gaze skimmed back up, past his expensive, well-cut morning coat and precisely knotted necktie to his face, noting a splendid square jaw, a pair of chiseled cheekbones, and a perfect Roman nose—strong features well suited to his athletic body. His eyes were green, the gray green of hoarfrost on a winter's day, but his hair was the warm, tawny gold of a wheat field in summer.

Delia stirred, turning completely around to face him. "My, my," she murmured, her natural feminine instincts stirring in the face of such splendid masculinity. "And just who are you?"

He bowed. "Simon Hayden, Viscount Calderon, at your service. You, I can only assume," he added as he straightened, "are the notorious Lady Stratham I've been hearing so much about."

Given that rather unflattering description, Delia wondered what exactly he might have heard about her. "Heavens," she said, working to keep her voice light, "my reputation precedes me."

"It does, indeed."

At this incisive reply, his attractiveness fell a notch in Delia's estimation. He seemed quite a cold fish.

What a waste, she thought, repressing a sigh as she cast a quick, wistful glance over his splendid body.

When she returned her gaze to his face, she saw that he was studying her as well, though his eyes were devoid of any discernible emotion. He said nothing, and as the silence lengthened, Delia began to feel like a butterfly on a pin under his unwavering stare. She refused to show any discomfiture, however. A woman had her pride.

"A pleasure to make your acquaintance," she said at last, using English in hope that he would do the same, thereby sparing him any need to continue in French, a language he was clearly uncomfortable with. "You've met Michel already, it seems, so now that we all know each other, Lord Calderon, do tell me what has inspired your interest in the affairs of the Savoy Hotel, particularly those that come under my purview?"

One corner of his mouth curved upward a notch, though it could hardly be called a smile. "You think I'm pushing in where I have no business?"

She smiled sweetly. "The thought did cross my mind."

"Then allow me to reassure you. I have an interest in the affairs of the Savoy because I am a member of the hotel's board of directors."

"What?" She couldn't help a laugh, for she was already acquainted with every member of the board, and she knew he wasn't among them. "Since when?"

"Since three weeks ago, Lady Stratham, when I acquired a substantial share of Savoy stock and was appointed as the board's newest member."

Delia stirred at that piece of news, suddenly uneasy. "I see."

"As to what has impelled my interference," he went on, "the power to do so has been bestowed upon me by a unanimous vote of the other members of the board. They have authorized me to study every facet of the hotel and its current practices and make whatever changes I see fit so that things might run more efficiently."

Dumbfounded, it took her several moments to think of a reply. "But Ritz is the general manager. Is that not his job?"

"Ritz has already agreed to give his full cooperation to my efforts."

"And if what you choose to do should go against his wishes?"

"Ritz's preferences," he said with a shrug, "must take second place to what is necessary."

With that dismissive reply, Delia knew just why everyone she'd encountered this morning was so touchy and out of sorts. Before she could speculate as to just how many other hotel employees this man had upset while she'd been in Paris, he spoke again.

"I sent you and every other head of staff a memorandum upon my appointment," he said, "introducing myself, explaining the situation, and requesting a meeting to discuss the changes that need to be made in each department for the coming year. As of this morning, you are the only one with whom I have not met."

Was he implying that she'd been negligent in her duties? "I've been away," she said, grimacing at the defensive note of her own voice.

"Yes, in Paris; I was told." His eyes narrowed a fraction. "Jaunting about on Ritz's behalf."

Choosing the decorations for the Parisian hotel Ritz was opening could hardly be considered a mere jaunt, but there was no point in saying so. "And what a pleasurable interlude it was, too," she said with an exaggerated sigh of rapture. "Paris is always so delightful, even at this time of year."

"I daresay."

Paris clearly held no charms for him, a fact that did not surprise her in the least. Resisting the impulse to needle him by waxing rhapsodic about the City of Light's witty salons, romantic cafés, and naughty cabaret shows, she said instead, "I was doing work for Ritz's hotel there."

"Ritz's own hotel, yes, quite so. Though I believe your entire salary is paid by the Savoy."

Delia stiffened, the last shred of his masculine appeal fading irretrievably away. "Just what are you implying, Lord Calderon?"

"I shall be happy to answer that question, Lady Stratham, and any others you may have in the meeting with you that I have already requested. Shall we say two o'clock this afternoon?"

"So sorry, but I have an engagement at two o'clock," she was happy to inform him. "In fact, my appointment diary is full for the entire day."

"Is it? So is mine, with one exception at two o'clock. Please rearrange your schedule so that we can meet at that time."

Such high-handedness made Delia bristle, and though her engagements today could easily be rearranged, she saw no reason to reward his arrogance by doing so. Besides, she had no intention of meeting with him until she had cabled Ritz in Rome and learned the true facts of the situation. Stalling, she decided, was her best option.

"You seem quite a busy man, Lord Calderon," she said, mustering all the charm in her arsenal, "and I should hate to see you waste your time, so let me assure you that a meeting between us is not at all necessary. I have always managed to do my job quite well without the assistance of any member of the board."

He gave a pointed cough. "Not as well as you might think, I'm sorry to say."

Those ominous words caused her uneasiness to deepen, but before she could ask what he meant, he spoke again. "After studying the fourth-quarter financial reports, the board feels that sweeping changes need to be made throughout the hotel. Your duties will be profoundly impacted by those changes and, given the fact that you have been gone so long, time is now of the essence—hence, my insistence upon a meeting today. If you would bring an estimate of your expenditures for the current year, that would be most helpful to our discussions."

Even if she chose to meet with him this afternoon—which was by no means a certainty, despite his presumptions on the matter—she wasn't about to spend the next four hours in the agony of suspense. "What sorts of 'sweeping changes' is the board thinking to make?" she asked.

"For a start, you will no longer be reporting to either Mr. Ritz or Mr. Echenard. The honor of being in charge of you now falls to me," he added with a most unflattering lack of enthusiasm.

"You?" Delia stared at him, appalled.

He seemed to perceive her feelings. "I see that you relish the prospect as much as I," he said dryly. "Still, there is little either of us can do about it. The deed is done."

Those words felt like a gauntlet thrown down, and Delia stiffened, bailing on charm—which was clearly wasted here—and readying herself to do battle. "Oh, is it really?"

"The board feels that the majority of your duties, particularly the events you arrange on behalf of the hotel for various clients, need to be managed with greater oversight than has been exercised in the past."

"Greater oversight?" she echoed. "Are you saying that I have been cavalier in such matters?"

His frost-tinted gaze slid past her, then back again, reminding her they were not alone. "This is hardly the appropriate place to discuss it. When you come to my office this afternoon, I will be happy to explain the situation—"

"Your office?" she interrupted in shocked surprise. "You have an office? Here in the hotel?"

"I do, yes. Right by your own, as a matter of fact."

This situation was growing worse with each passing moment. "So you're to be my nanny, is that it?"

He gave her a wintry smile. "I prefer to say that the board feels

Ritz is stretched much too thin to oversee your duties, and that both he and you would benefit from some outside supervision over your position, and those who report to you."

Delia couldn't imagine what had happened to bring about the board's concerns about her or this man's interference, but she had no illusions that any of it would be to her benefit. And as she envisioned working for this ice block of a man, she realized with a sick sense of dismay that her dream job had just become a nightmare.

2

She wasn't quite what he'd been expecting.

In his interactions with the hotel staff during the past few weeks, Simon had heard the name of Lady Stratham with tiresome regularity, usually during apologetic explanations as to why his ideas would be difficult to implement. In addition, Helen Carte, the wife of the Savoy Hotel's founder, had already told him quite a bit about the countess—that Ritz adored her; that she was a cousin of the Duke of Westbourne; that upon her launch into society many years ago, she'd been deemed one of the most outrageous and fascinating debutantes of the season; and that in the years since then, she had managed to make three most advantageous marriages, first to the son of a marquess, then to a French count, and, lastly, to a Scottish earl.

Helen suspected her of far worse sins than marrying well, and though Simon's first cursory examination of her expense accounts had revealed nothing definite to confirm those suspicions, the carelessness he had found in the countess's bookkeeping certainly made any fraud she might be committing easier to obscure. And even if she was innocent of any wrongdoing, the heedlessness with which she dispensed Savoy funds had taken Simon's breath away. No wonder Ritz adored her. She was his perfect protégé.

As a result of all this, the image formed in Simon's mind was of an outrageously flamboyant creature swathed in jewels and furs, whose once-captivating beauty had surely faded with time, whose cheeks now needed a touch of rouge to maintain their youthful blush, whose hair was streaked with gray, and whose figure required sturdy corsetry to overcome the inevitable weight gain of midlife.

Never had he imagined a slim, youthful woman with creamy skin, raven-black hair, and a piquant, heart-shaped face that made her seem more like an ingenue than a widow who'd buried three husbands.

How, he wondered, staring into a pair of enormous, indigo-blue eyes fringed by thick black lashes, had a woman so young managed to marry three times? He could only conclude she'd wasted little time mourning the demise of each husband before moving on to the next one.

It was also obvious, from this conversation with her and from those he'd had with other members of the hotel staff, that the countess was unaccustomed to being gainsaid—indulged and pampered her entire life, he'd wager, with not a single person to check her.

Until now.

She seemed to read the thoughts passing through his mind, and as he watched that pointed chin of hers lift a notch, he knew he'd have his work cut out for him in the days to come.

"As I already explained," she said, her voice bringing him back to the discussion at hand, "I am engaged all afternoon, and I am not in the habit of breaking engagements."

Her title and position aside, she was his subordinate, and he could not allow her to dictate the terms under which she would work, especially not in front of another employee. Best to make that clear straightaway, he decided. "One broken engagement is hardly a habit," he said, "so I suggest you notify the other party as soon as possible that something has arisen requiring you to reschedule."

"The 'something' in this case being you?"

"Just so. Unless," he added, offering the opportunity for compromise, "you would prefer to meet with me now? If Monsieur DuPont does not mind, of course." He leaned around her to give the florist an inquiring glance. "Would postponing our consultation until two o'clock be acceptable to you, Monsieur?"

Lady Stratham made a smothered sound at his address to the florist, and Simon—aware the word had come out sounding like *mon-sewer*—cursed himself for not having practiced his French more often as a boy.

Much to Simon's relief, however, Monsieur DuPont merely shrugged in the wake of this butchery of his native language and spread his hands in an expansive Gallic gesture, which Simon took to be an affirmative answer to his question.

"Excellent. I will return at that time." Turning his attention back to the woman before him, Simon gestured to the door. "It seems a space has opened in my schedule, Lady Stratham. And since you are clearly free as well, shall we take advantage of the moment and adjourn to my office?"

She looked as if she'd rather be tortured on the rack, but thankfully, she made no further objections and preceded him through the doorway of the florist's workroom. They did not converse as they crossed the long expanse of the hotel foyer to the other end and traveled the corridor where offices for the heads of staff were located. Passing hers, he entered his, expecting her to follow, but instead, she paused in the doorway, looking shocked.

"What happened to Madelaine?" she demanded, halting in the doorway. "This is her office, not yours."

Another thing for her to resent him for, he thought wryly as he circled his desk. "If you are referring to Mrs. Alverson," he replied, turning to face her, "she was let go."

"Let go?" the countess echoed, her elegantly arched brows drawing together in a frown. "Let go by whom?"

"By me, I'm afraid. You see—"

"You sacked my secretary," she interrupted through clenched teeth, "and took over her office?"

Simon met her resentful gaze with an imperturbable one of his own. "My obligation is to the Savoy shareholders, and that obligation requires responsible fiscal management. Eliminating unneeded staff is one of the best ways to increase efficiency, which is my primary task. And since this office became empty with Mrs. Alverson's departure, yes, my secretary and I have moved into it."

She glanced at the second desk in the crowded room, empty at the present moment, then looked at him again, a smile on her lips that did not reach her eyes. "How delightful to know that one of us, at least, still has a secretary," she murmured, her voice a purr. "But tell me," she added before he could reply, "just how does it increase efficiency to not consult me before deciding my secretary was one of the unneeded?"

Her voice trembled as she asked the question, revealing the anger behind it.

He couldn't blame her for that; he'd feel the same. No one liked being undermined, but it had been unavoidable under the circumstances. Still, given Helen's suspicions and his own observations thus far, he could not allow himself to be swayed by anyone's hurt feelings. "Had you been here, I would have informed you of my decision and why it was made," he began. "But—"

"You couldn't have had the courtesy to wait for my return?"

Interrupted for the third time since making her acquaintance, he could have pointed out that courtesy went both ways, but he refrained. "Obviously not," he said instead.

The hostility she displayed had become familiar to Simon these past three weeks. During that time, the other heads of staff had made it quite plain that their loyalty was to Ritz, Escoffier, Echenard, and Lady Stratham, and that he was an interloper. Some resentment was inevitable, but in this case, he was hampered by the staff's loyalty to Ritz, and also, oddly enough, by his title.

Because of his low birth and recent elevation to the peerage, many of the staff here considered him not as a lord, but as a poseur, his title nothing more than a bad joke. While he might secretly agree with them about that, he could not afford to show it. And respect, he well knew, had to be earned. But as he studied the resentment in the face of the woman before him, he also appreciated that earning that respect and straightening out the mess the Savoy had become were going to be far more difficult than he'd originally anticipated. He was beginning to feel like Hercules cleaning the Augean Stables.

Still, the difficulties did not matter.

Helen and Richard Carte had asked for his help, and he would have cut off his right arm rather than refuse to give it. He owed them more than he could ever repay. His own father's petty thefts and subsequent suicide fifteen years ago had devastated his mother, cost her her job, and tainted her good name. In the army and stationed in Africa, he'd been unable to be of much help, and if it hadn't been for Richard Carte, there was no telling what might have happened to his mother and his sister, Cassandra. Few people knew about his father's disgrace, and most of those who did had long ago forgotten, but Simon would never forget. His father's legacy of dishonesty and cowardice was one he was determined to destroy, not only for himself, but also for his sister's sake. Richard and the other members of the board had put their trust in him despite his father's criminal history, and he could not fail them.

"It's a complicated situation, Lady Stratham," he said at last, gesturing to the chair opposite his desk. "Please come in and sit down, and I will explain it as best I can. You can stand if you like, of course," he added pleasantly when she didn't move, "but with the full and fatiguing day you've indicated you have ahead of you, I'd have thought you would wish to sit while you can."

When she continued to hesitate, he pulled out his own chair and sat down, defying the protocol of always waiting for a lady to sit first, and reached for the manila folder containing his notes about her. He paused, opened the folder, and looked up at her again. "It's up to you."

She seemed to perceive the challenge behind his mild words. With a toss of her head, she came into his office and crossed to his desk. "I fear the most fatiguing aspect of my day shall prove to be you," she said making a rueful face as she sank into the offered chair opposite him.

"Whether that proves true rather depends on you."

"Does it?" she countered. "I seem to have little control over things within my purview, including my own staff, since you appeared on the scene."

"If you are referring to Mrs. Alverson," he began, but she shook her head.

"Not only her. I was also thinking of Michel, whose artistic sensibilities you've offended with your notions about his floral arrangements."

"I expect he'll recover."

If she perceived the dryness of that reply, she didn't show it. "And Mrs. Bates? The poor woman is cranky as a bear this morning, and I can only assume that is also because of you and your interference."

"Change is always upsetting."

"Especially when that change is not done through the proper channels. I can appreciate that you have a job to do—though what has precipitated it, I can't imagine. Nonetheless, protocol would dictate that you take your findings and recommendations to Ritz or

Echenard. They would then discuss them with me or with Escoffier, and we would discuss them with our own members of staff, deciding what to do with their help and cooperation. That's how things are handled here at the Savoy."

Simon rubbed a hand over his forehead, repressing the sound of exasperation that hovered on his lips, fearing that if he heard the prim, stonewalling little phrase "That's not quite how we do it here" one more time, he was going to put his head through a wall.

"Given that you now report to me, not to Ritz," he said aloud, "the protocol you describe is no longer relevant. And," he added before she could reply, "we can sit here all morning debating how the Savoy used to do things, but that would be a waste of time, since many of those procedures will be changing in the weeks ahead."

"Seems they've been changing quite a bit already."

"And will continue to do so. I suggest you accept the situation with as much grace as you can muster."

"Ritz has been a successful hotel manager for many years. Isn't it rather arrogant to assume you've got a better way than he does?"

"Hardly," he shot back, "given the abysmal lack of proper management I've been seeing here ever since my arrival."

The moment the words were out of his mouth, he wished he could take them back. Ritz, though he didn't know it, was in a precarious position, as were many other members of the hotel staff, including the woman before him. Profits had been eroding steadily during the past year, and when a detailed, damning anonymous letter had reached the board's attention last autumn—accusing Ritz, Echenard, and Escoffier of a slew of abuses—the members had voted to launch a secret investigation.

For months, private detectives had been secretly following those named in the letter and delving into the accusations mentioned by the author. The results so far had borne out the truth of those accusations, uncovering improprieties, foolish extravagance, and questionable decisions at every level. Worse, there were clear indications of fraud on a massive scale. As a result, the board had brought in Simon to supervise an audit of the finances, clear out the corruption, and put the hotel back on a profitable track.

As the owner of several hotels himself, hotels he'd salvaged from the wreckage of bankruptcy, he was uniquely qualified to handle this assignment. But, although he had gladly agreed to help the Cartes and he welcomed the challenge and opportunities this project afforded him, he could not say he relished the secrecy required here. He loathed subterfuge. It went against his nature.

"Let's not allow ourselves to be distracted from the matter at hand," he said, reminding himself sternly that discretion was the order of the day. "This meeting is not to discuss Ritz or the quality of his management. We are here to talk about you."

"My favorite subject." Her voice was light, her dimpled smile careless as she leaned back in her chair, but he could tell her ease of manner was a pose. There was unmistakable tensity in the set of her shoulders and in the tendons along her slender throat that told him she was nervous.

She should be.

She had not been mentioned in the anonymous letter, and no actual evidence had been uncovered against her yet, but the investigation was far from complete. Helen, however, was convinced of her guilt, and though that opinion seemed to stem mainly from the countess's long-standing friendship with Ritz, it could be enough to see her dismissed. Simon, however, knew better than anyone the damage that could be done from guilt by association, and until actual malfeasance was uncovered against the countess, he was prepared to keep an open mind.

"During the fourth-quarter shareholders' meeting a few weeks ago," he said, giving her the same speech he'd already given the other hotel managers and staff, "the investors in the Savoy were informed that they would not be receiving a dividend because the hotel's profits had plummeted again, falling 25 percent during the past year alone. Some areas have fallen even further and are barely paying expenses. The restaurant is currently operating at a loss."

"What?" She stared at him in astonishment. "But that can't be. We're busier than we've ever been. The restaurant is packed every night of the week. Even though it's only mid-January, the hotel is nearly full. I've got a dozen banquets and luncheons scheduled during the coming three months, and at least three dozen more over the course of the season." She shook her head, laughing a little. "How could hotel profits be declining?"

She seemed so confounded that Simon was taken aback. The letter had detailed a culture of corruption from top to bottom, one bolstered at every turn by the investigations of the private detectives. Even Lady Stratham's own secretary had been caught with her hand in the till. Even if the countess was innocent, Simon was hard-pressed to believe she was unaware of what the others were doing. As Michel DuPont had said, she seemed to know everything that went on here.

"Are you sure," she said, the sound of her voice bringing him back to the business at hand, "the hotel's accountants haven't made some sort of mistake?"

"Deloitte, Dever, Griffiths & Co. is a sound and reputable accounting firm. They are not in the habit of making mistakes. But on the infinitesimal chance that such a thing might have occurred, my first action has been to order a full forensic audit, which Mr. Dever is now conducting under my supervision."

"But why you? You're a peer, not an accountant."

"True, but I am a peer with a great deal of experience in matters of business."

"A peer with a head for business?" Her mouth curved, showing a glimmer of humor. "That's a bit of a unicorn."

More than a bit, he thought with a grimace. Since his elevation to the peerage a few months ago, he'd spent most of his time feeling like some sort of bizarre curiosity. He was the son of a hotel maid and a dishonest hotel cashier. His Harrow education had been obtained by scholarship, not by the privilege of a rich, titled family. His wealth had come by hard work and sound investments, not by inheritance. She, on the other hand, had been born into privilege and wealth, and possessed an aristocratic lineage that dated back to William the Conqueror.

"Perhaps it is out of the common way," he allowed, "but it is not unheard of for a man with a title to have an understanding of finance."

For some reason, that made her laugh. "Most of the boys I grew up with weren't taught anything as useful as accounting at school, but maybe your school was different?"

He knew what she was really asking, and it nettled him. "Harrow," he supplied. "That's what you wanted to know, wasn't it? After all, knowing where a man went to school is the easiest way to determine if he's the right sort or the wrong sort."

"That has nothing to do with my question," she said with an air of offended dignity he found highly suspect. "I was merely curious. But if you were at Harrow, perhaps you know my cousin, the Duke of Westbourne?"

"No," he answered, thinking of those long-ago days at school. "I have met your cousin, yes, but that was only a few weeks ago. We never met at school. He was two years behind me, I believe."

He didn't add that even if he and Westbourne had met, it probably wouldn't have mattered, since the sons of the wealthy peers had avoided scholarship students as if they had the plague. "As for my knowledge of finance," he said instead, "I acquired that by experience, along with my knowledge of hotels. I own three of my own and have substantial shares in five others, in addition to my stake in the Savoy."

"Oh."

She blinked, seeming disconcerted by this information, and Simon was human enough to take a bit of satisfaction in that. "To return to the point, the hotel is bleeding money," he said. "My task is to make any changes necessary to reverse this downward spiral. The investors fully expect a dividend at the end of the first quarter, and I intend to see that they get it."

He didn't tell her all that was also a very effective cover for the fraud investigation.

"And paying dividends to already wealthy investors is worth eliminating people's livelihoods?" she countered. "It's worth turning everything upside down and setting the staff's collective teeth on edge as they wait to learn if they are among the unneeded?"

"If the hotel cannot become profitable, it will go out of business and put every person here out of a job. If the Savoy is to survive, there must be proper resource allocation in every department." He reached for a file on his desk and opened it. "Which brings us, Lady Stratham, to you."

"All right, then." She straightened in her chair, assuming an impudent expression. "What's it to be? From the merciless look on your face, my guess is a firing squad at sunset. Or perhaps the gallows at dawn. I just hope I'm allowed a cigarette first."

Giving her a wry look in response, he pulled a sheet from the file. "The first thing we need to discuss is your operating budget."

She looked at him as if he had suddenly started speaking an unknown language. "My what?"

He found her bewilderment—not the first such response he'd seen during the past few weeks—aggravating as hell. For God's sake, he thought, did no one employed here understand the concept of profit and loss? "Your budget, Lady Stratham," he said, striving for patience. "Even a lady such as yourself must surely know what a budget is?"

"Why, yes," she drawled, but the dangerous narrowing of her eyes belied the careless lightness of her reply. "Even my poor, muddled feminine mind can comprehend the concept of a budget."

Simon, recalling the outrageous amounts billed to her expense account, was doubtful. "My question was not a belittling of your sex nor an indictment of your brain's ability. Rather, it stems from your profligate spending habits." He looked down, scanning the column of figures he'd jotted down in preparation for this discussion, then looked up again. "According to your expense diaries—"

"You went through my expense diaries?" she cut in, her voice rising. "The ones I keep in my desk? My *locked* desk?"

"Well, yes." He assumed an expression of mock regret. "Your desk will need a new lock, I'm afraid."

"I don't suppose you could have bothered to cable me in Paris and ask my permission before destroying my desk and going through my things?"

That would have put her on her guard were she guilty of any wrongdoing. "Not really," he said with a shrug. "Why?" Tensing, he leaned forward, watching her closely. "Was there something in your desk that wouldn't bear public scrutiny?"

"Of course not," she answered at once, "since I keep the letters from all my lovers in my suite upstairs."

If she was hoping to shock him, she was disappointed. Married three times, she was no innocent miss, after all. And even Simon could not deny that she was remarkably beautiful. Scanning her face, with its delicate features and thickly lashed dark blue eyes, he could well believe she had dozens of lovers.

"A very wise proceeding," he said gravely. "But while we are on the subject of your suite upstairs, it's paid for by the hotel, I understand?"

"Yes." Her face took on a wary expression. "The hotel allots me a room as part of my compensation. Why?"

"Your employment contract specifies a room, but not a suite. You'll have to move."

"You're such a harbinger of joy, aren't you, Calderon? Rather like cholera."

"Suites are a valuable commodity to the hotel," he went on, ignoring her comparison of him to a fatal disease. "We can't have a member of staff staying for free in one of the hotel's most desired rooms when those rooms can be let to the public for profit."

"Then I'll have the difference subtracted from my salary. With your permission, of course?" she added, her voice dripping with sweetness.

"That would be an acceptable alternative," he said. "By the way, I understand from Mrs. Bates that you have requested a hotel maid to act as your lady's maid? If so," he added as she nodded, "the hotel will be required to bill you for that service."

"I'm now paying to have a suite, but I don't suppose it would do me any good to remind you that suite guests are allowed maid and valet services at no charge?"

"No good whatsoever," he agreed with cheer, "since guests pay for those services now. All hotel maids and footmen are now required to report any and all tasks they do for suite guests to bookkeeping, just as they do for all the other guests who stay here. All tips, of course, will remain in place."

"How generous."

He ignored the sarcasm and returned his attention to his notes. "We've been far too generous, to my mind. Free valets, free maids, complimentary bottles of champagne to suite guests upon checking in, more free champagne to the tables—" He broke off, biting back any disparagement of Ritz's generosity in dispensing free wine from the

Savoy's cellars to the hotel's aristocratic clientele and began again. "As I was saying, the expenses for your department have been...lavish, to say the least. Thousands of pounds on flowers alone."

"I take it you are not one of those who believes in the axiom about flowers being as important to one's table as the bread?"

"Anyone who subscribes to that particular axiom has never been hungry," he countered without looking up. "Now—"

"Have you?" she interrupted. "Ever been hungry, I mean?"

He tensed, casting his mind back to the days of his childhood when his parents' meager wages had not stretched far enough, the periods when he had been pulled out of school to run errands for wealthy hotel guests in exchange for tips so his parents could make the rent on their lodgings. "Yes," he said brusquely. "I have. Now, might we return to the subject at hand?"

She made an exaggerated gesture of acquiescence in reply, and he continued. "I see that last year you acquired new paintings for the foyer, ordered new livery for the bellboys, and redecorated all the suites?"

"My dear man, those things had to be done. Bellboys *grow*, you know. Do you want them walking around in trousers that make them look like powder monkeys in the British navy? Or perhaps we should just sack them when they outgrow their uniforms and hire a fresh lot of smaller boys? As for the suites, the drapes were silk, which rots in the sunlight. They had to be replaced. The sheets were beginning to yellow, the mattresses were lumpy, and some of the settees still had the same hideously ugly upholstery from the hotel's opening. And the paintings?" She shuddered. "Ghastly."

The question of her honesty aside, he began to appreciate other reasons why Helen—who had chosen the upholstery, drapes, and paintings in question—didn't like her.

"Surely," she went on, her enormous eyes widening even further, "you wouldn't want the guests who stay in those precious suites of ours to sleep on lumpy mattresses with yellowing sheets and rotting drapes, would you?"

"Of course not. But expenses such as the ones you mention cannot be made on the spur of the moment. They need to be projected before the fiscal year begins. That is why a budget is necessary, particularly for you, since your department is not bringing in enough revenue to offset what you've been spending."

"That's not true!" she cried, bounding in her chair. "I bring in heaps of revenue. I am responsible for planning the banquets, the parties, and all the other events we hold here. People pay 25 percent above cost for those events, you know."

"Do they pay?" he countered, referring again to his notes. "The Marquess of Ravenlea held a dinner party last autumn for forty guests. The bill came to nearly six hundred pounds, a bill that—if the accountant's audits can be trusted—the good marquess never paid."

She grimaced. "Well, yes, that does sometimes happen, I'm afraid."

"It happens with nauseating regularity—so often, in fact, that because of it, your department has not made a profit in over two years. But," he added, attempting to soften the blow, "if it makes you feel better, you are not alone. Every department brings in too little and spends too much, hence my request for a budget from every member of management. I realize that you were not here to comply with my request, but time is of the essence if we are to pay a dividend at the end of March. So…"

He paused to pull a second sheet out of the file before him. "I took the liberty of drawing up a budget for you," he said, handing it to her across the desk.

"How thoughtful," she murmured with a smile that could have melted stone, but only a fool would have thought it genuine. "Your experience with hotel management must be vast indeed for you to predict how many parties I shall be arranging over the course of the year."

"My calculations are based on the reservations already made as well as your figures from last year."

She glanced down at the sheet in her hand. "Our revenue is likely to be much higher than this," she objected, looking up. "Your estimates are far too low."

His estimates were low for a reason. Within weeks, the investigation should be finished, and it was likely that Ritz would be gone, along with Escoffier, Echenard, and many others. Though in the long term, everything at the Savoy would come right, he could not predict what the result of their departure would be in the short term. Ritz and Escoffier were widely revered, not only by the staff, but also by the Savoy's wealthy clientele. Firing them would upset a great many people.

"Possibly," he conceded. "But I'd rather err on the side of caution. To that end, you and I will be meeting each month to discuss the expenses and revenue for your department."

"Yes, without you to rein me in, who knows what I'll do?" She leaned forward, adopting a confidential manner. "Why, without your guidance and sage wisdom, I might go completely off the rails and do something wild. Like buy new stair carpets or something."

Her past spending made her going off the rails quite likely without a firm hand to check her, but pointing that out would only increase her animosity, so he refrained.

"Speaking of my guidance and sage wisdom," he said instead as he pulled another sheet from the folder on his desk, "I have compiled a list of procedures and practices that might help you in running your department more efficiently."

"Goodness," she replied, taking the offered sheet. "Keep doing this, Lord Calderon, and I shall become so efficient, I shall have nothing to do all day but put my feet up and eat bonbons." She glanced at the list, then set it on the desk, along with the budget he'd made for her. "You're remarkably sure of yourself for someone who's only been here three weeks. Perhaps it's a bit premature to be offering me recommendations?"

"I've been here quite long enough to note the wanton extravagance displayed by every department of this hotel, especially yours."

His accusation merely seemed to amuse her. "But, my dear man," she said, laughing, "this is the *Savoy*. Wanton extravagance is how we do it."

"You mean that's how you used to do it," he countered, thinking that if he had a pound for every time he'd uttered that phrase during the past few weeks, paying a dividend to the investors would be easy. "Believe me or not, Lady Stratham, I fully realize the philosophy here has always been that one must spend more to make more."

"Quite rightly."

"Hardly, or there would be no need for me."

"Ritz knows what he's doing."

"Perhaps, but the fact remains that things can't go on this way. And if you wish to remain in your present position, you must understand that the lavish spending you're accustomed to will not be happening in the future. I hope—"

"But as I'm trying to tell you, that lavishness is precisely what we're known for. It's the very reason people come here. You can't expect—"

"It is not only what I expect, Countess," he cut in, feeling he was more than justified in an interruption of his own at this stage of their conversation, "it is also what I demand."

"So it's to be dogwood twigs in the flower arrangements even in the springtime? No more elegantly folded napkins in London's most elegant restaurant? No more valet service for the peers down for a quick vote in the Lords? No complimentary champagne for the Duchess of Moreland's table?"

"When the duchess stayed here last season, she failed to pay her bill," he answered at once, "so forgive me if I can't dredge up any regret that she'll no longer be enjoying our champagne free of charge."

"She'll pay her bill eventually," Lady Stratham countered with a breezy acceptance of the duchess's behavior that only heightened Simon's aggravation. It must have shown in his face, for she went on, "I realize it's frustrating, but surely you know as well as I do that most members of the ton don't have the same sense of urgency about these things that you seem to possess."

"A facet of the aristocratic lifestyle I find utterly reprehensible," he said crisply. "It will not continue. From now on, anyone who has made a habit of refusing to pay their bill promptly in the past will be required to submit a deposit of 50 percent on their rooms when checking in."

"Make a duchess pay half in advance?" she breathed, clearly scandalized. "You cannot be serious."

"But I am. And while we are on this subject, by the way, anyone who chooses to avail themselves of our banqueting facilities and your services will be required to pay a cash deposit of 20 percent up front. You're shocked, I see," he added, noting her expression.

"But…but surely…you realize…you must…" She paused, clearly finding it hard to come up with a reply. "But you're a viscount," she said at last. "Surely you know how these things work."

He didn't, of course, having been a peer for less than half a year, but he wasn't about to lose face by admitting it, especially not to someone like her. "That fact, funnily enough, does not prevent me from paying my bills on time. I intend to make sure others do the same."

"You don't understand," she murmured, giving him a look of pity that brought all his middle-class defenses to the fore. "You really don't understand. How is that possible?"

"What is it you think I am missing?" He clasped his hands atop the open file before him, striving to keep an open mind. "Explain it to me."

She lifted her hands, then let them fall in a gesture of surrender. "Very well, since you seem to need it spelled out. Allowing aristocratic guests leeway in regard to payment is part of a...a tacit understanding. Aristocrats bring a certain je ne sais quoi, an air of nobility and elegance that is necessary to a hotel of this quality. Your requirements will be regarded as an insult, and peers will go elsewhere. Without their presence, the Savoy will become just another comfortable, ordinary London hotel."

"Since a comfortable hotel in London is as rare as hen's teeth and therefore not the least bit ordinary, the Savoy will hardly lose money by following that example. In fact, if we don't make a far greater profit as a result of my efforts, I will be quite disappointed. The board will remove me from my position for it, and deservedly so."

"Profit, profit, the almighty profit," she muttered. "Is that the god you worship, Lord Calderon?"

"I save worship for church, Lady Stratham," he shot back, his patience at an end. "As for the Savoy, I'm not instituting these policies so the shareholders can lose money, that's certain. So I suggest you find a way to work within the budget constraints I've outlined or find ways to bring in additional revenue. It is that simple."

"It's not simple at all! As I've already tried to explain, your policies will cause us to lose the aristocratic clientele, and without that, the Savoy will cease to have that air of refinement that has always made it so extraordinary."

"Refinement?" he echoed, unable to hide his scorn for that concept. "So we should give things for free to people who can well afford to pay for them merely for the sake of aristocratic privilege? I suppose it's not surprising that you feel that way. You're a countess, after all. I can see why you think the titled deserve special privileges because of the fortunate happenstance of their birth."

"Are you…" She paused, her voice failing as her eyes narrowed with anger. "Are you calling me a snob, Lord Calderon?"

He shrugged. "Are you?"

"How dare you?" She jumped to her feet, glaring at him. "I am not a snob, and no one, by God, has ever accused me of being one."

"Perhaps I dare because no one else ever has? Not that I blame them, of course," he went on, ignoring her splutter of outrage as he also stood up. "Given your upbringing and powerful position, who would say it to your face?"

"You would, apparently, since tact seems to be an alien concept for you. If you converse with our aristocratic clients in the same odious way you speak to me, they'll all take their business to Brown's or the Bristol and we'll be broke in six months. And," she added as he opened his mouth to reply, "your conclusions about me are without any basis in fact. You do not know me, nor anything about me, nor have you bothered to ask the opinions of others about my character. If you had done so, you would never have made such an accusation. Your opinion of me—and, in fact, this entire conversation—demonstrates with painful clarity that I cannot possibly work under you."

Simon couldn't help feeling relieved. The last thing he needed was an uncooperative termagant under his supervision, however lovely she might be to look at. "Very well," he said imperturbably. "As I've said, you can no longer be under Ritz's supervision, but if you can't work for me, I'd be quite happy to put Helen in charge of you."

"Helen?" She stared at him, the anger in her countenance turning to horror at the mention of the Savoy founder's wife. "You don't mean Helen Carte?"

"The very same. Her husband is ill, and she has been taking on many of his tasks. She is the perfect person to be in charge of you, if you don't wish to work for me."

"But the woman loathes me."

"Really?" he drawled in pretended surprise. "I can't imagine why."

The sarcasm was not lost on her. "Helen is arrogant, judgmental, and impossible to work with. A lot like you, in fact."

"If by that you mean she is sensible, frugal, and understands the importance of solvency to an enterprise's success, then yes, she and I are alike."

"Frugal? Helen's so tight with money, if she dropped a shilling down a rabbit hole, she'd dig up the field to find it. But in making the comparison, I was thinking of her obsessive pettifogging, desperate need for control, and lack of trust in the staff to know best how to do their jobs."

That description flicked Simon on the raw, but he refused to be sidetracked by it. "Then it seems your only other choice is to resign."

At the throwing down of that particular gauntlet, her shoulders went back and her eyes narrowed. "If you think you shall rid yourself of me that easily, Lord Calderon, you'd best think again."

"Indeed? Then I expect you to comply fully with the conditions I have laid down. If you cannot, I shall expect your resignation. Do I make myself clear?"

"Quite clear, thank you." Snatching the sheets off his desk, she turned away, heading for the door between their offices without a backward glance, her hips swaying, the pleated silk hem of her blue skirt and the frothy white lace of the petticoat beneath it churning behind her heels with the force of her strides.

She reached the door and opened it, but if Simon thought their conversation was over, he was mistaken.

"By the way," she said, glancing over her shoulder at him as she paused with her hand on the knob, "since I am to be working for you for the foreseeable future, there's something you should know about me, something you might not yet have observed."

"What's that?"

Steel glinted in her eyes, like a duelist's sword in the sun. "I don't respond well to being lectured. I'm a woman, you autocratic bastard, not a naughty child."

Before he could reply, she had walked out, slamming the door behind her with enough force to rattle the painting on the wall.

"Woman?" he muttered in the wake of her departure. "Tornado is more like it."

But even as he spoke, the flaunting swing of her hips as she'd stalked away went through his mind, reminding him that *woman* and *tornado* were not, at least in this case, mutually exclusive concepts.

Simon eased back in his chair, letting out his breath in a slow sigh as he appreciated the inevitable storms that lay ahead.

3

Delia had never been the sort to let grass grow under her feet. After her meeting with Calderon, she marched straight to the Savoy's telegraph office and fired off a cable to Ritz in Rome. She then went in search of Ritz's second-in-command, but Monsieur Echenard had departed that morning for a winter holiday on the Riviera with his family. A sudden impulse, she was told by the assistant manager's secretary.

"Sudden impulse, my eye," Delia muttered as she departed Echenard's office. "Helen's responsible for getting him out of the way, I'll wager, and Ritz, too. Thereby giving that impossible man a free hand."

With half an hour to spare before her first appointment of the day, Delia made a few discreet inquiries among the staff, and though everyone with whom she spoke was as disgruntled about the changes being made and as worried about the future as she was, no one seemed able to add any details to what she already knew.

She did, however, have one more source of information available to her. When she returned to the hotel after her last appointment of the morning and found no reply from Ritz awaiting her, she went straight to the Duke of Westbourne's suite.

Her cousin, thankfully, was in.

"Delia? What a delightful surprise." Max opened the door wider for her to enter. "How was Paris?"

"Cold," she replied, giving his cheek an affectionate kiss before passing through the doorway into the sitting room of his suite. "Rainy. A lot like here. But it is January, so what else can one expect? Are you on your way out?" she added, noting his morning coat and the fresh carnation in his buttonhole.

"I'm having a late lunch with Marbury at Rules," he explained, closing the door behind her. "I'm only waiting for my valet to bring my hat, and I'm off. The blasted thing got crushed during the train journey down here, and Stowell took it to the Savoy's laundry to try and repair the damage. Did you come by to hear all the news from Gloucestershire?"

"I'd adore that, but I really came to talk with you about something else entirely. It's rather important, but I don't want to make you late."

"The later the better, to my mind. Marbury wants to bend my ear over the new Reform Bill before the Lords vote on it tomorrow, and I couldn't find an excuse to get out of it. Marbury's a worthy fellow, but deadly dull. He pontificates endlessly, which I suppose is what makes him so accomplished as an MP. Either way, we have a bit of time for a chat, I think. What's the trouble?"

Reassured, she took a deep breath and plunged ahead. "Dearest Max, I need your help."

His mouth took on a wry curve. "Knowing you, that spells trouble."

"I don't know how you can say that. The last time I asked you for help, you met a girl and got married."

"Exactly."

Delia was well aware that Max adored his wife, Evie, so she merely gave him a playful smack on the arm. "Do be serious. I've got a problem, and you are the perfect person to help me resolve it."

"Given that you've been away, I don't know how you even knew I was in town."

"I hear everything that goes on in this hotel. And what's going on now," she added, sinking onto the settee, "is a disaster."

"Ah," he said with a nod of understanding. "This is about Lord Calderon, no doubt."

She made a face at the mention of her newfound nemesis. "I've always admired your perspicacity, Max. It's why you're my favorite cousin."

He studied her face for a moment, then walked to the liquor cabinet. "Whisky or sherry?" he asked over his shoulder.

"Whisky," she answered at once. "Sherry is much too delicate for my present mood."

Max laughed, shaking back his dark hair as he poured a generous measure of whisky into a tumbler. "Calderon's giving the hotel a bit of a dustup, I imagine?"

"That's one way of putting it."

"And you've come to cry on my shoulder?" he asked as he brought her the drink.

She snorted, giving him an impatient glance as she took the offered glass. "I didn't come for sympathy," she corrected and took a generous swallow of whisky. "I already told you; I came for help. Specifically, I need information."

His eyes, the same dark blue as hers, widened as if in surprise. "Information about Calderon? I hardly know the man."

"He went to Harrow. Two years ahead of you."

"Even so, I don't believe we ever met until a few weeks ago."

"I thought all of you knew each other. The old school tie, and all

that. Either way," she went on as he shook his head, "you're a major
investor in the hotel. You must have been there for that shareholders'
meeting a few weeks ago."

"I came to London because two very important votes were scheduled in the House of Lords that week. I'm here again this week for the
same reason."

She waved aside politics. "Were you at that shareholders' meeting or not? Well, then," she added as he gave a nod, "you must know
what's going on."

"I may be an investor, Dee, but I'm not privy to the board's decisions regarding hotel operations. Besides, you got back from Paris
last night, didn't you? Given your uncanny ability to ferret out secrets,
you probably know far more about the whole affair by this time than
I do."

She didn't reply, but merely continued to look at him, waiting, and
after a moment, Max sighed and sat in the chair opposite her with
his drink, resigned to his fate. "What do you want to know that you
think I can tell you?"

"What happened at that meeting?"

"We got bad news. No dividend, yet again. That's four straight
quarters with investors receiving no return on our investment. Profits
are down, again, and by a very significant margin. There was a huge
outcry from the shareholders, as you might expect, and we demanded
that something be done."

"That something being Calderon?"

"Mrs. Carte regaled us with his qualifications, which are impres-
sive, and suggested he might be willing to turn things around. She
brought him into the meeting—"

"What, right then and there? Helen doesn't waste any time, does
she?"

"Calderon gave us his opinion on what changes were needed, and what he felt he could do in that regard. We were keenly impressed, agreed with his contentions, and despite the scandal of his father—"

"Scandal? What scandal?"

"It hardly matters. It was ages ago, and it had nothing to do with Calderon. So the board voted him in as a member with stock shares as compensation for his efforts."

"But why *him*? Couldn't your lot have chosen someone whose diplomatic skill is not equivalent to the tread of a bull elephant? Here three weeks, and he's already got everyone in an uproar. Chopping, changing, undermining Ritz at every turn. What's the good of that?"

"Dee, I appreciate the loyalty that Ritz has earned from all of you, but I'm sure everyone will cooperate with Calderon."

"Will they? The odds are long, in my opinion. I've heard very little about him that's positive."

"Perhaps you don't want to hear anything positive."

She ignored that. "It's hardly surprising, since he's high-handed, incredibly bossy, and absolutely determined to have things his own way."

"Is he?" Max lifted his glass, giving her a meaningful glance over the rim. "He sounds a bit like a cousin of mine."

"I'm nothing like that," she countered, aghast at the very idea that she and that impossible man were in any way alike.

"No?" Max cocked his head to one side, studying her with one raised eyebrow. "How many nannies did you wear out before your exasperated parents sent you off to finishing school?"

Delia made a sound of impatience at this unnecessary reference to her rather turbulent childhood. "I don't see what that has to do with anything," she protested, but when Max continued to subject her to his steady, unrelenting ducal stare, she sighed and gave in. "Four," she replied, "but I really don't see—"

"And how many finishing schools sent you down before you finally managed to graduate?"

"Three," she admitted and mustered her dignity, "but we're not talking about me and my rebellious youth. We are talking about the present, and Lord Calderon. He is not a rebellious adolescent but a grown man, one who seems unable to see any point of view but his own. Max, the man has no understanding of how things are done here and refuses to care. He isn't even bothering to consult with Ritz about the changes he wants to make. Is it any wonder the staff's noses are put out? And how does he expect to manage the staff anyway? Why, the man doesn't even speak proper French!"

Max's lips twitched. "A grievous sin, indeed," he said gravely.

"In this case, it is! Many of the hotel employees are French and are far more comfortable speaking in that language. Why, at least a third of the kitchen staff don't speak English at all, including Escoffier. Calderon's French is so painful to the ears that if Escoffier sees him coming, he'll duck into the larder and lock the door! How does that happen anyway?" she added, momentarily sidetracked. "How is it that a gentleman, a peer of the realm, speaks such abysmal French?"

Max, the wretch, actually laughed.

"What?" she demanded. "What has you so amused?"

"Nothing." He hastily stifled his laughter, but the smile at the corners of his mouth lingered, telling her it was only a token effort. "It's just that I'm remembering a conversation from a couple of years ago, when you called me out for wondering the very same thing about a certain young lady we both know."

Delia scowled, remembering the conversation in question. "That was different."

"Not so very different. You severely scolded me—and quite rightly, too—for wondering such a thing about Evie. And—"

"That is not at all the same," she cried, indignant at the comparison.

"Your wife might have done work for me before she met you, but she was never in charge of any hotel staff. And besides, Evie is a delightful person, while Lord Calderon is anything but. He called me a snob. I know," she added, giving a gratified nod as she noted her cousin's surprise. "Can you believe it?"

"Well, if memory serves, that's what you called me about Evie."

"I never said such a thing."

"Words to that effect, then."

"Nonsense. And again, we're not talking about me, or you, for that matter. We're talking about *him*. Who does he think he is, calling me a snob? Arrogant bastard."

"Well, I hope you didn't trade insult for insult and call him that to his face."

She shifted guiltily in her chair. "Might have done," she muttered. "In the heat of the moment."

"Oh, Dee." He laughed, shaking his head. "You do like to make things difficult, don't you?"

"I couldn't help it! You should have heard him, chastising me as if I'm a child, laying down the law, refusing to accept facts, denigrating other members of the aristocracy and talking as if he's not even one of us."

"Well, that last bit's understandable, I suppose. He's probably got a chip on his shoulder about our lot."

She frowned in confusion. "But why should he have? He's part of the aristocracy, too. Isn't he a viscount?"

"Yes, but it's a newly created title."

"Ah, that explains why I'd never heard of him."

"Exactly. He was awarded a peerage a few months ago for his bravery fighting the Boers."

"The Boers?" She paused to do some quick arithmetic. "He must have been very young."

"He was. Barely eighteen. He saved a general's life during the Battle of Majuba Hill, or Laing's Nek, or some such, and almost lost his own life in the process, I understand."

"That was very brave," she murmured, impressed in spite of herself—a reaction, oddly enough, that only made her more frustrated.

"Just so," Max replied. "The Queen finally recognized him for his action a few months ago, giving him a title and an estate somewhere in Berkshire."

"Better late than never, I suppose. The war was ages ago. Still, it's quite an honor."

"Indeed. Especially considering his background. Both his mother and father worked in the hotel trade."

"Did they?" Delia's mind flashed back to her conversation with Calderon about going hungry. In light of Max's information, that singular remark made more sense now. "I see. But then," she added, struck by another thought, "how did he manage the fees for Harrow? Inherited money? Scholarship?"

"If he were scholarship class, would that surprise you?"

Delia tossed her head. "He's intelligent enough for a scholarship, I suppose," she said grudgingly.

"A fine concession. I begin to understand why he called you a snob."

"What?"

"Perhaps he thinks you already know about his father's transgressions and his lowly background and are judging him for it?"

"First of all, I don't even know what his father's transgressions were."

She shot him an inquiring look, and he capitulated with a sigh. "Embezzlement."

"What?"

"His father was a hotel clerk who got caught with his hand in the till. The man was dismissed, of course—"

"Wait—" she pleaded, holding up one hand. "His father was a petty thief? But then, why on earth would the board agree to put him in charge of the Savoy? Did they not know about it?"

"They knew. Most of the board members were already acquainted with him. He and Richard Carte are partners in several other ventures, you see. And unlike his father, his own reputation in business is one of scrupulous honesty. As for the investors, Calderon told us about his father at the meeting. He felt it wasn't playing the game otherwise. Some of the investors weren't too keen on him after finding out, of course, but as I said during the meeting, one can hardly blame a son for his father's sins. Although," he added, watching her face, "I'm not sure you agree?"

Delia drew herself up, affronted. "I would never hold the circumstances of his birth or the actions of his father against any man. And whatever my opinion of Calderon himself may be, the accusation he leveled at my head was most unwarranted. I am not a snob, and you know it."

"True, but I'm not the one who needs to be convinced."

"I doubt I could convince Calderon that water's wet," she muttered. "Honestly, I don't believe I've ever met anyone so strong-willed, so determined to get their own way—"

"Just so," he murmured, cutting her off. "The pot has met the kettle, and she doesn't like it a bit."

"No one ever has trouble with me," she said with dignity. "I don't bully people into doing things I want."

"No, you just manage to convince them that what you want is all their own idea."

That stung, mainly because there was truth in it. But before she could reply, Max spoke again. "But here's the thing, Dee." He paused and leaned forward in his chair, looking uncharacteristically grave all of a sudden. "Nothing you've told me is relevant here. The investors—including me, by the way—will not continue to accept receiving no return on our investment. We require the board to do whatever is necessary to right the ship before it sinks."

"It's not sinking. Don't exaggerate."

"Even you must admit that the hotel has been spending an inordinate amount of money. Ritz is the worst offender, but you aren't much better. Don't deny it, Delia," he added as she opened her mouth. "I'm terribly fond of you, as you know, but you are a spendthrift."

Delia began to regret she'd paid this call. "All the decisions I make are sound, and none have been made without Ritz's full agreement. The hotel has an image to maintain. That costs money."

"Image is all very well, but things can't go on as they have. When Mrs. Carte brought Calderon in, it seemed to us like the answer to a prayer. This sort of thing is right up his street. He's taken over and turned around several other hotels. Very successfully, I might add."

Delia sniffed, no more impressed by that fact now than she'd been this morning. "I've made some inquiries about that. None of those hotels are in London, and none are up to Savoy standards."

"That's not a snobbish view at all," he murmured slyly.

"How does Ritz feel about what's happening?" she asked, wisely shifting the conversation. "Does anyone know?"

"Does it matter? He, Echenard, and Escoffier will be made to understand—if they haven't already—that there's nothing else to be done. Besides, Ritz has been stretched terribly thin, building this new Paris hotel of his and managing the new Savoy hotel in Rome, as well as running things here. You're his friend. Think of him. He's overwhelmed and could do with Calderon's help."

"Helping Ritz is supposed to be my job."

"Yes, I know. And I know how much the job means to you."

He didn't know, not really. No one could truly understand what a lifeline Ritz's offer of employment had been to her in the wake of her third husband's death. "Well, then," she began.

"But you, my dear, are not enough, and the lack of profit proves it."

"Not that horrid word again! Really, Max, you're already one of the wealthiest men in England. How much more money do you need to make?"

"Given the disastrous slump in income from land rents and what it costs to run the estates, I need all the income from other sources I can get. And most of the other investors—the titled ones, anyway—feel the same. Some of our lot are barely staying afloat. You know that."

"You're right, you're right," she conceded, appropriately chastened. "But the man's simply unbearable. What can I do?"

"Seems simple to me. Figure out a way to get along with him. Or," he added as she groaned, "quit."

"You sound like Calderon. He made that suggestion, too. Plain as a pikestaff he'd love it if I did. But I won't. I adore what I do. And I can't let Ritz down. And it's not as if I could go to work for another hotel anyway. None of them would hire a woman to be part of management."

"Would that be so bad?"

She stared at her cousin, confounded by the question. "But if I didn't work, what would I do with myself?"

"Charities?"

"I already run seven! I can't bear to take on any more. And what else is there? Spend my time drifting aimlessly from London in the season to country house parties in the autumn, to the Riviera or Egypt in the winter?"

"Nothing wrong with that. You might enjoy it. Or..." He paused to take a swallow of whisky. "You could marry again."

Delia stiffened. "Why on earth would I want to do that?"

"Why not?" He smiled faintly. "It's not as if you abhor the institution."

"Well, no, of course not, but—" She broke off, her chest tightening as her mind went back into the past, but the pain of those memories was too great to bear, and she veered her mind away from them at once, pasting on a smile. "Send yet another man to an early grave?" she said, her voice light. "I couldn't possibly."

"Darling Dee," he said gently. "You're not cursed, you know."

"Do the men of London know that?"

"Are you serious? Half the single men we know, including most of the young blades, would happily take a chance on you."

"I doubt that, but I love you for saying it. Even so, I see no reason to make a fourth venture into matrimony."

"What about children? Isn't that a reason? You adore babies."

The pain in her chest came again, stronger this time, and it took all the effort she had to hide it and keep her smile in place.

"I adore other people's babies," she joked. But Max didn't reply, so she added, striving to sound offhand, "The point is, I've been married three times, and don't have even one child to show for it."

"That doesn't mean—"

"Having children is clearly not something my body was meant to do, and I've accepted that. It's all right, truly," she added, noting the compassion in his eyes. "After all, I have my work here at the Savoy. That's my life now."

"Work is all very well, but it isn't everything."

"It is for me," she countered firmly. "And I love what I do here, Max. I have no intention of abandoning my duties, no matter how hard things get."

"That's the spirit," he said with approval, looking relieved, his eyes crinkling at the corners as he smiled. "And since you've asked for my advice, my first contribution in that regard would be to avoid calling Calderon a bastard. Second, accept the situation and learn to work with him."

That prospect impelled Delia to down the rest of her whisky. "How can I?" she asked as she set her empty glass on a nearby table. "The man's about as flexible as concrete. You should have seen him this morning, judging me, questioning my expenditures, and calling me to account for them as if I'm a young girl who's overspent her pocket allowance."

"I seem to remember your late father gnashing his teeth quite a bit about your lavish spending during your marriage to Armand. I feel some sympathy for Calderon."

She grimaced at the reminder of her woeful lack of restraint during the three years of her second marriage, but she refused to allow herself to be sidetracked. "The point is, Calderon made it quite clear he sees no value in what I do. Half the Savoy policies he's doing away with were my ideas. He has no use for me, and it's clear he doesn't like me."

"A horrible feeling," Max said amiably. "And one, I daresay, you're not used to."

"This is a fine state of affairs," she muttered, glaring at him. "You're my cousin. You're supposed to be on my side."

He sobered at once. "I am always on your side. But that's irrelevant here. The deed is done. I can't change it. And even if I could, I wouldn't. The indifference Ritz has displayed recently toward the Savoy—"

"Indifference?" she echoed, stung on behalf of her friend.

"Yes, Delia, indifference. I know you adore the fellow, but even you must admit his attention has been fixed predominantly on his other hotels, and the Savoy is suffering for it. If Calderon's efforts can succeed in putting Ritz's priorities back in order, I call that a good thing."

Having just been to Paris on Ritz's behalf, she couldn't really refute that point. "Even when everyone's grumbling? And they are, Max—at least the ones he hasn't already forced out. He dismissed Madelaine, you know."

"Madelaine?"

"My secretary, who, so far as I can see, hadn't done anything to deserve it."

"Sometimes staff are let go and it has nothing to do with performance. You know that as well as I do. And choices like that are completely within Calderon's purview. We gave him a free hand to cut any staff he deems unnecessary."

"Does that include me?" She sat up straighter, alarmed. "Max, is my job in jeopardy?"

The door opened before he could reply, and Stowell entered the suite, forcing Delia to wait for an answer to her question.

"Ah, my hat," Max said, standing up. "At last."

"Sorry it took so long, Your Grace," Stowell said as he crossed the room. "But the laundry is a bit overwhelmed just now. Short-staffed, I'm told. Lady Stratham," he added with a nod of greeting as he placed Max's top hat on his head.

"Tell me, Stowell," Delia said as the valet handed his master a pair of gloves, "is the situation in the laundry due to people being let go permanently?"

"I'm not sure, my lady." He paused to drape Max's cloak over his shoulders. "But I have heard that staff is being pared down, and that's very worrying for everyone. Things seem rather stressful at present."

"See, Max?" Delia murmured, feeling vindicated. "I told you so."

Her cousin was given no chance to reply.

"I do hope," Stowell said as he handed Max an umbrella, "the delay hasn't made you late to lunch, Your Grace."

"Not to worry," Max said cheerfully. "As I already told my cousin here, the later I arrive, the better. Walk down with me, Dee?" he added, gesturing to the door.

She'd have had to be held back by chains to do otherwise, with her question about her future at the Savoy still hanging in the air. "Well?" she asked once they had left the suite and started down the corridor toward the lift. "Is my job at risk?"

"Did Calderon say it was?"

"Not in so many words, but the implication was plain that he'd love to get rid of me. Any possible excuse will do, I'm sure."

"Then don't give him one."

"But he can terminate my job just because he wants to?"

"He can. So, since you've asked me what you ought to do, my advice—not that I think you'll take it—is to be as cooperative as possible."

"Bend the knee to that man?" She groaned, hating the prospect. "I don't know if I can. It would be so much better if you would help me find a way to get rid of him."

"Sorry."

She made a face at that breezy response. "No, you're not. But if he and I are found dead one day with my hands round his throat and his letter opener through my heart like a scene from some Shakespearean tragedy, it'll be all your fault."

"I'll give a beautiful eulogy at your funeral."

"Thanks," she countered dryly as they paused by the electric lift and he pushed the call button. "So you're leaving me to fight my battles alone?"

"Afraid so. Those battles will be epic, I'm sure, and I'm sorry I won't be here to see any of them."

"I can tell you every lurid detail when you and Evie come down for the season."

"No, you can't. Evie and I won't be doing the season this year."

"What?"

Before Max could explain, the lift doors opened, revealing a boy in livery. "Your Grace," he said, giving a respectful tip of his cap to the duke before turning his attention to her. "Lady Stratham."

"Samuel," she greeted him. "How's your mother?"

"Ever so much better, my lady. That liniment you sent over for her chest did her a world of good. It was very kind of you."

"Not at all. And I'm glad she's on the mend. Give her my best, will you?"

"Of course, my lady." He put his hand on the lever of the elevator mechanism. "Going down?"

"Yes," Max answered. "Ground floor, please." He turned, gesturing for Delia to precede him, then followed her into the elevator. As Samuel closed the doors behind them, she resumed the subject at hand.

"So why aren't you and Evie doing the season? Something exciting, I hope? Paris, perhaps? Or Biarritz?" she added as he shook his head. "Or sailing up to the Norwegian fjords?"

"We're not going anywhere this year, not even London. Evie doesn't want to travel in her condition."

"Her condition? Max!" she cried with a jolt of joy as she realized what he meant. "Evie's pregnant?"

At his confirming nod, she flung herself into his arms, oblivious to Samuel's presence, smothering her cousin in a hug and a slew of kisses. "That's wonderful news. Simply wonderful. How far along is she? Did the doctor say? Is she..." Delia paused, taking a deep breath. "She's all right, isn't she?"

"Of course. She's a little sick in the mornings," he added as they pulled apart, "but that's to be expected at this stage, I understand. She's about four months gone. Doctor Treves says she's in fine form."

"Excellent," she said with heartfelt relief. "And your sisters? Do they know about the baby?"

"They do. I telegraphed all of them and broke the news before I left Gloucester to come here. They were thrilled."

"Of course they were," she replied, laughing. "We shall all be spoiling that child senseless, I warn you."

"I have no doubt. Anyway, I won't be coming down to London again for ages, so I expect the next time I see you will be at Whitsuntide. You are coming up for the party?"

At this mention of the house party held every spring at Max's estate, she could only offer a helpless shrug. "I hope so, but it depends on how smoothly things go here. Given how they've started, I haven't much hope. Especially without you here to support my end," she added woefully.

"Oh, stop feeling sorry for yourself. You're perfectly capable of dealing with Lord Calderon without any help from me."

"Am I?"

"Of course. He's a man, isn't he?"

She thought of those imperturbable green eyes blinking at her in that cool, rather inhuman way of his. "I'm not sure. To me, he's more like the Grim Reaper."

Samuel choked, trying to suppress his boyish giggle, a reaction she found quite gratifying under the circumstances.

Max merely smiled. "Just be your usual charming self, and you'll have him eating out of your hand soon enough."

She made a face. "You talk as if I set out to charm people on purpose."

"Well—" he began, but she cut him off.

"I'm only charming to people I like. And as I've already told you, I don't like him."

"Like him or not," Max said as the lift jerked to a halt and Samuel opened the doors, "he's here, and you'll have to accept that and the changes he's making as best you can."

She didn't reply. Instead, she stared at her cousin, riveted, as an idea flashed into her mind—an idea so simple and so easy she was amazed she hadn't thought of it until now.

Max turned so that she could precede him out of the lift, but she didn't move.

Acceptance, she thought. That was the ticket. *Acceptance.* Things were already chaotic. Another week, perhaps two, and the consequences of his decisions would surely start coming back to bite him. All she had to do was sit back, do nothing, and watch him sail straight off the cliff.

"Delia, is something wrong?"

Faced with the inevitable consequences of his dunderheaded decisions, he might become more willing to listen to the opinions of others—the people who worked here, people who understood far better than he how a hotel like the Savoy ought to be run. And even if he was too obstinate to admit he was wrong and change course, the board would soon see the damage he was doing and stop him.

A put-down like that, she thought with a rather naughty sense of anticipation, would do that man a world of good.

"Delia?"

The sharp note of Max's voice succeeded in garnering her attention. "Hmm?" she asked, coming out of her contemplations with a shake of her head. "I beg your pardon?"

"You're standing there as if you've been turned to a pillar of salt. Is something wrong?"

"No, no, nothing's wrong. In fact," she added, smiling at him as she sailed past him out of the elevator, "I think everything just came right."

"I know that look in your eyes," he muttered, falling in step beside her as they crossed the foyer together. "Delia, what are you scheming?"

"Nothing."

That completely truthful reply didn't seem to impress him. "You really are a devil, Cousin."

"Max!" she chided. "What an odious thing to say."

"But accurate. I know you." He nodded to the entrance doors nearby, where the cab Stowell had ordered was waiting for him. "Can I drop you somewhere?"

"No, no." She gestured to the nearby dining room. "I have a lunch appointment here. Lord Synby wants a dinner for his club in February, and we're meeting to discuss the details. He'll adore it when I tell him we now require a 20 percent deposit in advance for banqueting services."

"I'm sure you'll handle the situation beautifully."

Synby was the sort of peer with whom one did not discuss such tiresome matters as money. He'd be heartily offended, she had no doubt, but if he were so put out that he canceled the affair or the members of his club went elsewhere, the consequences would be on Calderon's head, not hers. He'd be hoisted with his own petard.

The thought made her smile.

"Why are you looking like the Cheshire cat all of a sudden?" Max asked, frowning.

"No reason," she lied, even as her smile widened. "Goodbye, darling. Give Evie my best. I hope while the two of you are idling away your time, enjoying country life, you'll think of me down here slaving away."

"Delia," he began, giving her a look of warning. "I hope you're not going to make trouble."

She laughed. "I shan't dream of it. I mean what I say," she insisted, crossing a hand over her heart and looking as innocent as possible. "I will not do anything to cause trouble. Not a single thing. I promise."

She turned away, but Max's voice echoed back to her as she started toward the restaurant. "Poor Calderon. I almost feel sorry for the fellow."

"Me too," she murmured under her breath and laughed again. "Me too."

4

This is outrageous!" Lord Synby flung down his napkin. "Deposits in advance? Simply outrageous!"

"I know, I know," Delia murmured with the appropriate show of sympathy, spreading her hands in a helpless gesture. "But what can one do?"

"The members shall take our business elsewhere. The Bristol," he added with injured dignity, "will be delighted to host the banquet for one of London's most distinguished clubs without any nonsense."

His reaction wasn't a surprise to Delia, but she put on an expression of shock and dismay. "Oh, no! Dear Lord Synby, please don't go to the Bristol. Surely we can work around this bagatelle."

"Good woman, this is not a trifling matter. It's an insult. I shall tell Ritz so."

She bit her lip in apology. "I'm afraid Ritz is in Rome. And dear Mr. Echenard is on holiday. Lord Calderon is in charge while the two men are away."

"Calderon? Lord Calderon, you say? Don't know him."

"No? Viscount Calderon. Fought in the Boer War, I understand, and saved a general."

"Oh, that fellow." Synby, the twelfth of the Synby earls and a descendent of Tudors, gave a disparaging snort. "And he's running things?"

"For the moment. The Savoy has been so successful, and Ritz and Echenard so inundated—poor fellows—that the members of the board decided the two men needed help, so they have brought in Lord Calderon to assist."

"A peer managing a hotel?" Synby sounded scandalized.

"Calderon is a member of the Savoy's board of directors, you see, and the other members felt he could be of some assistance."

"And he made this decision about the deposits? Well, what can you expect from a man whose title is as shiny as a new penny? It's clear he doesn't know the ropes."

Delia took a bite of her baba au rhum and made a vague sound that might have been agreement with the earl's point of view or merely a sigh of appreciation for Escoffier's wonderful dessert.

"The Queen's handing out titles like candy these days," the earl went on, shaking his head. "It won't do, Lady Stratham. Won't do."

"You've clearly given the matter more thought than I. In light of that," she added, choosing her words with care, "perhaps you are just the person to offer Calderon a bit of guidance? If you were to take a hand…" She paused delicately and took another bite of her dessert as she let her idea sink in. "You would be able to explain things to him so well. A word or two from you, and I'm sure he'll realize that these new rules are completely unnecessary for gentlemen such as the members of the Godwyn Club."

"Hmm…perhaps, perhaps; but dash it, one shouldn't have to explain this sort of thing."

"I know," she replied with feeling. "Believe me, I know. But there it is. More coffee?"

Synby waved aside their waiter, Henri, who had paused beside the table with a silver coffeepot. "I've no time to idle over luncheon, Lady

Stratham. The banquet is less than a fortnight away, and this matter must be decided at once. Is Calderon anywhere about?"

"I believe he's in his office. It's just down the first corridor past the dining room. Shall we go together? That way, I can introduce you, then leave you gentlemen to talk things through. He's an open-minded fellow," she added, striving to keep a straight face as she put aside her napkin and stood up. "I'm sure you will easily make him see our point of view, and everything can be settled immediately, and no harm done."

"Splendid idea, Lady Stratham," the earl said as he rose to his feet. "Splendid."

She ushered him out of the restaurant and led him to Calderon's office. The viscount was in (a fact she had, of course, ascertained ahead of time), and was presently dictating letters to a short, sandy-haired young man. At the sight of her, Calderon stopped dictating and rose to his feet. "Lady Stratham."

"I hope I'm not interrupting," she said brightly as his secretary also stood up, "but there's someone I felt you simply must meet."

She pulled her companion through the doorway. "Lord Calderon, this is Lord Synby. And this is..." She paused, giving a pointed glance at the sandy-haired young man before returning her attention to his employer.

"My secretary, Mr. Ross," Calderon supplied. "Ross, this is Lady Stratham, and...er...Lord Synby."

"How do you do, Mr. Ross?" She beamed at him, holding out her hand. "Such a pleasure to see that the Savoy's new policies allow the truly important people to have secretaries."

She did not miss Calderon's wry look as she shook hands with the young secretary, but she ignored it. "Lord Synby and I have just been discussing the upcoming banquet for the Godwyn Club. It seems there's a bit of a muddle over the deposit requirement. Of course, I..."

She paused, pressing a hand to her bosom and attempting to look the picture of wide-eyed innocence. "I, being a mere woman, know little of finance, so I felt the best thing was to bring Lord Synby to you, Lord Calderon. I'm sure you can explain the Savoy's new policy far more effectively than I ever could. Now," she added before Calderon could reply, "I simply must be off. I have a meeting with Lady Malvers about her widows and orphans luncheon, and the dear baroness is such a stickler for punctuality. Good afternoon, everyone."

Giving all three men her brightest smile, she departed. Pausing in the doorway to her own office, she reached for her hat from the coat-tree, and as she put it on, the earl's booming voice echoed from the office next door.

"Lady Stratham tells me the Savoy is requiring deposits now. Whose idiotic idea was that?"

Chuckling under her breath, Delia shoved in her hatpin, reached for her cloak, and left her office to break the bad news about deposits to Lady Malvers.

Lady Malvers was every bit as insulted by the prospect of paying money in advance as Lord Synby had been, and by the time Delia had departed from the Malverses' sumptuous apartments in Park Lane, the baroness, like the earl, was complacently confident that a word or two in Calderon's ear from a peer of the realm would straighten out the mess. She heartily approved Delia's suggestion that Lord Malvers discuss the situation with Calderon directly, and she promised that the baron would be calling upon the viscount in very short order.

By the end of the following day, Lord Malvers had also expressed his displeasure with the new policies to Calderon, and had, like Lord Synby, vowed to take his business elsewhere. Delia might have been able to persuade them not to do so, of course, but as much as she hated to lose business to a competitor, she could see no other way to make Calderon see that his method of doing things was wrong-headed. No, he needed to be hit with the painful consequences of his decisions as quickly and decisively as possible. Faced with a slew of complaints, canceled parties, and lost revenue, he'd soon be forced to change course, and she consoled herself for the business lost by imagining the delicious moment when Calderon would be forced to eat some humble pie.

Lord Synby and Lord and Lady Malvers were not the only ones to abandon the Savoy. Within a few days, three more of her clients had moved their upcoming banquets and luncheons to rival establishments, just as she had predicted. She could only hope that Calderon saw sense in time for her to repair the damage before Ritz returned. The poor man had enough to concern himself with these days, and the last thing he needed was to come back and find his beloved Savoy in shambles and all his favorite customers in a rage.

A week after Lord Synby and the Godwyn Club's departure for the Bristol, however, Delia discovered that not everyone was as willing as she to take the long and patient approach to the situation.

She was in her office, still wading through the pile of correspondence that had accumulated during her Paris trip, when she was interrupted by a torrent of angry French.

"It is insupportable, Madame. Insupportable!"

Delia looked up as Auguste Escoffier came striding into her office, and the look of fury on his face made her grimace. "What's the trouble?" she asked, responding in the Frenchman's native language, though she was sure she was going to regret the question.

"That I should suffer such insults, such treatment!" He ran a hand through his thinning silver hair and puffed out his chest, actions that made him look less like the world's greatest chef and more like an agitated banty rooster. "That he and his minions should do this to me? To *me*? I am Escoffier, not some third-rate cook in an East End tavern."

Delia had a pretty fair idea of who the man in question might be, but the mention of his "minions" piqued her curiosity. "Who are you talking about, Auguste, my darling? Lord Calderon?"

"Him and the others."

"What others?"

"That pig of an accountant, Monsieur Deloitte. He and his clerks are with Calderon in my office as we speak, looking through my papers. What business have they to look through my private papers?"

Delia's gaze slid to the broken lock on her splintered desk drawer. "Believe it or not, I know how you feel," she said with a sigh. "But I hardly see what I—"

"I cannot come in, they tell me. I must stay out, they say. Keeping me out of my own office? How dare they? And not only that, Madame. They go through the wine cellars, the larders, even my kitchen. My kitchen, Madame! They go everywhere. They even talk to my suppliers about me, and about Ritz, too, and Echenard—poking, prying, asking questions. I am not supposed to know about that, but my suppliers are loyal. They tell me about this."

"Your suppliers?" she echoed, surprised and baffled. "But why talk to them? Whatever the accountants want to know, why don't they just ask you directly?"

"You ask me to tell you why they do what they do?" He lifted his hands to the sky in exasperation and let them fall. "They snoop, they spy on us. They dismiss members of my staff without my consent. They—"

"What?" Delia cried in dismay. "More people gone?"

"Two of my waiters were dismissed last week. And one of the kitchen maids today."

"Heavens! We shall soon have no staff at all."

"We are not the only ones who suffer. Agostini has lost two cashiers. Calderon says they cost too much, they must go, and *pfft*—" He paused to snap his fingers. "They are gone. No notice, no warning. They are told to leave at once, and they are shown the door."

"This is absurd!" she cried, too furious at such unfair treatment toward the staff to remember her newfound strategy of staying neutral. "Oh, that man is impossible!"

"As you say," Escoffier agreed. "How shall we serve the food? My dishes, so meticulously prepared, shall be cold before they reach the tables! And who shall wash the dishes? Me? Can you not do something, Madame?"

At that question, Delia's anger faltered, and she gave a frustrated sigh, remembering harsh realities. "Unfortunately not," she admitted, the words bitter on her tongue.

"I cannot operate under such conditions as this. What are they looking for in my papers? Do they wish to steal my recipes, and then fire me?"

As much as she disliked the man, Delia could not see Calderon doing such a thing. "I don't think you need worry about that," she murmured soothingly.

Escoffier was not pacified. "Nowhere else would I be treated this way. Nowhere! At any other hotel, they would fall to their knees and beg to acquire me."

That, Delia knew, was not an exaggeration. He'd be snatched up in a heartbeat if he ever left the Savoy, and though that would be just what Calderon deserved, it would be a calamity for the hotel and for Ritz, and that was a price she wasn't willing to pay. She tried again to apply oil to the troubled waters. "My darling Auguste, you know we'd never survive without you. The hotel wouldn't last a day."

"And I should care about that? If I did not have a contract, I would have departed already, *Madame*."

The reminder that a contract bound him filled Delia with profound relief. "Of course," she murmured. "And you have every right to feel as you do. It's completely understandable. But—"

She broke off as a movement from the doorway caught her attention, and she looked up to find a most welcome sight in the doorway. "Kay?" she cried in delighted surprise. "What a treat to see you! Come in, come in," she added, beckoning her friend into the room as she rose and circled her desk. "Heavens, how long has it been?"

"Ages," Lady Kay Matheson replied as she entered Delia's office. "A year, at least."

"That long? Well, the passing time certainly does you justice. You look lovely."

Kay, never comfortable with compliments, made a scoffing sound. "Oh, stop. You'll turn my head."

Delia doubted such a thing was possible, for Kay had always been painfully self-conscious about the generous curves of her figure, her flaming red hair, and the smattering of freckles across her nose and cheeks, and who could blame her? The scandal sheets had been vicious to her upon her debut fifteen years ago, deeming her England's least desirable debutante and making her vulnerable to the machinations of scoundrels with bad intentions. Her disastrous elopement one year later with notorious hellion Devlin Sharpe had not only broken her heart and torn apart her family, but it had also put her decidedly beyond the pale in the eyes of society.

"It's true," Delia insisted, moving past Escoffier to give her friend an affectionate kiss on each cheek. "You're looking absolutely radiant. But what brings you to town at this god-awful time of year? Off to the Riviera with your parents?"

"Oh, no, we're far too busy for that. No, no, I've come to ask you for a favor."

"How splendid. I adore doing favors for people."

Behind her, Escoffier gave a cough, and she stepped sideways. "Kay, do you know Monsieur Escoffier? Escoffier, this is Lady Kay Matheson, daughter of the Earl of Raleigh."

"Monsieur," Kay greeted him with a pleased smile. "I have partaken of your magnificent culinary creations so often, I feel as if I know you, but it is a pleasure to truly meet you at last."

Despite having lived in England for years, Escoffier still spoke no English, but Kay's warm and friendly smile communicated her point so effectively that the chef's thunderous frown was soothed away at once.

He responded with some equally flattering words in French, and Delia, hoping to preserve his momentary good mood, took full advantage. "Thank you, Auguste," she said, taking him by the arm and propelling him past Kay to the door, "for bringing this matter to my attention. As soon as Ritz returns from Rome, we will sit down, all three of us, and decide what to do. Until then, we must soldier on and continue to do our part."

With a few more platitudes, she finally rid herself of the temperamental chef and closed her office door behind him with relief.

"Oh, dear," Kay murmured. "I seem to have interrupted something terribly important. Sorry."

"Don't apologize. Believe me," she added, making a face, "your arrival was a blessing and your timing impeccable. Things are a bit chaotic just now with Ritz away, and Escoffier hates it when things don't go smoothly, but there's little I can do for him but commiserate. It makes one feel so helpless. So," she added, happy to change the subject, "doing a favor for you will be a most welcome distraction. How can I help?"

"I need the Savoy's biggest, most lavish banquet room for the seventh of June, along with the finest plates, silver, and linen you've got and the most exquisite dishes Escoffier can make."

"Heavens! What's the occasion?"

Her friend drew in a deep breath and let it out slowly. "I'm getting married."

"Kay!" she cried, wrapping her friend in a hug. "Now I know why you're glowing. What delightful news."

"Yes, it is, isn't it?"

There was an odd, wistful note in her voice, and Delia pulled back to look into her face. "Isn't it?"

"Of course it is!" Kay said at once. "It's just that it's all so overwhelming. And so unexpected at my age."

"Nonsense! You're only a year younger than I am."

Kay made a rueful face, her pert, freckled nose wrinkling up. "But a fetching widow of thirty-three has a bit more appeal to the average male than a disgraced spinster of thirty-two."

The fact that darling Kay was a spinster of thirty-two could be laid directly at the feet of Devlin Sharpe. Even after all this time, Delia still felt outrage on her friend's behalf. She didn't express her feelings aloud, however, for there was no point in rehashing the past, not when Kay seemed close to happiness at last. Before she could think of a reply to her friend's self-disparaging view of her situation, Kay spoke again.

"Either way, Dee, you're right to say it is delightful news. You'll help plan the wedding banquet, won't you?"

"You know I will. But first you must tell me, who is he?"

"Wilson Rycroft."

"Rycroft?" She blinked, startled. "The American millionaire?"

"The very same." Kay gave a short laugh. "You seem surprised. Not that I blame you. The family could hardly be expected to view a man from the wilds of America's Middle West as much of an improvement over a penniless fortune hunter."

Delia bit her lip, appreciating the pain her friend had endured.

"That's not how I feel, darling. If you're happy, I'm happy. It's just that I know your family's approval has always meant so much to you."

"Dearest Dee," Kay said with warm affection. "There's no need to worry about my family. After all, things have changed a great deal since Papa died."

Delia nodded with understanding, well aware that Kay's father had been, to put it kindly, a domestic tyrant, obsessed with controlling anyone and everyone within his power. "It's good to know they accept your choice of husband this time."

"As I said, everyone is relieved, especially my mother."

"And you?" Delia asked gently. "Are you relieved?"

"How could I not be? Wilson is as unlike Devlin as a man can be."

Delia couldn't help being glad about that. She'd never met the American millionaire, but it was reassuring to know that he was not as dangerous to her friend's heart, soul, and reputation as Devlin Sharpe had been.

"Well, that's all right then," Delia said. "It's nearly time for dinner. Are you free? We can go over to the Criterion and discuss all your wedding plans over some lovely food and obscenely expensive champagne."

"The Criterion?" Kay laughed, the shadow passing from her face. "Don't you want to eat here?"

"Heavens, no. I eat here every day. I'm dying to dine somewhere else for a change. But if you tell Escoffier I said so, I'll denounce you as a liar. Shall we?"

Delia gestured to the door, but before they could depart, another visitor arrived, one whose hard breathing told her he must have run the full length of the corridor.

"Michel?" Delia stared at him, noting the gleam of excitement in his eyes. "What on earth?"

"You'll never believe what's happening," the florist gasped, pressing a hand to his narrow chest and sucking in air as he glanced at the closed door into Calderon's office. "Ross anywhere about?"

"No, he's on an errand," Delia replied, growing more surprised by this mention of Calderon's secretary. "What is going on that has you looking so excited?"

"Darling, it's just too delicious." Michel stepped inside Delia's office and closed the door behind him. "Calderon's in the lobby being shredded into spills by the Duchess of Moreland as we speak."

"No!" Delia gave a laugh, hardly daring to believe such delightful news. "Not really?"

"Yes, really. I was right there, placing the new flower arrangements, and saw it all. He was talking to Ricardo at the registration desk when the duchess swept in, interrupted them, and demanded a room. Calderon stepped aside so that Ricardo could assist her, but when Ricardo told her she had to pay her previous bill before he could offer her a room, she tore him to bits. Calderon jumped into the fray, and she turned her ire on him. I thought you'd want to know."

"Quite right," she applauded, hooking her arm through Kay's and starting for the door. "Come on, Kay. I've simply got to see this."

"You're looking terribly gleeful, Delia," Kay commented, allowing herself to be hauled down the corridor at what was almost a run, with Michel following close on their heels.

"I suppose I am," Delia admitted, unrepentant, as they turned the corner and entered the lobby. "It's a flaw in my character, I confess, but I do love it when I turn out to be right."

Simon's own hotels ran like well-oiled machinery, and he was determined to see that the Savoy did the same. But as the Duchess of Moreland dressed down the poor reception clerk, the Savoy, and him in withering tones, Simon appreciated that changing things around here was going to require more on his part than mere determination.

"I realize," he said the moment he could get a word in, "that this new way of doing things is a bit disconcerting, Your Grace—I mean, Duchess," he corrected at once, remembering the rules of etiquette his newfound position required only after seeing the duchess's mouth twist with contempt at his faux pas.

Cursing the entire ridiculous slew of aristocratic rules that now governed his life, Simon planted a firm but polite smile on his face and persevered. "Perhaps you would care to accompany me to my office?" he suggested, well aware that every eye in the lobby was upon them. "That way we can discuss—"

"I see no need to be shuttled off to some little cubbyhole," she said haughtily. "Nor do I see the need for any discussion. I merely require a suite for the next two nights until I depart for Paris, where the *Méditerrannée Express* shall take me to the Riviera. If you will kindly comply with this simple request, we can end this most unpleasant encounter."

Simon, who had already explained the hotel's new policy three times in the most delicate fashion he could manage, decided it was time to be blunt. "That will not be possible, Duchess, until you pay your bill and make the required deposit."

The duchess was a frail, elderly woman, but her eyes were imperious, her manner supremely confident, and though Simon had little understanding of and even less patience with the aristocracy, he couldn't help admiring the way they stubbornly clung to the notion of their superiority. "Are you refusing to oblige me, Lord Calderon?"

"The Savoy is not a bank, Duchess, and we will no longer be granting credit to those who have a history of not paying their debts in a prompt fashion. If you were to pay the balance you already owe, then of course we can—"

"How dare you?" The duchess's jewel-like eyes narrowed, and he knew that if they were living a few centuries ago, he'd be seized by guards, dragged away, and hurled off the nearest rampart. Fortunately for him, this was 1898, and they were not in some medieval castle.

He gave a slight shrug, his polite smile still firmly in place. "It is my job to dare such things, Duchess. As I have already explained, when you have paid your outstanding bill and have put down a deposit on your pending reservation, I will be happy to oblige you with the finest suite the Savoy has available."

"I have no intention of rewarding your insults in such a way. I shall be informing all my friends of the Savoy's outrageous new policies. Furthermore, I shall go to Claridge's. At Claridge's, the managers are not fueled by naked ambition. They know their place. And," she added, glancing over him with disdain, "they stay there. They do not presume to elevate themselves above their birth."

There it was. His place. Everything always came back to that, didn't it? His new title notwithstanding, to people like the duchess, he was a nobody from nowhere and he always would be. He'd accepted that fact of life a long time ago, and yet, somehow, the duchess's words succeeded in flicking him on the raw.

Still, it wouldn't do to show it, and Simon gave a nonchalant shrug. "That, of course, is your prerogative. But," he added as she turned away, "if you would be so kind as to tender payment for your outstanding bill before you go, it would be much appreciated."

The duchess, unsurprisingly, did not comply with that request. Not even bothering with a backward glance, she marched toward the exit doors, oblivious to every avid stare.

As Simon watched her depart, he was reminded of another imperious female who'd stalked away from him a week ago in a blaze of offended aristocratic sensibilities.

Your requirements will be regarded as an insult, and peers will go elsewhere.

As much as he hated to admit it, the days following Lady Stratham's prediction had proven her right, for several members of the ton had already broken with the Savoy over the new policies. He thought he'd been prepared for that, but with Lady Stratham's words ringing in his ears as he watched the duchess walk out the doors, he felt a sudden, unwelcome glimmer of self-doubt.

In instituting the new credit policies for guests, he'd been absolutely certain that any fury would quickly pass, and that the lack of quality hotels in London would lure people back. Even if the board were forced to fire Ritz, he had been confident that eventually everything would work itself out.

You're remarkably sure of yourself.

He had been sure, true enough, but what if he was wrong? What if they did not return? What if others followed in their wake and things kept getting worse? Aside from the galling prospect of Lady Stratham crowing about it, he'd be letting Helen and Richard down. He'd also be tossed from the board, his compensation in stock shares would not be paid, and his chance to finally gain a foothold in a London hotel would be lost. And he'd still be trying to lay his father's ghost to rest.

Simon rubbed four fingers across his forehead, feeling a headache coming on, and he couldn't help wondering if he could have avoided Lady Stratham's predictions by being less blunt.

Tact seems to be an alien concept for you.

Another accusation of hers he could not refute at this point. He preferred to call a spade a spade, but as he watched the duchess sail out the exit like a victorious battleship, he appreciated that in the rarefied air of the Savoy, blunt speaking was costly.

If you converse with our aristocratic clients in the same odious way you speak to me ... we'll be broke in six months.

As more of Lady Stratham's words from a week ago echoed through his mind again, Simon muttered an oath.

"Having trouble?"

Those sweetly murmured words penetrated his consciousness, and he turned to find the very object of his thoughts standing a few feet away, arm in arm with a friend, a tiny smile curving her lush pink lips.

The sight of that smile caused Simon to stiffen. "No," he said, shoving self-doubt away, reminding himself that customers who didn't pay their bills were no great loss. "Not at all."

"That's good to hear. I was on my way to dinner and saw you with the duchess. You seemed to be having a bit of trouble with her, and I was about to inquire if I could help, but you managed to settle things with her before I could jump in."

He'd have hurled himself in front of a train before asking her for help, and besides, if that provoking smile of hers was anything to go by, any help she gave would end up doing him more harm than good.

"I appreciate your thoughtful offer," he lied. "But I had things well in hand."

"Of course you did."

Oddly, this quick and mild agreement was more galling than her smile, but thankfully, the clerk on the other side of the registration desk gave a little cough, and Simon offered Lady Stratham and her friend a polite bow of farewell. "Enjoy your evening."

She gave a nod and turned away, and with relief he returned his attention to the clerk, who was waiting expectantly. "Yes, Ricardo, what is it?"

"Before the duchess arrived, you were asking me about a certain Mr. Sharpe?"

"Yes, Devlin Sharpe," he confirmed, happy to return to the subject that had brought him to the lobby in the first place. "Mr. Sharpe is a friend of mine, and he's staying at the Savoy for a day or two. We are dining together this evening, and I wanted to inquire if he had checked in yet?"

The clerk opened the registration book and scanned the most recent names that had been added. "Not yet, my lord," he said, looking up. "Do you wish to be notified when he arrives?"

"Yes, thank you. And if you could please ask the maître d'hôtel to reserve a table for us in the restaurant for..." He paused to pull out his pocket watch. "For nine o'clock, I would appreciate it."

"Of course. And where can we find you when Mr. Sharpe arrives?"

"I'll be in my office," Simon answered, but as he shoved his watch back into his waistcoat pocket, his gaze slid past Ricardo and down the long foyer in the direction of the American Bar, and he reconsidered his decision. The Savoy's famous barkeep, Frank Wells, was said to make the best cocktails on this side of the pond.

He'd never been much of a drinking man, but Lady Stratham was the sort of woman who could make even the staunch teetotaler break the pledge, and he was glad Mr. Wells hadn't been one of the corrupt people he'd had to fire during the past few weeks.

"On second thought, I'll be in the American Bar," he said, and as he headed in that direction, he wondered if Mr. Wells's repertoire of famous cocktails included one called a Tornado. With Lady Stratham's damnable smile still in his mind, it seemed an appropriate choice.

5

He was in the Savoy's American Bar, sipping a bizarre concoction of whisky, gin, and crème de menthe that had been recommended to him by the barkeep, waiting for Devlin, and imagining various ways he might rid himself of Lady Stratham, when a voice intruded on his thoughts.

"Difficult day?"

Simon looked up to find the Duke of Westbourne standing by his chair, faultlessly attired in white-tie, a drink in his hand and a smile on his face.

Simon leaned back in his chair, giving the other man a rueful look. "Is it that obvious?"

Westbourne's smile widened into a grin, one that bore a strong resemblance to that of his provoking cousin. "Well, it's rather a safe bet when a man's drinking alone in a bar. May I join you?"

Simon hesitated, for he'd quite had his fill of aristocrats for one day. But then, he remembered the shareholders' meeting, where he'd told the investors of his father's disgrace. Helen and Richard had advised him not to, but he felt he'd had no choice; honor demanded full disclosure of that information, even though he'd been sure it would sink his chances. It was Westbourne who had pointed out to the other investors that a man could not be blamed for his father's sins.

"But," the duke went on before he could reply, "if you would prefer to drown your frustrations with the Duchess of Moreland all by yourself, I would completely understand."

Simon sighed. "You saw the whole encounter, I suppose."

"I think everyone in the lobby saw it."

He grimaced, knowing that was probably true.

Westbourne, however, merely laughed. "Don't worry about it, old chap. Being a duke myself, I ought not to say it, but a more odious woman than the Duchess of Moreland never drew breath."

Simon gestured to the empty chairs at his table. "Please join me, but know that it won't be for long. I'm waiting for someone, and when he arrives, we're going to dinner."

"And I'm off to dinner with friends at my club, where they intend to bore me for the remainder of the night with discussions of politics. So please, take pity on me," he added, taking the chair opposite, "for this is my only chance this evening to be in congenial company. What is that green stuff in your glass, by the way?"

"Mr. Wells called it a Savoy Hurricane." Simon held up his glass to study the emerald-colored contents, then he took a swallow, almost relishing the cocktail's medicinal, ice-cold burn. "He didn't have anything in his repertoire called a Tornado. This," he added as the duke gave him a dubious look, "was the best he could do."

"I've no idea what tornadoes have to do with anything, but either way, that drink looks absolutely vile."

"It is rather," Simon agreed, and in a contradictory spirit, he downed the contents of his glass and signaled for Mr. Wells to bring him another. "But the taste seems to improve as one goes on."

"That's both the delight of cocktails and their danger."

"Indeed? I don't imbibe often enough to know. I dislike the effect strong drink has on me. That's probably because," he added as he remembered Lady Stratham's words from their first meeting, "of my obsessive need for control."

"I beg your pardon?"

"Or," he mused, ignoring the question, "it might be my need for efficiency. After all, cocktails are a much faster way for a man to get sodding drunk than port, claret, or beer. And efficiency, so I've been told, is the god I worship. Or it might be profit. I can't quite remember which."

The duke shook his head, laughing in obvious bafflement. "You seem determined to speak in riddles, Calderon."

Simon did not enlighten him. "It's all your fault, really," he said instead. "If you hadn't spoken in my favor at the shareholders' meeting, I doubt I'd be here now."

"It's the least I can do for a fellow Old Harrovian."

"I'm not sure how much good my public-school education has done me so far. I've got members of the nobility dressing me down and hotel staff loathing the sight of me. Nothing at Harrow prepared me for that."

"Minor problems to a man of your abilities," Westbourne countered lightly.

"Perhaps," he acknowledged as the barkeep whisked away his empty glass and set a fresh cocktail on the table. "But as a fellow Old Harrovian, couldn't you have at least warned me what I'd be in for?"

"If you mean the Duchess of Moreland—"

"I'm not talking about her. I'm talking about that black-haired tornado you are forced by familial obligation to acknowledge as a cousin." He lifted his glass in a toast. "My condolences on that, by the way."

"My cousin?" he echoed, still clearly puzzled, but after a moment, his brow cleared. "Ah, now I understand your references to torna-does," he said and grinned. "Delia is lovely, isn't she?"

"In appearance or temperament? If you mean the former, I am forced to grant it. But if you mean the latter, I must disagree. Never have I met a more exasperating female—"

He broke off, for even in his own decidedly middle-class upbringing, one didn't disparage another man's relations to his face. "Sorry. I don't mean to insult a member of your family."

"Please, don't apologize. I've gotten crosswise with my cousin a time or two, so I know how you feel. And truth be told, I'm rather amused to discover that there is at least one man in the world who refuses to fall immediately at Delia's feet."

Simon found such a prospect so appalling that he emptied his glass in one hefty swallow, making the duke laugh.

"She seems to have gotten under your skin," Westbourne commented.

"It would be more accurate to say I got under hers," Simon clarified and once again signaled for Mr. Wells.

"So, what's Delia been up to? You needn't mind telling me," the duke went on as Simon hesitated to reply. "I won't take offense, and I might be able to offer you some insight you'll find useful, so feel free to be frank."

Frankness in this place was a luxury he couldn't afford. Westbourne was one of the Savoy's major investors, but he was not a member of the board. He was not privy to the infamous letter, the hiring of private detectives, or Helen's suspicions about the duke's beautiful and exasperating relation. And if Westbourne got any inkling of how deep the rot within the Savoy had gone before proper measures could be taken, he'd surely tell the other investors, they'd all run to dump their shares, the value of the Savoy's stock would plummet, and the fat would be in the fire.

It wasn't quite fair, he supposed, to pump Westbourne for information about his cousin when she was one of those under suspicion. On the other hand, the duke had freely offered some insight regarding her, and Simon could certainly use it.

"I had my first meeting with her last week," he said, choosing his words with care. "Just as I have with every other member of hotel management."

"Yes, so I heard."

"Went running to cry on your shoulder afterward, did she?"

"Delia? God, no. She's not the crying sort. There was some gnashing of teeth and cursing your name, however. Along with some dire predictions about the hotel's future if the things you want to do are implemented."

"The things I want?" Simon echoed with some heat. "As if what I want has anything to do with it. I'm doing what's necessary."

"You don't have to tell me that. I supported your nomination because I'm sure you have the experience and skill to turn things around."

Simon had been sure of that, too, but the events of the past week were giving him cause to doubt. "She declared she could never work for me. I offered to put her under Mrs. Carte's supervision, but she wasn't having that, either. I then pointed out that her only other choice was to resign, and as you might guess, that suggestion did not serve to improve her opinion of me."

"Ultimatums," Max said gravely, "are not among Delia's favorite things."

"Yes, I realized that when she declared I'd never force her to resign, referred to me in a way that put my mother's honor in doubt, and stormed out of my office."

"You were lucky," Max assured him. "Remind me to tell you about the time I read her diary."

Diverted by this rather unsavory admission, he eyed Max with doubt. "You read her diary?"

"What can I say? I was only twelve at the time. Delia's revenge was to shred the essay I'd just completed for my tutor, which had taken me a week to compose. She also hid my best cricket bat in the attics and put itching powder in my socks."

From what Simon could see, the years hadn't changed her much. "I suspect she'd adore exacting similar revenge upon me."

"For your sake, I hope not. As you have seen, my cousin's got a bit of a temper."

"Thank you for the reminder," he replied as Mr. Wells set his third cocktail before him, "but what I'm waiting for is some of that insight you promised me."

"The most useful thing I can say is to quote the old proverb that one always catches more flies with honey than with vinegar."

Simon stared, appalled at the idea.

The duke grinned. "You look as if I've just suggested a visit to the dentist."

"Forgive me," Simon said at once. "It's just that flattery is not my strongest talent. And even if it were, I daresay your cousin is far too clever to be taken in by such a tactic—"

"No, no, you misunderstand me. I'm not suggesting you attempt to charm Delia. As you've already pointed out, it wouldn't fool her for a moment. No, in this scenario, Delia needs to be the honey. If you can gain her support, she can convince others to accept the policies you've introduced. She might even be able to get the duchess to pay her bill."

"Gain her support?" he echoed in disbelief. "Haven't you heard a word I've said? She despises me. How on earth can I gain her support when she feels that I'm undermining Ritz and that everything I'm doing will bring the hotel to ruin?"

"The loyalty to Ritz runs deep around here. That is especially true in Delia's case. They are close friends. Nonetheless, if you can get her on your side, she can be of great assistance to you. She knows a great many people, and she's got a persuasive way about her when she chooses. Most of the scrapes I got into as a boy were at her instigation."

That was no surprise to Simon, but before he could think of a more tactful reply, another voice entered the conversation.

"Simon, what the devil are you doing in a bar? The last time I saw that was in Cape Town. About fourteen years ago, as I recall."

Simon looked up to find Devlin standing behind the duke's chair, a look of amused disbelief on his dark, rakish face.

"I had to find something to occupy my time waiting for you," Simon countered. "You're late, as usual."

He stood up, a move that brought the duke to his feet as well, but when Westbourne turned in Devlin's direction, Simon saw the amusement inexplicably vanish from his old friend's face and a wooden expression take its place.

"Duke," Devlin greeted the other man with a stiff, barely perceptible nod of acknowledgment.

"You two know each other?" Simon asked, surprised by the sudden, unmistakable tension in the air.

"Not well, I'm afraid," the duke answered, "but we have met. Mr. Sharpe," he added. "Pleasure to see you again."

"Is it?" Devlin's smile was back, a mocking curve that Simon knew from long acquaintance could mean trouble. "Afraid I can't say the same."

An offensive remark, but oddly, the duke did not seem offended. "Quite understandable," he replied, "given the circumstances. And now," he added, turning to Simon, "I must be off. It won't do if I'm late to dinner. Good evening, gentlemen."

With a nod to both of them, the duke departed, and Simon turned to Devlin, frowning in puzzlement. "What was that all about?"

"Nothing." Devlin took the chair vacated by the duke. "Just a bit of ancient history."

"Between you and Westbourne?" Simon resumed his own seat. "I wasn't aware you two had ever met."

"Only once. When I was spared from making the worst mistake of my life."

At this mention of the night fifteen years earlier when Devlin had been jilted at the altar, Simon began to understand. They hadn't known each other at the time, but from what the other man had let slip over the years, Simon knew his friend had every right to resent anyone associated with the bride's defection. "The duke is a friend of Lady Kay, I take it?"

"Not him. But they move in the same circles, and one of his sisters was her bosom companion. Kay was staying with them the night she agreed to elope with me. The duke and his sisters are the ones who came after us. While his sisters persuaded Lady Kay to change her mind, the duke reminded me that, because I am the fifth son of a baron, I am a gentleman of birth, breeding, and absolutely no prospects, without so much as two shillings to rub together."

"But that last bit's not true. You've got heaps of money."

"Ah, but I didn't back then. I was only nineteen, after all, and wholly dependent upon my minuscule quarterly allowance. Lady Kay's family, the duke informed me, felt she could do better. Lady Kay, I soon discovered, agreed with them."

"Sorry. I didn't know of the connection."

"Not to worry." Devlin flashed his characteristic mercurial smile. "As I said, I was spared from marrying the wrong girl, and it was a blessing in disguise; believe me. Especially since I'm now about to marry the right girl."

"What?" Simon laughed. "Engaged already? You've only been home from Africa a week."

"What, you don't believe I could sweep a girl off her feet in a week? All right, all right," he added as Simon gave him a pointed look. "I'll own up. My intended is Lady Pamela Stirling, beloved only daughter of the stone-broke Marquess of Walston. We met in Cairo last autumn when she was on holiday with her family."

"You must have fallen for each other straightaway."

"Yes, well, it's amazing how much more appealing a baron's fifth son becomes once he's amassed an obscenely large fortune. Lady Pamela is quite willing to tie the knot with me in order to help me spend it."

"That's rather a cynical way of approaching matrimony. Shouldn't love play a part in this sort of thing?"

Devlin laughed. "Good God, Simon, you really are the golden boy so beloved in English literature. Decorated war hero with unimpeachable morals, a stout heart, and remarkably good looks. You've even got the right color hair. I can't think why we're friends."

"You have to have at least one honorable friend. Especially now that you've decided to do something as honorable as matrimony."

"A man's got to settle down sometime. Which reminds me...the wedding is the seventh of June, and Pamela's mother is inviting half the damn ton. Any chance we can have the wedding dinner here at the Savoy? We'll need the largest banquet room you've got."

"If it isn't already reserved, it's yours." He stood up. "Let's go to dinner. We can inquire at the front desk on our way out."

"Out?" Devlin echoed as he rose. "I thought we were dining at the restaurant here."

Simon shook his head. "Let's not. I need to get clear of the Savoy and all the refinement of your damned aristocracy."

"Don't be spiky. It's not my fault I was born into this ridiculous institution of so-called nobility. Tell you what." He clapped Simon on the shoulder as they started out of the bar. "Let's find an East End pub and wrap our bellies around a pair of underdone steaks, a plate of chips, and an old-fashioned plum tart."

"As long as there's plenty of ale to go with it all."

Devlin laughed. "First cocktails, then pints of ale? What's brought on this sudden uncharacteristic impulse to drink?"

"A tornado, my friend." Simon picked up his glass and drained the remaining contents. "A black-haired, blue-eyed tornado."

"A woman," Devlin said at once, giving a nod of sympathetic understanding. "Best batten down the hatches then."

An image of Lady Stratham and her provoking smile came into Simon's mind. "I intend to," he said as he set his now-empty glass on a table by the door. "Believe me, Devlin, I intend to."

The following morning, Delia was in her office before eight o'clock. She wasn't usually an early riser, but she had no intention of allowing Calderon any excuse to fire her. No, she would be the picture of a cheerful, cooperative, and industrious employee, and when she saw him, she wouldn't crow about being right. Well, she amended as she sat down at her desk, she might crow a little.

She smiled, remembering how the duchess had torn Calderon apart the night before. He'd held his own end up all right, she had to admit—no easy feat in front of all those people. But in the end, it hadn't mattered; for not only had the duchess departed for Claridge's, but she had also not paid her outstanding bill. A few more incidents like that, and Calderon might be prepared to start listening to those who understood the Savoy and its clientele.

Delia's smile faded, however, as she eyed the piles of work on her desk. Many of the letters that had accumulated during her absence were still unopened. In addition, she had to plan a luncheon party for Lady Gray, a regimental dinner for the City of London Royal Fusiliers, and a banquet for Viscount Ridley, the British home secretary, and she could only hope none of them would walk away from the Savoy before Calderon saw sense. In addition, the invitation cards for the East India Club dinner had arrived from the printer and were now waiting to be filled in, placed in envelopes, and sent out.

That event, thankfully, was too close to be canceled, but the fact that it was only two weeks away meant the invitations were her top priority, so Delia shoved aside her unopened letters, opened her inkwell, and reached for a pen.

"You rang for tea, my lady?"

She looked up to find a waiter in the doorway. "Ah, yes, James, thank you. Come in. Goodness," she added, eyeing the extra teacups and heaping plate of breakfast pastries on the tray as the waiter came toward her desk. "How much does Auguste think I'll be able to eat?"

"I believe he thought you might be meeting with clients. You usually have morning tea sent to your room, my lady, not your office, and never this early unless you have a meeting."

Delia, notorious for rising late, made a face. "You needn't remind me I'm awake before the birds today," she said, clearing space on one side of her desk to make room for the tray. "But with Calderon in charge, I don't dare slack. What's this?" she added, noting an envelope on the tray.

"A cable from Rome, my lady. It arrived this morning, so I brought it along."

"At last." Relieved, she plucked the envelope off the tray and tore it open, pulling out the printed missive inside. But if she'd been hoping for some advice from her mentor that would be helpful, she was disappointed.

Calderon wants to ruin everything I've built at the Savoy.
Do not help him do it.

—Ritz

"That's not very helpful, César," she murmured under her breath.

"My lady?"

"Nothing, James." She shoved the telegram in her skirt pocket. "How is the staff adapting to the new regime?"

"It's been a bit hard, my lady, I admit. We've lost two waiters and a kitchen maid in the restaurant."

"Yes, I heard," she murmured, thinking of Escoffier raging about that fact in her office the evening before. "Cost-cutting measures, I was told."

"We were told the same. And it's not just the restaurant. Two cashiers and one of the maids were let go as well, and rumor has it they aren't done yet. It's got us all on tenterhooks, wondering who might be next to get the boot. Most of the staff live hand to mouth, you know. We can't afford to lose our jobs."

Delia nodded, sympathetic but not surprised. "I know, and I'm sorry. I wish I could do something."

"Couldn't you talk to him, my lady? Tell him that we're working 'round the clock and we can't afford to lose any more people?"

"Calderon doesn't listen to me, I'm afraid," she replied, the words bitter on her tongue. "He doesn't like me."

"Oh, my lady, I don't believe that for a moment."

She smiled at this show of loyalty. "It's a shock, I know," she said wryly, "but it's true, nonetheless. We got off on the wrong foot from the moment we met, and it's gotten no better since then. In fact," she added lightly, "the next person let go might very well be me."

"He'd never fire you. Why, you're a countess, my lady. He wouldn't dare give *you* the sack."

From what she could see, Calderon would dare anything in the name of his precious profits, but she didn't say so. "The same could be said of you, James," she said instead. "The restaurant is so busy; I can't imagine he'll dismiss any more waiters."

"I hope not, my lady. And in the meantime, there is one benefit to being short-staffed. Our share of the *tronc* is bigger for those of us who remain."

She knew at once what he meant. The *tronc* was the accumulated total of all the day's tips, which were divided equally among the waiters who had worked that day, and it was the only pay they received. "I suppose that's something. And the extra money is quite a help to you right now, I imagine. How are you enjoying fatherhood, by the way? Your wife had a boy, I heard?"

The young man beamed at her mention of his newborn son. "A fine, healthy boy, my lady."

"Excellent. And Lizzie? She is recovering well, I trust?"

"Oh, yes. She's already back in the laundry, hard at work."

"Already? But she only had the baby two weeks ago. She shouldn't be working! At least, not yet."

"She vows she's up to it, my lady. And as I said, we need the money."

"Of course," Delia said at once, appreciating that not everyone had the luxury of working only when and if they wanted to.

"Anyway, Lizzie and I are just crossing our fingers Calderon doesn't decide to let either of us go."

"Let's hope that doesn't happen. But please don't allow Lizzie to overtire herself. And tell her I have a gift for the baby. It should be arriving any day now."

"Thank you, my lady. That is most generous of you. Will there be anything else?"

"No, thank you, James. You may go."

The waiter departed, and after a sip of tea and a bite of croissant, Delia once again picked up her pen, but she had barely dipped her pen in the inkwell before she was once again interrupted.

"Good morning, Lady Stratham."

Turning her head, she spied Mr. Ross in the doorway between her office and Calderon's, and though she couldn't help feeling a little bit resentful that Calderon had decided his own secretary was necessary while hers was not, she knew none of that was Ross's fault, and she gave him a sunny smile.

"Good morning," she replied and gestured to the tray at her elbow. "Would you care for some tea and croissants? Please have some," she added as he hesitated. "The kitchen sent up far too much, and if you don't help me, I fear I shall eat all of them by myself, and then I'll have to loosen my corset, something a lady never wants to do."

The young man blushed to the roots of his hair at the mention of corsets, but when she poured a cup of tea and held it up with an encouraging nod, he came into her office. "Your ladyship is very kind."

"Not at all. Do sit down," she added, gesturing to the chair opposite her desk. "Would you like sugar? Milk?"

"Neither; thank you, my lady," he replied as he took the offered cup and saucer and sat down.

"Your employer seems to be running a bit later than you this morning," she commented, nodding to the empty adjoining office as she set a croissant on a plate for him.

"I have been informed that his lordship will not be in today."

"Oh? Early meeting?" she guessed, handing over the croissants and a napkin.

"Oh, no, my lady. His valet sent word that he was feeling a bit under the weather this morning."

"Indeed?" Taking pleasure in news like that, she reminded herself sternly, would be very, very wrong. "It's not serious, I hope?"

"Oh, no. He'll be quite all right by tomorrow, his valet has assured me. But it leaves me rather at loose ends in the meantime, with nothing much to do."

It was an opportunity she could not resist. "Really? I'm sure it must be difficult to be idle, but..." She paused, assuming a woeful expression as she gestured to the heaps of files, letters, and papers on her desk. "I'm so inundated with work, I can't help envying you."

Like a magnet to steel, the young secretary responded at once. "Can I help you in any way?"

"Oh, would you?" She clasped her hands, looking hopeful. "Would you really?"

Fifteen minutes later, the tea and croissants had been consumed, and the invitations, envelopes, and list of invitees for the East India Club dinner had been transferred from her desk to the secretary's. "You're an angel, Mr. Ross," she told him with relief and gratitude. "An absolute angel."

At this gushing praise, Mr. Ross's fair, freckled face once again turned bright red. "Not...not...at all, my...my lady," he stammered. "It's my pleasure."

"I know it isn't, though you're terribly sweet to lie and say it is. But please understand," she added before he could protest, "that I am in your debt. If there is anything I can ever do for you, I insist you let me know."

Delia returned to her office, sat down, and prepared to tackle her correspondence, but then she noticed the note she'd scribbled on her blotter last evening during her conversation with Kay: a reminder to reserve the banquet room for the other woman's wedding dinner.

Deciding it was best to handle that now while it was at the forefront of her mind, and happy to avoid tackling the pile of letters on her desk for a few more minutes, Delia left her office and headed for the lobby.

When she arrived at the registration desk, she found young Ricardo on duty. Frowning over a slip of paper in his hand, he didn't even notice her until she gave a little cough.

The clerk looked up. "Lady Stratham," he said, straightening respectfully and setting aside what he'd been reading. "Good morning, my lady. You're out and about quite early today."

Delia made a face. "I know it."

He smiled, but it was an abstracted smile, and watching him, Delia grew concerned. "You seem rather preoccupied today, Ricardo. Can I help?"

"Oh, no." He sounded shocked. "I couldn't possibly trouble your ladyship."

"By all means, trouble me." She gave him a wink. "You should know by now how much I adore trouble."

He hesitated, then said, "Two cashiers were let go this week, and Mr. Agostini asked if I would help with the charge tickets." He held out the slip of paper. "This was waiting for me when I arrived this morning."

Delia glanced at it, recognizing that it was a ticket for charges from the American Bar to one of the rooms, and aside from the brow-raising amount of liquor consumed, she saw nothing particularly extraordinary about it. "Yes, and...?" she asked, looking up, not understanding the problem.

"It is for room 538. Lord Calderon's room," he added as she remained unenlightened.

"Indeed? All this is from last night?" At Ricardo's nod of confirmation, Delia thought again of Calderon's set-to with the duchess, and she had a pretty fair idea of why the man had decided to embark on a bout of alcoholic excess afterward. It was also, she reflected in amusement, why he was feeling unwell today. "Poor fellow," she said and had to bite her lip to hide her smile. "He seems to have accumulated quite a bill."

"He and his friend were in the bar before dinner, and then they came back a few hours later and stayed the rest of the evening. I can't be sure, but I believe they were still there when I departed at midnight."

"Quite a night," she replied, donning as grave an expression as she could manage. "But I'm not sure what the problem is, Ricardo."

"He's management, my lady. The hotel usually doesn't charge management for liquor, as you know. I can't imagine why Mr. Wells would even do up a ticket for it, but it was here with the other tickets when I came in this morning. And since Mr. Wells is not in yet, I can't ask him about it."

"Why don't you just put the ticket through with all the others and let the bookkeepers sort it out?"

"I don't know what Mr. Agostini will say about that, I really don't." As he mentioned the head cashier's name, his frown of worry deepened, and Delia immediately knew what was needed.

"Put the ticket through and charge Calderon's room," she told him. "If Mr. Agostini questions you about it, tell him I told you to do it."

"Thank you, my lady." Clearly relieved to cede responsibility to a higher authority, he set the ticket aside. "What can I do for you this morning?"

"I need the reservation book."

Ricardo pulled the volume in question out from behind the counter and placed it before her. Opening it, Delia began flipping pages as she reached for a pencil, but when she located the page for the seventh of June, her fingers froze.

> *Devlin Sharpe. Wedding banquet. Sixty guests. HMS Pinafore Room.*

She stared at the page in disbelief, not only because the Savoy's largest banqueting room had somehow been reserved without her knowledge, but also because of the name of the man who had reserved it.

"Devlin Sharpe?" she murmured, reading the entry again, hardly able to believe it. "Devlin Sharpe is getting married?"

"It sounds as if you know the gentleman, my lady."

At the sound of Ricardo's voice, Delia looked up. "Not really," she said slowly and looked down at the book again.

It had to be the same man. The name was not a common one. So, Kay's long-lost love, the scoundrel who had persuaded her to an underhanded elopement fifteen years earlier, then ruined her reputation when she changed her mind, was getting married on the same day she was, and he wanted the same banqueting room? It was such an incredible coincidence that Delia couldn't help wondering if his choice was deliberate. She'd never met Sharpe herself, but from what she knew of the man, it would be just like him to try to throw a spanner in the works and hurt Kay's plans. But how, Delia wondered, had Sharpe managed to reserve the same banquet room that she had promised Kay? The only people who were allowed to reserve banquet rooms were Ritz, Echenard, and herself. How had this happened?

"Ricardo?" She looked up again. "Echenard isn't back from his holiday yet, is he?"

"No, my lady."

And Ritz, she knew, was still in Rome. "Then who put this entry in the reservation book?" she asked, tapping the appropriate line on the page with her finger as she spoke. "Do you know?"

The young clerk leaned over the desk to glance at the entry. "Oh, that was Lord Calderon," he said as he straightened.

Of course. She should have known. That man had his finger in every pie. Was it any wonder Ritz resented him?

"He came by here with Mr. Sharpe as they were going out to dinner and had me put the entry in the book. They seem to be quite old friends."

The fact that Calderon would do something like this without consulting with her wasn't a surprise, but that a man like Devlin Sharpe was his friend did take her aback a little. Calderon was so damned buttoned-down and straightlaced that having Devlin Sharpe as a friend seemed rather incongruous.

"Being he's in charge now," Ricardo went on, sounding anxious in the wake of her silence, "I thought it was all right. It's for Mr. Sharpe's wedding banquet. He's marrying an earl's daughter, I understand, and it's to be a big affair. Sixty guests, I heard them say. That's why Lord Calderon wants the HMS Pinafore."

"Oh, he'll get the Pinafore all right," Delia muttered and slammed the book shut. "Over my dead body."

"My lady?"

But Delia had already turned away, and as she headed back to her office, she realized that her current method of dealing with Calderon was just not going to work. Granted, it had been amusing to hand the outraged Lord Synby over to him and duck out, and an absolute delight to watch him face down the formidable Duchess of Moreland. But such pleasures, she appreciated with chagrin, were very short-lived and would not be at all helpful in solving her immediate problem. But what could she do? As she asked herself that, the words of Ritz's telegram echoed through her mind.

Calderon wants to ruin everything I've built at the Savoy. Do not help him do it.

Easy for César to say, she thought in aggravation. He was a thousand miles away. She was here, and she had a problem that only Calderon could resolve. In this case, at least, her strategy of standing by while his policies backfired was untenable.

Kay's wedding would be in the midst of the London season. By the time the consequences of Calderon's other decisions came back to bite him, Kay would have been obliged to choose a different venue for her wedding banquet. Kay had been through hell at the hands of Devlin Sharpe. Allowing that man to cause her any more grief was a nauseating prospect and one Delia absolutely refused to accept.

And if things kept on this way and Calderon did not change course, Kay wasn't the only one who would suffer. Half a dozen employees had already been dismissed, and they might not be the only ones. As James had said, many of the staff lived hand to mouth and could not afford to be without employment. Having grown up in the aristocracy, Delia had been raised with a strong sense of responsibility for one's staff. It was the duty of people like her to provide employment for others whenever and wherever possible, not to stand by silently as they were dismissed without cause. And with Ritz and Echenard away, she felt that sense of duty and responsibility even more keenly.

There was also the matter of the hotel's image as London's finest hotel, an image Ritz had worked hard for years to cultivate. How could she continue to watch helplessly as that image and Ritz's legacy were tarnished? But damn it all, how could she stop it?

Delia stopped in the corridor. Taking deep breaths, she tried to cool her temper and think logically of a solution.

Can't you talk to him, my lady?

James's words echoed back to her, a repeat of Escoffier's plea from last night, but she didn't see how talking to Calderon would make a difference. Unless…

Just be your usual charming self, and you'll have him eating out of your hand.

The memory of Max's solution to the problem made Delia groan.

"Not that," she muttered. "Anything but that."

She rubbed a hand over her forehead, her mind working desperately to come up with a less nauseating prospect. But there was no other course she could think of that had a prayer of succeeding, and at last, resigned to her fate, she turned around.

"I hope everyone appreciates the enormous sacrifice I'm about to make on their behalf," she grumbled as she headed for the kitchens. "My pride may never recover."

6

The first time Simon awakened, it was due to the customary clink of drapery rings sliding back and the scent of early tea. But upon opening his eyes, he'd been hit with a shaft of bright morning sunlight that felt like a spike piercing his skull, a painful reminder of why he didn't drink. Closing his eyes again, he'd ordered his valet to shut the damn drapes, take away the tea, and send word to Ross that he was ill.

He had then drifted back into blessed sleep, only to be awakened again sometime later by the sound of a knock on his door and the low murmur of voices.

This time, he opened his eyes gingerly, but though the light in the room was now much dimmer than before, his head was still aching fit to split, his eyes felt as if they had sand in them, and he could only wonder how someone had managed to stuff cotton wool into his mouth while he slept. With a groan, Simon pulled the covers over his head.

"My lord?"

His valet's voice was a soft murmur, but to Simon, it sounded like a gunshot, making him wonder why he'd ever thought becoming a viscount required a valet. He pulled the counterpane down, bestowing a malevolent glare on the unflappable man standing there with a tray in his hands. "Morgan, if you don't go away and leave me in peace, I swear to God, I will sack you."

Even as he spoke, the smell of coffee and bacon, neither of which he had asked for, hit his nostrils. His stomach rumbled. "And I thought I already told you I don't want any breakfast."

"I didn't order it, my lord. The waiter who brought it said it was sent up by Lady Stratham."

"Lady Stratham?" That information was so astonishing that Simon abandoned any thought of firing Morgan and sat up. "You must have heard wrong. Or you're going daft."

Morgan gave a cough and nodded to the tray he carried. "If you'll notice, my lord, there is a note."

Simon pulled the folded slip of paper off the tray, broke its wax seal, and opened it.

> *You'll feel better if you eat. And drink the tomato juice. You won't like it, but it will help. Trust me on this.*
>
> *—Delia*

"Trust her?" he muttered as Morgan shifted the tray to one arm and lifted the lid off the plate for his inspection. "God help me if I ever become that big a fool."

He leaned closer, eyeing with suspicion the heaping plate of eggs, bacon, potatoes, and baked beans, the glass of tomato juice, the pot of coffee, and the stack of buttered toast. "Where do you suppose she's put the arsenic?"

Morgan deigned to smile. "If you'll notice the vase, my lord, it's clear Lady Stratham bears you no ill will."

"It's not clear to me." Still skeptical, he glanced at the bud vase on the tray, unable to fathom what a few flowers had to do with anything. "But even if you're right, she's probably sucking up because she's afraid I'm about to fire her."

"A countess would never do anything like that," Morgan murmured, looking shocked; bless his trusting soul. "She's probably just being kind," he added before Simon could reply. "She's ever so nice, her ladyship is."

At once, an image of her came into Simon's mind. Her sooty-lashed blue eyes sparkling with amusement, her full pink mouth curved in a mischievous smile, the smothered laughter in her voice—all at his expense. "Nice?" he echoed, chagrined to realize that he might have found her quite nice indeed if she weren't so damned aggravating. "Who says so?"

"A great many people."

"A great many people think the world is flat, too," he muttered, tossing the note back on the tray.

"But the earth is flat, sir. Why, one has only to use one's eyes to know that."

Simon was in no condition for a debate on astronomy with a follower of the flat-earth movement. "Just send it back, Morgan."

But even as he spoke, he inhaled the scent of bacon again, and he realized to his surprise that, despite the pain in his head and the unsteadiness of his stomach, he was actually hungry. "On second thought," he said as his valet turned away, "put it on the table over there and bring me my dressing robe."

A short time later, and much to his own surprise, Simon had wolfed down every crumb of food on the tray. As Lady Stratham had predicted, he was less enthusiastic about the tomato juice, for it had the sharp, unmistakable tang of liquor in it, and liquor was something he'd had far too much of the night before. But his mouth was dry as dust, and he ended up drinking all of it, as well as the entire pot of coffee.

Afterward, he had a hot bath and a shave, and by the time he was dressed, he felt considerably better.

Deciding that he might be able to get some work done today after all, he ventured downstairs, and as he passed Lady Stratham's office on the way to his own, he found her at her desk opening letters. "Slaving away, I see," he remarked, pausing in the corridor.

At the sound of his voice, she looked up. "He lives!"

Simon gave a little bow. "To paraphrase Mark Twain, the reports of my death have been greatly exaggerated."

That made her smile. "Having some breakfast helped, I trust?"

"It did, yes." He paused, feeling strangely awkward and a little bit guilty that he'd been so quick to judge her motives. "Thank you. Though I confess, I almost sent it back, fearing you might be trying to poison me."

"I would never do such a thing. I might think it," she added, her smile widening, "but I would never do it. I like living too much to risk being hanged. You're safe as houses."

"That's reassuring."

"And even if that weren't the case," she added, "I'd never do away with someone while simultaneously attempting to broker a truce with him. That would be blatant hypocrisy and quite dishonorable."

Somehow, Simon felt that attempted poisoning might be a greater breach of honor than hypocrisy, but her remark was sufficiently surprising that he didn't bother to say so. "Was that your intent?" he asked instead. "To broker a truce between us?"

"Of course! I thought the flowers made that quite obvious."

"The flowers?"

She groaned. "Don't tell me they didn't send the vase up with the breakfast?"

"There was a bud vase of flowers on the tray," he said. "Purple, spiky things. But what do flowers have to do with anything?"

"Not just any flowers. Hyacinths."

"Oh, well, I didn't realize they were *hyacinths*," he said with a nod, still utterly at sea. "That explains everything."

She sighed, shaking her head, demonstrating that his attempt to look ho-hum and wise hadn't fooled her for a second. "I begin to see why you find winter flower arrangements in springtime acceptable," she said sadly. "In the language of flowers, hyacinths signify a new beginning."

He stared at her askance. "Flowers have a language?"

"Of course! If you wish to express your feelings to someone, you send them flowers that have the meaning you wish to convey." She laughed at his doubtful expression, and despite the fact that their conversation about flower arrangements was the rocky start that had led to the present need for a truce, he couldn't help laughing, too.

"Why, Lord Calderon," she exclaimed, bolting up from her chair with a suddenness that startled him. "What is that?"

"I beg your pardon?" he asked as she circled her desk and walked toward where he stood. "What is what?"

"You're..." She paused, halting before him and squinting as she leaned closer, studying his face as if confounded. "You're laughing."

"I have been known to laugh on occasion."

"Not in my hearing. My goodness." She pressed a hand to her chest. "The miracles that can result from giving a man a hearty breakfast and a little hair of the dog that bit him."

"Hair of the dog?"

"Frank's special tomato-juice cocktail."

"The Savoy's barkeep invented that vile concoction I drank this morning?"

"Well, he says he invented it, but for my part, I'm inclined to doubt. Every barkeep worth his salt claims he's invented some exciting new cocktail when he really stole it from someone else. Either way, he says it's an excellent cure for the aftereffects of alcoholic excess. And looking at you, its effectiveness speaks for itself."

"But how did you know—" He broke off, not willing to admit he'd been so careless as to imbibe enough that such a remedy was necessary.

"How did I know you needed it?" she finished for him. Leaning closer, a distinctly mischievous look in her dark blue eyes, she whispered, "I have my spies. I hear everything that happens in this hotel."

That was just what worried him. "You shouldn't pay attention to gossip," he said.

"You're right," she agreed at once, straightening and donning a contrite expression. "They told me you'd gone on rather a bender, but having listened to such wicked rumors, I feel thoroughly ashamed of myself."

As if to illustrate the point, she hung her head, looking so woebegone that he couldn't help laughing again.

"Another one?" she cried, looking up. "Well, that proves it."

"Proves what?"

"That you're not nearly as stiff and haughty as you pretend to be."

He was a bit taken aback by the description. "I'm not the least bit haughty."

Even as he spoke, however, he watched one of her dark brows arch upward, and he appreciated that haughty might be a fair assessment of his behavior to date—at least from her point of view.

"I'm so glad to see this side of you," she said breezily. "Now, every time you poker up and frown so ominously, I shall know it's all a hum, and our friendship can remain intact."

"Ah, so we're friends now, are we?"

The laughter in her expression vanished. "I'd like us to be."

He met her gaze, and something in her eyes made him catch his breath. He stirred, and when she moved closer, the faint but unmistakable scent of her perfume wafted to his nose—a spicy, exotic scent so blatantly sensual that his body responded at once. Warmth flooded his limbs and his muscles tightened as arousal flickered to life inside him. "You sound as if you mean that," he murmured.

"I do mean it."

She sounded so sincere, and when she moved a step closer, the arousal in him rose a notch. Involuntarily, he bent his head a fraction, but then he stiffened, reminding himself of all the reasons he could not afford to trust her. "I'm not sure I believe you."

"But what—" She broke off and her tongue darted out to lick her lips, drawing his gaze to her mouth. "What can I do to convince you?"

What, indeed. Erotic possibilities at once began going through his mind, but of course, he was too much of a gentleman to ever act on them. She was under his supervision. She was also an extravagant spendthrift, probably an accomplished liar, and might very well be guilty of embezzlement and fraud.

Sadly, however, his baser masculine nature proved woefully unimpressed by such considerations, and his gaze slid downward, his mind conjuring images of what might be beneath the soft blue cashmere dress that clung so provocatively to the generous curves of her figure.

"The truth is," she said, her voice barely discernible to his ears above the hard thud of his heartbeat, "I've had a sort of epiphany. I've realized it makes sense for us to be friends."

He blinked, trying to think past the sensuous haze enveloping him. "Friends?"

"It's the best thing for everyone, don't you agree?"

Given what he was feeling right now, being friends with her sounded like the most nonsensical thing he'd ever heard, but by sheer force of will, Simon hauled his gaze back up to her face and his mind out of the gutter. "Absolutely," he said with more enthusiasm than he actually felt. "It's an excellent idea."

"Oh, I'm so glad." She laughed, pressed a hand to her chest. "Such a relief to know we can get along if we try."

"Yes," he agreed, rather surprised. "I suppose it is."

"And it's certainly better for the hotel if we're friends."

"Indeed."

They both fell silent, almost as if neither of them knew quite where to go from here, but at last, she gave a little cough, took another step back, and gestured to the desk behind her. "In this new spirit of friendship, perhaps we could discuss a matter of hotel business, if you are feeling up to it? It won't take more than a minute or two, but it is somewhat urgent."

"Of course." Relieved by the possibility of distraction from the lustful thoughts in his mind, Simon followed her to her desk, where they paused side by side. As she began rummaging amid the untidy piles of papers, files, and letters heaped on its surface, he worked to regain his equilibrium and remember his priorities.

When she pulled a large leather-bound ledger from beneath an untidy pile of letters, he seized on it like a lifeline. "You want to discuss the reservation book?" he asked as she opened the volume and began flipping through the pages.

"Yes. There's a mix-up with one of the reservations, I'm afraid, and we need to get it sorted."

She paused at a particular page, her finger tapping at one of the lines written there, and he leaned over the book to have a better look. She did the same, her shoulder brushing his. It was innocuous contact, barely discernible through layers of clothing, and yet, it nearly sent all his efforts to regain his control to oblivion.

He jerked sideways a fraction. "What sort of mix-up?" he asked, mortified that his question was a strangled rasp in his throat.

Fortunately, she didn't seem to notice.

"It's for June seventh. You've reserved the Pinafore Room for Mr. Devlin Sharpe, but that room is already taken for that date."

He took a deep breath, striving for equilibrium, reminding himself of their newfound friendship. "How could that be? There is no entry in the book but mine."

"Well, yes, but nonetheless, it's already reserved. I reserved it last night."

"Without putting it in the book?"

"I'm afraid there wasn't time to do so. You see, my friend Lady Kay Matheson came to see me and requested the—"

"Lady Kay Matheson?" he interrupted, startled, the sensuous haze around him dissipating as he spoke. "You mean the Earl of Raleigh's daughter? She is a friend of yours?"

"Yes. We came out together." She turned toward him. "Do you know the family?"

"I know of them," he replied grimly, remembering the voluptuous redhead who'd been standing arm in arm with Delia in the lobby the night before. No doubt that was the infamous Lady Kay. "Devlin Sharpe is a friend of mine."

"Oh?" She seemed surprised, and yet, looking at her, he had the vague, uneasy feeling she wasn't surprised at all. "Well, that's good news," she said with a laugh. "I mean, if you're his friend, it makes the whole thing so much easier to resolve."

"Does it?" he countered, turning to face her, suddenly wary. "How so?"

"Isn't it obvious? Being your friend, Mr. Sharpe will surely be more understanding than another customer would be when you explain the situation and we move him to a different room."

With those words, the vague, uneasy suspicion hovering at the back of his mind became certainty, and all this morning's events came into focus with sharp, stinging clarity.

The thoughtfully provided breakfast, the offered truce, the pretense of friendship, the come-hither look in her eyes, the seductive perfume—all part of a deliberate strategy. Had she dumped a bucket of water over his head, she could not have extinguished the fire smoldering inside him more effectively.

So much for hyacinths and new beginnings.

"Now, why," he murmured, feeling like an utter fool, "would we move Devlin's event to a different room?"

"But I've just told you. When you reserved it, it was already taken."

"No," he corrected, his voice hard, "it was not taken. If it's not in the reservation book, it is not reserved."

"But, Simon—"

"Simon, is it?" he muttered, shaking his head in disbelief. "My God, woman, you've got brass. I'll give you that."

"I don't know what you mean."

"Don't you?" He folded his arms, studying her through narrowed eyes. "I'm referring to your sudden concern for my health and well-being, and the motives so clearly behind this pretense of friendliness and amiability."

She actually had the temerity to seem offended. "There is no pretense," she said, bristling. "I am attempting to broker peace and forge a friendship between us so that we can better work together."

"You're doing it to soften me up."

"That is a horrible way of putting it," she muttered.

"But accurate."

"Is it? Alternatively, someone who didn't have odious and unfair preconceived ideas about my character might credit me with enough wits to know not to ask for something I need when the person I need it from is not feeling well!"

He couldn't help a laugh. "That's some fine hairsplitting, right there."

"Call it what you want. For my part, I call it common sense. I deemed making you feel better a priority so that we could tackle a mutual problem and maybe rub along better for the good of the hotel."

"You did it to get your own way. And," he added as she made a sound of impatience, "this problem is hardly mutual. Your lack of planning has nothing to do with me, and a plate of eggs and bacon, a vase of flowers, and a melting glance or two from those big blue eyes of yours doesn't change that."

"Obviously not," she agreed, scowling at him, "since, despite all my efforts to put you in a reasonable frame of mind, you're still as grouchy as a bear."

"Perhaps that's because I don't like being manipulated with feminine wiles under the guise of friendship."

She gave a snort of derision. "As if my feminine wiles would ever work on you! There'd have to be blood in your veins instead of ice water."

Those words implied that she hadn't perceived his inexplicable moment of weakness where she was concerned, and Simon drew a breath of profound relief. "Now that's a brilliant tactic," he said. "Seduction didn't work, so you resort to in—"

"Seduction?" she interrupted, staring at him as if appalled. "I wouldn't seduce you if my life depended on it."

"Good, because I'd never fall for that trick," he shot back, painfully aware that he nearly had.

"No? Darling, if I ever set out to seduce you, you'd never be able to resist me. And anyway," she added before he could protest, "I wasn't playing a trick!"

"Like hell you weren't. I suppose you wear that seductive perfume and dresses that cling to your curves when you meet with duchesses and debutantes, too?"

She gave an indignant huff, and in her eyes, Simon saw that steely glint he was coming to know well.

"As I said, my only intent was to wipe the slate clean, put you in a more agreeable frame of mind, and show you that I don't hold grudges. I thought if we could become friends, you would be better able to see my point of view on things, not just about Kay, but about everything you're doing here. The deposits on banquet rooms, the poor employees you're dismissing left and right, the snooping in people's private papers—"

"Your expense accounts are not private."

"And Escoffier? He came to me in a rage yesterday because you and the accountants were snooping through his desk. Are his personal letters and recipes not private?"

"Nothing in the offices of employees is private. As I told you, if you want privacy, keep your papers in your room."

"But what are you looking for?" she cried. "What possible reason could you have for going through Escoffier's desk? Or mine?"

"I already explained that. We are auditing the records of every head of staff."

"Even Ritz?"

Especially Ritz, he thought. "Everyone. And before you go racing off to send Ritz a cable, let me add that he already knows about our efforts, and he has tendered his full cooperation. You and Escoffier could both profit from his example."

"That's exactly what I was trying to do!" she countered. "And for my efforts, you have accused me of selfish motives and trickery, when all I was doing was employing the same tactics you'd have used on me if our positions were reversed. Oh, yes, you would have," she went on as he opened his mouth to dispute her contention. "Though I'd never accuse you of trying to seduce me, since seduction is clearly beyond your capabilities."

It had been ages since he'd seduced a woman, unfortunately, but Simon wasn't about to fall into the trap of defending his ability to do so. "It's beyond your capabilities, too, obviously," he was happy to point out. "Since it didn't work."

"Oh, for heaven's sake! If I were attempting to seduce you, I'd never have chosen to do it here, with the door into the corridor wide open and your secretary in the very next room. And if you would only stop huffing and puffing and congratulating yourself for your imperviousness to my charms, you'd be fair and admit that what I was trying to do is the only sensible thing."

"Sensible?"

"Of course. You're a man of business, aren't you? If you wanted to make a business deal with someone who didn't like you or trust you," she added as he started to reply, "wouldn't you attempt to change their unfavorable view and gain their trust before you made your proposition?"

"Trusting you is asking for trouble. And your example hardly applies here."

"Oh, really? Why not?"

Because he'd almost fallen for it. A galling fact he had no intention of admitting aloud. "What you're talking about is a hypothetical situation, one in which I can't possibly know what I would do until I had all the facts. And it doesn't really matter anyway, since in this case, I have no intention of yielding. I will not cancel a room Devlin has reserved in good faith just because you failed to put your friend's reservation in the book when you had the opportunity."

"But there was no way I could have known you would involve yourself in the making of reservations. The only people authorized to reserve banquet rooms are Ritz, Echenard, and myself."

"And me."

"I didn't think of that."

"No," he agreed. "You didn't. And that is exactly why you have a problem."

"It's your problem, too."

"How so?"

"You're here to make the hotel as profitable as it can be. If we don't move your friend's booking, we will lose Kay's. How do you think the board is going to feel about losing one of the biggest social events of the upcoming season because you're being unreasonable?"

"Perhaps they'll share my view that the unreasonable one in this scenario is you."

"And yet I'm under your supervision. Doesn't the responsibility for my mistake ultimately rest with you?"

He sucked in an exasperated breath, unable to deny the truth of that. "If so, then what would the remedy be? Should I dismiss you?"

"Don't you think you've dismissed enough people already? Because of that, by the way, you've got everyone on edge. They're all waiting, wondering if they'll be the next casualty of your cost-cutting measures."

He could not tell her the true reasons for that. "That's neither here nor there," he said instead. "As for the rest, are you suggesting I should keep an even closer eye on you?"

Her eyes widened in horror at the prospect. "You wouldn't dare."

"Wouldn't I? The more I think on it, the more I think it's a wise idea. In fact, given your clever, scheming brain, I ought to be watching you twenty-four hours a day."

"Don't be absurd. You've obviously got far too much on your plate to bother with hovering over me. And it isn't at all necessary. Why can't we just learn to get along?"

"I'm all for that. We can start with you giving your friend your sincerest apologies for the mix-up on her reservation and suggesting she book an alternate room as soon as possible."

"A course open to you as well."

"Tell Devlin he has to give up the banquet room his fiancée wants because his previous fiancée wants it, too? The previous fiancée who abandoned him and broke his heart? Hell, no. I will strip naked and dance a jig on the Savoy rooftop before that happens."

"As much as I'd love to see a hilarious display like that, I feel compelled to point out that when it comes to Lady Kay and Devlin Sharpe, you've got the story all wrong."

"Which part? The part where she agreed to marry him and then reneged? The part where she jilted him at the altar, or—"

"There was no altar to jilt him on!" she cut in. "Devlin Sharpe is a scoundrel who persuaded a respectable young lady of barely eighteen to defy her family and sneak off with him to Gretna Green when he didn't even have an income to support her! Who could blame her for realizing it would be a mistake? Thank God my cousins found them at that road-side inn and were able to bring her home before they got to Scotland. Not that it mattered in the end, of course. That blackguard decided that if he couldn't have her, no other man could. He made sure everyone knew she'd run off with him, ruining her in the eyes of society."

Simon stared at her, astonished. "Wait, you think he told—"

"And now," she went on before he could set her straight about Devlin, "after she's spent over fourteen years as the most unwanted heiress in England, she's finally found a man to marry, and I'm supposed to tell her that the banquet room she wants is unavailable because the man who shamed her and ruined her wants it for his new bride? Never! And none of this would even be an issue if you had bothered to consult with me before you booked the room."

"It also wouldn't be an issue if you had put the reservation in the book when your friend first requested it. Perhaps you ought to have been doing that instead of gloating over my difficulties with the duchess last night."

She tossed her head, showing he'd hit a nerve. "Oh, stop," she muttered, looking guilty as hell. "I was not gloating."

"Oh, yes, you were."

"Well, maybe I was," she conceded. "A little. But either way, that's beside the point. What do we do now? The Pinafore is the only room big enough to seat Kay's guest list."

"What about the basement? Didn't Ritz spend an obscene amount of money turning that into a banquet room a few years ago?"

"It's booked also. The British Archaeological Association. They always reserve the basement for their annual dinner. Makes them feel like they're in a cave, I suppose. We paint cave drawings on the walls with chalk, lay animal skins on the floor, serve them fire-roasted joints of beef and mutton—it's all very silly, to my mind, but they simply adore it. Including, I might add, the Prince of Wales, who is their primary sponsor. Moving them into another room is out of the question."

"Then, unless Lady Kay wants to go to another hotel, she will have to shorten her list of invited guests and make do with one of our smaller rooms for her wedding dinner."

"This is so unfair."

"On the contrary, the rule of first come, first served is completely fair."

"I *was* first!"

"The reservation book begs to differ."

"How?" she murmured, shaking her head as if baffled. "How is it that only moments after I might start to like you, you prove yourself to be absolutely impossible?"

"We have something in common, then. Only moments after I started to like you, I realized I was being played for a fool, and I came to my senses." As he spoke, he couldn't resist a glance over her, and every alluring curve seemed like another slap in the face. "If you don't want to admit your mistake to Lady Kay, you can always go to Devlin and ask if he's willing to give up the room for her. Who knows? You may have better luck with him than you've had with me."

"I'd have better luck with the devil than with you."

"Well, perhaps you can offer Devlin your *friendship* in exchange. Though being an engaged man, and an honorable one—"

"Honorable? Him? That's rich."

"I doubt he'll play your game," he finished, ignoring her scornful interruption. "Now if you will pardon me, I have work to do."

Ignoring her sound of outrage, he crossed to the door connecting their offices, but before opening it, he paused to say one more thing.

"And by the way," he told her, his hand on the knob, "don't wear that damned perfume around me anymore."

With that parting shot, he opened the door and departed, and it took everything he had to close the door gently rather than slam it behind him.

"My lord," Ross greeted him in surprise, rising to his feet. "I was told you were ill."

"I was. Now I'm better." The moment he uttered those words, he realized how false they were, for anger and arousal were still coursing through him like hot lava. "Or at least," he amended, "I'm a little bit wiser."

The secretary looked understandably puzzled. "I'm gratified to hear it, my lord," he murmured.

"So am I, Ross." Taking a deep, steadying breath, he shoved thoughts of Delia Stratham out of his mind and started past the secretary's desk toward his own. "Now—"

He broke off, noticing the stacks of hand-addressed envelopes on one corner of the secretary's desk, and came to a stop. "What on earth are you doing?"

"Invitations for Lady Stratham. For the East India Club's annual dinner."

"Lady Stratham?" Simon rubbed a hand across his forehead. "Of course. That woman's always got her eye on the main chance."

"I thought it would be all right. Since you were ill, I had very little to do this morning. And she was in desperate need of help."

"Now she's usurping my secretary. I'll wager," he added, noting the teacup and crumb-laden plate on the opposite corner of the desk, "she brought you breakfast, too, before she asked oh-so-sweetly for your assistance? That seems to be a favorite tactic of hers."

"Begging your pardon, my lord, but she didn't ask for my help. I offered it."

He gave the other man a look of profound pity. "I daresay that's how it seemed."

"Did I do wrong, my lord?" The secretary looked at him anxiously. "Are you angry with me?"

The one he was angry with was himself. "No, of course not," he answered with a resigned sigh. "You did what any other mug would have done in your place, so finish the task now that you've taken it on. But in the future, please see me before you do any more work for that woman."

The secretary nodded. "Would you care for your letters, my lord? There's one I know you'll want to read immediately. It's from your sister."

"Cassie?" Simon's spirits brightened at once, and the infuriatingly seductive Lady Stratham was forgotten. "At last. She never responded to my last letter, and it's been almost a fortnight. I was becoming worried." He took the sealed pale pink envelope from Ross's outstretched hand. "Anything else?"

"A letter came this morning from Mrs. Carte, requesting a meeting with you. It's urgent, she says."

That could only mean the auditors and detectives had news regarding the investigation. "Contact Mrs. Carte and see if she is available to meet for luncheon."

"Today, my lord?" The secretary pulled out his watch. "It's past noon already."

"Go to the front desk and use the telephone there. If Helen feels it's urgent that we meet, then I want that meeting as soon as possible."

"Very good, my lord."

The secretary bustled out of their office to follow instructions, and as Simon watched him go, he could only hope that whatever news Helen had for him would establish the guilt or innocence of a certain provoking, curvaceous, blue-eyed devil.

Five minutes of being friends with that woman had been enough to light him on fire, and he didn't know how much more of her friendship he could take before she burned him to a crisp.

7

*D*elia scowled at the closed door, almost wishing she had lived up to that impossible man's expectations and dosed his breakfast. Not with arsenic, of course, but would a harmless little emetic in his coffee have been so bad? That, she couldn't help but feel, would have been poetic justice.

Still, playing such a trick, as satisfying as it might be in her imagination, would not be quite so satisfying in reality, since it would also get her fired. And it certainly wouldn't solve the problem at hand.

She heaved an exasperated sigh, circled her desk, and plopped down in her chair, knowing she needed to come up with a more practical course of action than making Lord Calderon throw up.

She'd offered peace in the hope it would enable them to get along, help him see her point of view, and generally make things easier for everyone, but she'd clearly muffed it. So now what?

Going to Sharpe was out of the question. She wouldn't give that scoundrel the time of day, and besides, it probably wouldn't do any good. He knew Kay was her friend. And Simon would regale the other man with twisted stories about her motives as soon as he possibly could, warning the other man not to trust a single thing she said.

Nor could she go to Kay. After all her friend had suffered at Devlin Sharpe's hands, Delia would not heap more pain and worry on her, especially not now, when she finally had the chance for some happiness.

And talking to Calderon, trying again to persuade him to see her point of view, was also out the window. Having had three husbands, Delia knew quite well when a man could be persuaded to a certain course and when he couldn't. This man was definitely in the latter category.

The reason for that, of course, was that he was stubborn, unreasonable, and quite possibly off his onion. He not only disliked her for the most unjust reasons, but he now thought her some kind of scheming seductress as well.

What an insufferable presumption. As she'd tried to explain, all she'd been thinking to do was be nice, forge a truce, and become friends, and she'd gotten soundly snubbed and insulted for her trouble.

And why was that? she wondered in baffled irritation. What the devil was wrong with her? Most people *liked* her, damn it all. So why didn't he?

Not that it mattered, of course. She didn't, she reminded herself sternly, care two straws for his opinion of her. As for seducing him, the thought had never even occurred to her. Why would she ever want to seduce a cold fish like him?

Suddenly, the image of his face came into her mind. The lean planes of his cheekbones, the straight Roman nose, the hard line of his mouth so close to hers, the spark of heat in those cool green eyes as they had homed in on her mouth.

She was no green girl. She knew what a look like that *usually* meant. And when she'd seen it in Simon's eyes, her body had responded at once, her pulses quickening with a faint, answering thrill.

The heated look she'd seen in his eyes must—must—have been her imagination, or a trick of the light. But what if it hadn't been?

With that tantalizing question, Delia leaned forward, resting her elbow on her desk and her chin in her hand. What if the man she'd deemed such a cold fish wasn't so cold after all? If he had kissed her, what then? What would it have been like, to have his arms around her and his lips on hers?

Again, she felt that thrill of excitement, that heated longing in her blood. It had been years since she'd felt such a thing, and it was wonderful. Quixotic, exciting, and wonderful.

It was also absurd. Simon wanting to kiss her? Not bloody likely.

I will strip naked and dance a jig on the Savoy rooftop before that happens.

For some reason, an image of him standing naked before her flashed through Delia's mind—his wide shoulders, his narrow hips, his—

Appalled by the wayward direction her thoughts had taken, Delia veered her mind firmly away from carnal imaginings of Calderon's manly attributes. She didn't know which was more unlikely: being kissed by him or watching him dance naked on the hotel roof. But either way, such speculations were hardly helpful. Unless—

Suddenly, without any warning, a possible solution to her current problem flashed through her mind. She jerked upright in her chair, jolted by a shot of renewed hope.

It was a wild idea, she told herself. A wild, extravagant, perhaps even mad idea. But wasn't the Savoy known the world over for its wild, extravagant, mad ideas? And if she could pull it off, Kay would have a wedding banquet so unique, people would talk about it for years to come.

There was only one problem: how to get Simon to agree. After this morning, she doubted she could get him to agree with her about the color of an orange.

Once again, his face came before her eyes, and her own question echoed through her mind again.

What can I do to convince you?

Delia drummed her fingers on her desk, thinking hard. Convincing a man to see things her way wasn't usually such a problem, but in this case, it was painfully clear that the easiest tactics—putting on a pretty dress and a dab of perfume and being friendly and nice—were not going to work. No, to convince Simon of the soundness of her idea, she'd have to present it to him in terms he could accept, terms of viability, cost, and profits. That meant some serious research on her part.

After another moment or two of consideration, she stood up. A trip to Westbourne House, she decided, was the first step.

As his secretary had predicted, Simon opened the letter from his sister straightaway, and just the act of slitting the envelope and pulling out the sheets of notepaper banished all his frustrations, filled him with pleasurable anticipation, and made him smile.

A few moments later, however, his smile was gone, and an ominous frown Delia Stratham might have recognized took its place. Slowly, grimly, he reread some of the lines penned in his baby sister's round, generous handwriting.

> *I encountered Miss Maberly and Lady Mary Nasby in the village last week, but though I was as friendly as I could be, they were not inclined to be the same. I fear they do not like me very much.*

What the devil was there not to like? he wondered with all the baffled fury of a protective older brother. Cassandra was a sweet, pretty, lively girl who'd never in her life had a spot of trouble with making friends. At least, not until now.

> *I invited them to come for tea one day, and they assured me they would do so if it were possible. But two weeks have passed since then and neither of them has called upon me. I can only think they must be terribly busy.*

Busy? Simon's hand tightened around the sheets of notepaper as a fierce, protective anger rose inside him. It was January in the country. How could two young ladies be too busy to visit a new neighbor and have a cup of tea?

> *In fact, none of our neighbors have come to call. I rattle around in this big, cold, empty house all day long, with no one for company but my governess and the servants. It makes the days seem endless.*

At those words, pain joined his anger, squeezing his chest like a fist around his heart, for even in a letter read from miles away, he could hear the forlorn note in his sister's voice.

> *Dearest Simon, I know you are terribly busy just now and it is hard for you to get away, but I miss you so. I know it is not as bad as the days when you were in Africa and I only got to see you once a year, but somehow, it feels worse because I don't even have Mama. I am so lonely here, I can hardly bear it.*

"My lord?"

Simon looked up to find his secretary standing in front of his desk. "Yes, Ross, what is it?"

"Mrs. Carte is happy to have lunch, but only if you can meet her immediately, for she has another engagement scheduled for half past two. She suggested Rules, which is a very short walk from her office and yours. I took the liberty of confirming the engagement, and I reserved a table at Rules."

"She doesn't want to dine here in the hotel?"

"She said it might be best if the Savoy staff didn't see the two of you with your heads together."

"That's probably wise. Very well, then," he added as he stood up, "I'd best be on my way. Helen hates to be kept waiting."

He tucked the letter from Cassandra into the breast pocket of his jacket and started for the door, but on the threshold, he stopped, struck by another thought. "Ross, do I have any engagements for the weekend?"

"No, my lord. Ritz is scheduled to return from Rome tomorrow, and you had planned to leave him in charge here and go to Dover so that you could see to things at the Bainbridge. I have tickets for us on the ten o'clock train tomorrow morning, returning Friday afternoon."

He waved aside the trip to his Dover hotel. "Yes, but I'm free for the weekend? Then," he added as Ross gave a confirming nod, "I think I shall go straight from Dover to Berkshire and spend a few days with my sister."

"Oh, she'll love that, I'm sure. It's been a month, I believe, since you last went down."

I am so lonely here.

"A month too long, I fear," he muttered. "I'll return Monday night, so you'll need to reschedule any engagements I have for that day. Now, I'd best be on my way."

With that, he exited his office, left the hotel, and made the two-block journey to Rules. He walked quickly, but by the time he arrived, Helen was already seated at one of the restaurant's famous red booths, waiting for him.

"Helen," he greeted the dark-haired, sloe-eyed wife of the Savoy's founder with the affection and respect of long acquaintance. "How are you?"

"A bit tired, Simon, I confess. Between Richard's ill-health, running the Savoy Theatre, and this awful business with the hotel, I'm worn to a nub."

"I can imagine," he replied as he slid into the seat opposite. "How is Richard?"

"Still ailing."

"Really? But when I last saw him, he assured me he was doing better."

"My husband has always been so optimistic." She gave a weary sigh, pressing a hand to her forehead. "But the doctors are not."

"I'm sorry. I shall make a point to visit more often."

"He'd appreciate that. He has a great deal of affection for you, you know."

"It's mutual, Helen. After the scandal with my father came out, Richard took my mother on at the Bainbridge when no one else would hire her."

"It wasn't your mother's fault that your father was dishonest. To this day, Richard says making her the head of housekeeping at the Bainbridge was one of the best decisions he ever made. Letting you buy half that hotel and take over its management was another. You doubled the profits in less than a year."

"Still, the fact remains that at the time of my father's death, no one wanted to hire a woman whose husband was a thief." Simon paused, his father's shame still a bitter taste in his mouth even after all these years. "I owe Richard more than I can ever repay."

"Well, we are grateful to you as well, Simon. Especially now, I find your help with this Savoy business a godsend."

He cast a worried glance at her. "Helen, please don't distress yourself about the Savoy. Given Richard's illness, I can manage things with the auditors and solicitors on my own if it's too much for you. You needn't be involved at all if you don't wish to be."

Her tired face took on a hard, determined look. "If you think I can bear to stand by, doing nothing as Ritz robs my husband blind, you don't know me at all."

He smiled at that. "I know you well enough to have known that's what you'd say, but nonetheless, the offer stands. I take it our solicitors and detectives have made some progress in the investigations?"

"They have, and I'm afraid things are even worse than we previously suspected."

"Worse?" Somehow, that surprised him, though he didn't know why it should. "How much worse?"

Helen hesitated, but her grim expression told its own tale, and Simon drew a deep breath. "It's that bad, is it?"

"Let's just say we'll be dismissing a great many more people before it's over."

As she spoke, an image of Lady Stratham stole into Simon's mind. "Which people?" he asked, his voice harsh to his own ears.

"Let's have lunch first." Helen picked up the menu in front of her, and Simon forced images of Lady Stratham out of his mind. Over an excellent meal of turtle soup, filet of beef, and apple tart, the two of them discussed other topics, avoiding the matter of the Savoy altogether.

Only after the last crumb of tart had been eaten and they were both sipping their coffee did Simon once again broach the question uppermost in his mind. "Who will we be firing? Ritz, obviously, but then, we already knew it would come to that in the end. Who else?"

"Many of the restaurant staff will have to be replaced. As the anonymous letter said, half the waiters are collecting bribes from customers for the best tables, charging customers for flowers that were never ordered, and pocketing commissions on cigar sales instead of putting them in the *tronc*. They are also granting restaurant credit to the biggest tippers and then giving the cashiers a part of the *tronc* as a bribe to ensure the bills never get collected."

"So these generous tippers never end up paying for the food and wine they consume."

"Exactly. By the way, you recall how the author of that letter accused Ritz, Echenard, and Escoffier of helping themselves to the hotel wine and liquor without paying for it?"

"Yes, but then we learned that Madelaine Alverson, two of the waiters, and a kitchen maid were colluding to steal wine out of the Savoy cellars and sell it. The detectives caught them red-handed."

"Yes, but we have now confirmed that what they were taking was only a drop in the bucket. When the accountants audited the wine inventory, they realized there was far more wine unaccounted for than those four could possibly have taken."

"So another of the accusations of the letter writer has now been confirmed beyond doubt."

She nodded. "And there's more. Ritz, Escoffier, and Echenard have not only been taking wine for themselves, but they've also been dispensing additional hotel wine and liquor to their personal friends and charging it as an expense to the hotel. We estimate they've taken over ten thousand pounds' worth during the past twelve months alone."

"Ten thousand pounds' worth of wine in a single year?"

"And they've been engaging in this practice from the very beginning, right under Richard's nose. The accountants tell me that
between them, those three men have stolen over fifty thousand
pounds' worth of wine and liquor during the past eight years."

"If that's so, then the head cashier must know all about it. Which
explains why when Ritz was hired, he insisted on bringing in his own
man for that position."

"Oh, yes. Mr. Agostini is in this up to his neck. And it isn't just the
wine. As the letter said, they've also been helping themselves to the
Savoy's food stores, as have Agostini and both restaurant managers."

"How can they get away with that? What, do they all just walk
into the larder whenever the mood strikes and take what they want
and no one notices?"

"Oh, no, it's much more subtle than that. The food is given directly
to them by the hotel's suppliers as gifts. Vast quantities of groceries
are being sent every week from the Savoy's suppliers directly to these
men's personal residences."

"But how can the suppliers make any profit if they're giving so
much food away?"

"Because the food supplied to the Savoy kitchens is being delivered
short in order to make up the difference. If the hotel is charged for a
dozen eggs, only ten are delivered. A fifty-pound bag of flour is really
only forty-five, and so on."

"The arrogance of these people," Simon muttered, shaking his
head in disbelief. "The absolute arrogance."

"Arrogant is the word. They haven't even bothered to try to cover
their tracks. Once the auditors started delving into things, they had
no trouble uncovering what's been going on and how."

Simon considered for a moment. "Escoffier must be aware that the
hotel is being shorted on food supplies in order to pay for these gifts."

"Oh, he knows." Helen's voice vibrated with outrage as she spoke.

"He knows. Even worse, we have also confirmed that he's taking bribes from suppliers."

"In addition to the gifts and shorted supplies?"

Helen nodded. "Bellamy's and Hudson Brothers, among others, are marking up the prices for all foodstuffs they sell the hotel. They charge the higher price and give Escoffier the difference. Five percent on every food order. Among themselves, they call it a commission."

"Commission?" Simon made a sound of contempt. "That's rich. What about Ritz himself? What bribes is he receiving?"

"Ritz?" Helen fairly spat the name. "As the letter said, he's been giving away the Savoy's food and wine to favored guests and giving them unlimited credit at the restaurant. The total outstanding unpaid debt accumulated by Ritz's friends and associates is nearly fourteen thousand pounds."

Simon was staggered by the amount, though he knew he shouldn't be. "Ritz isn't the sort to do anything halfway, is he? Not even theft."

"Adding insult to injury, there is a definite quid pro quo involved. For example, not long ago, Ritz hosted a party for a group of railway executives, and—"

"Let me guess," Simon interjected, "he got free railway passes in exchange."

"Exactly. His stockbroker and his doctor have dined for free at the restaurant numerous times. In exchange, it's understood that Ritz pays no brokerage fees and no medical bills to these gentlemen. A year ago, Ritz hosted a party for a group of wealthy businessmen in the restaurant. The bill, which came to over five hundred pounds, has never been paid. Many of those businessmen are now investors in his Paris hotel, which has nothing to do with the Savoy or my husband. And there's something else the detectives have uncovered," she went on before he could ask for more details, "something that wasn't in the letter."

Simon braced himself. "Go on."

"The detectives noticed big, unmarked bundles being delivered to the Savoy laundry every Tuesday and taken away every Friday. They became curious about this practice and started investigating, and they learned those bundles contain laundry."

"Ritz is getting his personal and household laundry done for free?"

"Him, Echenard, Escoffier, and God only knows who else."

"And no charge tickets are ever written for this service?"

"No, but Mrs. Henderson, the head laundress, has brought her family and friends to dine in the restaurant numerous times without paying."

"Good God," Simon burst out, at the end of his tether. "These men already get exorbitant salaries. Can't they at least pay for their own damn laundry?"

"Why should they?" Helen countered grimly. "They don't seem willing to pay for anything else."

"The question is," he countered as he picked up his coffee cup, "what do we do about it? At the very least, anyone involved will have to be dismissed."

"Dismissed?" Helen made a sound of derision through her teeth. "I want far more than that. They have turned the Savoy into a den of thieves. I want them criminally prosecuted. Ritz, Escoffier, Echenard, Agostini, Lady Stratham—all of them."

Simon's coffee suddenly tasted bitter on his tongue. "Lady Stratham?" he echoed, careful to keep his voice indifferent. "What evidence have the detectives uncovered against her?"

"Nothing that can be considered criminal, but they haven't begun investigating her yet. If you recall, we decided to concentrate our investigation on the specific accusations in the letter, and she wasn't mentioned. But already, there are some very clear indications of her culpability."

"Such as?"

"We know her own secretary was stealing wine and selling it."

"Guilt by association is not guilt. What else?"

"The head florist, Michel DuPont, is involved, and he's under her direct supervision." She gave a huff of outrage. "Had Ritz never hired that woman and allowed me to continue handling the flowers and the decorating, I might have caught on to all these schemes long before I got that letter. Now I know why Ritz was so eager to boot me out and hire her."

The florist's involvement still didn't prove anything against Lady Stratham, but Helen's animosity toward the other woman was so deep and unwavering that he saw no point in saying so. "How is DuPont involved?" he asked instead. "Are the managers getting free flowers, too?"

"Ritz and Escoffier definitely are. Flowers delivered to their homes whenever they like, and they never pay for them. The flower sellers, like the food suppliers, deliver the hotel orders short to make up the revenue."

"And in exchange for his inability to count how many roses are in a dozen, does Monsieur DuPont enjoy free meals in the restaurant like our head laundress?"

"We don't know yet. But in auditing the cashiers, the accountants discovered that when DuPont's daughter was ill, the hotel paid for her to have a very exclusive Harley Street doctor—Lady Stratham's doctor, as it turns out. The private detectives confirmed that it was the countess herself who made the arrangements. The bill is recorded as a debt from Monsieur DuPont, but it's been sitting on the books for two years without ever being paid."

Simon drew a deep breath. "And is there any proof of a quid pro quo between him and Lady Stratham?"

"Not yet, but I'm sure they'll find it."

"Will they?" He felt compelled to point out the obvious. "She is a countess, Helen. And quite wealthy in her own right, from what I understand. She can easily afford to buy her own wine and flowers."

"Ritz is wealthy, too, and it hasn't stopped him from stealing us blind."

"No, but—"

"Are you *defending* her?"

"Of course not. But until her guilt is established—"

"How could it be doubted? She feels every bit as entitled and privileged as the rest of them, believe me. And her loyalty to Ritz and her friendship with him are well-known. Thick as thieves can be, those two." Her eyes narrowed accusingly on him before he could reply. "And why should I even have to remind you of all that? You seemed quite willing to entertain the possibility of her guilt when you first came. What's changed? Working her wiles on you, is she?"

A picture of midnight-blue eyes and a dazzling dimpled smile came into his mind, and he shoved it out again at once, reminding himself how Delia had tried only an hour ago to do the very thing Helen was accusing her of. But even that was not enough to condemn her as a thief.

"They call her the merry widow, you know," Helen went on before he could reply. "Black widow is more like it. Three husbands and counting. Someone told me," she added when he didn't reply, "that she stole her first husband from another girl. He was engaged, I was told, unofficially, of course, but still..." She paused and sighed. "Once a thief, always a thief, I suppose."

He set his jaw and met Helen's eyes with a hard gaze of his own. "Using unrelated gossip to make your point is unworthy of you, Helen."

She had the grace to look ashamed.

"As for the rest," he went on when she didn't reply, "as we discussed only minutes ago, my own mother was dismissed from her post because of my father's thefts. I won't do that very thing to someone else, Helen. Not without proof."

"Your mother was innocent. You can't possibly believe the same about Delia Stratham!"

"It doesn't matter what I believe. It only matters what can be proved, particularly in the case of Lady Stratham. She's quite highly placed in society."

"So because she is a countess and the cousin of a duke, you think she should be allowed to walk away unscathed?" Her eyes narrowed. "Perhaps I was wrong. Perhaps your recent elevation to the peerage, rather than Lady Stratham's charms, has influenced your view, then."

"I don't give a damn if she's a cousin of the Queen," he shot back, stung and almost insulted by the idea that his useless new title and considerations of aristocratic privilege held any sway with him. "As I said, if she's guilty of embezzlement, I'll happily vote to fire her. But a criminal prosecution?" He shook his head. "It would be unwise, in my opinion, and I'm not just talking about her, but all of them."

She sighed, her shoulders sagging a little. "You sound like Richard. He wants them all fired. But he is reluctant to prosecute any of them criminally. He says it would be the deuce of a mess."

Simon nodded, not surprised by his old friend's view of the matter. "Ritz is highly respected, even adored, by many influential people. So is Escoffier. The scandal would be enormous. Some of society's most highly placed people would have to admit they've been receiving things for free and giving quid pro quos in exchange, and they'd blame the Savoy for dragging them into it. As gratifying as it might be to prosecute, it's wiser to just dismiss those involved without any fuss, as we did with Mrs. Alverson and the others we've let go, and keep things as quiet as possible. The threat of criminal prosecution and the possibility of public humiliation will be enough to ensure their discretion. But," he felt compelled to add, "in Lady Stratham's case, the accountants have yet to find the evidence."

"You took a look at her expense accounts. Was there nothing there to tell against her?"

He shook his head. "Some sloppy bookkeeping, a few questionable expenditures."

"Nothing that could be considered suspicious?"

"Not really, but then, my examination was cursory. When will the accountants be doing a full audit of her records?"

Helen lifted her hands in a gesture of exasperation, then let them fall into her lap. "They have to finish with Ritz, Escoffier, and Echenard first. They tell me it will be several more weeks, perhaps a month, before they can delve into Lady Stratham's involvement."

"A month?" An image of Delia came into his mind again, and a month suddenly seemed like an eternity.

"That is what the auditors are telling me," Helen said, breaking into his thoughts. "They are too cautious, in my opinion."

"I approve of caution, but can't they move any faster? The investors want a dividend at the end of March, and that would be much easier to do if the hotel could stop pouring money into the pockets of Ritz and his cohorts. And though I know Ritz agreed to give his full cooperation to an audit, the more intrusive these investigations become and the longer they go on, the more likely he is to smell a rat."

"He already does. He sent Richard a most irate cable from Rome, demanding to know why his staff was being harassed. And even though we managed to get Echenard out of the way by sending him on holiday, he also cabled Richard. I can only assume that Escoffier, Agostini, and Lady Stratham have been keeping both of them informed of the changes you are making and the audits the accountants are conducting."

"Yes, I daresay they are starting to realize there's more to this than cost-cutting to satisfy the investors. We knew they would, of course, but I'd hoped to be finished before they truly appreciated what dire straits they're in."

"It doesn't make your job any easier, of course, but there it is. Mr. Dever tells me they need another month."

"Very well, but the minute they learn anything more, let me know."

"Of course."

Forced to be content with that, Simon paid the bill, and he and Helen went their separate ways. But as he walked the short distance back to the Savoy, he decided that although the accountants would not be able to start investigating Lady Stratham for four more weeks, there was no reason he could not do some investigating of his own. He'd have to tread carefully, however; for though Delia was aggravating as hell, she was also devilishly clever.

Rather a shame now that he'd thrown her offer of a truce back in her face this morning. On the other hand, if he'd agreed to make peace and be friends, pumping her for information now wouldn't be quite playing the game.

Nonetheless, as he reentered the hotel and started toward his office, he appreciated that there were ways to delve into her activities and find out more about what she might be doing without pretending to be her friend. He was her employer, after all. He could keep as close an eye on her activities as he wanted.

A glance through her doorway revealed that she was out, and he questioned Ross as to her whereabouts the moment he entered his office.

"Lady Stratham is at an appointment this afternoon, I suppose?" he asked as passed the secretary's desk on the way to his own.

"Oh, no, my lord," the secretary replied as he stood up. "I don't think Lady Stratham left for an appointment. I believe she went down to the laundry."

"The laundry?" He stopped halfway to his desk and turned, sud-denly alert. "Did she say why?"

"No, not to me. But I'm sure it must have been because of the duf-fel bag."

"What duffel bag?"

"When I returned from luncheon, I noticed this enormous duffel bag on Lady Stratham's desk. A few minutes later, when her ladyship came in, I heard her give an exclamation of annoyance and say out loud—she was talking to herself, you understand—that the bundle ought to have been delivered to the laundry. Then," he added, gestur-ing to the open door between offices, "I saw her pick up the bundle and go out again. I presume she was going to the laundry."

The detectives noticed big, unmarked bundles being delivered to the Savoy laundry every Tuesday.

As he remembered Helen's words from a short time ago, he also remembered that today was Tuesday.

"Thank you, Ross." Feeling grim, he turned away. "I'll be back later."

Helen's investigation into Lady Stratham's activities might have to wait, but right now, he decided, was the perfect time to begin his own. Leaving his office, he started for the laundry.

8

"But how are you feeling, truly?" Delia cast a concerned glance over the dark-haired young woman who was ironing on the other side of the worktable. "Are you absolutely sure you haven't returned to your duties too soon? If money is a concern, I'm sure something can be worked out."

Lizzie Welton smiled as she set the iron back on the plate to warm. "Please don't worry about me, my lady. Mrs. Henderson has been very kind to me, saying I could take breaks if I needed to rest, but honestly, I feel right as rain. But then, I was only in labor for twelve hours."

"Twelve sounds like a lot."

"Oh, no, my lady. It's nothing, especially when you consider that this is my first baby. The midwife couldn't believe it. I was born to have babies, she said."

Pain hit Delia square in the chest, but she swallowed hard and shoved the feeling aside. "A blessing, to be sure, but even so, dear Lizzie, you mustn't tire yourself out."

"No worries on that score. I have help at home." Lizzie's plump face took on a rueful expression, her pert nose wrinkling up. "My mother-in-law," she said with a profound lack of enthusiasm, "has moved in with us."

"Ah." Delia gave her a knowing look in return. "Now I see why you were so eager to return to work."

Lizzie grinned. "Exactly so, my lady."

Delia watched her pick up the iron again and appreciated that she'd taken enough of the young woman's time. "I had best allow you to carry on with your duties or Mrs. Henderson will scold me." Gesturing to the half-open duffel bag on the worktable, she added, "Can I put this somewhere, so it won't be in your way?"

"If you could just put it by the lift on your way out, my lady, I'll take it with me when I finish here."

Nodding, Delia pulled the edges of the cloth bag all the way up and tightened the drawstring, then she wrapped her arms around the enormous bundle and carried it out of the ironing room. But as she stepped through the doorway and turned in the corridor, she ran straight into something solid, something that shouldn't have been there.

"Oh!" she cried, the force of the collision sending her stumbling backward, but thankfully, two strong hands grasped her arms before she could fall to the hard stone floor.

"Careful," a deep male voice cautioned, and Delia's good mood slipped a notch as she recognized who that voice belonged to.

"Calderon?" she cried in dismay. "Is that you?"

She lowered the bundle in her arms so that she could see, and when she looked into a now-familiar pair of green eyes, she groaned. "Can't I ever get away from you? What on earth are you doing down here?"

"I might ask you the same question," he replied. "Do you always bring your laundry down yourself?"

She blinked, taken aback. "My what?"

"Your laundry," he repeated, nodding to the soft, pillowy bundle between their bodies. "Isn't that yours?"

She burst out laughing. "Heavens, no! When my laundry needs doing, Molly brings it down, not me."

"Who is Molly?"

"Molly Grimes. One of the hotel maids," she added as he continued to look bewildered. "She's doing it for me until I find a new maid of my own. Don't worry," she continued, making a face. "The hotel is charging me an outrageous sum for her services."

He frowned, clearly not taking her teasing in the proper spirit, which didn't surprise her in the least. "Stop complaining," he muttered, his hands sliding away from her arms. "You get enough other things for free."

"If you mean my suite, I pay for that now, too, remember? And I can only conclude you are glowering at me in such a disagreeable fashion because you're still out of sorts about this morning. And why," she went on before he could make any attempt to deny it, "are you skulking about in the hotel service corridors?"

"I was not skulking."

"Were you spying on me? After all," she went on before he could reply, "you think I'm some schemer forever attempting to trick you with my wiles. Just what," she added, her ire growing as she thought of the accusations he'd laid at her door a few hours ago, "do you think I'm getting for free? Laundry service?"

Her words had been spoken half in jest, but when his gaze lowered speculatively to the bundle in her arms, she realized they were nothing less than the truth.

"Oh, my God, that's exactly what you do think." She shook her head, appreciating with mingled dismay and irritation just how low his opinion of her really was. "So that's why you were hovering just outside the door in that clandestine manner. You thought you'd catch me out."

"I hardly had time for such a thing. I had only just stepped out of the service lift," he added, gesturing to the still-open elevator doors beside him, "when you appeared in the corridor and cannoned into me. But I admit, I am curious as to why you are bringing bundles of clothing down to the laundry. As you pointed out, it's something your maid would usually do."

"Oh, for heaven's sake, do you ever stop thinking the worst of me?" Taking a step back, she bent down to set the duffel bag on the floor between them, then she loosened the drawstring and pulled the edges of the sack down to partially reveal what was inside. "Does this look like clothing to you?" she demanded, lifting the bundle as she straightened.

He blinked, staring at the enormous furry brown head now visible above the edge of the sack. "It's a bear."

If she weren't so exasperated with him, she might have relished the stupefied look on his face. "Yes, exactly." She held the enormous toy higher, shaking it in his face. "A bear."

"What the devil are you doing, carting enormous stuffed animals around the hotel?"

Lowering the bear, she glared at him over the tips of its fuzzy ears. "It's...a...present," she explained, pausing between each word to illustrate just what an idiot he was being. "For...the...baby."

"The baby?" he repeated. "Whose baby?"

"Lizzie's baby, of course!"

This, sadly, did not enlighten him.

"Lizzie Welton," she explained, giving a nod to the doorway behind her. "Lizzie works here in the laundry, and her husband, James, is a waiter in the restaurant. They just had a baby. I bought them a baby gift, and because Harrods made a muddle and delivered it to me by mistake rather than taking it to her, I brought it down to her myself."

He opened his mouth to reply, then closed it again, and if she weren't so irritated by his asinine assumptions about her character, she might have found his inability to speak immensely gratifying.

"And if you're going to run things around here," she went on, fighting the impulse to take the bear and bash him over the head with it, "perhaps you ought to know the names of those who work here and make an effort to learn more about them, instead of wasting your time trying to catch me in the act of doing something naughty! That would be a better use of your time, wouldn't you agree?"

"I—" He broke off and looked down at the bear again, shaking his head as if in disbelief. Then suddenly, unexpectedly, he started to laugh.

The sound of his throaty chuckle caused Delia's aggravation to fade away as pure astonishment took its place. "You're laughing," she said, her surprise making her words seem almost like an accusation.

"Sorry," he apologized in a choked voice. "It's just that—"

Another chuckle escaped him, and he pressed a fist to his mouth to smother it, staring at the bear.

"All this amusement out of you in one day?" she murmured, jerking her chin. "I had no idea I was such an excellent source of entertainment for you."

Giving a cough, he let his hand fall and lifted his head. "Yes, well," he said, "there are times when all one can do is bow to the absurd. And seeing you carrying an enormous toy bear through the corridors of the laundry is one of those times."

"Maybe you think so," she countered, "but I don't find being accused of illicitly obtaining things for free something to laugh about."

His amusement faded and a hint of what might have been regret crossed his face. "Forgive me. It seems I have jumped to an unwarranted conclusion."

"Yes," she said, not quite ready to forgive, "you have. But that doesn't surprise me. You are always ready to think the worst of me. I just wish I knew why."

She waited, but he did not explain. Instead, he held his hand up, palms toward her in a gesture of truce. "I made a presumption that was both unfair and untrue, and I have no explanation or excuse to offer. But if it's any comfort to you, I now feel like a prize fool."

She sniffed, slightly appeased. "That's some consolation, I suppose."

"My assumption was unwarranted, and my behavior terribly rude. I can only ask again that you accept my sincerest apologies."

No one could ever accuse Delia of not taking advantage of heaven-sent opportunities.

"Hmm…" She bent down, pretending to consider his request as she wrapped the toy for Lizzie's baby back within the protection of its cloth bag. She took her sweet time tying the strings into a bow, quite happy to relish his discomfiture.

At last, however, she put the baby's gift to one side, straightened, and returned her attention to him. "I just might see my way to forgiving you," she said. "That is, if you agree to do something for me."

"I suppose I should have seen that coming," he muttered, giving another laugh. "The answer is no."

"How can you say no to my request already?" she demanded. "You don't even know what it is yet."

"I'm not giving the Pinafore Room to Lady Kay." As if that were the end of the matter, he turned, gesturing to the doorway of the service lift for her to precede him inside.

"The Pinafore Room?" she repeated over her shoulder as she walked into the lift. "Oh, but I'm not asking you for that."

"You're not?"

"No, no." She turned to face him. "I've quite given up trying to persuade you there. Aren't you coming?" she added in surprise, noting he hadn't followed her.

He shook his head. "So, if you're not going to try to change my mind about the banquet room," he added as he grasped the handles of the steel lattice doors and began to close them, "what do you want?"

She smiled at him through the doorway, her widest, prettiest, most persuasive smile. "I want you to have dinner with me."

The doors stilled, and he stared at her through the gap, understandably surprised. "Dinner?"

Not even the sunniest optimist could have thought he sounded enthusiastic. Still, she could hardly take back her invitation, and if she wanted to help Kay, the staff, and the hotel, she had no choice but to persuade him. "Yes, dinner." Noting his expression, she made a face, taking refuge in teasing. "Don't look so delighted by the notion, or it'll turn my head."

At once, the dismay on his face vanished and an expression of polite regret took its place. "I seem to do nothing but offend you," he murmured. "But—"

"Well, then..." She forestalled the obvious refusal he'd been about to utter. "To make it all up to me, you really have to come. Would Friday night suit you? Are you free?"

"Actually, no. I'm off to Dover for the rest of the week, and then I was planning to go straight to my country house from there. I haven't been home for over a month."

"You could come back here after Dover, have dinner with me, and then go to your country house on Saturday, couldn't you? There's an early train to Berkshire out of Charing Cross. You'd arrive home before noon."

"Delia, I'm not at all sure the two of us having dinner together is a good idea."

"Really, Simon," she said with a sigh, "you're perfectly safe in my company. It's not as if I intend to ravish you over the saddle of lamb." With a wink she added, "After all, every woman knows ravishing a man should always be done over dessert."

He was looking as if he'd rather eat rocks than be ravished by her, and though she supposed she shouldn't be surprised by his response to her invitation, it was rather disconcerting to know how little he relished the prospect.

Truth be told, she wasn't accustomed to this sort of reaction from men. Without being unduly conceited, she was old enough and experienced enough to be aware of her own power to attract, and his reluctance to accept even a mere dinner invitation made her feel off-balance, humbled, even a little apprehensive.

"Heavens, you really do dislike me, don't you?" she murmured. "I realize you and I have gotten crosswise a few times—this morning being a perfect example—but would having dinner with me be so very awful?"

"That's not it," he said at once. "I am always happy to have dinner with a beautiful woman, believe me, but I feel obliged to point out that you do work for me."

Beautiful? She stared, too taken aback to reply. She'd thought for a moment, this morning, that he felt some attraction for her, but then, he'd shut her down so ruthlessly that she was sure she'd been mistaken. But now, in light of this unexpected compliment, she didn't know what to think. Was he—

"It might be considered inappropriate."

The sound of his voice interrupted her reverie, and she forced herself to say something. "Please don't accuse me again of plying you with my feminine wiles."

"I wasn't—"

"It's just that," she said in a rush, "I have a project idea I want to put before you and presenting it over dinner is the best way. I can't explain, but if you come, you'll see why."

He considered, then gave a nod. "Very well, then; I accept. Shall we meet in the restaurant?"

"No. Be in the Savoy lobby Friday evening at half past seven. I'll have a carriage waiting for you."

"A carriage? We're not dining here?"

"No, no. That would be far too predictable. In fact, we won't be dining in a restaurant at all." Oddly nervous, she forced a laugh. "But you'll be relieved to know I was only teasing about ravishing you over the dessert."

"Relieved?" Something flickered in those impenetrable eyes, a flash of gold on green. "That's not quite how I'd describe it."

"No? How—" She paused, her voice failing her, and she had to swallow hard before she could continue. "How would you describe it?"

His lashes lowered, then lifted, and as he met her gaze again, Delia saw again that flash of gold and realized what it was—the same spark of desire she had seen this morning, and she felt again an unexpected, gratified thrill. When he spoke, however, his voice was aggravatingly indifferent. "I shall see you Friday evening, then."

Disappointment pierced her—a baffling, highly irritating response—and it took her a moment to muster her poise and think of a reply. But before she could utter some offhand reply as a show of indifference equal to his, he shut the lift doors between them with a clang, bowed, and turned to go, leaving her staring at his back between the steel lattice grates with chagrin as he walked away.

Simon couldn't imagine the reason behind Delia's invitation to dinner. She wanted something from him, that much was clear, but he was hardly in a position to object to that, since he wanted something from her, too. Dinner together gave him the perfect opportunity to further his investigation regarding her. Granted, she had seemed quite indignant about the notion of having her laundry done for free, but though it had seemed genuine enough, he could not afford to assume her innocence based solely on that. He needed more information. In the meantime, there was no point in speculating.

He journeyed down to Dover to check on things at his hotel there, and during the next three days, he was kept very busy with work, but despite that, and despite his refusal to speculate about her motives, he wasn't able to keep her completely out of his thoughts.

At unaccountable moments, images of her laughing eyes and witch-black hair would steal into his mind, and before he knew it, his imagination would be conjuring pictures of shapely breasts and long, slim legs. She was a dangerously seductive femme fatale, possibly a liar, and perhaps even a thief, but nonetheless, it took every scrap of willpower he possessed to shove enticing imaginings of her naked body out of his mind so he could work.

Thankfully, by the time he returned to London on Friday, he had his imagination under control and his priorities back in order. Arriving at the Savoy late Friday afternoon, he had just enough time to bathe, shave, and change into white-tie attire, and he arrived in the hotel lobby only two minutes late. He expected Delia to be waiting for him, but instead, he found someone else coming toward him as he entered the lobby, someone who did not look the least bit happy to see him.

"Monsieur Ritz," he said, his voice coolly polite. "Back from Rome, I see."

The hotelier, a dandy of a man with an enormous mustache, a balding forehead, and the vanity to insist on wearing shoes that were too small for his feet, came toward him, limping a little in his tight patent leather ankle boots. "Lord Calderon," he said with a stiff little bow.

Simon bowed as well, feeling a bit as if he and the other man were duelists en garde. The hostility in Ritz's voice as he spoke again confirmed that impression.

"I have only just returned, but I already see that you have implemented many changes while I have been away."

Simon met the resentment in the other man's eyes with a level stare of his own. "Yes," he agreed mildly. "I have. If you wish to discuss them, we can meet next week—"

"Alas," the other man cut him off, "I must go to Paris on Monday. In any case, what is there to discuss?" He gave a careless shrug, but only a fool would have found it convincing. "Would discussions cause you to modify the changes you are making to my hotel?"

"I'm always happy to hear another's point of view."

"Are you? The staff seems to feel otherwise. They don't think you quite understand how things are done here."

Perhaps because you keep stirring the pot.

Thankfully, another voice entered the conversation before Simon could utter that biting retort.

"Lord Calderon?"

He turned to find Ricardo at his elbow. "Yes, Ricardo?"

"Your carriage is here, my lord."

"Excellent. Thank you." He turned to Ritz. "If you will pardon me, Monsieur, I have a dinner engagement, and I must go."

"Of course."

Their gazes locked, the two men bowed again, then Simon turned away. Passing through the entrance door held open for him by a doorman, he walked into the courtyard, where a driver in elegant livery waited for him beside a carriage with an aristocratic insignia.

"My lord," the driver greeted, tipping his cap with his left hand as he opened the door with his right. "I'm Reeves, your driver this evening."

"Reeves. Where are we going?"

He smiled. "Begging your pardon, my lord, but Lady Stratham has instructed me not to tell you. It's a surprise, she said."

"Then I shall not attempt to spoil it."

He stepped into the carriage, settling back against the black leather seat as Reeves closed the carriage door. A few moments later, the vehicle jerked into motion, pulled out of the Savoy courtyard, and began rolling along the Strand. They traveled up Drury Lane, then turned onto New Oxford Street, making for the West End. A short time later, Reeves was opening the carriage door for him in front of a four-story mansion on Park Lane.

Exiting the carriage, Simon walked through a pair of wrought iron gates, across a flagstone courtyard, and up a trio of stone steps, where a tall man in livery was standing by the massive front doors.

"Lord Calderon?" he said with a bow. "I am Hardwicke, the butler here. Lady Stratham is expecting you. This way, please."

He led Simon through the front doors, across an opulent marble foyer, up a curving staircase, and into a luxuriously appointed drawing room on the first floor, where Delia was waiting for him.

"Lord Calderon, my lady."

Simon had always prided himself on his discipline and self-control, but when she turned at the sound of his name, his throat went dry and his body began to burn, reminding him with undeniable force why pride so often went before a fall.

9

Dressed in a cashmere gown of vivid cyclamen pink, she stood out against the green walls of the room like an exotic flower on a mossy embankment. Impeccably cut, the soft woolen gown seemed to hug every curve of her figure. Her black hair was piled high atop her head in a riot of curls that looked ready to come tumbling down at any moment, and the way the low neckline clung to her full, round breasts shredded all Simon's efforts not to think about her without her clothes.

"You came."

The surprise in her voice forced him out of his reverie, and he drew in a deep, steadying breath. "Did you think I wouldn't?"

"I wasn't sure, to be honest," she confessed as she came toward him. "All week, I've been thinking you'd find some excuse to cry off."

"I would never do such a thing. It wouldn't be right."

She halted in front of him, tilting her head a little to one side. "Do you always do what is right?"

"I try to," he said, keeping his gaze firmly fixed on her face, trying to ignore the erotic scent of her perfume. "That, I daresay, also surprises you."

"Funnily enough, it doesn't." She smiled, the corners of her almond-shaped eyes tipping upward. "Though I expect we might often differ in our definition of what's right."

That was probably true and a good reminder for him to keep his wits about him. He glanced around, noting the elegant mahogany furnishings, rich velvet draperies, and gilt-framed paintings. "Whose house is this? Yours?"

"Heavens, no. This is Westbourne's London residence. At this time of year, the only person on the premises is usually Hardwicke, but I brought a few of Max's other servants down from Idyll Hour to prepare the dinner and do for us this evening."

"Idyll Hour?"

"Max's ducal estate in the Cotswolds."

"You brought servants all the way from Gloucestershire?" He laughed, a little confounded. "Just to serve us dinner?"

"Wanton extravagance, I know, but I believe in creating the proper atmosphere."

"The proper atmosphere for what?"

She didn't answer that question. Instead, she turned, putting a hand on his arm.

"Come with me."

Tucking her hand into the crook of his elbow, she led him out of the drawing room. He took it for granted that she was leading him into the dining room across the corridor, but unexpectedly, she turned, propelling him away from that room and back toward the stairs.

"Where are we going?" he asked.

"You'll see."

"You're being very mysterious."

"Am I?" She looked at him as they started up the stairs, a tiny Mona Lisa smile on her lips. "Good."

It was clear she wasn't going to tell him anything, but as they ascended to the second floor, then the third, his curiosity grew. When they reached the top of the stairs and stepped onto a wide landing flanked by corridors leading to what were clearly servants' rooms, he couldn't resist trying again. "We're having dinner in the attics?"

"Of course not. That would be silly."

"What's left, then?" he asked jokingly as they crossed the landing to a set of double doors. "The roof?"

"As a matter of fact…" She paused, opening one of the doors. "Yes."

With that singular remark, she pulled him through the doorway into what seemed at first to be a grove of trees. When he looked up, he saw branches strung with fairy lights, but despite it being early February, the branches were thickly covered in leaves, and the air was balmy and warm, and he realized the place she had brought him was actually a hothouse.

All around him were potted trees and ferns, and the mingled scents of flowers, peat, and boxwood hung in the air. Faintly, in the distance, he could hear music, a soft, delicate melody.

"I feel as if you are Hermia and I am Lysander," he commented as Delia led him along a path among the trees lit by more fairy lights. "And we've just entered the forest of Shakespeare's *A Midsummer Night's Dream*."

"An apt analogy," she replied, "except that, unlike Hermia and Lysander, we are not lovers."

With those words, his mind started conjuring carnal images again, and he could not for the life of him think of a reply. Fortunately, they emerged into a clearing at that moment, and Hardwicke stepped forward, a tray with two filled glasses in his hands.

"Sherry, my lord?"

"Yes, thank you," he replied with fervent gratitude, and as he plucked a glass off the tray, it occurred to him that if he remained in charge of Delia much longer, he might well become a dipsomaniac.

Taking a much-needed swallow of sherry, he followed Delia as she led him to a round table by a fountain that had been set for two, its white tablecloth, silver, and crystal gleaming in the soft light. To his left, a footman stood beside an enormous rosewood sideboard laden with covered dishes. To his right stood a gramophone, its turntable spinning and the notes of a Mendelssohn concerto drifting from its horn into the languid air. All around them were more trees strung with fairy lights, and above his head, a framework of glass and iron formed a domed ceiling. Beyond it was the inky blackness of the night sky.

"What is this place?" he asked.

"Evie's garden. Evie is my cousin's wife," she added as he looked at her in puzzlement at the unfamiliar name. "Evie grew up in London, but after marrying Max, she developed a passion for country life, especially gardening. So Max built this for her as a present on their first wedding anniversary so that she could always have a garden, even here in town—though they're usually here only during the season. The rest of the year, the house is closed up and empty. Except for Hardwicke, of course. He's here all year round—he takes care of Evie's garden and generally keeps an eye on things when the family's not in residence."

"And you brought me here because...?"

"Welcome to the Savoy's newest banqueting room," she said, gesturing to their surroundings with her glass. "Well, a facsimile of it, at any rate."

"You want to build a structure like this on the roof of the Savoy?"

"Yes." She laughed at his dubious expression. "You're looking at me as if you think I'm crazy."

"Well," he began.

"You can't say the hotel roof isn't big enough."

"No," he agreed. "You could easily seat a hundred people up there."

"But . . . ?" she prompted when he fell silent.

He didn't reply. Instead, he walked to the other end of the clearing, sipping his sherry, considering the idea. "It would certainly be a unique setting," he said as she joined him.

"Exactly. No hotel in London has a banquet room like this."

"That's probably because of the difficulties."

"Such as?"

"The logistics, for one thing. It's a long way from the kitchens to the rooftop, remember. The waiters will have to go up and down seven flights of stairs, serving seven courses of food to a very large group of people. How will you manage that without the food getting cold?"

"The waiters can use the service lifts and the wheeled restaurant carts to bring up the food. I've already borrowed one of the waiters and tested the timing. Believe it or not, it takes no longer to deliver food to the roof than it does to take it to the Pinafore Room. Service won't be a problem."

He looked around again and shook his head, bemused. "You want to do all this just to ensure that your friend has a place to hold her wedding dinner? A bit over the top, isn't it?"

"I'm not only thinking of Kay, although she was the impetus for my idea. If we had another large banquet room, we would certainly make good use of it. And besides," she continued in a rush as if afraid he'd argue that point, "we are talking about the Savoy. As I told you during our first meeting, being over the top is what we're known for."

"You're not the only one to tell me that. The staff reminds me daily that the merely mundane and practical is not up to Savoy standards."

"Having trouble getting everyone to embrace your oh-so-sensible changes, are you?" she murmured, giving him a look of feigned surprise over the rim of her wineglass.

"The changes are sensible, Delia. More importantly, they are necessary. Because of that, the staff's opinion on the matter cannot be my primary concern."

"No," she allowed, "but you can't blame them for being worried about their future. How many of their jobs will you decide are unnecessary before the investors can make an acceptable profit?"

He took a moment to reply, appreciating the fine line he was walking. "I can't make any blanket promises," he said at last, "but I don't plan on dismissing anyone else except for just cause."

Her radiant smile was his reward. "Do I have your permission to pass that information on to everyone?"

"Would my lack of permission stop you?" he countered wryly.

Her smile faded to a serious expression. "If you swore me to secrecy, I wouldn't tell. I hope, however, that I can reassure them?"

"Of course. But," he added with a sigh, thinking of Ritz, "I'm not sure how much good it will do."

"What do you mean by that?"

Thankfully, Hardwicke's voice interrupted before he could reply.

"My lady, dinner is served."

They returned to the table, but if Simon thought the distraction of dinner would enable him to sidestep the issue, he was mistaken, for they had barely sat down before she resumed the subject.

"If you're having trouble with the staff," she said as the footman set their soup in front of them and took their sherry glasses, "perhaps I can help."

That offer brought to mind the Duke of Westbourne's advice from a week ago.

If you can get her on your side, she can be of great assistance to you.

Sadly, he wasn't sure how much help the duke's advice could be. His biggest problem was Ritz, and in that battle, he knew quite well which side Delia would come down on. And besides, until her innocence or guilt was determined and this whole fraud business decided once and for all, he could not afford to trust her an inch. "Do you truly want to help?" he asked.

"Of course! I'll help you any way I can." She gave him an impish grin. "As long as you let me put a hothouse on the roof."

He laughed at that. He couldn't help it. "God, woman, you are relentless. Do you never take no for an answer?"

"Only when I hear it. And sometimes," she added irrepressibly, "not even then."

"I can well believe it. But I hope your offer of help means that you've decided to stop standing in my way?"

"I haven't stood in your way," she protested. "I haven't," she repeated as he gave a laugh of disbelief. "I've merely...allowed you to see for yourself that changing things isn't as simple as you may have thought it would be."

"A neat distinction." He gave her a wry smile. "You also, I notice, enjoy crowing over my discomfort when your lot tears me to bits."

If he was hoping for apologetic regret, he didn't get it. Instead, she grinned back at him. "If you're talking about the duchess, I did offer my help."

"Only after the woman had already left," he grumbled. "But I'm not really worried about people like the duchess. I was prepared for the resentment of the clients who are no longer getting things for free, and I do think eventually it will pass. It's the stonewalling by the staff that I find most frustrating at present."

"You said yourself that change is upsetting. And surely you've done this sort of thing with other hotels. Haven't you ever encountered this problem before?"

He shook his head. "With one exception, the other hotels I've acquired were already bankrupt and closed."

"The exception being the Bainbridge, which you own in partnership with Richard Carte?"

"You've been making inquiries about me, I see. But," he added when she merely smiled, "you're quite right. Richard asked me to step in and take over that hotel a year ago when he first became ill."

"Is he really so very ill? The man doesn't look well, of course, and there have been rumors, but nothing definitive has been said."

"Doctors never seem able to be definite about these things. But to return to the point," he said, choosing his words with care, "the staff at the Bainbridge did not feel as if their loyalties were being divided when I took over. It's different here. I understand the loyalty everyone feels toward Ritz and his way of doing things, but it hampers me at every turn."

"And that surprises you? Ritz has earned their loyalty over a number of years. While you . . ."

She stopped, but he knew what she hadn't said. "While I am a usurper who's been here a mere five weeks," he finished for her. "I do realize that, but I wish I could make everyone understand that if the hotel can't be made to run at a profit, many more people will lose their jobs than those few I've already let go. Stonewalling me and what I'm trying to do will not serve them in the long run. As I said, I don't want to fire anyone else, but I will do so if they refuse to follow those policies. If you truly want to help, perhaps you could impress that fact upon them."

"I can do that, of course, but—" Breaking off, she leaned back for the footman to take her soup plate, then she went on. "But it would be better coming from Ritz than from me. He will be returning very soon, and when he does, I'm sure you can persuade him to work with you to gain everyone's cooperation."

Simon knew that wasn't going to happen. Aside from the fact that Ritz was directly countermanding his orders, in light of what Helen had told him, it was now clear beyond doubt that the other man would have to be dismissed, and soon, though just how and when that would happen were open to question. "Ritz has returned," he said, sidestepping the issue of the other man's fate. "I saw him in the lobby earlier."

"He's back from Rome?"

"He arrived this afternoon. But it hardly matters, since I have no intention of asking for his help."

"You'd really let pride stand in your way?"

"It's not pride. It's—" He broke off, knowing he couldn't tell her the truth, chagrined to realize he wished he could.

Thankfully, the footman appeared, taking his soup plate. Hardwicke followed, presenting a tray of sole Véronique, giving Simon time, and as he helped himself to the fish, he considered what explanation to offer that would satisfy her without requiring him to lie and without giving anything away.

"I have to do what I think is best for the future of the hotel, Delia," he said at last. "Ritz will have to accept my way of doing things, and frankly, I'm not sure he can. When we saw each other earlier, he made his resentment of me quite clear."

"You can't blame him for that," she replied as Hardwicke moved to her side of the table. "I felt the same."

"Felt?" he echoed and frowned, wondering if he'd misheard. "You sound as if that's in the past."

To his surprise, she shrugged as she set a sole fillet on her plate and put the silver fish slice back on Hardwicke's platter. "I'm a pragmatist, I suppose," she said as the butler moved away. "I've never seen the point of beating dead horses. You're here, the rest of the board wants you here, and as you said, changes have to be made if the hotel is to survive. That's why I wanted to make peace with you. It wasn't to gain my own ends, truly. Nor was it just for my friend Kay. For the good of everyone, I accepted that the only thing to be done was to help you as best I can. Ritz will come to the same conclusion, I'm sure."

He'd never be given the chance, but of course, Simon couldn't say so.

"He might," he said instead.

She stopped eating, a forkful of fish halfway to her mouth. "What if he doesn't? The board won't fire Ritz, surely?"

He began to wish he'd never agreed to this dinner. Dodging her questions without lying was like dodging raindrops without getting wet. "I can't discuss with you what the board may or may not do. That sort of information is confidential. In any case," he rushed on before she could probe more deeply, "Ritz and I will have no opportunity to discuss anything involving the hotel for some time. I'm off to Berkshire for the weekend to see my sister, and he's off for Paris on Monday."

That, he was relieved to see, diverted her attention. "You have a sister?" she asked and resumed eating. "What's her name?"

"Cassandra." He smiled. "She's my only sibling, but she's much younger than I am. Only seventeen."

"And where is she now?"

"At my estate, Ivywild. In Berkshire." His smile faded as he remembered the troubling words of Cassandra's last letter. "It's a bit hard for her just now," he found himself saying. "She's back from finishing school, and none of her friends from school days live anywhere near. And when it comes to helping her, I'm a bit lost, to be honest. She was born the year I went into the army, so I didn't have much opportunity to see her until she was twelve and my military service was over. Now that both our parents are gone, watching over Cassandra is my office, and I spend most of my time feeling I'm in way over my head."

"Young girls are never easy. Is there no female relative who can guide her?"

He shook his head. "Unfortunately not. And I sense that my elevation to the peerage has made things even harder for her."

"How so?"

He forced a laugh. "I know nothing about being a peer," he confessed.

"I grew up in the hotel trade. My father was a cashier and my mother was a maid. When I wasn't in school, I worked as a bellboy and a lift attendant. What I know of the aristocracy is only by observation, and as a result, I'm finding my new social position difficult to navigate. The ton, I've discovered, isn't particularly welcoming to those who are elevated to the peerage rather than being born within it."

"Perhaps not."

"It doesn't bother me. I don't really care what other people think. But the lack of acceptance bothers Cassandra a great deal. All the more reason I wish I'd had the means to refuse the title when it was bestowed."

"Refuse it?" She straightened in her chair, staring at him in astonishment. "You can't be serious."

"I am. I didn't want the blasted thing. I hope you won't think me rude for saying it, but I'm not the least bit impressed by the aristocracy; I care little for its pretentions, snobbery, and silly rules."

"With that sort of attitude, I'm shocked the aristocracy hasn't accepted you with open arms," she murmured, giving him an amused look across the table.

"I realize I ought to be falling to my knees in gratitude for my elevation," he countered dryly, "but that would be hypocritical."

"But doesn't your elevation offer you the opportunity for more business contacts?"

"Hardly; and you know that already, since you are the one who reminded me that peers are not particularly good at business nor much impressed by it."

"Well, you've got me there. But what about the social considerations? It's not so important for you, perhaps, but your sister will benefit greatly from being an honorable."

"Will she?" Simon was doubtful. "It hasn't benefited her much so far. I wish I knew what to do to help her assimilate to our new life, but as I said, I'm lost."

"Would you like some advice?"

"Are you offering any?" he countered with a laugh.

The moment the joking words were out of his mouth, he cursed himself, but it was too late to take them back.

"I'd be happy to," she answered. "But will you take my advice? That's the question."

It was indeed.

"What do you think, Hardwicke?" she asked before Simon could answer, turning to the butler as he paused beside her chair with a platter of lamb chops. "Do you think I am an acceptable guide for a young girl entering society?"

"Lord Calderon's sister could not do better, my lady," Hardwicke answered loyally as he moved to Simon's side of the table. "Any young woman would be fortunate indeed to have your guidance."

"Well, there we are then." Laughing, she returned her attention to Simon. "How can you refuse me after such a ringing endorsement?"

Allowing his sister to be guided by the advice of a woman suspected of embezzlement and fraud was an insane idea. And he wasn't sure it was quite right to allow her to do him a good turn when he might very well be firing her in a month's time. But even as he reminded himself of these facts, the forlorn words of his sister's letter echoed through his mind.

Dearest Simon, I am so lonely here.

He capitulated. "I'd be grateful for any insight you can offer, Delia."

She blinked, clearly showing she hadn't expected that. "You mean it?"

He gave a shrug. "Should I not? You're well placed in society, influential, and popular. You possess a quick wit and a keen mind, and given that we're having dinner in a greenhouse, you clearly have ingenuity."

"I do love butter," she purred. "Especially when it's poured over me by a man who has so little use for me."

He froze, staring at her across the table as a wild fantasy of literally pouring butter on her naked skin and licking it off flashed through his mind.

Good God, what was wrong with him?

Something of what he was thinking must have shown on his face, for her amusement vanished and her eyes went wide. "Why are you looking at me like that all of a sudden?" she whispered.

He stiffened, forcing his countenance into the blandest expression he could muster. "How was I looking?"

"I don't know. As if…" She paused, her tongue darting out to lick her lips. "As if I'm Little Red Riding Hood and you're the big bad wolf."

That analogy was so apt, he had to take a hefty swallow of wine before he could reply. "You're wrong in my assessment of you, by the way," he said, desperate to divert the subject. "I confess I sometimes find you exasperating, aggravating, and too devilishly clever for my peace of mind, but—"

Her groan interrupted him. "First you butter me up, then you slam me down. I'm getting dizzy."

"Nonetheless, despite how it might seem, I do value your opinion. I wouldn't have asked for it if I didn't."

"Very well, then." She ate a few more bites of her food, then set down her knife and fork, picked up her glass, and leaned back in her chair. "Can you tell me specifically what the problem is?" she asked as the footman took her plate. "Who has snubbed your sister, and when, and under what circumstances?"

"I'm not sure of the details, but from what she's written, the county girls her age are quite unfriendly toward her. She's such a sweet girl who's never had a problem making friends, and she's taking it hard."

"You think their standoffishness is due to snobbery?"

"What other reason could there be?"

"Well, we British are rather standoffish by nature, aren't we? And it's always hard on girls when they leave school and have to make new friends all over again. When you bring her out—"

"Bring her out?" He stopped eating and set down his knife and fork with a clatter, staring at her in dismay.

"Of course. She'll be doing the season, she'll be presented at court—" She broke off as he shook his head. "Simon, you're a viscount. Your sister will have to be presented. I'm happy to put her name in for consideration. I'd have to meet her first, of course, but once that's done, I can easily write to the Lord Chamberlain and make the request. The Queen can hardly refuse, since she's the one who bestowed a title on you in the first place."

"Coming out, being presented…is all that really necessary?"

"Of course! A girl of her position must make her coming-out, do the season, and be presented if she expects to do well in society and make a good marriage."

"Marriage?" His dismay deepened. "She's far too young to be thinking about marriage!"

"But she's not. She's seventeen."

"Exactly. She's a child."

"No, she's a young lady. Most young ladies are brought out at that age. And many marry after their first season. I did."

"Did you?" he asked, momentarily diverted as he recalled his own surprise at his first glimpse of her. "So that explains it, at least partly."

"Explains what?"

"When we first met, I was shocked at how young you are. I had thought a three-time widow would be older."

"And here I was thinking Helen had been whispering in your ear about how dreadful I am."

He didn't miss her inquiring look across the table, but he refused to be drawn. "I form my own opinions about people's character, I assure you. But I confess, I did have a certain image of you in my head that was partly due to what she told me."

"What sort of image?"

"Gray haired, stout, wearing too many cosmetics, and flamboyantly middle-aged."

She laughed merrily, not seeming the least bit insulted. "Well, I like that! Stout and middle-aged, indeed."

"As I said, I was shocked to discover how mistaken I was. In any case, even if I do decide to bring my sister out this season, that's several months away. I'd dearly love to see her make a few friends before then. She's terribly lonely, and I'm so busy here. She's only got her old governess for company."

"It would certainly be easier for her if she made some new friends before the season begins. Your neighbors in Berkshire are the obvious choice."

"I know, but as I said, they don't seem willing to be her friends."

"How do they treat you? With similar indifference?"

"I can't answer that, since I haven't yet met any of them."

"You haven't? Well, then," she added, laughing as he shook his head, "that explains it."

"I don't see how."

"No one in the county is going to call on your sister until you've called first. The newest gentleman to the neighborhood always calls first. You need to visit the other gentlemen of the county, who will introduce you to their female relations. Then, and only then, the ladies can call upon your sister. Until then, they are prevented by etiquette."

"It's as simple as that?" He shook his head, baffled anew at how the most minor failure to observe the rules could have such a powerful impact. "So it's not snobbery? How can you be so sure? The Duchess of Moreland seemed to think I was beneath her notice."

"She's like that with everyone. And I'd be lying if I said there weren't more like her. But if you call on the local families while you're home this weekend, your sister will probably find the other young ladies of the county willing to reciprocate."

"And if that doesn't happen? If there's more to this than mere etiquette?"

"Then you'll need to bring out the heavy guns."

"Such as?"

"Me. I can easily put in a good word with your neighbors. I once lived in Berkshire, near Reading, so I know quite a few people there. I can easily facilitate any needed introductions. I can also help launch her when she comes to London for the season. Introduce her about, chaperone her, that sort of thing."

Such a plan was unlikely to come to fruition. If she was guilty, she couldn't be allowed anywhere near his sister. And if she was innocent, she'd hardly be willing to help him once the truth came out and her beloved Ritz was booted out and perhaps arrested. And who could blame her? "Oh, I don't think that's really necessary," he began.

"She'll need a chaperone, Simon."

"Well, I suppose she will, but I can't possibly impose on you."

"If it were an imposition, I wouldn't have offered. You don't seem to relish the idea," she added, making a rueful face. "But really, you don't have to make excuses. If you don't want me around her because you don't like me, you can just say no."

"It isn't that," he assured her. "It has nothing to do with my opinion of you. But there's something you need to know," he added, improvising as he spoke. "And once you do, you'll probably want to take back your offer."

"Oh?" She set down her knife and fork, giving him her full attention. "What is this awful piece of news?"

He met her eyes across the table, dread like a knot in his stomach. "My father was a thief. When he was a cashier, he embezzled money from the hotel where he worked."

"Oh, that." She waved her hand in a dismissive gesture. "I know all about that. Max told me."

"I see." He hesitated, but something in him, something he couldn't quite define, drove him on. "There is one thing your cousin didn't tell you, because he doesn't know."

"Oh? What's that?"

"After he was caught out, the hotel intended to prosecute my father for the thefts, and he shot himself rather than face the disgrace."

Again, her reaction was not what he'd expected. Instead of looking appalled, she tilted her head, studying him. "You're angrier about that than about the theft, aren't you?"

"Should I not be?" he countered. "He committed a criminal act, and when it was about to be exposed, he shot himself rather than face it."

"Yes, but sometimes," she said, her voice soft, "people are in such pain, suicide can seem like the only way out."

Strangely enough, he'd never stopped to consider it from that angle. "Nonetheless," he said, watching her closely, "he was a thief."

She shrugged. "There are worse things."

That nonchalant reaction confirmed his worst fears about her view of theft and thieves, but oddly enough, he couldn't seem to work up any indignation over it, and he feared perhaps he, like everyone else at the Savoy, had fallen under Delia Stratham's charming spell. But then—

His gaze slid to her lips. There were, as she had just pointed out, worse things.

"You know, Simon," she said, breaking the silence and forcing him to veer away from the naughty direction his mind was taking, "if you're afraid people in my set will judge Cassandra for what your father did, you can rest easy. Some will; most won't. We all have thieves and suicides in our family history. So, I'm not taking back my offer. Unless," she paused, studying him, "that's not the reason for your reluctance?"

He was in a cleft stick now, damn it all. "I'm not ungrateful for the offer, Delia," he began.

"But…?"

"I'm just not sure Cassandra's ready to do the season," he parried.

"Being the protective older brother, are you?"

"I am that, I admit it. As I said, I'm all she's got. And we haven't been in society long enough for her to know the ropes. What if out of ignorance, she makes some ghastly mistake?"

"A few weeks with me, and she'll be right as rain. I know all about the rules. How to obey them. How to bend them. And—" She paused to give him that dazzling, dimpled smile. "How to break them."

"That's rather what I'm afraid of," he admitted, only half in jest.

She sobered at once. "I would never do anything to hurt your sister's reputation. And though I was a bit wild myself as a girl, any of my peccadilloes were forgiven long ago."

"Let me think on it." He paused long enough for the footman to take his plate, then he went on, "Don't misunderstand me, Delia. As little as I know about the aristocracy, I can well imagine what a responsibility it must be to help bring a girl into society, and I appreciate your offer very much. But as you said, I need to pave the way first. Let me do that, see how she gets on, and go forward from there."

"Very well, but know that I'm happy to help. That is, if you truly want me."

Want her?

He froze, his wineglass halfway to his lips, staring at her across the table as heat once again curled in his abdomen. He did want her. Of course he did. How could he not?

Almost since the moment they met, he'd wanted her. He'd tried to deny it, then he'd tried to ignore it, but the past three days had proved his efforts were in vain. He also knew that lusting after her was like playing with fire, and as Hardwicke returned with their dessert, he decided it might be best to once again divert the conversation.

"I didn't realize," he said as the butler placed a crystal dish of sylla-bub in front of him, "that you had ever lived in Berkshire."

She nodded. "My first husband's family comes from there. His father was the Marquess of Forley."

"Your husband didn't inherit the title? Was there an older brother?"

"No, and my husband would have taken the title, but he died before his father, so his younger brother became the marquess when the old man died. That was probably a blessing for the estate."

He was watching her face as she spoke, and he did not miss the pensiveness in her expression. "How so?"

"When I met Roger, I was seventeen and he was twenty," she said, and it didn't escape his notice that she hadn't answered his question. "When he proposed, my parents were delighted. He had the right pedigree and plenty of money, you see."

"And what about you? Were you delighted?"

"Me? I was over the moon. I thought he was the handsomest man I'd ever seen. He was also a poet and a tortured soul. Girls are roman-tic and terribly naïve at that age. I fell in love with him the first time he wrote me a poem."

"That's not love, then. It's infatuation."

"You're right, of course, but at the time, it felt like love. At least, until I found out he had another love besides me."

"Another woman? That bastard."

"Not a woman," she corrected, shaking her head. "Cocaine."

"Your first husband was a cocaine addict?"

"Yes. He developed the habit when he took his Grand Tour. It's terribly fashionable, you know."

"A foolish fashion," Simon muttered, shaking his head.

"I can't disagree with you there."

"Couldn't you have stopped him?" Even as he spoke, he knew what a futile question it was. "Never mind. I suppose if someone is bent on that sort of self-destruction, it's impossible to stop them."

"I'd have tried, though, if I'd known. But as I said, I was young and naïve. I did notice his violent changes of mood, but we'd been married almost a year and a half before I learned that the stuff in his snuffbox wasn't snuff."

"That must have been quite a shock." Setting down his spoon, he pushed aside his empty dessert dish, propped one elbow on the table, and rested his chin in his hand. "What did you do?"

She shrugged. "What could I do? When I questioned his doctor, the man brushed me off. He was so damnably smug about it, too." She looked down, toying with her dessert. "He wasn't quite so smug at Roger's funeral. That was a few weeks later."

"So cocaine was the cause of your husband's death?"

She nodded. "He died nineteen months after we were married. I just wish…" She paused, sculpting syllabub meditatively with her spoon, and she was silent so long, he thought she wasn't going to finish what she'd started to say. "I just wish," she said at last, "I'd had the sense to learn my lesson."

"What do you mean?" he asked, frowning, puzzled. "What lesson?"

She set down her spoon and lifted her head, shaking back the tendrils of hair that had fallen over her forehead. "Let's just say I'm not a particularly good judge when it comes to men. I can be a bit blind sometimes."

Given her faith in Ritz and her refusal to see what the man was doing right under her nose, her declaration didn't surprise him. On the other hand, it was highly possible she did know and didn't care or was a fully active participant. Which of those came closest to the truth, he was here to find out. But before he could think of a way to begin that process, she abruptly stood up. "It's a bit warm in here. Do you mind if I get some air?"

He rose at once. "Of course not, but it's quite chilly this evening. Are you sure you want to go out?"

She opened her arms, nodding to her long sleeves. "My dress is wool. Besides, I don't mind the cold."

"Shall I accompany you?"

"No, no, please stay and have your port." She signaled to Hardwicke, who appeared at once with a bottle and glass. "I won't be long."

Following her lead, he acquiesced, remaining behind as she walked to a nearby glass door, opened it, and stepped outside, vanishing out into the night.

He found it rather ridiculous to sit here sipping port by himself, but it was clear she wanted a few moments alone. Nonetheless, when she did not reappear after a quarter of an hour, he decided to go in search.

He stepped out into the cold, crisp air. From the light of the hothouse, he was able to find her at once. She was standing by the balustrade, staring pensively beyond the streetlights into the inky blackness of Hyde Park.

"Delia, are you all right?" he asked as he started toward her.

At once, she turned, her pensive expression replaced by a smile. "Right as rain," she said brightly as he halted beside her. "Should I not be?"

"I wondered if I might have said something to offend you."

"No, no, of course not. I was just a bit hot in there, that's all."

He sensed there was more to it than that, but he didn't press her.

"The air inside the hothouse was a bit oppressive," he said instead. "The humidity, no doubt."

"If you agree to my plan, we shall have to conduct some experiments to get the temperature just right."

There was a question in that statement, but he couldn't answer it. Not until he knew more. "Do you have any idea how much it will cost to do something like this?" he asked.

She sighed, shaking her head, staring at him as if he were a hopeless business. "Really, Simon," she said with good-natured exasperation, turning to lean against the balustrade as she looked at him, "is there no romance in your soul? Imagine for a moment how splendid it will be—the view of the river, the moon, its light on the water—"

"This is London," he felt compelled to remind her. "All the coal soot in the air makes it impossible to see the moon."

"Oh, don't be so literal," she chided. "We'll hang an enormous paper lantern to look like a moon. And people can dine amid the trees and flowers no matter what time of year it is, and no matter what the capricious English weather decides to do. And when the weather is fine, we can open everything up and do outdoor events. Picnics, cotillions, that sort of thing. The parties there will be the talk of London."

"That's the heart of my problem, right there," he countered ruefully. "Everyone at the Savoy thinks of the party, not the price."

"Then think of it as an investment, if that helps. It will pay for itself in one London season, I promise you."

Simon was usually inclined to regard such blithe assurances with a grain of salt, but he couldn't deny the idea had possibilities. It would be a setting unlike any other in London. With the proper publicity—

"Well?"

He looked up at the sound of her voice to find her watching him, biting her lip and crossing her fingers as she waited for his reply.

"I'm not saying no," he replied at last. "But," he added as she gave a chortle of triumph, "I can't say yes, either. Bring me a full proposal of the project, including an engineer's report on how to build the glass structure, a detailed cost estimate, and your fairest projections on the annual revenue you think it will generate. Then I can decide how to proceed."

"I'm already working on that information. I should have a full report for you in two to three weeks."

"Even if the numbers are favorable, it will still be costly, so I shall have to get the board to agree, which won't be easy. We're in the midst of trying to cut costs, if you remember."

"The board will listen to you, I'm sure. And if you need additional support to persuade them, Ritz will be happy to add his voice to yours. He'll adore this idea, believe me. It's right up his street."

Simon had no doubt of that at all, given Ritz's tendency to spend money like water. "I'm sure it is," he said tactfully. "I can't promise anything, but it is an ingenious idea, and quite unique."

For some reason, that made her smile.

"What's so amusing?" he asked.

"You and I seeing eye to eye about something. It's . . ." She paused, considering. "It's nice."

Nice? He lowered his gaze to the deep *V* of her evening gown. Dangerous was more like it—at least for him.

"Isn't it?"

He studied her face, the wide smile, the sadness still lingering in her eyes. "Yes," he admitted, surprised by the fact. "It is nice."

The breeze picked up, stirring the tendrils of hair at her temples and making her shiver. "Ooh," she said, rubbing her arms. "You can tell it's winter, can't you?"

"Should we go in?"

"Oh, no, not yet. At this time of year, I feel I spend all my time indoors, and it's not raining for once. Do you mind if we stay out here a little bit longer?"

She shivered again even as she spoke, and Simon unbuttoned his dinner jacket. "Here, then," he said, sliding it off his shoulders. "At least put this on."

"Don't you need it?"

"Not as much as you. Turn around."

She complied, and he slung the garment over her shoulders. As he did, the delicious scent of her perfume floated to him on the light breeze, and just like that, the arousal he'd been trying to keep at bay for days flared up again, hotter than before.

He ought to tamp it down, but even as he told himself that, he leaned in and closed his eyes, inhaling deeply.

"Well, now," she murmured. "It seems I was wrong."

Simon opened his eyes and took a deep breath of the bracing winter air, trying to think. "Wrong about what?"

She turned toward him, clasping the lapels of his jacket in one hand to hold the edges together as she pushed a wind-tossed tendril of hair away from her face with the other. "I accused you of having no romance in your soul," she said. "I stand corrected."

He almost laughed with her, but not with humor. There was nothing the least bit romantic about what he felt at this moment. Arousal, not romance, was thrumming through his body. "I didn't realize," he said, trying to think when his wits felt thick as tar, "that it was romantic for a man to give a woman his jacket."

"Oh, but it is—at least from a woman's point of view. Though being a man, you might see it as simply being chivalrous, I suppose."

"Chivalrous?" He paused, his gaze raking over the luscious curves of her figure. "I'm not feeling the least bit chivalrous right now, believe me," he muttered.

"No? Then what—" She paused, and to Simon, it seemed an eternity before she spoke again.

"What are you feeling?" she asked at last, her voice so low, he barely heard it over his thudding heart.

He didn't answer. Instead, he simply stood there, wordless, unable to conceal the dark hunger surging through his body.

Her eyes were the color of the midnight sky overhead. A lock of her ebony hair flew across her face, and without thinking, he reached up, pulling it back and tucking it behind her ear.

Those midnight eyes widened as if in shock, but she didn't move. She didn't pull away.

Slowly, his fingertips traced the velvety curve of her ear and moved down the column of her throat. The tendons in her slender neck felt taut as harp strings, and when he felt the pulse at the base of her throat, as rapid as his own pounding heart, the arousal in him flared into outright lust. With an abrupt move, he slid his hand to the nape of her neck and pressed his thumb beneath her chin to lift her face.

Her lips parted, but she didn't protest.

She was close enough that he could feel the warmth of her body, and the arousal inside him deepened and spread, making his heart pound in his chest like a trip-hammer. He pressed his fingers into the nape of her neck, urging her to come closer.

She complied, and the knuckles of her hand brushed his chest. It was the barest contact possible, but he sucked in a sharp breath just the same, and somehow, that sound succeeded in penetrating the sensuous haze enveloping him.

"Good God." He jerked, letting her go and taking a long step back, staring at her in dismay. "What the hell am I doing?"

She laughed, a low, throaty chuckle that threatened to send the last vestiges of his control to the wall. The tendrils of her hair floated around her laughing face, making her look a bit like a witch in the night. "I think you were about to kiss me."

He wanted to deny it, but that would have been a lie. "We should go," he said instead and took another even longer step back, putting some much-needed distance between them. "It's late, and I have to catch the early train for Berkshire in the morning."

Her smile faded away, and the laughter went out of her eyes. Puzzlement and a hint of what might have been hurt shimmered across her face. It was gone before he could be sure, but nonetheless, the mere possibility that he'd hurt her cut him to the quick.

But kissing her would be a serious mistake. It was unethical, for one thing, since he had full power over her job. It would also cloud his judgment, muddy his thinking, and make it impossible for him to be objective when the time came to decide her fate, and that would be a betrayal of the trust Richard and Helen had placed in him.

He had to walk away now, while he still could. It was the only honorable thing to do.

He turned abruptly and started back toward the hothouse, but as he did, it felt as if he were ripping himself in half, making him curse his sense of honor. Being a cad, he thought, would have been easier. And far more enjoyable.

10

Delia watched as he walked away, her head in a whirl, her heart thudding hard in her chest, her emotions tilting from pleasure to amazement and back again.

She knew now that she had not been mistaken. That look in his eyes the other day in her office had not been her imagination or a trick of the light. It truly was desire.

"But how can that be?" she whispered, staring through the glass, watching as he vanished amid the fig trees and ferns of the hothouse. "He hates me."

Even as she said it, she gave a delighted little shiver, remembering how he'd touched her, tracing his fingertips over her ear, caressing her neck, and she gave an incredulous laugh as she realized he didn't hate her as much as he'd led her to believe.

But then, why hadn't he kissed her?

Her laughter faded away as she contemplated that question.

Of course, Simon was one of those upright, straightlaced, honorable men. He was stubborn and often infuriating as hell, but he was not the sort to do anything improper. He played by the rules.

On the other hand, it wasn't as if she were a young girl, with chaperones hovering about. There was nothing improper about kissing a widow, for heaven's sake. She had no innocence to protect and no reputation to keep pristine. Granted, he'd tried to avoid coming to dinner by using some lame excuse about how it wasn't appropriate because they worked together, but that was ridiculous, too. Who would know? Who would care?

He emerged from the trees again and glanced around. When he saw that she hadn't followed him inside, he turned his head in her direction, and though she knew he couldn't see her out here in the darkness, she could see him, stone-faced, looking as if he'd rather eat nails than kiss her.

But it was too late for that sort of pretense to fool her. Delia smiled, hugging that knowledge to herself as she straightened away from the balustrade and started for the door into the hothouse. In one unbelievable moment, they had both felt the same spark of desire. The question now was what she intended to do about it.

She considered her options as they journeyed together back to the Savoy. She could ignore the whole episode, of course, which was quite proper and horribly dull. She could shamelessly fling herself at him the next time, a much more agreeable possibility, at least until she slid a glance at him in the seat opposite. He was looking out the window, and the grim set of his profile warned her that hurling herself into his arms was a risky business. He was just as likely to toss her out of the carriage and into the street as he was to kiss her back.

Despite his desire for her, it was painfully clear he didn't like her much. And that, she acknowledged with a grimace, was the reason he intrigued her so. He wanted her, but he didn't want to want her, and she found that both deliciously enticing and aggravating as hell. Especially since she wasn't sure why.

Delia took a deep breath, hoping she wasn't about to make a complete fool of herself. "There's three of us in this carriage, it seems."

At the sound of her voice, he turned his head to look at her. There was a quizzical line between his brows, but other than that, his expression was unreadable in the dim light. "I beg your pardon?"

"You, me, and the elephant. You know," she prompted when he didn't reply, "the big, obvious elephant sitting right here between us. Maybe we should talk about it?"

His frown deepened, his expression turning wary. "I'm not sure I understand you."

His attempt to dissemble didn't fool her for a minute. "Has anyone ever told you you're a terrible liar?"

He looked away, but he didn't reply.

Pressing a man on something like this was a violation of feminine decorum, no doubt, but Delia had never been one to care about things like that, and when the carriage turned into the Savoy courtyard, she tossed aside euphemisms and cut to the chase. "You wanted to kiss me," she said. "Why didn't you?"

He gave a laugh, a harsh sound in the closed confines of the carriage. "God, woman," he said and looked at her again. "You can certainly be direct when you want to be."

"I can. Can you do the same? And please," she added as he opened his mouth to reply, "don't give me some excuse about how we work together, and it wouldn't be honorable."

"It's not an excuse. It's the truth."

"Perhaps, but it's also not the real reason."

He stirred in his seat, confirming the fact. "It's a very large part of the reason, believe me."

"There must be more to it than that."

His lashes lowered, his gaze raking over her in a way that made her breath catch and her toes curl in her shoes.

"Very well, if you must know." His voice was harsh, without a shred of romantic tenderness, and yet, by the time he looked into her eyes again, her pulse was hammering. "Kissing you would be like lighting a match in a room full of gunpowder. And explosions like that can annihilate a man."

Her heart slammed into her ribs with enough force to steal the breath from her lungs, and it was a long moment before she could manage a reply. "Heavens," she said, trying to make her voice offhand and lightly flirtatious, but despite her efforts, the word came out in a breathless rush. "What a delightful prospect."

"Not for me," he said grimly as the carriage came to a halt. "But I hope," he added as the doorman opened the door for them, "your curiosity is now satisfied."

"Not really," she confessed, stepping out of the carriage and turning toward him as he followed her out of the vehicle. "I've never been in an explosion like that. I'd love to find out what it's like."

"You won't, not from me."

A rejection if ever there was one, but strangely, she wasn't the least bit insulted by it. "That sounds like a dare," she said, smiling. "And I never, ever refuse a dare."

With that parting shot, she turned away, but behind her, she heard him mutter under his breath, "God help me now."

She didn't reply, but as she walked toward the entrance to the hotel, she felt a delicious little thrill of anticipation, and she laughed aloud. This was going to be fun.

This was going to be hell.

Simon followed her into the hotel, her laughter ringing in his ears, and as he studied the slim, straight line of her back, the deep dip of her waist, and the sultry swing of her hips, he couldn't help wondering just how a man could escape a hell as delectable as that.

That he wanted her was aggravating, and the fact that she knew only made it worse. But the most damnable part of it all was that he knew she didn't want him, not really. She just wanted the challenge of bringing him to his knees. And if he didn't find a way to shore up his defenses, she might very well succeed.

What a humiliating thought.

He could dump her in Helen's lap, he supposed. That would be no more than she deserved, the flirtatious devil.

His second option was to just fire her, thereby sparing everyone the bother of investigating her and spare himself the frustration of keeping her at arm's length and pretending he was immune to her charms when they both knew damn well it was a hum.

But even as these possible solutions to his problem went through his mind, he knew neither of them were viable. As to the former, Helen had enough on her plate. She didn't need one more burden. As to the latter, firing Delia because he found her unbearably tempting was both unfair and cowardly. And both options were an admission that he was as weak as water where she was concerned. He'd rather be tortured on the rack than make an admission like that.

No, he decided as he followed her across the lobby toward the lift, the only thing to do was keep up a wall of indifference until this Savoy business was settled and he could get clear of her.

That resolution had barely gone through his head before she came to an abrupt halt and turned to smile at him as if she'd known he was behind her the entire time.

"Why, Lord Calderon, are you following me to my room?" she asked, making the question sound every bit as naughty as the thoughts that had been going through his mind when he'd kissed her.

"No," he corrected, his voice as firm as he could make it. "I'm going to mine."

She sighed. "How disappointing."

He wouldn't have been human if the teasing glimmer in her eyes hadn't made him smile at least a little. But when another feminine voice spoke behind him, his smile vanished.

"Darling Simon, at last!"

He knew that voice as well as he knew his own, but it wasn't possible. He looked over his shoulder, thinking his ears were playing tricks on him, but one look at the round, laughing face, golden hair, and big brown eyes of the girl behind him, and he knew his hearing was perfectly sound.

"What the devil?" he muttered, turning to stare at her, appalled.

"Thank goodness I saw you across the lobby," she said, pressing a hand to her chest with another laugh as Ricardo came up beside her, out of breath. "I've been waiting for ages, and no one seemed to know where you'd gone. And Mr. Esteban here," she added, gesturing to the man beside her, "was terribly reluctant to give me a room."

"I'm sorry, my lord," Ricardo interjected. "I wasn't sure what to do with her, to be honest. Without you here, and her being an unchaperoned young lady, it didn't seem right to just give her a room, if you understand me. And your valet didn't know what to do with her, either. So we decided to wait for your return so you could decide what to do. I hope that wasn't wrong?"

"No, no," Simon assured him at once. "You did the right thing."

Looking relieved, Ricardo gave a nod. "Shall I have a room prepared for her?"

"Put her in a suite," he replied. "Have a maid put her things in one of the bedrooms, and have my valet move my things into the other."

Ricardo departed, but before Simon could return his attention to the more serious problem at hand, Delia moved forward to stand beside him, giving a little cough. "Perhaps," she murmured to him, "you ought to introduce me to your friend?"

"She's not my friend," he replied with a long-suffering sigh. "She is my sister."

"Sister?" Delia smiled, looking delighted and not at all surprised. "How lovely."

Both women turned to him expectantly, and he was forced to give in to the inevitable. "Lady Stratham, allow me to present my sister, Cassandra. Cassie, this is the Countess of Stratham."

"Countess?" Cassie echoed, clearly impressed. "Heavens."

"How do you do, Miss Hayden?" Delia held out her hand. "I'm delighted to meet you. I've heard so much about you."

"Have you?" Cassie laughed as they shook hands. "None of it good, if the look on my brother's face at this moment is any indication. But," she went on before he could reenter the conversation, "I'm glad he is making friends here in London."

"She's not my friend, either," he cut in, but as he spoke, he realized how rude that sounded, and he quickly added, "We work together."

"He's my boss," Delia said, leaning closer to Cassie in a confidential manner that made Simon decidedly uneasy. "He's very good at it. Being bossy, I mean."

Cassie rolled her eyes. "Don't I know it," she agreed with feeling.

Simon was in no mood for this sort of banter. "Cassandra Jane Hayden," he said incisively, "what in God's name are you doing here?"

"Uh-oh," Delia murmured. "He just used your middle name."

Cassie nodded, grimacing. "I think I might be in serious trouble."

"You are indeed," he muttered, feeling decidedly grim. "Now answer my question."

"I came to see you, of course. When you didn't reply to my letter, I got worried."

"Letter? What letter? The last one I received from you arrived only three days ago."

"Three days? But it's been a fortnight since I sent it. I waited and waited, but you never replied."

"It must have been lost in the post then, because I only got it this past Tuesday. Either way, it doesn't matter. How did you get here? And why are you unchaperoned? Where is Mrs. Morrisey?"

"She's at Ivywild, of course. Don't worry," she added as he groaned. "I left her a note. As to how I got here, I came by train. How else? I thought—" She broke off, giving him a look of injured innocence that didn't fool him for a second. "I thought you'd be happy to see me. Haven't you missed me?"

Beside him, Delia made a choked sound of smothered laughter, and he shot her a warning look. She immediately pressed her lips together to hide her smile, but her eyes were still alight with mischief. "Are you in town long, Miss Hayden?" she asked, turning her attention to Cassie.

"No," Simon put in before his sister could reply, giving the girl his sternest frown. "She is going straight back home. First thing tomorrow."

"Oh, that's such a shame," Delia said. "I was hoping the two of you could join me tomorrow night at the opera. I have a box at Covent Garden."

"The opera?" Cassie echoed before he could refuse the invitation. "Oh, that would be lovely. I've never been to Covent Garden."

"And she's not going now," Simon assured them both. "She's going home to Berkshire with me."

He was ignored.

"Several friends of mine are coming," Delia went on. "One of them is a young lady about your age. I know you'll like her. You two might even become friends. I know it can be lonely for a girl," she added with a pointed look in Simon's direction, "once she's left school. It's hard to make friends."

Simon felt a stab of conscience, just as he suspected Delia had intended, and the look he gave her in return was wry.

"It's Puccini," she told him irrepressibly. "*La Bohème*. It's an excellent production. I saw it when it first came to London last autumn. You really ought to see it." She turned to Cassandra. "We can have supper here at the Savoy afterward."

"Oh, it all sounds so wonderful," Cassie said wistfully and turned to Simon. "Can we go?"

Simon felt compelled to point out the obvious. "You're already in serious trouble, young lady."

"I know," she agreed at once. "And I'm sure there will be consequences, which I absolutely deserve. But," she went on before he could emphatically concur, "before then, can we go to the opera with Lady Stratham? I promise I'll be good as gold from now on."

He knew his sister well enough to know how laughably ridiculous that promise was, but Cassie gave him no chance to say so.

"Oh, dear brother, do say yes. Please, please."

He glanced from Cassandra to Delia and back again, any shred of stern brotherly resolve fading.

"Two peas in a pod," he muttered, knowing he'd just lost the battle. Their radiant smiles told him that they knew it, too, and he feared that he was the one in serious trouble.

11

The following morning, Delia found a note from Ritz on her breakfast tray, asking for a meeting with her that afternoon. He was spending Sunday at home with his family and then departing for Paris first thing Monday morning, the note said, and he wanted to discuss hotel business with her before his departure.

She had a pretty fair idea that the hotel business in question involved Simon, however, and that made everything terribly awkward. On the one hand, she understood Ritz's misgivings—his dislike of being undermined, his concern for the staff, and his resentment of the changes. She had felt the same, in the beginning. But during the past few weeks, she had also come to see Simon's point of view. A hotel that lost money could not stay in business. Both Simon and Max had forced her to accept that brutal truth, but Ritz still seemed to be under the illusion that nothing had to change.

Easy for him to be so cavalier, she thought, tossing the note back on her breakfast tray, since he was never around for more than a few days at a time. He had clearly not yet appreciated that the changes Simon was implementing were going to be made, no matter how many of the employees he rallied to stand against them.

Delia bit her lip, staring at the note on the tray, feeling torn. She owed Ritz so much, and she honestly didn't know where she'd be today if it weren't for him. But she also knew when to accept the inevitable. And she had the feeling that the entire purpose of the meeting Ritz wanted was to force her to choose a side, and that was a position she did not want to be in. Stalling, she decided, was her best bet.

Fortunately, she had the perfect excuse to avoid a meeting. Her day, she knew, was going to be full, for she had to pave the way for Cassandra's introduction into society tonight. Inviting Simon and his sister to the opera had been an impulse on her part, but if Cassandra hoped to move in society, the poor girl was clearly going to need some help. Simon might understand balance sheets and income statements, but he was clueless about what a seventeen-year-old girl required to make a successful debut.

The opera was an excellent way to begin the process. The boxes that lined the perimeter of the Royal Opera House at Covent Garden were the perfect place to see and be seen by anyone who mattered, and though early February in London wasn't the most exciting time, there would still be plenty of the ton's aristocratic members in attendance to see just who Lady Stratham had invited to share her box for the year's first performance of Puccini's new opera.

Despite the ideal setting, it was a tricky business to launch a girl, and Delia knew choosing whom else to invite had to be done carefully. Adding to the difficulty, she didn't have much time to make the arrangements.

With that reminder, she dashed off a note to Ritz explaining that she was fully engaged all day and evening, expressing her sincerest apologies, and suggesting they meet the minute he returned from Paris. She then summoned Molly, got dressed, and left the hotel to begin making her arrangements for the evening ahead.

As she'd suspected, filling the remaining five seats of her box was not an easy task. No one liked receiving last-minute invitations, particularly for the benefit of a girl they'd never met whose brother had not been to the manor born. In addition, word of Simon's new policies at the Savoy had gotten round, ruffling quite a few aristocratic feathers, requiring her to send one telegram, make a dozen calls upon acquaintances, and use every bit of her skill at persuasion. But these efforts proved worthwhile, and in the end, those in her box that evening included one baroness and her daughter, one very eligible baronet and his sister, and one very exasperated duke.

"Really, Delia," Max grumbled as they stood by the refreshment table, waiting for Simon and his sister to arrive, "the favors you ask."

"Oh, stop," she replied as she accepted a filled glass from the footman pouring champagne. "I've asked bigger ones of you in the past."

"That's hardly a point in your favor. You realize I'm a busy man?"

She negated that point with a scoff. "In February? Hardly."

"Even in February, it's not a simple matter to drop everything and come all the way to London. Especially when I was given no explanation."

"I did explain."

"Not really." He pulled a slip of paper out of the breast pocket of his dinner jacket. "'Need you in London immediately stop,'" he read. "'Your investment in Savoy may depend on it stop Take two o'clock train stop Will reserve room for you tonight stop Bring white-tie stop Much love Delia stop stop.' That," he added, giving her a wry look, "was not very illuminating."

"Well, a telegram doesn't allow for long-winded explanations. And it piqued your curiosity, didn't it?"

"Which it was obviously designed to do," he agreed, shoving the telegram back in his pocket. "So, how does my investment in the Savoy hinge on my presence at the opera?"

She bit her lip, giving him a look of apology. "That might have been a bit of an exaggeration on my part. But you can't complain," she added as her cousin made a sound of aggravation, "since I'm really just following your recipe for success."

"Which is?"

"I'm sucking up to my new boss. Who," she added, spying Simon and his sister in the doorway, "has just arrived."

"Using me to suck up to Calderon wasn't precisely what I had in mind," Max muttered in her ear as they started forward together to greet the new arrivals.

"I'm doing this for his sister. She's a lovely girl, and a duke's condescension would be very helpful to successfully bringing her out in May. So I expect you to follow the same advice you gave me and be your most dashing, charming self."

There was no time for more.

She halted by the doorway to greet the new arrivals, and as she did, her heart gave a strange little flutter. Simon looked every bit as handsome in his white tie and tails as he had the night before, and it took her a moment to find her tongue.

"Lord Calderon," she managed at last, hoping she didn't look as gauchely nervous as she felt. What on earth was wrong with her?

"Lady Stratham." He bowed. "I hope we're not late."

"Not at all."

"If we are late, it's my fault," Cassandra put in. "It was a mad scramble trying to find something to wear, for I didn't bring anything suitable with me." She brushed her hand nervously over her pale pink silk gown. "I hope this is all right."

"You look lovely," Delia hastened to reassure her, then she turned, gesturing to the man beside her. "Lord Calderon, I believe you already know my cousin, the Duke of Westbourne. Max, allow me to present Lord Calderon's sister, Miss Cassandra Hayden. Miss Hayden, my cousin, the Duke of Westbourne."

Wide-eyed, looking suitably impressed, Cassandra dipped her knees in a deep curtsy. "Duke."

"Miss Hayden," Max replied, playing up beautifully with his most elegant ducal bow. "A pleasure to meet you. And may I say that if you were late, one look at you and all would be forgiven at once."

Delia feared such a lavish compliment might have been a bit over the top, but Cassandra's face lit up like a candle, and she breathed a soft sigh of relief.

"I didn't know you'd be here this evening, Duke," Simon said, joining the conversation.

"I didn't have much choice. I was pressed into service."

Delia's sideways kick in his ankle was ignored. "I understand," Max went on, "you've been making some significant changes at the hotel?"

"I have. I'd be happy to discuss them with you, if you're willing."

"Of course."

The two men exited the box to talk business, and Delia turned to the girl with a rueful smile. "I think your brother is trying to avoid me."

"Oh, no! Why would he?"

"The obvious reason, perhaps?"

"You think he doesn't like you?"

Delia considered, then admitted the truth with a laugh. "I don't know what your brother's opinion of me is, to be honest. But dislike is quite possible."

"I doubt that." Cassandra shook her head so adamantly that Delia was startled. "Simon never pretends. He despises hypocrisy and dishonesty. If he disliked you, he'd never have accepted your invitation for tonight."

"Even though an event like this is a good entrée into society for you?"

"Especially then. If he didn't like you, he'd have good reasons for that opinion, and he'd do all he could to keep me away from your influence. Both our parents are dead, you see, so we only have each other."

"You have no other relations at all?"

"A few scattered cousins, but we hardly know them. So Simon feels his responsibility for me very keenly."

Delia smiled. "You don't have to tell me that. It's plain as a pikestaff. When I mentioned to him last night that he'd need to bring you out, he looked as if I'd just asked him to jump off a cliff."

"He worries that society won't accept me." She bit her lip. "I'm afraid that's partly my fault. I rather cried on his shoulder about some things in my last letter."

"He doesn't want you to be snubbed and get hurt, which is perfectly understandable. And that is where I come in. Stick with me, my dear, and you'll soon have more friends than you know what to do with. Now," she added, putting her arm through the girl's, "come with me, and I will introduce you to my other guests."

She suited the action to the word, and before long, the four youngest members of the party were all seated together, chatting away like old friends as they waited for the performance to begin. But Delia had barely congratulated herself on finding Cassandra a group of suitable companions before Baroness Ferridale was standing by her side, making inquiries about England's most recently elevated viscount.

"I'm told he's exceedingly rich. Is that true?"

Delia saw the speculative gleam in the other woman's eyes, and, given that the baroness's very pretty daughter was about to be put on the marriage mart, that could only mean one thing. Delia froze, dismayed, her glass of champagne halfway to her lips.

"Delia?" the other woman prompted when she didn't reply. "Are you all right?"

Delia recovered her wits with an effort. "Of course," she lied.

"Well, then?" the baroness urged with a hint of impatience. "Is he rich or not?"

She gave the other woman her most innocent stare in return. "Heavens, Selina, I've no idea."

"No? Really, Delia, I feel quite let down. You usually know these things."

"In this case, I'm afraid I don't," she was happy to reply. "I've no idea what he's worth."

"When you invited me for this evening, you told me he's quite a successful captain of industry," Selina reminded her. "And that he's terribly clever. So he must be rich, mustn't he? And so handsome, too. Quite possibly the handsomest man in London. Don't you think so?"

"His looks are all right, I suppose," she countered with a shrug, almost wincing at such a palpable understatement.

"All right?" Selina echoed, laughing. "Is that all you can say? Really, dear, your eyesight must be going. It starts to happen at about your age, you know."

That was a bridge too far. "For heaven's sake, Selina, I'm only thirty-three!"

"Exactly." With that last catty remark, the baroness moved to join her daughter and the others, leaving Delia to glare resentfully at her back. Thirty-three, she told herself, was *not* old.

"And they say eavesdroppers never hear good of themselves."

Simon's murmured voice behind her made her jump. "Goodness!" she gasped, turning around. "I didn't know you were there."

He grinned. "Your failing eyesight must be to blame."

"Don't you start," she said, giving him a warning scowl.

"I'm just getting a bit of my own back. After all, you said I'm merely all right. Still, you did sing my praises to her this afternoon, so I suppose that's some consolation."

Delia mustered her dignity. "I was singing your praises for your sister's sake. It was necessary so that the baroness would come this evening and bring her daughter. I thought Miss Ferridale would be a good companion for her, since they're coming out together."

"Of course," he said gravely, but there was a distinctly knowing glint in his eyes that made her decidedly uneasy. "Nonetheless," he went on, "it's gratifying to know the baroness considers me a handsome fellow, even if you don't. But the crucial question, really, is what does her exceedingly pretty daughter think?"

Aghast, she stared at him. "It shouldn't matter. You're far too old for her."

"Your ability to wound me knows no bounds, it seems. But my masculine pride demands that I point out you're only three years younger than I am. As for Miss Ferridale…" He paused to study the girl on the other side of the box as he took a sip of his champagne, seeming to actually consider the question of becoming her suitor. "A baron's daughter…quite pretty. I daresay I'd be a lucky man."

"Don't be absurd," Delia shot back. "As I said, she's too young for you."

To her immense irritation, he laughed. "No man ever cares about things like that."

"Well, you should. She's only eighteen, almost the same age as your sister, for heaven's sake."

"So?"

Delia couldn't believe what she was hearing. "You said just last night that your sister is far too young to be married!"

"Ah, but we're not talking about my sister, are we? We're talking about my possible future wife."

Delia made a sound of utter exasperation. "Men. You are all such hypocrites about these things."

He laughed again. "What's wrong, Delia?" he asked, looking mortifyingly pleased with himself. "Are you jealous?"

She was. Oh, God in heaven, she was. And he knew it, too, the wretch.

She opened her mouth to deny it and declare him quite off his chump, but the knowing amusement in his eyes told her further denials would only prove his point. He knew the truth—had known it before she had.

Given all that, there was only one thing a woman with any sense could do.

Delia took a deep breath, downed the last of her champagne, and met his amused gaze head on. "I am, actually," she confessed, and as she noted his stunned expression, she felt an odd, dizzying thrill. How liberating, she thought, how intoxicating to admit one's feelings to a man openly, instead of dancing around them, dropping delicate little hints in the approved ladylike fashion. It had been a long time since she'd felt so free.

After her last husband's death, she'd left all notions of romance and desire behind her. But now, for the first time in over five years, she felt them coming to life, a breath of wind stirring the ashes.

With that in mind, Delia took a deep breath and burned her boats completely. "I'm jealous as hell," she said and gave an exhilarated laugh. "So put that in your pipe, Simon, and smoke it."

With that parting shot, she turned away and took her seat beside Max. Her cheeks were flushed, her heart was racing as if she'd been running, and she felt as giddy as a girl of sixteen.

It was glorious.

Had anyone asked Simon to offer a considered opinion of Puccini's new opera, he'd have been hard-pressed to do so. Sitting directly behind Delia, he'd been far too distracted by the slender column of her neck, the scent of her perfume that occasionally wafted to his nose, and the graceful tilt of her head whenever she turned to whisper something to her cousin to pay any attention to the performance on the stage below.

Her throaty laughter from earlier this evening continually overrode the music of the orchestra and the soaring voices of the performers, and her words kept coming back again and again to torment him.

I'm jealous as hell.

Even now, he could hardly believe he'd heard her correctly. The idea that Delia, of all women, could be jealous of a girl barely out of finishing school was ludicrous in the extreme. But he had to admit, every time her confession echoed through his mind, it made him smile with pure, manly satisfaction.

And that, he appreciated, made his warning to her in the carriage truer now than ever before. Being anywhere near Delia threatened to destroy his objectivity, hurt the investigation, and betray two of his dearest friends. Besides, Delia was the sort of woman who could wreak havoc on a man and deem it nothing more than jolly good fun, and he had no intention of being that sort of amusement.

Good thing he was going to the country on the morrow, for that would give him some breathing space, enable him to get clear of her and the desire for her that was beginning to bedevil his sleep and muddle his thinking. Unfortunately, there was something he had to discuss with her before he caught the morning train, something that could not wait for his return.

As the evening progressed, he watched for any opportunity to speak with her, but there was none. During the intermission, the short walk back to the Savoy after the performance, and supper in the hotel restaurant, her attention was commanded by others. And when the supper was over and goodnights were being said, he was cornered by Lady Ferridale, and she slipped away.

It took him at least five minutes to extricate himself from the baroness and her obvious matchmaking and go in search of Delia, but he soon discovered she had not gone to her room. That, he supposed as he stood outside her door, was probably a good thing, since it would have taken all the willpower he had to stand in the doorway to her room without giving in to temptation, hauling her into his arms, and showing her she had no reason to be jealous of a slip of a girl.

He knocked again, but there was still no reply. Not knowing whether to be frustrated or relieved, he turned and started toward his own room at the other end of the hotel, but as he passed the elevator, he realized there was one person who might know where she'd gone, and he pressed the bell to summon the lift.

A few minutes later, his search was over and he was on the roof, watching her.

She was standing by the balustrade overlooking the Thames and wrapped against the cold winter chill in her full-length opera cloak of black cashmere, a lamp on the balustrade beside her casting a glow on the pale skin of her profile.

He gave a cough, alerting her to his presence, and she turned. "Hullo. Finally extricated yourself from Lady Ferridale, I see."

"It took some doing." He started toward her across the rooftop. "Why are you up here? Thinking about your hothouse idea? Remember," he added before she could reply, "I can't approve it until I have all the information, and even then, the board will have to agree."

"I'll have a full proposal on your desk as soon as I possibly can," she promised.

"Is this where you want to put it?"

She nodded. "I think so. There's enough space on this side, and it has the best view."

He glanced around, noting the inky blackness above their heads, the faint, snaky outline of the Thames beyond the balustrade, and the glow of the streetlights lining the Embankment below. "Not much to see now, though."

"Not at this time of night, no. But for luncheons and cotillions, there's no better prospect." She turned toward him, leaning one hip against the balustrade. "Is that why you're up here, too?" she asked. "To envision my idea in its proper setting?"

"Actually, no. I came looking for you. I tried to catch up with you after the party, for I wanted to speak with you before I leave for the country in the morning, but the baroness cornered me, and I couldn't get away."

Delia sniffed. "Wanted to sing her daughter's praises to you, no doubt."

He grinned as he remembered her admission of jealousy earlier, but she gave him no time to enjoy it.

"So you came looking for me up here?"

"No, actually. I assumed you'd gone to your room, so I went there first—"

"Coming to a lady's hotel room in the wee small hours? And when I recently accused you of this nefarious intention, you denied it, you liar."

"I want to talk with you, not have an assignation." Even as he said it, he thought of how he'd felt standing outside her room, the doubts and temptations that had momentarily flitted through his mind, and his throat went dry at the memory.

She sighed. "You really know how to flatter a woman, don't you?"

"I've never been very good at that," he admitted. "But to return to the point, I asked the lift attendant if he knew where you might have gone, and he told me he'd brought you up here. He was quite surprised by that, it seems."

"I daresay. It's not the sort of thing the guests would be inclined to do, is it? But why did you come in search of me? Hotel business, I suppose?"

He shook his head. "No, I wanted to talk with you about something else entirely. My sister," he supplied when she frowned in puzzlement.

"Ah." Her brow cleared and she gave a laugh. "Want to know if she passed muster with my aristocratic friends?"

"In a way. Is she sufficiently prepared to do the season, do you think?"

"Absolutely. The question is, will you let her?"

He made a face. "Do I have a choice?"

"Not really, no."

He nodded, not surprised. He'd already accepted the inevitable fact that he was going to have to put his baby sister into the teeth of high society. He just hoped she would not get hurt. "I'm taking her back to Berkshire tomorrow. As you suggested, I'll call on my new neighbors to pave the way for her so that she can make some friends there. In light of that, do you have any advice?"

"Don't ever let them think they're better than you. They're not."

That made him smile a little. "Are you saying that because you want me to know you're not a snob?"

"No, I'm saying it because it's true. But if you now appreciate that I'm not a snob, all the better."

"Any other sage wisdom to offer?"

"No, but—" She broke off, considering, then she gave a nod. "Actually, yes; I do want to say one very important thing. It's not advice, exactly. More like a warning."

"That sounds ominous."

"Your sister is remarkably pretty, and very sweet. And she's been quite sheltered for most of her life. She is also, as you know, very young. A scoundrel will be quick to see that."

"I'm painfully aware of that," he said with a grimace. "Thinking about all the rotters out there who'd take advantage of her has kept me up at night more than once."

"I daresay. Any girl without a mother to keep a sharp eye on her every minute is a tempting target, but girls of Cassie's temperament are especially susceptible to men of that ilk."

"As you were?"

She shook her head. "My first husband wasn't a scoundrel. Roger was an addict, and he was weak, perhaps, but he wasn't a scoundrel. And besides, I may have been as young as your sister back then and equally sheltered from life's harsh realities but—" She broke off, giving him a grin. "I was never sweet."

He laughed. "I can well believe that. But what makes you say it?"

"At Cassandra's age, I was regarded as something of a hellion."

"Really?" he said dryly. "Imagine that. What did you do?"

"Well, for one thing, I was an accomplished poet."

"Writing poetry makes one a hellion?"

"Well, my poems did. At finishing school, I composed a long and lurid ode to the gardener's handsome young assistant, particularly the way his trousers hugged his shapely, muscular legs."

"Indeed?" He was tempted to glance down and imagine how trousers would look on a certain pair of wholly feminine legs, but he refrained.

"But I think," she went on, "it was my limerick about the headmistress's lack of internal organs that did it for me in the end."

He frowned in puzzlement. "Lack of internal organs?"

"My headmistress was born in Park Lane," she recited. "She has no heart and no brain—"

His shout of laughter interrupted this impudent epistle. "I begin to see how you acquired your reputation. What happened?"

"My parents, God rest their souls, were advised to come and collect me forthwith. That was my first finishing school."

"I take it there was more than one?"

"I was expelled from three."

"Three? Good God."

"I did manage to graduate from the fourth one. Either way, I may regret these confidences, for after hearing them, you're probably not too keen on the idea of me befriending your sister."

She was right about his lack of enthusiasm, but not for the reasons she was assuming. "Why were you at finishing school at all? I mean, Cassie was in finishing school only because our mother had died and I had another year to serve in the army. Reserves, of course, but I was still stationed in Africa, so boarding school was the best thing for her. But aren't girls of your class usually schooled at home by a governess?"

"Usually, but having been through a slew of nannies and governesses, my parents thought perhaps finishing school would be a better choice for me. Obviously, they were wrong."

"Your poor parents."

"Just so. That's why they allowed me to marry so young. I was wildly in love with Roger. He was a poet, too, you see. We were mad about each other, and my parents thought a husband would straighten me out."

"Given what you've told me about your first husband, and what I know of you, that plan doesn't seem to have succeeded."

"Not a jot. Roger was far too weak to control me."

"And your second husband?"

"Armand?" She shook her head. "Heavens no. He was a French count, insanely attractive, and a stone-broke fortune hunter. He was also reckless, dangerous, and completely without regard for consequences. He drove motorcars, sailed yachts, and chased women. When he chased me, I fell for him like a ninepin. I'd never met anyone like that, you see, and he harkened to my own adventurous side. We ran off together a month after we met, got married in Gibraltar, and spent the next three years living off my money in the south of

France—gambling at Nice, sailing the Mediterranean, and driving his favorite motorcars along the Côte d'Azur."

"You didn't mind him living off your money?"

She shook her head, giving him a rueful smile. "I probably should have, but the truth is, I loved every minute of it. Until…"

"Until?" he prompted when she fell silent.

"Until he died in a car crash."

"I'm sorry."

"Don't be." She paused again, staring down at her gloved fingers. "When Armand died, I wasn't in the car. I wasn't even in France at the time. He was with another woman. They both died. She wasn't…she wasn't the first, I learned later."

He studied her bent head, thinking of last night when she'd escaped outside after dinner. "I see."

"What do you see?" she whispered, not looking at him.

"Why you said you're a bit blind about men."

She gave a deep sigh and nodded. "Just so."

"What was your third husband like?" he asked after another moment. "Another waster, I suppose?"

"On the contrary. Hamish was over twenty years older than me, mature and sensible."

"A complete contrast to your previous husbands, then."

"Oh, yes. He was quite fond of me. He *said* he wanted children."

Her emphasis on one particular word did not escape his notice, but she rushed on before he could even think of a way to inquire further.

"So did I, more than anything. I fell in love with him—partly, I admit, because he was a safe choice. At least—" She paused and laughed again, but to Simon's ears, there was no humor in it. "At least I thought he was."

He tensed, his misgivings growing. "What do you mean? What was wrong with him?"

"Well, for one thing, he had a dicky heart. It gave out less than a year after we married. And then—"

She broke off abruptly, her face twisting with sudden pain.

"And then?" he prompted.

"It doesn't matter." She turned her head, meeting his gaze. "Some in society call me the merry widow, you know."

"I've heard it said."

"But my enemies have a different name for me. They call me the black widow."

"I've heard that, too," he admitted.

"From Helen, I daresay. I can't blame her," she added, looking away when he didn't deny it. "After all, that nickname is probably closer to the truth. Sometimes I wonder..." She paused, taking a deep breath, staring out over the water. "Sometimes I wonder if that's my destiny. That I'm cursed or something."

"Nonsense."

His stouthearted denial made her smile a little. "Somehow," she murmured softly, "I knew that's what you'd say. You're not the superstitious sort."

"Bad luck can happen to anyone, Delia. It doesn't mean anything more than that."

"Oh, I know. Still, three husbands in ten years is a bit thick. Either way, society loves to speculate about who my next husband's going to be. How long after the wedding, they wonder, will the poor chap drop dead? Whenever it looks as if I have an admirer, bets are laid about it at White's and Boodles. Everyone thinks I ought to stay as far away from men as possible."

"And you don't agree?"

"Should I?" she flared, a note of defiance in the question. "Why should I put myself on a shelf to wither away and collect dust?"

His mouth curved, a hint of a smile.

"What?" she asked, her defiance faltering. "What's so amusing?"

"The idea of you ever sitting on a shelf collecting dust."

She stirred, tossing her head. "Just so," she muttered. "In spite of everything, I still like men. I like romance. And I like lovemaking. I may have forgotten these things for a while, but I still like them and want them. There, I've shocked you, I daresay."

"Not really, no," he said. "But," he added, his smile widening, "I suspect you were hoping you would."

"Maybe a bit," she admitted, laughing, her usual good humor restored. "But it's your own fault, you know."

It was his turn to laugh. "You needle me and tease me and say outrageous things solely in order to provoke me, and that's my fault?"

"Yes. Teasing you is irresistible. It's because you're so . . . straight, so upstanding and honorable."

He wondered suddenly how honorable she would think him if she knew his real mission at the Savoy, and he hastened into speech. "My friend Devlin says the same."

She made a face at the mention of that name, clearly not impressed by the comparison. "Speaking of scoundrels . . ."

"He's not. I know you disagree," he added as she opened her mouth to argue the point. "And your loyalty to your friend Lady Kay does you credit, but I've known him for fourteen years, and I know the soundness of his character. I started life with nothing, and I'd probably still have nothing if it weren't for him. He persuaded me to stake him in a gold-mining venture in Africa, and I put every shilling I could spare into it. It paid off, giving me enough to buy my first hotel when I returned to England."

"That doesn't mean your friend isn't a scoundrel when it comes to women."

"There's usually blame on both sides when love affairs go awry. But please, Delia, let's not argue. I enjoyed myself far too much this evening to let an argument spoil it."

"Did you enjoy yourself?" She blinked as if that was an unexpected admission. "Really?"

He looked into her eyes, his gaze steady. "Yes, really."

She smiled, a wide, radiant smile of pure pleasure she made no effort to hide, and Simon felt something sharp and sweet pierce his chest, a reminder that he'd best tread carefully. A few more smiles like that from her and his heart might be in jeopardy.

He swallowed hard, hoping to hide it, but despite his efforts, she seemed to sense, at least a little, the thoughts passing through his mind. "You'd better watch out," she warned, her voice carelessly light. "Too many more nights at the opera together and people will start to think I'm after you to be husband number four. You could be endangering your life."

It wasn't his life he was worried about, but before he could think of a way to set her straight without giving himself away, she spoke again. "It's clear the only safe thing for any poor chap who becomes entangled with me would be a torrid affair." She heaved a sigh. "I'd only do that if there could be explosions."

At once, delicious images of her naked in his bed crossed his mind, and arousal hit him square in the groin. Desperate, he curled his hands around the balustrade in front of him, gripping it hard as he fought for control, reminding himself of all the reasons this woman was out of bounds. She might be a thief, for one thing, but he was beginning to appreciate that his masculine nature didn't care one bit about her morals or lack of them. Hell, if she were caught robbing the Bank of England, he'd probably still want her. She was flirting with him, but he suspected that flirting with men was as natural to her as breathing; it didn't mean anything. And even if she were genuinely attracted to him, she'd surely change her tune once the truth came out.

"It's a good thing," she added dryly, breaking the silence, "that I'm not holding my breath waiting for those explosions to happen."

"That," he said in a harsh whisper, "is probably wise of you."

"You really are the most vexing man," she cried. "Any other chap would take these shameless hints I'm throwing his way and start planning a wicked weekend for us in an obscure country cottage somewhere. But of course, you're far too good and honorable for that sort of thing."

Exasperation flared up inside him, mixing with his lust. "For God's sake," he muttered, letting go of his death grip on the balustrade and turning to face her, "stop talking as if I'm some sort of saint."

"You mean you're not?"

"Hardly," he said. "If I were—"

He broke off, his gaze sliding irresistibly to her mouth. "If I were a saint, I wouldn't find you such a damnably tempting little morsel, would I?"

"Am I tempting?"

He met her eyes, and the desire he saw in their midnight-blue depths called to the lust within him like a siren song. Lying, he realized, was pointless. "You know you are. I daresay plenty of other men have found you so."

Her full pink lips took on a rueful curve. "Well, I'd like to think so, but with you, I'm never really sure where I stand, to be honest."

That was a bit reassuring, but then she moved closer, the heat within him flared even higher, and any sense that he might actually gain the upper hand with her went straight out the window.

"Most of the time," she murmured, "I feel as if you can't stand me."

He swallowed hard. "Indeed?" he managed.

"But then..." She paused, her tongue flicking out to lick her lips, and heat curled in his belly. "But then you look at me the way you're looking now, and I wonder."

He didn't reply. The night air was crisp and cold, but the heat of her body seemed scorching hot, even from several inches away. The scent of her perfume was in his nostrils, his heart was thudding like a trip-hammer, and his wits were hopelessly fogged.

"What about you?"

He frowned at the sound of her voice, trying to think. "Me?"

She stirred, moving a few inches closer. "Don't you want to know? I know I do."

His wits felt thick as tar, his body was fully aroused, and he had no idea what she was talking about. "Know what?"

Her lashes lowered, but there was nothing demure about her glance over his body. "What it would be like."

She looked up at him again as she closed the last scrap of distance between them. Her breasts brushed against his chest, her hip touched his groin, and the pleasure of the contact nearly drove him to his knees.

He groaned, and the sound impelled him to grasp one last time for sanity. "What *what* would be like?"

She lifted her hands between them, cupping his face in her palms as she rose on her toes. "Lighting matches," she whispered and kissed him.

12

Having been married three times, Delia had experienced many kisses in her life. The sweet, shy kisses of youth, the knowledgeable ones of experience, the tender ones of mutual affection. But no kiss had ever been like this.

No kiss had ever turned her blood to molten lava, burning away all her strength and melting her very bones. No kiss had ever ignited desire this quick or pleasure this hot.

Until now.

Simon had warned her that it might be like this, at least for him, but she hadn't been able to believe such a thing was possible for herself. How could she? Bit by bit, husband by husband, disillusionment, heartbreak, and grief had eroded any romantic or sexual feeling she'd ever had, and for the past five years, no man had ignited even the tiniest spark of her feminine interest. But from their very first meeting, this man had aggravated her, provoked her, and challenged her in ways no man ever had before, and in the process, he had somehow reawakened longing and lust within her, two things she never thought she would feel again. Now, his kiss was doing far more than reigniting long-forgotten needs and desires; it was transmuting them into something beyond all her previous experience. She had dared to play with fire, and this was the result: an exhilarating, dizzying, blazing-hot ride. Like flying into the sun.

She ought to pull away now, she supposed, before either of them could get burned. She had a history with men, one that didn't bode well for Simon, or for her. And yet, this awakened hunger was too strong, and her starved body refused to listen to her mind's reminders of past pain. Hungry for more of this intoxicating pleasure before life inevitably snatched it away, she wrapped her arms around his neck, pressing her body against his.

His response was all she could have hoped for. He made a rough sound against her mouth and his arms came up, wrapping around her waist, pulling her closer as his tongue pressed against her closed lips, urging them to part.

Happily, willingly, she complied, raking her hand through his hair as she tasted his mouth and reveled in the sensual storm. She felt the throb of life surging through every cell and every nerve, and the pleasure began to seem like pain, the pain of pure joy, as her frozen heart began to thaw.

His hands slid down, cupping her buttocks as he lifted her onto the very tips of her toes, until her hips were pressed to his. In a position of such scorching intimacy, there was no mistaking his arousal, and Delia moaned against his mouth. "Come to my room," she heard herself say. "We can—"

His hands gripped her shoulders, hard, cutting her off midsentence. "God, you are the most relentless woman alive," he ground out through clenched teeth. "Why are you doing this?"

She could hear her own rapid breathing and his; she could see it, too, white clouds mingling in the still, cold night air. She could hear her heart thudding in her chest, and she'd have sworn on her life that she could hear his, too. Desire was like a living thing, pulsing and seething between them. And she knew the only answer she could give him was the truth.

"Because I want you," she said simply. "And," she added as he gave a humorless laugh, "I know that you want me. Deny it if you must," she added as he shook his head, "but we both know I'm right."

He shook his head again, but he didn't let her go. Instead, his hands tightened on her shoulders. "I can't do this," he muttered and gave her a little shake. "Damn it, Delia, I can't. I won't."

"Why not?" She gave a wild little laugh. "You wouldn't be taking an innocent virgin. I'm a fully experienced woman, and I know what this means. And anyway, who's to know?"

"I would." He let her go then, his hands sliding away, his voice telling her there was no point in further discussion. "I would know."

She stared at him, feeling suddenly raw, exposed, and vulnerable in a way she'd never felt before.

With an abrupt move, he turned and left her, striding away into the darkness beyond the ring of lamplight, vanishing from view before she could even assimilate that he was gone.

She didn't follow him. Her knees were so weak, she wasn't even sure she could walk, and she sagged back against the balustrade, her lips burning, her nerves raw, her body aching with unfulfilled need.

Delia pressed her fingers to her mouth with a grimace, appreciating that she had just been kissed within an inch of her life, and then, without any reason or warning, spurned and decidedly rejected. Not that she could blame him, really, given the fate of all the men who had come before.

So much, she thought ruefully, for lighting matches around gunpowder.

Simon didn't get a wink of sleep. Instead, he lay in bed, staring at the ceiling, cursing himself, his body in full rebellion against what he'd done. It had been ages since he'd been with a woman, and when he had one, warm and willing, in his arms, he'd pushed her away. When, as she had pointed out, no one would have seen, no one would have known.

He was an idiot.

And yet, had he taken what she'd so temptingly offered, had he gone to her room and done what he'd been imagining for weeks, he'd still be lying here afterward, wide awake, cursing himself—not for being an idiot, no, but for being a dishonorable bastard who let his cock do his thinking for him.

A no-win situation if ever there was one.

It was a good thing indeed that he was leaving for the country today. Perhaps he ought to stay in Berkshire longer than a few days. It could easily be managed. Ross would be here to deal with anything that might come up in his absence, and he would only be a few hours away by train if anything happened at the hotel that required his return. He hadn't had a holiday in ages, and Cassie could certainly do with the company.

All those reasons made perfect sense, and yet, he knew his real motive for wanting to linger in the country had nothing to do with being sensible. He needed to get clear of Delia. He needed time and distance so that he could regain his perspective, put his priorities back in order, and cool the desire for her that ran through his blood.

He heard the clock on the mantel chime the hour. Six o'clock. With an oath, he tossed back the sheets, giving up any idea of sleep, and got out of bed. He slid on a dressing robe, fetched a towel and a cake of soap, and went to take a cold bath.

An hour later, he was in his office with a stack of financial reports and correspondence in front of him. Given the early hour, and the fact that it was Sunday, this part of the hotel was quiet as a tomb, but if Simon thought he could get clear of Delia by immersing himself in work, he was very much mistaken.

The door to her office was open, and every time he looked up at the darkened room next door, he remembered the first time she'd awakened his arousal with her attempts to call a truce. Though she was not here, he seemed to catch the scent of her perfume with every breath he took, and in the quiet of a Sunday morning, he could hear her whispered words of a few hours ago.

Come to my room.

His body responded at once, heat curling in his groin, temptation beckoning.

I want you and I know that you want me.

Want? God, he ached with wanting.

Tossing the pencil aside, Simon closed the accounting ledger in front of him, plunked his elbows on the desk, and rested his head in his hands with an aggravated sigh. He had no one to blame for this mess but himself.

The question now was what to do about it.

The most agreeable answer was obvious, but not one he could act upon. But perhaps when this mess with the Savoy was over, and Ritz was gone—

He cut off that hopeful possibility at once. Guilty or innocent, there was no way in hell she'd ever make him that delectable offer again. If she was guilty, she'd be fired along with the rest, and blame him for it. If she was innocent, she would only hear what had happened from Ritz, for Simon had signed confidentiality agreements upon his appointment, and he could not break his word to give her the true facts.

The idea that he even wanted her at all was baffling to him. Morality and honest dealing were not just words to him, they were a way of life, and wanting a woman like her, a woman who, at best, played fast and loose with the rules, was an aggravating thing indeed. At worst, she was a thief, but even if the evidence proved her so, he feared it would not be enough to dampen his desire for her.

"Ah, so here you are!"

The sound of a strident feminine voice broke into his thoughts. He looked up to find Helen in the doorway, and the look on her face told him Delia was not the only female giving him grief today.

"Helen." He stood up. "What brings you out so early on a Sunday?"

"That you can even ask that question amazes me. What in God's name are you thinking?"

He had no idea what she was referring to, but the question almost made him want to laugh just the same, for he'd been asking himself that exact question for the past six hours with no answer in sight. Still, given her anger, laughing at this moment, even if that laugh was an ironic one, probably wasn't a good idea. "I beg your pardon?"

She crossed the small office in three quick strides. "Don't pretend you don't know what I mean," she said, halting before his desk. "I saw you."

"What?" He stared at her, dismayed and appalled, and those torrid moments on the roof with Delia came roaring back. How the hell could Helen have seen them? The steel lattice doors of the lift, when opened, rattled loud enough to wake the dead. Surely he'd have heard. The moment that thought went through his mind, however, he grimaced, remembering the state of arousal he'd been in at the time, and he appreciated that a herd of water buffalo could very well have rumbled across the rooftop without gaining his attention.

"Really, Simon," she went on, her voice vibrating with the force of her fury, "sitting in that woman's box at the opera? Are you mad?"

"The opera?" he echoed, relief beginning to displace his dismay as comprehension dawned. "Oh, the *opera*."

"Yes, the opera! What did you think I meant?"

Guiltily, he looked away. "Well," he began, but she spoke again before he could articulate some sort of answer to that question.

"I was there, Simon. I saw you sitting in her box, plain as day. I daresay half of London saw you!"

He took a deep breath and got firm hold of his scattered wits. "My sister is in town, and I wanted to take her out for the evening. Lady Stratham kindly invited us to share her box at Covent Garden."

"Oh, my God!" she burst out, staring at him in unmistakable horror. "She's done it to you, too."

"Done what?"

"All Delia Stratham has to do is crook her little finger and men everywhere come running. But you? Really, Simon," she added as he opened his mouth to reply, "I thought you had more sense than to be taken in by that schemer!"

"I'm not taken in by her," he said, but even as he spoke, he remembered the taste of her mouth and the feel of her in his arms, and he was forced to admit, much to his own chagrin, that Helen's accusation had a degree of validity.

"I warned you about her," Helen went on, oblivious to his denial. "I told you what she's like. But I see that my warning was in vain. You've fallen under her spell, just like every other man in London. My God, that you could be such a fool!"

Helen made a sound of exasperation and looked away, shaking her head, and he decided perhaps he ought to try to handle this matter in a way she was more likely to appreciate.

"I have to work with her, Helen, at least for the time being."

"But you don't have to go to the opera with her!"

That was a point he could not refute. "No," he agreed mildly. "But it seemed harmless enough."

"Harmless? Delia Stratham is not harmless."

The venom in her voice was unmistakable, and he tilted his head, studying her thoughtfully, his curiosity piqued. "Why do you dislike her so much?"

"Why?" she echoed, staring back at him in disbelief. "Because she's dishonest!"

"So you've found proof of that since our last conversation?"

"No, but as we discussed that day, the indications are clear. Her secretary, the florist—"

"Those indications are slim enough to border on absurd."

Her eyes narrowed, warning him she didn't appreciate having her opinion called absurd. "I was right, then," she said flatly. "That day at lunch, you were defending her. You still are. You've taken her side."

"I'm not taking anyone's side," he shot back, feeling defensive and hating the feeling. "I'm working damned hard not to do so."

"Why should it be such a battle?"

That was a question he'd been asking himself for days now, but he'd be damned before he'd admit that to Helen, of all people. "I appreciate your concerns, Helen. I do. But if her innocence were proved beyond any doubt, I have the distinct impression you would still dislike her. Why? Is it because of her friendship with Ritz? You've never liked him, I know, but is it really fair to condemn someone else so wholeheartedly because of that?"

"Fair?" Helen cried. "You wish to talk about what's fair? That woman has always been able to do whatever she wants and never suffers any consequences for it. She's feckless and careless and she spends money like water, and everyone loves her for it. While I—"

She broke off, her face twisting with pain, and she looked away.

Simon studied her bent head with both compassion and understanding, appreciating that jealousy lay at the heart of her resentment. "While you, on the other hand, are sensible, responsible, and suffering," he said.

"And universally disliked," she added with a humorless laugh. "Don't forget that. The staff loathes me."

"I doubt that. And you know as well as I do that anyone with power over their livelihoods is going to earn the resentment of some among the staff. I have felt it, too. But there's another side to that coin. Ritz is loved, but he has enemies as well. If that were not so, you never would have received that anonymous letter. And Helen," he added as gently as he could, "it's not as if Lady Stratham has not suffered, too. Losing one husband is tragic enough, but three? Her life has hardly been perfect."

With a sound of impatience, Helen lifted her head. "I see that my warnings are useless," she said coldly, making it clear she was in no frame of mind to sympathize with someone she disliked and distrusted. "But there is one thing I must ask you, and I expect an honest answer."

He stiffened, offended by the implication that he would offer her any other. "Of course. What do you want to know?"

"We're nearly done investigating Ritz, then we will be doing the same with Lady Stratham. Once the evidence against that woman is presented to you, how will you vote?"

"If there is such evidence, I will vote to have her dismissed, along with all the rest. How can you doubt it?"

"You're a man, that's how." She turned away abruptly. "But for the sake of our friendship, I hope you mean what you say."

He watched her as she walked out of his office. "I hope so, too, Helen," he said under his breath. But he had the uneasy feeling that his choice, when it came, was not going to be so simple.

From the moment she woke up Sunday morning, Delia resolved to forget about those fiery moments with Simon on the roof. But during the two weeks that followed, fate seemed determined to circumvent her. He remained at his estate in the country, so she didn't have to see him, but reminders of him seemed to be everywhere.

When Michel came to her to discuss the flowers for Lady Gray's upcoming luncheon party, she thought of the day six weeks ago when she'd first met Simon, and how baffling it seemed now that she had ever thought him cold.

When she left the hotel one afternoon to meet Kay for luncheon, she saw that the hyacinths were starting to crop up in the Embankment Gardens, and her mind went back to the day she'd sent him breakfast and flowers and tried to broker a truce with him. He'd tossed her efforts quite decidedly back in her face and questioned her motives, and why? For the flimsiest, most ridiculous reasons.

I suppose you wear that seductive perfume and dresses that cling to your curves when you meet with duchesses and debutantes, too.

To hear him talk that day, anyone would have thought she was a shameless opportunist for putting on a little perfume and a pretty dress. What woman didn't do that when she wanted a man on her side? Would he have preferred her to don sackcloth and ashes and smell as if she hadn't bathed for days? Would that have persuaded him to make peace and see her point of view?

As she requested bids and worked on the proposal for the rooftop hothouse, there was no way she could avoid thinking about their dinner together at Westbourne House, and how, after giving her every sign in the world that he found her deuced attractive and wanted to kiss her, he'd walked away. His explanations for that had managed to be both delightfully flattering and maddening as hell. They had also, she was forced to admit, only served to make him more attractive than ever.

And then, when at last her curiosity had gotten the better of her, when she had thrown all caution and feminine decorum to the winds and kissed him, she'd been thoroughly spurned for her trouble.

God, you are the most relentless woman alive.

Delia grimaced and leaned back in her chair, shoving aside her notes for the greenhouse and staring glumly at the ceiling of her office. That's what a girl got for taking the initiative with a man. Rejection and insults. She was a fool, and this mooning over him was becoming ridiculous.

He'd made his opinion of having an affair with her perfectly clear. Why keep reliving it?

Because when she'd been in his arms, with his mouth on hers, it had been the most intoxicating, glorious kiss of her life. That was why.

But it hadn't stopped him from walking away, *again*, had it?

How many times, she thought, angry with him and with herself, was he going to spurn her before she got it through her head that what she wanted—what she knew they both wanted—wasn't going to happen? And why was she more wildly attracted to him than ever?

Because she was deranged.

Delia sat up in her seat, scowling at his empty desk through the doorway, frustrated beyond belief. He was the most impossible, unfathomable man she'd ever met, and yet, he'd awakened in her desires more powerful than any she'd ever experienced. Unfortunately, he welcomed her advances about as much as he'd welcome a plague epidemic.

On the other hand, given her history, who could blame him? She was the black widow, after all. Was it really so surprising that even if he wanted her, he would run from her as fast as he could?

"He probably doesn't want to die," she muttered, half in jest.

But even as she tried to joke about it, her shoulders slumped, and she gave a sigh.

Despite how much he exasperated and infuriated her, the truth was that she had really begun to *like* him, damn it all. She actually liked his implacable will. She admired his honorable, upright nature

and his insistence upon playing by the rules, and she was vastly enter-
tained by his almost puritanical notions of sexual conduct, even after
he'd just kissed her within an inch of her life. That combination of
qualities made him unlike any man she'd ever had a pash for, including her late husbands. Especially her late husbands.

Melancholy stole over her suddenly, a misty, brooding fog as gray
as the late February day outside, and she realized in horror that she
was rapidly sinking into a hopeless morass of self-pity. How ghastly.

With that thought, she resolved to stop thinking about that
man, stop feeling sorry for herself, and get back to work, but she'd
barely picked up her pen before she was interrupted with yet another
reminder of him.

"Good morning, my lady."

She looked up as his secretary came through the doorway with
a handful of letters. "Morning post," he added, placing the letters
beside her.

"Thank you, Ross. Do you know," she added on impulse, "when
Lord Calderon will be back?"

"I am not certain, my lady, I'm sorry. Perhaps next week, he told
me. But we correspond daily. Was there something you needed?"

"My sanity," she sighed.

"I beg your pardon?"

"Never mind. Thank you, Ross. You may go."

He returned to the office next door, closing the door behind him,
and Delia picked up the first letter on the pile he'd given her, reminding herself she had work to do.

Her virtuous intentions lasted about three seconds, long enough to
read the name of the sender penned on the back flap of the envelope.

"Oh, for heaven's sake!" she muttered in complete exasperation,
staring at Cassandra Hayden's name. Was she never going to stop
being reminded of that man?

She stared at the letter, torn between curiosity and the rather craven impulse to shove it in a drawer. Curiosity won.

"Oh, dear," she murmured a few moments later, staring at the penned lines , sympathy replacing her earlier aggravation. "Poor girl."

Her own troubles forgotten, at least for the time being, she read the letter again, wondering how she could be of help. The girl was clearly in over her head. Perhaps she could write to the ladies of the county and put in a word? But there wasn't much time. And in any case, would that be—

"Delia, my dear!"

She looked up, and at the sight of the balding, mustachioed man in the doorway, she dropped the letter in complete surprise. "César?"

He bowed. "In the flesh."

"Back at last!" She jumped up, circled her desk, and flung herself into his arms with the familiarity of their long acquaintance. "I was beginning to think you'd vanished from the face of the earth, and I'd never see you again," she declared, pressing a kiss to each of his cheeks with profound affection. "How was Paris?"

He rolled his eyes, his smile fading. "Chaos, my dear. I wish you had been with me to help straighten out the mess. How we'll ever be ready to open by June, I cannot think."

"You could delay the opening," she replied, moving to return to the chair at her desk and gesturing for him to take the chair opposite. "Give yourself more time."

"Only if I must. How have things been here?"

There was a nuance in his voice as he asked the question, a casual indifference that was unlike him, making her appreciate at once what he was really asking, and she decided a bit of flattery wouldn't go amiss. "As well as they can be when you are away."

"Yes, yes, you try to put the good face on, but the staff is unhappy. This I know."

"There has been some grumbling," she admitted. "But things are getting better."

"Are they? I do not think so."

Delia gave a diplomatic shrug. "I can only say that no one has come to me with any complaints for several weeks now. I take that as a good sign."

"You are always so optimistic, my dear friend. But I appreciate your honesty."

"I'm always honest, César. You know that."

"Yes, of course. You are too honest, sometimes, I fear."

That took her aback a bit, but before she could ask what he meant, he went on, "And what of our friend Lord Calderon?" he asked. His voice was light, almost unconcerned, but Delia heard the tension beneath the question. "What is your honest opinion there?"

She wriggled a little in her chair, sensing that in this case, César would definitely not appreciate her honesty. "Well, it's early days yet," she hedged. "I think it's too soon to judge."

"You form no opinion, even though he makes the Duchess of Moreland and Lord Synby take their parties elsewhere?"

"You heard about that, did you?"

"Of course. But I am curious why I didn't hear it from you before I left for Paris."

The rebuke was plain, making her grimace. "I was completely inundated the day you wanted to meet. And then you left for Paris, and you've been away ever since. And you know how bad I am at writing letters, darling!"

That was something he could not refute, and she was relieved when he nodded his head. "I know, but I need you to help me against Calderon. If we let him have his way, he will be the ruin of everything we have built here."

"That was my opinion, too," she acknowledged. But before she could point out that for the good of the hotel, she had changed her mind, Ritz spoke again.

"We must fight him, all of us. Together."

"Fight him?" Delia echoed in dismay, appreciating that what she'd blithely assumed was a minor skirmish between two powerful men was in fact a full-fledged war. And she was caught squarely in the middle. "I'm not sure what can be done in that regard," she murmured tactfully.

"Ah, but I do. I know." He smiled, rubbing his hands together as if quite pleased with himself. "We shall have a party."

Delia blinked. "A party?"

"But of course!" he said, laughing. "What better way to reassure our friends that nothing has changed?"

"But, César, things have changed," she pointed out.

She was ignored. "We will invite the most influential people in society—Lady Gray, Mrs. Williams...and your cousin, the duke, of course, and his delightful wife. You will make the arrangements?"

"I could," she murmured doubtfully. "But we can't really afford to host such a lavish affair, can we? We're supposed to be cutting costs these days, you know."

"Nonsense!" he scoffed, brushing that objection aside with a wave of his hand. "We do not worry about such trifles here. This is the Savoy. We do not pinch the pennies."

"I realize that, darling. Still, it's not as if we have much choice these days."

"It shall be a dinner," he went on as if she hadn't spoken. "Twelve courses. For the dessert, Auguste shall carve an ice sculpture in which to put a serving for each guest. The best wines, of course, and the best champagne. I wonder if there is enough of the Clicquot '91 for eighty people?"

"Eighty people?" She stared at him, aghast. That particular champagne was the most expensive one in the Savoy cellars, and to serve it to eighty people would run up an exorbitant sum.

"We shall engage a salon orchestra to play through dinner," Ritz went on happily, not seeming to notice her shock. "Then we can have dancing afterward."

Suddenly, Simon's words from their first meeting echoed back to her.

I've been here quite long enough to note the wanton extravagance displayed by every department of this hotel.

Remembering those words as Ritz prattled on about this wholly unnecessary party when everyone's livelihood—including that of the man before her—depended on austerity, she truly appreciated for the first time the validity of Simon's criticism. But before she could remind Ritz again of the constraints on their finances these days, her friend spoke.

"I shall leave the arrangements to you, dear Delia, of course. The decorations must be superb. Orchids, of course, and perhaps some of those—" He broke off, waving his hands in the air. "What is that flower? The one of New Guinea that is orange and purple, about so big, and has the shape of a bird?"

"Bird-of-paradise?" she murmured faintly, remembering the cost of those ran about six shillings each.

"That is the one, yes. We shall have them at every table. I wonder—should the vases be crystal?"

She'd never been one to let cost get in the way of a good party, God knows, but as agreeable as all this sounded, she knew she simply must bring Ritz back to reality.

"I'm happy to arrange a party, if you like, but I'm not sure Calderon will approve the expense."

"Him?" In that one word, there was no mistaking his opinion of the other man, and Delia winced. It wasn't surprising, of course, that Ritz didn't like Simon. He clearly resented the other man's power over him and he was accustomed to being in absolute control.

Nonetheless, it was not like Ritz to show such open contempt for a peer. He was a snob from head to toe. But then, she thought, remembering the Duchess of Moreland's odious condescension, Simon's title was terribly new, and in consequence, perhaps Ritz didn't deem it worthy of his usual obsequious deference.

Either way, Delia knew that Ritz was going to have to do what she had done: accept the inevitable and call a truce. Perhaps, she thought, studying her friend's resentful expression, she could help that along. Before she could decide how to set about it, he spoke again.

"You think I care what that contemptible tyrant approves?" he demanded, his voice rising a notch.

She stared at him unhappily as more of Simon's words came back to her.

Ritz will have to accept my way of doing things, and frankly, I'm not sure he can.

How right he had been.

"Well," she said in reply, trying to take a reasonable, middle-ground sort of approach, "he is in charge of hotel expenses these days. A party such as this will require his permission."

Ritz drew himself up. "This is my hotel. I do not ask permission to do what is best here. Especially not from men like him. Men who do things on the cheap, who do not have the vision to see beyond a quarterly profit? *Non.*"

Delia feared that reminding her friend of tiresome facts was only making matters worse, but she persevered. After all, she was the one being asked to plan this party.

"Of course you are," she said soothingly. "Of course you are. But we must consider whether or not this is a good time for a party. The investors are expecting a profitable first quarter, and we won't be able to meet that expectation if we throw any lavish parties. Perhaps when the season starts, we can work with him to plan something acceptable to both of you."

"I have no intention of working with him. He must work with me."

"But, César—"

He stood up. "I can see," he said coldly, "that you have made up your mind to side against me."

"I'm never against you!" she cried, stung. "I am your friend, and you know that."

He opened his mouth to reply, but she rushed on: "As your friend, I tell you it would be unwise to go against Calderon at this stage."

"If you don't wish to plan this party for me," he said, his voice now like ice, "I will do it myself. But I never thought you, of all people, would take the side of my enemy."

With that parting shot, he stalked out of her office in a fury, and she let out her breath on a slow sigh, appreciating that getting these two men to cooperate with one another and work together was not going to be easy.

Perhaps she ought to just stay out of it. After all, she didn't seem to be very good at brokering truces these days. On the other hand...

Her gaze strayed to Cassandra's letter, and she wondered if perhaps she could accomplish two good deeds in one fell swoop. It was, she decided, worth a try.

13

Simon was town bred. Though he'd spent most of his military service in Africa and trekked through the bush with Devlin a time or two when he was on leave, in all the thirty-six years of his life, he'd never lived in the English countryside. But he knew it was considered a peaceful, serene sort of life, and peace and serenity were things he badly needed just now.

Delia's kiss had left him a hot, hard, unholy mess, and walking away from her had felt like ripping himself in half, but thankfully, there was little cause at Ivywild to think of her, though he did take her advice. He paid calls upon his neighbors, and just as she had predicted, the county returned the favor, ensuring that Cassandra would have the pleasure of company and amusements whenever he could not be with her. When she suggested a dinner party for their new-found friends in the county, he gladly agreed, his only qualification being that he did not have to plan the menu.

Since receiving the estate along with his title eight months ago, he'd spent very little time here—an occasional weekend to see his sister, a week at Christmas, and that was all. But to keep his mind away from thoughts of Delia, he threw himself into estate business and country life, and as the last days of February slipped away and March began, he found that tramping muddy lanes in the rain, visiting the cottages, and touring the farms with his land agent, Mr. Beecher, cooled his blood more effectively than all the willpower he possessed ever could. And much to his own surprise, he discovered that he liked country life.

Two weeks after his arrival, he and Beecher decided to tour Lowe's Farm and see how his pigs were getting on. When they arrived, they found that six of the pigs had gotten out and were happily rolling around in the mud of the field beyond. Both of them were roped in to help by Lowe and his two sons, and by the time all the recalcitrant animals were safely back in the pen, all five men were covered in muck. It was nearly dark by the time Beecher's wagon pulled back into the drive at Ivywild.

To his surprise, Cassandra was on the front steps as his boots hit the gravel, and she came running down to greet them.

"At last!" she cried, stopping beside the wagon. "I thought you'd never return. You were supposed to be back ages ago. Heavens," she added, looking them over in dismay. "You two look as if you've been rolling in the sty with the pigs."

"Perhaps because we have been. After a fashion." Simon glanced down over his muddy trousers and boots and those of Mr. Beecher, and he laughed, shaking back his wet hair. "God, we do look a sight, don't we?"

"One of the hazards of country life, my lord," his land agent replied. "If we're finished for the day, I'll be off home."

"Yes, of course. Thank you, Beecher. Perhaps we should have a look at the warrens tomorrow?"

"If you like." Beecher tipped his cap to Cassandra. "Miss Hayden."

The land agent departed, and Simon turned to his sister. "I'm going up to bathe and change before dinner."

"Excellent idea," she approved, her nose wrinkling up. "But, Simon, I have something to tell you before you go up."

"Walk with me, then."

He gestured to the house, but to his surprise, she hung back, shaking her head.

"I can't," she said, glancing past him down the drive. "It's best if I tell you right here. We don't have much time, you see."

Puzzled, he studied her, and when he saw her lift her hand to her neck and begin twirling a loose tendril of her hair around her finger, he felt a hint of misgiving. Cassie only twirled her hair when she was nervous.

"Time for what?" he asked, bracing himself.

She opened her mouth to reply, but before she could, the sound of wheels on gravel and the rattle of horses' traces told him a visitor was coming up the drive. But when he turned, he was surprised to see the vehicle approaching was his own carriage, with his own driver on the box.

"What the devil?" he muttered in surprise.

He glanced at his sister, who was looking decidedly guilty, then back at his approaching carriage, which was now circling around the fountain in the drive, and when he saw the face of the passenger inside, a delicate face of dark blue eyes, finely arched black brows, and a dazzling, dimpled smile, all the composure he'd spent the past two weeks striving to achieve went sailing straight off into the wind.

The carriage pulled to a stop, his driver rolled out the steps, and Delia exited the vehicle, giving him a tantalizing glimpse of her filmy petticoats, dainty foot, and stocking-clad ankle beneath the hem of her dark green traveling suit, and Simon was caught between wanting to haul her into his arms and kiss her senseless and shoving her into the carriage to send her straight back to London. It wasn't until she stopped in front of him and her gaze traveled down over his body did he remember the state he was in, and when she pressed her lips together against a smile, he felt as foolish and painfully embarrassed as a schoolboy caught writing a love letter to the girl next door.

She lifted her gaze to his face, the corners of her almond-shaped eyes crinkling with unmistakable laughter. "I take it you were not expecting me."

Without waiting for a reply, she turned to his sister. "Cassandra, my dear," she said, holding out her hands to give Cassie's a squeeze. "Lovely to see you again."

"I was so glad to get your telegram," Cassie said with a profound and obvious relief he did not understand. "And I'm so glad you're here."

"Why *is* she here?" Simon asked his sister. "And what telegram?"

He was ignored.

"I was happy to come," Delia replied. "I just hope I can help."

"Help with what?" he asked, but he was again ignored as Delia turned expectantly toward the handful of servants who had now joined them in the drive.

"This is Mr. Filbert, our butler," Cassandra supplied, "and Mrs. Knight, our housekeeper. And Mrs. Morrisey, my governess-companion."

"How do you do?" Delia murmured. "Mrs. Knight, I'm afraid my maid was obliged to remain in town. If it isn't too much trouble, could you perhaps have one of the housemaids do for me while I'm here?"

"I will see to you myself, my lady," the woman replied.

"Oh, no, I wouldn't dream of causing you any inconvenience of that sort. No, no, a housemaid will do quite well. As you can see," she added, gesturing to the pile of luggage footmen were now removing from the boot of the carriage, "I didn't bring much with me. I won't be wearing anything too elaborate."

To Simon's decidedly middle-class eyes, a trunk, two hatboxes, and three valises seemed like an alarming amount of luggage, and he wondered in consternation not only what she was doing here, but also just how long she intended to stay. When she moved toward the house with Cassie beside her, he decided he was going to find out that information right now.

He reached out, putting a hand on her elbow before she could move out of reach. "We need to talk, Countess," he said in a voice that brooked no opposition. "If you will excuse us, Cassandra?"

He didn't wait for an answer, but immediately began steering Delia across the drive to get her out of Cassie's earshot.

"We don't really have time for a conversation just now, do we?" Delia said as he turned the corner of the house with her in tow. "It's half past six already, and I need a bath before dinner. So do you, obviously—"

"Later," he cut her off, and as he pulled her along a moss-covered flagstone path, just the contact of his hand on her arm was enough to start arousal flickering to life inside him. "We are going to have a little chat first."

He led her under the arch of an arbor, where he finally stopped amid the bare canes, iron pillars, and wooden trellises of the rose garden. Letting her go, he faced her, plunked his hands on his mud-encrusted hips, and launched into speech.

"My God, woman, do you never take no for an answer? I begin to see why you've had three husbands. The poor devils couldn't run fast enough to get away."

She made a sound of outrage. "You think I came down here chasing after *you*? What unbelievable conceit!"

"Is it?" he shot back, feeling trapped and frustrated, not by her, but by his own traitorous, ungovernable feelings where she was concerned. "After what happened a fortnight ago?"

"You mean when you kissed me?"

"I didn't kiss you," he took great satisfaction in pointing out. "You kissed me."

She tossed her head, a gesture he was coming to know well, one that told him his shot had gone home. "Well, you weren't exactly pushing me away."

"I did push you away!"

"After you practically kissed my mouth off."

He sucked in a sharp breath, and any satisfaction he felt dissolved in the wake of that undeniable point. He decided it was time to change tack. "Either way, what are you doing here?"

"I'm not here for you, so you needn't worry I'll fling myself into your arms. I made that mistake once, and believe me, once was enough. It will not happen again, I assure you."

"Then why are you here?"

"To help Cassie, of course. Didn't she tell you I was coming? Well," she added as he shook his head, "she probably hasn't had time. After all, I only telegraphed her from the station two hours ago. Still, I had assumed she would—"

"Wait," he cut in, his frustration deepening, "you sent her a telegram from the train station inviting yourself down here on the spur of the moment?"

"I didn't invite myself! Good heavens, pushing in like that would be the height of bad manners."

"Somehow," he muttered, glaring at her, "I doubt if that fact has ever stopped you before."

"Cassie asked me to come, you impossible man!"

He blinked, startled, his frustration faltering a notch in the wake of that information. "What? She didn't discuss it with me."

There must have still been some skepticism in his voice, and she heaved a sigh. Reaching for the handbag hooked over her arm, she opened it and pulled out a letter. "Your sister wrote to me," she said, waving the slip of paper under his nose, "and asked for my help. I got her letter in this morning's post."

"Help with what?"

"Her dinner party tomorrow night. She invited three of the most prominent families in the county to dinner, I understand, but once the deed was done, she must have panicked. It's a perfectly understandable feeling, of course, for it's her first time hosting such an affair. She wrote to me, confessed she felt in over her head, and begged me to come and assist her. I was delighted to do so."

He stared at her, the last of his ire fading away in the wake of that information. What was it about this woman, he wondered in utter bafflement, that made him so often act like a prize idiot? And more importantly, why did her talent there only make him want her more? He was a sensible man, rational and even-keeled. He wasn't the sort to lose his temper or reason with emotion rather that facts. Never had a woman made him feel so off-balance, so out of control, so absurdly vulnerable.

Delia reached out, breaking into these grim ruminations as she shoved the letter into the front pocket of his filthy tweed jacket, crumpling it in the process. "Read her letter for yourself, if you don't believe me. Now, since it is less than ninety minutes to dinner, I'm going to go find my room, bathe, and change. Then I'm going to see Cassie and determine what I can do to help make her party a smashing success."

She turned and stalked away, hips swaying and skirts churning, reminding him of their very first meeting when he'd likened her to a tornado.

Under the arbor, the tornado paused to level his defenses one last time. "As for you," she said, her blue eyes glinting like steel in the evening twilight, "you can go hang."

There was nothing for it, of course. He had to apologize.

"Lift your chin, my lord, if you would."

Morgan's voice intruded, and Simon complied, tilting his head back so that his valet could shave his neck.

How many times, he wondered, thoroughly aggravated with himself, was he going to act like a fool in front of Delia and be obliged to apologize for it? Too many to count, he suspected, if he remained near her much longer. Worse, he'd have to get her alone to offer said apology, and that, he was already appreciating, would be a serious test of his hard-won willpower and restraint.

Morgan set aside the razor. "There we are, my lord," he said, wiping away the traces of shaving soap from Simon's face and neck. "I've laid out white-tie for you this evening, of course," he added, nodding to the clothes that had been placed carefully on the bed. "Which studs and links would you like?"

"White-tie?" Simon echoed as he untied the sash of his dressing robe. "Is formal dress really necessary?"

The valet looked at him with patient gravity, reminding him—not for the first time in the six months of their acquaintance—that when it came to the wardrobe of a gentleman, he knew far more than Simon on the subject. "An ordinary evening suit *might* be considered tolerable when dining only with one's own sister," he said, expressing again his disapproval of Simon's usual attire for the dinner table. A viscount, Morgan felt, was above the standards of ordinary, middle-class mortals. "But you are dining with a countess."

"Don't I know it?" he acknowledged with a sigh. "And when one has a countess to dinner, white-tie is de rigueur."

Morgan, accustomed to Simon's awful French accent and fully aware he was winning the battle over his master's wardrobe, gave him an indulgent smile. "Just so, my lord."

Dressed at last to his valet's satisfaction in the formal dress of tails, high collar, a white tie, black onyx studs and links ornamenting his shirt, he journeyed down to the drawing room.

He had hoped to pull Delia aside and offer his mea culpa straight-away, but he was given no opportunity. The ladies had joined him for less than a minute before Filbert came in to announce dinner, and Simon was obliged to wait.

Delia was seated beside him at dinner, which he initially thought was a blessing, for it kept her stunning face and low-cut evening gown out of his direct line of vision unless he turned his head. But he soon found that fact wasn't enough to keep desire for her at bay, because even if he kept his eyes fixed firmly on his plate or on his sister across the table, the faint traces of Delia's perfume drifted under his nose, and the delicate scent was enough to trigger every sensual memory and erotic dream of her that he'd ever had.

Dinner was a tantalizing torment, but afterward, much to his surprise and relief, Cassie suggested that she and Delia go through so that he could enjoy his port. Though he usually found the idea of sipping port alone in his enormous drawing room both unappeal-ing and downright silly, particularly since he wasn't wont to drink much anyway, he was glad of it tonight, and by the time he rejoined the ladies in the drawing room, his baser desires were firmly rele-gated to the back of his mind, and he felt quite capable of offering Delia his apology without yanking her into his arms and kissing her senseless.

When he entered the drawing room, she was sitting with Cassan-dra on the sofa, and the two of them had their heads together, bent over a sheet of paper in Cassie's lap.

"Lady Bassington has no sense of time at all," Delia was saying as he came in. "She'll be a quarter of an hour late, at least."

"Isn't that considered rude?" Cassie asked.

"Well, she's quite elderly, you know, and one must make allowances. Because of that, I should advise against soufflés for the first course. And Lord Nasby can't abide goose liver—it's terribly hard on his gout. So pâté might not be a wise alternative."

"Going over tomorrow night's menu, I take it?" Simon said, settling into a chair opposite.

"We are," Cassie replied. "And, oh, Simon, I can't tell you what a help it is to have Lady Stratham here to advise me."

He noted his young sister's expression and heard the relief in her voice, and he knew that, although Delia's presence might be causing him any amount of personal frustration, it was a small price to pay for Cassandra's sake.

"I'm glad," he said. "You'll have to tell Mrs. Melrose as soon as you've decided things, though, for you're not giving her much time."

"No," Cassie agreed, "and I fear she will be absolutely wild with us. We are changing nearly everything."

Delia patted her arm. "She may try to bully you about it, but you can't let her."

"Won't you come down to the kitchens with me and talk to her?"

Delia shook her head. "That won't do. You are the mistress here. You must take charge. The trick with servants," she added as Cassie groaned, "is to listen, acknowledge their concerns, consider their opinions, and then, if you still disagree, express your gratitude for their advice, and politely but firmly reiterate what you want. And keep doing that until they give in. Sometimes it takes a while. You just have to be more stubborn than they are."

Cassie, he noted, cast a nervous glance at Filbert and Thomas, but the butler and the footman both remained impassive, clearly accustomed to being discussed as if they weren't in the room.

"So, no soufflé and no pâté," she said. "But then, what shall I serve as the first course?"

"Oysters," Simon and Delia said together, and when she smiled at him, he felt the earth shift again, settling into something new and curiously right, and he decided this was the moment he'd been looking for.

"Are the two of you finished discussing the menu?" he asked. "Because if so, I'm thinking our guest might like to see more of the garden. I'm happy to give her a tour," he added before either of them could reply, offering Cassie a pointed glance.

His sister's eyes widened a fraction, making him appreciate what she was thinking, but that couldn't be helped, and he turned his attention to Delia, who was looking equally surprised. "Shall we, Lady Stratham? There's plenty of moon tonight."

She hesitated, a wary, puzzled look in her eyes. "If Cassie doesn't mind?"

"Heavens, no, I am glad, quite glad, to stay here," the girl replied with perhaps overdone enthusiasm. "I shall…" She paused, casting a frantic glance around, then she reached for the book on the table beside her. "I shall read my book. It's such a fascinating story, and I've been dying to get back to it all evening. I'm so glad you've given me the perfect excuse."

He didn't point out that the book was his, not hers, but once he and Delia had donned warm coats and were walking a path lined by lilac trees, she spoke, making him realize that she, too, had seen through Cassie's excuse to stay behind.

"I didn't realize Cassandra was so interested in the workings of the internal combustion engine."

"You saw that, too?" He turned his head, giving Delia a rueful smile. "I fear she's thinking to do a bit of matchmaking."

"Well, we both know that's a lost cause."

Her voice was light and humorous, but he heard the tartness

beneath it, reminding him forcibly of his obligation. "Do you mind if we stop a moment?" he asked.

He suited the action to the word, and she stopped as well, facing him on the path. Her face was pale, luminous in the moonlight, and the cold breeze stirred the loose wisps of hair that curled at her neck, stirring his arousal as well.

He snuffed it out and clasped his hands firmly behind his back. "I wanted this moment to offer you my apologies," he said, stiff, embarrassed, and keenly aware of his own vulnerabilities where she was concerned. "My accusations earlier were uncalled for and most ungentlemanly. I seem to always assume the worst about you," he added with a sigh, "and though I can't explain quite why that is so, I appreciate that apologizing for it is becoming a habit with me, one I daresay you are coming to find quite tiresome."

"On the contrary." She smiled, a wide, winsome smile that was so unexpected, he could only stare. "I actually rather like this habit of yours."

"Like it?" he repeated, dazed as usual by the power of that smile and completely bewildered by the words of her reply. "Why?" he added wryly. "Because it gives you the upper hand?"

"As agreeable as that sounds, no, since I never feel like I have the upper hand with you."

Another surprising bit of news. "Oh" was all he could think to say.

"I like this habit of yours," she went on, "because it then allows me to ask you for something in return."

He laughed at that. She was so outrageous, he couldn't help it. "Fair enough. So what am I to do to make up for my insufferable conduct earlier? Hire you a secretary? No, that can't be. You seem to have already appropriated mine."

She pulled a twig of lilac, still bare, from the nearest tree and rewarded his teasing jibe by tossing it at his head. He ducked, it sailed past him, and he guessed again. "My consent to the hothouse? Another dinner?" he added when she shook her head. "Or perhaps an extravagant party for a hundred guests that's going to cost the hotel a thousand pounds?"

Something flickered across her face, a hint of surprise that indicated his guess might have been right, but when she spoke, her words told him he was wrong again.

"Not a party, no. Nothing like that." She paused, then said, "Ritz came to see me this morning."

"Ah," he said with instant comprehension. Undermining him, after all, was Ritz's favorite pastime. "Came to cry on your shoulder, did he?"

"In a way. He is worried about the hotel."

"The hotel? You mean me."

She didn't deny it, and he sighed, bracing himself. "What did he say? That I'm a tyrant of epic proportions I suppose?"

"Can you blame him for feeling a bit like that? I did at first."

He opened his mouth to say there was a world of difference, because Ritz was crooked. But then, he remembered, much to his chagrin, that he still wasn't certain about the extent of her involvement in Ritz's schemes. All his instincts warred against her guilt, but given his passion for her, he knew his instincts could not be trusted. He took a deep breath and tried to speak impartially. "We've talked about this, Delia. We cannot afford to do things Ritz's way anymore, and he simply has to accept that."

"With as much grace as he can muster," she said, offering back to him the suggestion he'd made regarding her in their first meeting.

"Yes."

"Can't the two of you just make peace?"

"What do you want me to do?" he asked, keeping his voice light. "Send him some hyacinths?"

She didn't seem to take his teasing in the proper spirit. "I'm sure," she said earnestly, "that the two of you could learn to work together."

He shook his head, staring at her. "I just do not understand your loyalty to that man," he said, both envious of Ritz's appeal to her and baffled by it.

"He said much the same about you. He thinks I'm taking your side against him."

"I wish you would," he muttered, rubbing a hand over his forehead. "It would make my life so much easier."

"But if the two of you could work together, wouldn't that benefit everyone? Couldn't you try?"

He lifted his head to study her face. Her hopeful expression was unmistakable, and he appreciated that this was why everyone at the Savoy loved her. Liniment for the lift boy's mother, baby gifts for the laundress, her desperate attempts to make everything right and help anyone who needed it, and once again, his instincts whispered to him that she had no clue what Ritz was doing. His head, however, told him there was no way she could be that blind.

"Delia, listen to me." He put his hands on her arms. "I appreciate that you want to help, but you can't. Your concern for the hotel and the staff does you credit, and your loyalty to your friend is laudable, but let me handle Ritz. I'm asking this as a favor: please don't meddle."

She sighed and looked away, but after a moment she nodded, and he let his hands fall away.

Suddenly, in the silence, he remembered they were quite alone, making him appreciate again his vulnerability where she was concerned, but before he could suggest that they rejoin Cassandra, she spoke again.

"You said you don't understand my loyalty to Ritz. Shall I tell you how he earned it?"

Her voice was musing, almost detached, its very softness impelling him to stay where he was.

"If you wish to tell me, Delia," he said, "I'm happy to listen."

She stopped and gave a laugh, but he sensed there was no humor in it. "It's not an easy story to tell." With an abrupt move, she turned to face him again, looking not at him, but into the lilac trees and the darkness, and she was silent so long, he thought she'd decided against telling him anything at all.

"When Lord Stratham died," she said at last, "I was with child."

A blunt statement like that, especially on such a delicate subject as pregnancy, made him blink. But he knew she had no child living, and when she looked at him again, the pain in her face hit him like a blow to the chest as he realized what she hadn't said.

When he spoke, however, he was careful to keep his voice neutral. "Indeed?"

She nodded. "I was about six months gone. It was quite astonishing that I conceived at all. I'd never been with child before, and this time, it was only because I—"

She stopped and gave a laugh. "This isn't the sort of thing a lady is supposed to talk about, but Hamish's state of health had made him impotent. In the first six months of our marriage, we were only..." She paused and gave a little cough. "We were only together a few times, and on all three occasions, things ended in epic failure for him and frustration for me. He stopped coming to my room after that."

He studied her profile in the moonlight, the pensive curve of her mouth. "Some women might have been quite relieved by such an arrangement."

She turned her head, her smile a quick, impudent flash of white teeth in the moonlight. "I wasn't."

The naughty implications behind those words and that smile were plain, but it was clear she wasn't flirting with him. She often used impudence, he realized, as a shield, to hide her true feelings, to avoid inconvenient questions—or, in this case, to ward off pity. "I see."

She laughed. "Such a polite reply, but I fear you're thinking I'm a completely depraved female—"

"That's not what I was thinking at all," he cut in. "And in any case, depraved is both an inaccurate and cruel way to describe it, Delia. A young wife with an impotent husband is bound to have some degree of frustration. Only natural."

She turned, tilting her head to study him. "You're an incredibly easy person to talk to, do you know that?" she said after a moment. "I've never discussed this with anyone before."

Yes, he thought, *I'm an excellent father confessor.* "Not anyone?"

She didn't seem to hear the wry note in his voice, and she shook her head in reply. "I think it's because I just…trust you. You're so upright and honorable."

Simon grimaced, feeling like an utter hypocrite, but thankfully, she didn't notice.

"Anyway," she went on, "my…ahem…frustrations weren't my only consideration."

"No?"

"I wanted a baby," she said simply. "So much, I'd have done anything. I had come into my first marriage with precious little knowledge of male-female relations, but my second marriage had proved to be quite an explicit education in that regard."

How explicit? he wondered, and his muscles tightened, desire flickering to life. Reminding himself how inappropriate that was at such a moment, he set his jaw and said nothing.

"Hamish knew before we married that people called me the black widow. He knew how much the nickname hurt me and how worried I was that it might be true. He also knew how badly I wanted children. If he had told me of all his health difficulties before the wedding, I would not have married him."

"He deceived you?"

"It might be more accurate to say he was deceiving both of us. I think he hoped a young wife might turn the tide. Obviously, he was mistaken."

"Such a condition might be grounds for divorce."

"Perhaps, but even I'm not outrageous enough to try something so scandalous. Instead, I employed a different approach. Two years after we were married, I decided I'd had enough of kisses at the door and a pat on the cheek, so I seduced my husband shamelessly. I used every trick I could think of. And it worked. By some miracle, I conceived. Not that any of it did much good in the end," she added softly. "Three days after Hamish died, I lost the baby."

A shaft of pain hit him, obliterating the desire inside him like a candle flame snuffed out. He had no idea what to say, but he could not bear to offer the trite, conventional replies most people were wont to utter at moments like this. "Ah" was all he said.

That simple reply seemed to act on her like a cork popping off a bottle of champagne, and more words came spilling out of her mouth. "I know that all three of my husbands had in some way deceived me, but I loved each of them passionately and I grieved each of them when they died. In their deceptions and their deaths, I thought I'd felt all the pain a woman could feel, but I was wrong. When I miscarried, when my beautiful little boy followed Hamish to his grave, I wanted to die, too."

He pressed a fist to his mouth, his heart hurting for her. She may have been born into privilege and wealth, but none of that could keep away misfortune, pain, and loss.

"I wandered around inside Stratham House for months," she went on, "hiding from the world, drowning in grief, unable to get past my pain. Hamish's son and his wife wanted to move into the house," she went on, "as was their right. He'd become the earl, so it was now his house, but I went into absolute hysterics. I would not let them in. I stayed in the house alone, refusing to see anyone for over six months. I stopped eating. I reached a point where I could barely find the will to get out of bed. My family was terribly worried about me, but I couldn't seem to care about that. Or about anything else for that matter. I couldn't see any point in living. There were times when I…" She paused and swallowed hard. "When I even contemplated killing myself."

He studied her face, twisted with pain, and her eyes, haunted and dark, and his own emotions—dismay, sadness, and a deep, profound compassion—almost overcame him, but he knew she wouldn't welcome expressions of pity, so he offered none. "Now I understand what you meant that night at dinner when I told you about my father. But," he added when she nodded, "nothing stopped him. Something stopped you. What was it?"

She smiled, but it wasn't one of the winsome or impudent or downright naughty smiles he was used to. Instead, it was a sad smile—sad and unexpectedly sweet. "It was Ritz."

Suddenly, it felt as if a fissure in the earth had opened under his feet, sending him hurtling down, down, into a dark abyss. "How so?" he asked, his voice a tight rasp to his own ears.

"He came to see me. I refused to see him, but when it comes to not taking no for an answer, Ritz puts me to shame. He talked and wheedled and bullied his way past my butler, burst right into my bedroom, and told me this tale of woe—how he was in desperate need of help with the hotel, how he was just too overwhelmed to handle it all by himself, he didn't know what to do, and how much he needed my help."

As much animosity as Simon had for Ritz, he couldn't help admiring the other man for finding the one tactic guaranteed to work with
Delia. "So," he murmured, "that's how you came to work for the
hotel?"

"Yes. He offered me a job. I made all sorts of excuses, but he countered them all, insisting again and again that I was the only person
he could hire who understood him, who could truly see his vision.
I accepted—which raised quite a few eyebrows in society, let me tell
you, but I didn't care. It was as if he'd tossed me a lifeline in a stormy
sea. To this day, I'm still not sure if he did it for himself, or for the
hotel, or for me, but—"

She broke off and gave a shrug. "Whatever his motives," she went
on, "he gave me purpose, a reason to get out of bed. At the most vulnerable moment of my life, Ritz gave me the courage to hang on until
things could get better, and for that, he will always have my gratitude
and my loyalty. Had your father had someone like Ritz, someone of
boundless optimism and possibility, he might not have done what he
did."

Simon didn't know how to reply. After all, what was there to say?
Ritz had given her a purpose in life, but Simon knew that if Helen
had her way, that purpose would be destroyed. And what, he wondered, would happen to her then?

"Goodness," she said, her voice changing with mercurial suddenness to an airy tone. "Listen to us. How on earth did this conversation
become so maudlin?"

She moved, stepping around him, adding, "We should rejoin your
sister before she thinks you've spirited me off to Gretna Green. A girl
of that age is so terribly romantic."

She walked away, but he didn't follow her immediately. Instead, he
watched her for a long moment, and before her figure had vanished
around the corner of the house, he realized what had been baffling

him from the first moment they'd met. He realized why she set off sparks of both temper and arousal in him, and why, no matter what she knew or what she'd done, he could never treat her with the indifference and impartiality of a mere employee.

Because he was falling in love with her.

Simon groaned. Turning his back, he stared out into the night, wondering what the hell he was going to do now. But even as he asked himself that question, he knew the answer. No matter her innocence or the level of her guilt, there was only one course of action open to him, and he could only hope that when this was all over, his heart wouldn't be in shattered pieces on the ground.

14

The telegram arrived at breakfast.

Simon had barely helped himself to eggs and bacon from the warming dishes on the sideboard and sat down with the *Times* before Thomas presented the missive to him on a salver. When he opened it and read the typewritten lines, any appetite he had vanished at once.

> More evidence uncovered stop Even worse than thought stop
> Richard has called meeting of board Monday morning at
> nine to vote immediate termination stop Suggest you return
> at once stop Helen stop stop

Simon frowned, surprised and puzzled. Helen had assured him that the detectives would not be finished until they had delved into Delia's activities, and that any such investigation would not be commencing for another week, at least.

Unless, he realized, a sick knot twisting his gut, some of the new evidence to which Helen referred was against Delia. If so, it would make any further investigations unnecessary.

But what was that evidence?

"Well, that's settled at last," Cassie said, her voice interrupting his thoughts as she entered the room. "Mrs. Melrose is such a tartar! The way she was protesting, you'd think changing the first course for tonight was akin to tumbling the walls of Jericho. I know nothing about cooking, of course," Cassie went on as she opened chafing dishes one by one to survey the contents, "but I can't imagine how raw oysters on ice could be harder to prepare than cheese soufflés."

Simon scarcely heard. Today was Friday, and there was, he knew, a midmorning train. If he managed to catch it—

"Lady Stratham's advice was absolutely right," his sister's voice intruded on his thoughts. "I stuck to my guns, so oysters it is, but it took some doing, let me tell you."

Simon did not reply. "Filbert," he said, glancing to where the butler stood at attention beside the sideboard, "doesn't the morning train to London depart at half past ten?"

"It does, my lord," the butler replied. "Every day but Sunday."

"London?" Cassie turned from the sideboard in surprise, diverted from domestic concerns.

Simon kept his gaze on the butler. "And is there one in the afternoon?"

"No, my lord. The next train would be tomorrow at the same time. The Sunday train is half an hour later, after early services."

"Why all these questions about trains?" Cassie asked as she set her filled plate on the table opposite him and sat down.

Simon pulled out his pocket watch, noting he had less than forty minutes to pack and get to the station if he wanted to make that train. He could telephone Helen, he supposed, find out what new information the detectives had uncovered, but that meant a trip into the village, and he might not reach her. Did he really want to spend the next twenty-four hours in suspense? And besides—

"Simon?" his sister prompted, breaking into his thoughts. "Why do you need to know about trains to London?"

He stood up, shoving his watch back in his waistcoat. "Something has arisen that requires me to return to London today," he told his sister, tucking the telegram into the breast pocket of his jacket. "Urgent business. It can't be helped."

"What?" She stared up at him in obvious dismay. "But what about the party?"

"Lady Stratham will be here to help you. She's far better at this sort of thing than I am. Don't worry," he added gently, noting the panic in her face. "It will be a raging success, I have no doubt."

"But this business can wait until Monday, surely?"

If there was anything against Delia, he might have time to mitigate the damage before Monday's meeting. He had to at least try. "I'm afraid not, love."

He turned to the butler. "Filbert, I'll be in my room, packing. Fetch Morgan, tell him we have to catch the train at half past ten, and send him up to assist me. Then have Hever harness the horses and bring the carriage round."

"Very good, my lord."

The butler glided out of the room to follow these instructions, and he once again turned to his sister. "Tell Lady Stratham I've gone and give her my apologies for not waiting to say goodbye," he said as he came around the table. "I'm sorry I'll miss the party. You do know that if it weren't absolutely critical, I'd stay?"

"I know," she said with a sigh. "I just hope I don't make a mess of the whole thing."

"Stuff," he scoffed and bent down to kiss her forehead. "You'll be splendid."

Twenty minutes later, he was in the main foyer waiting for the carriage as his valet brought down the last suitcase. "Morgan, where's my dispatch case?"

"I believe it is in the library, my lord."

He nodded. "I'll fetch it. You and Thomas take the luggage out to the drive. That way," he added as he turned and started for the corridor that led to the library, "we won't waste any time once Hever's brought the carriage."

He went to the library. It took him several minutes of searching to locate the dispatch case, but at last he found it, tucked underneath the malachite table beside the settee. Grabbing it by the handle, he straightened and turned to exit the room, but at the sight of Delia in the doorway, he came to a dead halt.

She was wearing some sort of loose-fitting tea gown, but though the garment of corn-colored silk made her appear fully dressed, her hair was scandalously loose, falling around her shoulders and down to her waist in blue-black waves, making her look as if she'd barely risen from bed. Her next words confirmed the fact.

"Your maid Susan told me you were leaving when she brought my breakfast tray up. Is it true?"

"I'm afraid so. I must go back to London at once."

He made the mistake of glancing down as he spoke, and when he saw her bare toes, pretty pink-and-white toes, peeking out from beneath the ruched hem of her gown, his body responded at once, desire flickering to life within him.

"But you'll miss Cassie's party."

Somewhere past this rising desire, he regained a measure of his wits. "Yes," he replied, jerking his gaze back up to her face, but sadly, that wasn't much help, for her loose hair made him think of what it would be like to wake up in her bed and see her this way, all rumpled and mussed and enticing as hell.

"It must be terribly important."

"Yes." He looked into her eyes, struggling to remember priorities. "My apologies for deserting you both. But I'm very grateful you're here to help my sister."

"Of course. I'm happy to help, though I fear I shall have to walk by myself tonight, since I doubt anyone but you will be willing to endure the chilly weather with me." Those magnificent dark blue eyes softened. "I'll miss you, Simon."

In the wake of those softly uttered words, overwhelming gladness pinched his chest, squeezing his heart. Almost at once, however, misgiving took its place as he remembered what lay ahead, what might happen, and what it might cost her.

"Delia," he began and took a step toward her. Then, abruptly, he stopped, and apprehension tightened in his throat, making him forget whatever he'd been about to say. "You'll be all right," he said instead. "Quite all right."

A puzzled little frown creased her forehead. "Well, of course I'll be all right," she said in some surprise, making it clear how nonsensical his words must have sounded from her point of view. "Is there some reason I wouldn't be?"

Suddenly, the frown vanished, her brow cleared, and a teasing glimmer came into her eyes, crinkling them at the corners. "I won't be prostrated with sadness just because you've gone back to London a day or two ahead of me, if that's what you're thinking." She smiled, her nose wrinkling up impudently. "I won't miss you *that* much."

He didn't smile back. He didn't reply. Instead, he stared at her in silence, because he didn't have the freedom to say all that he wanted to say.

He wanted to say that he would fight for her, that he would do whatever he could to defend and protect her. That if things went badly, he'd be there to pick up the pieces—if she'd let him. But then, she probably wouldn't. Her loyalty, after all, was to Ritz, not to him. When this mess was over, she might very well never speak to him again. He'd never touch her, he'd never kiss her again.

That thought was like a dam breaking. His dispatch case hit the floor with a thud, and then he was striding toward her, reaching for her, hauling her into his arms.

She was already lifting her face and twining her arms around his neck before his mouth captured hers, and the moment it did, her lips opened beneath his in willing accord.

She tasted like tea and marmalade. She smelled intoxicating, like oranges and flowers and warm, sweet woman, and her kiss was making his head spin. He wanted more.

He moved, stepping backward and pulling her with him as he kissed her, maneuvering their bodies behind one of the marble columns of the library and into a small reading alcove at the other end of the room. Pressing her back against the wall of books, he lifted his hands to cup her face as he tasted her in long, lush kisses that flared his desire even higher and banished any thought as silly as leaving. But he still wanted more.

Easing his hold, he slid his hands to her breasts, making a sound of appreciation as he realized there was no confining corset to impede him. He cupped her breasts in his hands, shaping them through thin layers of silk and muslin, finding them every bit as round and full and luscious as they'd been in his imagination.

He tore his lips from hers to press kisses along the column of her throat as he shaped her breasts in his palms, and her soft moan against his mouth was far more erotic than anything his imagination could ever have conjured. But it still wasn't enough.

His hands moved lower, his palms gliding over the generous swell of her hips as he trailed kisses up to her ear.

She shivered in response. "We'd better stop," she gasped, even as her arms tightened around his neck. "Simon, you'll miss—"

He captured her lips again, silencing her before she could remind him of the damned train and what would come after. He shoved his hands between her body and the bookshelves, cupping her bum and lifting her off the ground, pressing her hips to his as he tasted deeply of her mouth and his hands shaped her buttocks.

This time, she was the one who broke the kiss, her breath coming in shuddering gasps as she moved her hips against his.

The pleasure of it was so exquisite, he groaned, and he knew he'd explode if he didn't ease back. Lowering her to the ground, he grasped at the folds of her gown, pulling them up to get his hands beneath, and as his palms glided up her thighs, her body felt scorching hot through the thin fabric of her drawers.

His head was swimming, his wits eroding more with every inch his hands went higher. His one, his only coherent thought now was to touch her bare skin, but before he could act on that delicious impulse, he heard Cassie call his name.

"Simon, the carriage is here."

A sane man would come out of an erotic haze at once upon hearing the sound of his sister's voice, but Simon proved he'd gone quite off the rails by ignoring it completely. Instead, he eased his hand between Delia's thighs.

She was damp, ready, and when he slid his fingers into the slit of her drawers, she made a faint keening sound, her hips stirring against his seeking fingers. "Simon," she wailed softly against his ear, her arms tightening convulsively around his neck.

She was close to orgasm, he knew. So, so close.

"Simon, we have to stop," Delia gasped, even as her hips worked frantically against his caressing fingertips. "We have to stop. We have to stop."

Suddenly, her legs tightened around his hand, and her protests ended in a startled gasp of surprise and pleasure as she came in a rush, her arms tightening around his neck. He relished the moment, savoring her orgasm as much as he would have his own. He continued to caress her with his thumb as he slid his index finger deeply inside her. She came again at once, and then again, and then again.

At last, she sagged against him with a sigh of pure feminine satisfaction, and he eased his hand out from between her thighs. His cock was aching, his entire body demanding release, and he moved to unbutton his trousers.

"Simon?" Cassie's voice came again, more insistent this time.

Not yet, he thought, wanting, hungry with need. *Not yet, for the love of God.*

"Simon, where the devil are you?"

Her voice was drawing closer, and he gave a groan, knowing he had to stop. He could not let Cassandra catch them in here like this.

Drawing on willpower he didn't even know he possessed, he jerked Delia's skirts down and stepped back, withdrawing until she was safely out of his reach, but even then, even when they were no longer touching, he could not bring himself to leave her. He didn't have enough strength for that.

"I have to go," he heard himself say.

"Yes," she agreed.

Neither of them moved.

"Simon?" Cassie's voice, sounding quite alarmed by now, caused him to take a frantic glance around the column toward the doorway.

"I'm in the library," he called back, his voice absurdly normal—a miracle, all things considered. "I'll be along in a minute."

"The luggage is stowed and Morgan's already in the carriage, waiting for you."

"Coming," he called back. "Tell Morgan I'm coming."

He returned his attention to Delia. She was staring at him, wide-eyed, disheveled, and delectable, her breasts heaving with her rapid breathing, her lips puffy from his kisses. He might never have the chance to see her this way again, and he drank in the image of her now like the parched desert soil soaked up rain, knowing he would remember it as long as he lived, no matter what happened.

"You said your business was urgent, but—" She broke off, her tongue flicking out to moisten those kiss-tinged lips, driving him mad. "But can't you postpone it?"

"I can't." The words were an agonized whisper. "But—"

He broke off and took a deep breath. "But when it's over, when it's all behind us, perhaps—"

"Simon!" Cassie called, her voice frantic, almost strident in its insistence. "The train is in the station. I can see the smoke."

With an oath, he bent and grabbed his dispatch case, then he straightened, turned away, and started for the door. Behind him, he heard Delia's voice, breathless and bewildered.

"When what is behind us?"

He didn't pause until he had stepped safely through the doorway. Then he turned to find her staring after him in bafflement, waiting for an answer he could not give.

"Don't hate me," he said. "That's all I ask, Delia. For God's sake, don't hate me."

He left her then, striding away across the foyer and out the front doors without a backward glance.

15

On his instructions, Simon's driver drove the carriage like a bat out of hell, and it was only that fact that enabled Simon to make the train. He jerked open the door of an empty first-class carriage and leapt aboard just as the train was pulling out of the station, earning himself an indignant oath from the porter on the platform. But upon seeing his face through the window, Simon was given a respectful tip of the cap and a hushed, reverent greeting of "My lord," and for the first time since his elevation to the peerage, Simon appreciated the fact that having a title did have its uses.

"I'll pay for my ticket, I promise," he called through the window, then fell onto the carriage seat as the train pulled out of the station and started on its ninety-minute journey to London.

On the way, he stared out the window, striving to think of some other reason Richard would call a meeting before Delia had been investigated, but there was only one, and he knew it. Not that it mattered, really, for his own course was already decided.

He arrived back at the Savoy at a quarter past one to find his secretary anxiously waiting for him. "You did catch the morning train," Ross exclaimed as he entered the office. "I didn't know if you'd manage it."

"You knew about the telegram Helen sent me?"

"Oh, yes, my lord. Mrs. Carte called first thing this morning. She told me she'd sent it, and that you might be returning from Berkshire today as a result. She also asked me to give you this."

Ross plucked a large sealed envelope from the stack of papers on his desk and held it out to him. "She said she'd be at the Savoy Theatre until five o'clock, my lord, if you wish to call on her after you've read it."

That, he reflected, might be a good idea. "Anything else?"

"She also instructed me to tell you that the Savoy board is assembling for the Monday meeting at the Carte residence. Nine o'clock in the morning. She did not say what it was about, only that—"

"I already know," he cut in. "Thank you, Ross. I'll be out for the rest of the day. But if you are free this evening, I'd appreciate it if you'd stay. I might need your assistance later."

"Of course."

Simon paused, considering. Delia, he knew, was coming back tomorrow. "Make a reservation for me and Morgan at another hotel for tomorrow night."

"Another hotel?" The secretary blinked at these unexpected instructions, but being an excellent secretary, he recovered at once. "Very good, my lord. Just the one night?"

"Yes. I'll return to the Savoy sometime Sunday evening. Very late. Just don't tell anyone where I've gone."

"Do you have a preference for any hotel in particular?"

"No," he added as he turned and walked away. "But make it as far on the other side of town as you can."

Having ensured that he would be nowhere near Delia when she returned and in no danger of repeating his behavior of a few hours ago until after the vote was over, Simon then left the Savoy and went to a pub, where he ordered a plate of sandwiches and a pot of coffee, broke the seal on the envelope, and pulled out the sheaf of papers. After taking a deep breath and saying a little prayer, he began to read.

Cassandra's party was a raging success. As Delia had predicted, Lady Bassington was late—thirty minutes to be exact—and Lord Nasby expressed his gratitude that no organ meats were on the menu. Everyone accepted Lord Calderon's absence with good grace, though Lady Nasby did sniff a little and murmur to Delia that a gentleman earning a living wasn't quite proper. Delia smiled back, reminded herself that these were Cassandra's closest neighbors, and refrained from reminding the other woman that she, too, held a job.

Cassie, she was relieved to note, proved an able conversationalist, managing to be both a lively talker, which pleased the silent, rather dour vicar, and an encouraging listener, which helped the shy Lady Mary Nasby emerge from her shell. The party was such a triumph, in fact, that by the end, Lady Nasby deigned to mention her *unmarried* son to Delia, and inquired if Cassandra would be coming out in May.

It was the wee small hours of the morning before the last guests departed. Tumbling at last into bed around half past one, both relieved and exhausted, Delia expected to fall asleep at once. But sleep, perversely, refused to come.

The day had been so busy she'd had no time to think about what had happened with Simon that morning in the library, but now, as she lay in bed, wide awake, staring at the ceiling of her dark and silent room, those extraordinary moments came roaring back.

So long since she'd felt desire, even longer since she'd enjoyed its completion. But instead of proving to sate her, those moments had only served to make her remember what she'd been missing. Even now, hours later, his kisses still burned her lips and sexual desire pulsed through her body, making her ache with need from head to toe.

If anyone had told her when she'd first met Simon that a mere six weeks later, she'd be engaging in torrid sexual escapades with him against the wall of his library, she'd have laughed in that person's face, not only because of their mutual animosity during their first meeting, but also because she'd never have thought Simon capable of feeling such deep and ardent passions. Even now, the discovery seemed something of a revelation.

With three marriages to her credit, Delia had always thought herself fairly adept at managing the sterner sex, but when it came to Simon, her prior experience was no help at all.

She never knew quite where she stood with him. He could go from extraordinarily reserved to hotly erotic in the space of a heartbeat. One day he spurned her; the next day, he had her up against a wall with her skirts around her waist.

And the things he said were equally baffling.

Don't hate me.

What a thing to say. Considering that she'd willingly let him pull up her skirts, that she'd shamelessly reveled in his mouth on hers and his hand between her thighs, and the orgasms that had rocked her body, the idea that she could ever hate him seemed ludicrous in the extreme.

Delia groaned and turned over, pressing her hot cheek into the pillow, his desperate, baffling words echoing in her head.

When it's over, when it's behind us...

What on earth did *that* mean? When what was over?

Suddenly, Delia felt a shiver of foreboding that dampened her desire, a far less delightful feeling. It was like the stirring of wind and the darkening of the sky that preceded a thunderstorm. Clearly, something was coming, something that he thought would make her hate him, but what was it?

Maybe he intended to fire her. The moment that thought entered her head, every instinct she possessed rejected it. Granted, she wasn't always the best judge, but she just couldn't believe Simon, of all men, would kiss her within an inch of her life, touch her the way he had, if he intended to fire her.

There were men, of course, who would have no pangs of conscience about that sort of thing, but Simon wasn't one of them. He wasn't that type of man at all, and despite her epically bad judgment in the past, there was nothing in the world that would make her believe him capable of such duplicity.

He might be intending to fire Ritz. Given that the two men didn't get along, that might be a much more likely prospect, except that it seemed so unfair, and as aggravating as Simon could be sometimes, he was scrupulously fair. And even if he wanted to fire Ritz, he alone didn't have the power to do it. Ritz had an ironclad contract. Only the board could revoke that contract with a vote, and even then, only for cause. What cause could they possibly have? A few unprofitable quarters? It seemed absurd.

Simon's stringent fiscal management was all very well, and obviously necessary in the present circumstances, but Ritz *was* the Savoy. It was his imagination, his vision, that had created the most extraordinary hotel in the world. Firing him would be madness.

Throughout the night, Delia's mind spun round and round in these futile circles. It was nearly dawn when she finally fell into a deep, exhausted sleep, and she only awakened when Susan, the housemaid, shook her shoulder with the urgent whisper that if she didn't wake up soon, she could miss her train.

An hour later, she and Cassandra stood by the carriage saying their farewells as footmen loaded her luggage onto the boot.

"I am so grateful, Lady Stratham," Cassandra said for the second time in as many minutes. "I really couldn't have done it without you."

"Nonsense. My contributions were quite minor. Never sell yourself short, my dear," Delia added as Cassie started to protest. "Maidenly modesty is all very well, but be aware enough of your talents to have some self-confidence. You were an excellent hostess last night, and that's what made the party go. Whenever your confidence starts to flag in the future, remember that."

"I'll try, but I still shudder to think how things could have gone— collapsing overcooked soufflés, or poor Lord Nasby being carried out on a stretcher with his gouty foot all wrapped up. So I can't thank you enough."

"The luggage is loaded, my lady," the footman said, coming around to open the carriage door for her and roll out the steps.

"Thank you, Thomas," Delia called over her shoulder, then reached out to give Cassandra's shoulder an affectionate pat. "I shall see you in London when the season starts."

"If Simon lets me come," Cassie replied as Delia stepped into the carriage and settled herself on the tuck-and-roll leather seat. "He hasn't agreed to allow it, you know."

"He will once he is assured by me of how well you'll do. I shall be giving him a full report of last night's triumph, I promise you."

But keeping that promise, Delia found upon her return, wasn't going to be easy, for Simon proved as elusive as the wind. Ross could give her no clue as to his whereabouts, other than to say he was away. And when she tried to probe for more information, the secretary mumbled something about an errand he simply had to run before he went beetling off.

Monsieur Echenard, who had only just returned from his holiday in the south of France, assured Delia that he knew nothing of Lord Calderon, his whereabouts, or his schedule. And Ritz, when she asked him where his fellow manager might be, flew into a rage and suggested she stop sucking up to Calderon and tend to her own job.

Delia, though a bit stung by the implication that she wasn't paying attention to her duties, tactfully retreated and didn't pursue the matter any further, but during the next twenty-four hours, Simon's ominous words continued to echo in her head, causing her apprehension to deepen.

She got even less sleep that night than she had the night before, and by Sunday evening, she was exhausted. She wished she could just fall into bed, but unfortunately, she had already made plans that evening to attend a dinner party at the home of Lord and Lady Malvers.

Returning to the Savoy afterward and hoping for a good night's sleep, she ordered a hot-water bottle and a cup of warm milk and retired to her room, but she'd barely gotten settled beneath the sheets with the water bottle at her feet before a careless remark from her maid sent Delia's plans skidding sideways.

"You were wondering this morning where Lord Calderon's been, my lady? Well, I think I know."

The girl's expression contained such a degree of suppressed excitement that Delia was surprised. "Really? Do tell."

"His valet was in the laundry not an hour ago," she said, offering Delia the cup of warm milk. "And Lizzie heard him say something about a house in . . ." She paused, leaning closer in a confidential manner, and whispered, "St. John's Wood."

"St. John's Wood?" Delia blinked, even more surprised. "What was he doing all the way up there?"

"Talk is that his lordship's got a mistress there and he stayed the night with her."

"What?" A pang of raw, outraged feminine jealousy radiated through her, and Simon's last words at Ivywild once again whispered insidiously into her ear.

Don't hate me, Delia.

Delia recovered her poise with an effort and worked to scuttle such unfounded gossip. "Nonsense. It's not," she added firmly, "the least bit like him."

"Well, I wouldn't have thought so, either, my lady. He's never chatted up any of the maids. Never flirts with us or nothing. He's ever so polite, always, just like a proper gentleman. Never loses his temper. And he's a fair man; no one can deny that. Though I don't much like the new way of having to keep count of every single thing I do every minute so Mrs. Bates can write charge tickets for it, and so I told her—"

"What makes anyone think Calderon's got a mistress just because he stayed the night in St. John's Wood?" Delia cut in, returning to the vital point, but even as she asked the question, she knew the answer. St. John's Wood, though quite posh and respectable on the surface, was well-known as the place where rich men bought villas in which to keep their mistresses.

The little maid colored up. "Oh, well," she mumbled, embarrassed, as if suddenly remembering she was talking to a proper lady, "it's only talk. He might have been there for some other reason altogether, mightn't he?"

The maid's tone was wholly unconvincing, telling Delia she didn't believe her own words. And when Delia thought back to what Simon had said to her in the library, she realized in dismay that the gossip might well be true.

When it's over…

Those words, she realized with a pang, made more sense now.

Don't hate me.

"Will that be all, my lady?"

Delia came out of these agonizing contemplations with a start. "Yes, thank you, Molly. You may go."

The maid departed, and the moment she was gone, Delia set aside the milk and got out of bed, her hopes for rest forgotten. After hearing this sort of news, what woman in the world could fall asleep?

A *mistress*, she thought, and began to pace. She'd never, she appreciated with chagrin, thought of such a thing. Perhaps she ought to have done, and yet, it seemed curiously out of character. Not the part about having a mistress—she knew quite well by now that he was passionate enough under his starchy surface to have half a dozen mistresses. But to toy with her at the same time? Try as she might, she just couldn't imagine Simon doing such a thing. On the other hand…

Delia turned at the wall and started back across her bedroom, nibbling absentmindedly on her thumbnail, her thoughts racing. On the other hand, did a woman ever really know the truth about men? Given her history, she certainly didn't.

The real question, however, was why it even mattered. Why should she care if he had a mistress? It wasn't as if that episode in the library was her first sexual experience. She knew her way around, knew that such an event, even if deliciously pleasurable, didn't really mean much. There was no deflowering of an innocent virgin, no possibility of pregnancy, no consequences. Hell, even if someone had caught them, it would have been a bit embarrassing, but hardly a scandal. She and Simon were both mature adults, capable of a quick romp in a library without any long-lasting repercussions. So why should she care if he had a mistress?

But she did care. Cared like hell. She wanted to find that woman and rip her throat out. She wanted to find Simon and slap his face. And as she realized that, Delia also made another astonishing discovery. She cared because she was falling in love with him.

She stopped pacing, tilting back her head with a groan of dismay. Love was something she'd really hoped never to feel again. She was horrible at it. She didn't want it. Things always got messy, complicated, and painful, leaving one bruised, battered, and thoroughly disillusioned—a consequence that seemed highly likely in this case, since she could not see Simon ever falling in love with her. Hell, half the time, he didn't even like her. And yet...

She thought back to those moments in the library at Ivywild in agonized uncertainty. Could he really have held her, kissed her, caressed her in that scorching-hot way when he had some beautiful courtesan available to him anytime he wanted her?

Men did. Armand had taught her that.

But Simon was not Armand. Nothing like. Besides, his words to her only made sense if he'd had a mistress and had decided to break with the woman because of Delia.

If that was true, she thought with a sudden flare of outrage, why had he stayed away last night? It didn't take that long to break off an entanglement with a courtesan.

But then, mistresses could be very artful. Had the woman persuaded him to enjoy one last fling in the hope he would change his mind and keep her? Had she succeeded?

Delia decided she was damn well going to find out.

She strode over to the armoire, opened it, and studied the contents for several moments, considering. Then she pulled out a dressing robe of gold, tangerine, and purple silk. She slipped the garment on over her cream-colored chiffon nightdress as she crossed the room to her dressing table. There, she unraveled the braid of her hair, dabbed on a bit of perfume, and pinched a bit of color into her pale cheeks. After surveying her reflection for a moment, she gave a satisfied nod, slid her room key into the pocket of her robe, and left her suite.

Tonight, she was going to end this unbearable suspense once and for all. She'd ask her questions, and depending on his answers, she was either going to throw him down onto the bed and shamelessly have her way with him at last, or she was going to tear his philandering male heart into pieces, grind it into dust, and drive him away for good.

She could only hope that his fate was the former and not the latter, and as she padded down the darkened empty corridor toward Simon's room, she crossed her fingers that her usual tendency to fall for a cad proved to be wrong this time around.

Simon liked to think that in the six years since he'd left the army, he'd become a pretty good man of business. He'd learned how to size up a situation, weigh his options, decide a course of action, and negotiate a satisfactory outcome. Today, he'd had to do all of those things, but how successfully he'd done them, he didn't know.

Tucking his hands behind his head, he stared at the ceiling of his darkened room, reflecting on the frantic events of the past thirty-six hours.

Things had started out splendidly. The final report from the solicitors revealed that Ritz, Echenard, Escoffier, and Agostini had committed even more abuses than the ones Helen had already told him about, but in that report there had not been a single shred of evidence against Delia. Not one bottle of wine taken by her left unpaid, not one piece of clothing laundered without a charge ticket, and not a single admission from Savoy's suppliers that she'd received any gifts. Wonderful news, and he'd arrived at the Savoy Theatre relieved and in good spirits.

And then, he'd seen Helen's face, merciless and implacable, and from that moment on, everything had gone completely off the rails.

She'd wasted no time on polite greetings. "Did Lady Stratham enjoy her visit to Ivywild?" she'd asked in a voice as cold and hard as ice, and he'd known that at least one vote in the board meeting was not going to go Delia's way. No lack of evidence or words from him were going to change Helen's opinion or her vote. He knew her well enough to know that. He'd tried anyway, to no avail.

But fortunately, Helen was not the only one who had a vote, and he'd spent his evening and all day today calling on other members of the board to discuss the situation.

Helen, he soon discovered, had been busy during his absence in the country, plying the other board members with implications that Lady Stratham's innocence was still in doubt, her loyalty to Ritz absolute, and her ability to be trusted nonexistent. He'd combated those concerns, emphasizing to the other members of the board the lack of evidence against her. He'd also shamelessly used her gender and her position as a countess to bolster the idea that she was wholly ignorant of what Ritz had been doing. Women, after all, he'd said with the dismissive, superior amusement many men were wont to use when discussing the fairer sex, knew little of finance and were easily deceived by a man of Ritz's smarmy charm. It was laughable, of course, for no one who knew Delia could believe such nonsense, but it was the only play he'd been able to think of, and he could only hope that he'd managed to become adept enough at dodging the truth to pull it off.

And other women, he'd added, feeling no pangs of conscience about throwing Helen under the trolley after she'd gone behind his back, were known to be jealous of other women's beauty and charm, and could be vindictive.

He arrived back at the Savoy just before midnight Sunday night, bone tired and with no idea if his efforts would bear fruit. He'd fought the good fight, but he knew that with Helen on the warpath, Delia could very well lose her job anyway.

Fortunately, he had a new post in mind for her—if she'd give him the chance to go down on one knee and propose it. Given her quick temper, he knew she might not.

Ritz, her dear friend and the mentor she revered, would be fired, disgraced, and humiliated. Like all the other men she had trusted in her life, Ritz would fall off his pedestal and all her illusions about him would be shattered. In addition, she would know the part Simon had played in bringing about the other man's downfall, and she'd probably lay a good bit of the blame at his door. And she'd undoubtedly subject him to a thorough tongue-lashing as well.

He might mitigate the damage to his own image in her eyes by voting in Ritz's favor, but he could not do it. He could not vote against his conscience, not even for Delia. The man was guilty and the evidence undeniable, and even though it would be hard for her, she would eventually have to accept the truth that the mentor she revered so much was crooked as a fishhook. She might also face the loss of her own job and blame Simon for that, too.

Regardless, he knew his own course was set. After it was all over, he intended to be by her side. And there he would remain, whether she wanted him or not, because that was the only way he could prove to her that there was one man in her life who would never let her down, and that man was him.

She'd need that sort of reassurance if she was ever going to agree to marry him. And marriage it had to be, for he was not the sort of man who could ever accept less. Her hints about a torrid affair were all very well, but free love had never appealed to him and never would. He was old-fashioned that way. And she wanted children; she must, or her miscarriage would never have grieved her so deeply that suicide had seemed a viable alternative.

He stared into the darkness, daring for the first time to imagine what married life with Delia would be like. Glorious, if those quixotic

258 LAURA LEE GUHRKE

moments in his library were any indication. Tumultuous, no doubt, with fights and makeups, and probably many, many times when he'd act like an imbecile. Ah, well.

One thing he did know, and it made him smile: life with Delia would never, ever be dull.

By this point, he'd almost decided permanent bachelorhood was his destiny, for in his entire thirty-six years, he'd never met a woman he could see sharing a lifetime with. But then, he'd never been in love before. Lust, of course. Infatuation, certainly. But love? Never.

Until now.

He honestly had no idea if Delia felt about him as he did about her. He'd liked to have been able to say with certainty that those hot moments in the library proved her feelings and that they would remain unshaken, despite the events that would soon change her world, but he knew quite well that with Delia, nothing was certain. That was, he acknowledged ruefully, part of her charm.

But it could very well be that she did not feel as he did. She might never forgive him for keeping the truth from her. What then?

Before he could even begin to contemplate that wrenching possibility, a soft knock sounded at his door.

Simon frowned, lifting his head. What the devil?

Perhaps he'd imagined it, he thought, but then, the knock came again, a bit louder this time, and he got out of bed. He switched on the nearest electric lamp, then retrieved his dressing robe from the armoire. He slipped it on and tied the sash as he crossed the room, hoping to hell Cassandra hadn't taken it into her head to come for another unannounced visit or that Ritz hadn't somehow learned of his looming comeuppance and had come to his room to shoot Simon with a pistol.

Both of those possibilities seemed extremely unlikely. It must be, he decided as he reached for the doorknob, a member of the staff. Some hotel emergency, no doubt.

He opened the door to find that his third guess had been right, but the member of staff wasn't Ricardo, or Agostini, or even his own secretary. Instead, much to his astonishment, he found Delia standing in the corridor.

She was scandalously clad in a filmy nightgown with some sort of silk kimono over it, and at once, hope leapt in his chest and desire flared in his body. Sadly, however, there was a frown on her face that made it unlikely she was there to fling herself into his arms and make mad, passionate love to him. Could she know already? he thought wildly. Could Helen, perhaps, have told her? But why would Helen—

"Just tell me one thing," she said, cutting off the speculations rattling through his head, her voice low, brusque, and unmistakably urgent. "Do you or do you not have a mistress?"

"What?" The question was so unexpected and so ludicrous, he couldn't help a laugh of disbelief.

"You were away last night," she went on, "and the rumor going around the hotel is that you've been with your mistress at a house in St. John's Wood."

He rubbed his eyes, still not quite able to believe she was standing here and baffled by this nonsensical conversation. "Delia, what are you doing here? It must be after one o'clock in the morning."

"Is it true? If it is true…" She paused, her chin lifting proudly even as her cheeks flushed a delicate, embarrassed pink. "I think I have the right to know."

Simon didn't know quite what to say. He knew all about St. John's Wood, of course; most men with money did. But why Delia was coming to him at this hour to ask him about some silly rumor defeated him utterly. But then, he noted her lower lip caught worriedly between her teeth and the hint of what might be jealousy in the frown drawing her dark brows together, and he began to understand.

"People think I've been staying with my mistress in St. John's Wood?" he asked, striving to sound nonchalant even as a powerful wave of exultation rose within him.

"And that you keep her in a house there," Delia went on. "Do you deny it?"

Her jealousy was unmistakable now, and it took all the sang-froid he possessed not to smile. "I do deny it," he said gravely, rather enjoying that he wasn't the one assuming things for once. "I was not in St. John's Wood. I was in Hanover Terrace. Granted, that's right below St. John's Wood, but not actually in it. And it wasn't a house. It was a hotel."

"Oh." She looked away, and her chin quivered. "I see."

"Why do you ask?" he said, watching her, wanting so badly to haul her into his arms and kiss her. "Are you jealous?"

She sniffed and looked at him again, donning an expression of extreme indifference that didn't fool him for a second, sending his exultation rising higher. "Not in the least."

"No?" he asked, unable to stop the grin that spread across his face. "Then why did you come to ask me this in the middle of the night? Why…"

He paused, his voice going dry and his grin fading away as his gaze slid down to her bare toes peeking out from beneath the frothy hem of her nightdress. It was a sight he knew he might not see again for quite some time, if ever. But at least he now knew that she cared about him. That was a start. "If you're not jealous, why are you here, dressed like that?"

She made a scoffing sound, all her feminine pride plain to see. "You think I came because I want to show you how much more alluring I am than some courtesan in St. John's Wood? You're dreaming."

One kiss, he thought. It wouldn't be fair to take it to full completion, at least not for him, not until after she knew the truth. But a kiss, he told himself, was different; they'd already crossed that bridge and then some.

"Perhaps." He lifted his hands to cup her face. "But if I am dreaming, for God's sake, don't wake me up yet."

With that, he bent his head and kissed her.

16

Her lips were as warm and soft as they'd been a few days ago, but hotter, somehow, and sweeter. So, so sweet. Her lips parted beneath his, her tongue touched his, and he groaned into her mouth, sliding his arms around her, tightening his hold until her body was pressed fully against his own.

The desire he'd been trying so desperately to curb, desire he'd tried to keep at bay by staying away last night, was rushing through him now, through every cell and nerve of his body. His heart was pounding so hard in his chest that it sounded like a trip-hammer.

But past all that, he heard a door open in the distance—the doors of the lift, he realized vaguely—and then voices, echoing softly around the corner and along the corridor where they stood, reminding him that he had to stop now, while he still could.

He tore his mouth from hers. "You've got to go," he muttered, grasping for sanity. "We can't stand here making love in the corridor."

Instead of answering, she reached around him with one hand and opened the door, while her other hand flattened against his chest. "Good thing we have a room then, isn't it?" she whispered, pushing him to urge him backward.

He shook his head vehemently and didn't move. "Not now. Not yet."

"So you do have a mistress, then?" She rose on her toes and kissed him, sending his resolve tilting dangerously sideways.

"What? No." He grabbed her arms. "Delia, we can't do this. It wouldn't be right. I'd be taking advantage of you. You don't know—"

"Really, Simon," she interrupted, a soft, grumbling sigh as she kissed his chin, "all these rejections are beginning to hurt my pride."

This reminder that he'd been blowing hot and cold with her from the beginning added a hint of guilt to the quixotic mix of his emotions, but before he could reply or pull away, she spoke again. "Your sense of morality is quite honorable and one of your most endearing qualities, but you really needn't worry." She paused, her arms tightening around his neck as she kissed him again. "I'll still respect you in the morning."

The voices around the corner grew louder, coming closer, and this time, when she steered him backward, he gave ground, stepping backward into the room before anyone could see them. Delia followed him, closing the door behind them, and as it clicked into place, he cursed himself for thinking kissing her once and saying goodnight would ever work. Where Delia was concerned, his oh-so-laudable morality, along with his restraint and good sense, went straight out the window.

Valiantly, he tried again. "Delia, listen to me. We can't do this."

She sank back on her heels with a sigh. "Why not?"

"Because I'm in love with you, that's why. And if—"

"What?" She stared at him as if he'd just grown a second head. "You are?"

"Yes. You see—" He broke off, watching as a radiant smile lit her face, and he forgot completely what he'd been about to say next.

"How marvelous," she said, her hands sliding up his chest, her arms winding round his neck.

"Is it?" His voice was strangled, desperate, and his arousal was growing impossible to contain. "It doesn't feel marvelous to me. It's been hell, if you want to know the truth."

"Goodness, as bad as that?"

"And if I take advantage of you this way now, it'll be worse, because you'll never fall in love with me."

"Oh, well, it's too late to worry about that," she said as she rose on her toes and began pressing kisses to his lips, his chin, his neck. "That particular deed's already done, I'm afraid."

"What?" He pulled back, staring at her askance, not sure if he could believe his own ears.

She nodded, laughing. "I'm in love with you, too. I realized it when I found out about your mistress."

Joy and jubilation rose up inside him like fireworks, and as torturous as all this was, he knew he'd never be happier than he was at this moment. "I don't have a mistress. That's a groundless rumor, and I have no idea how it got round, but—"

He broke off, realizing he was getting into the weeds and away from the vital point. "You mean it?" he asked and grabbed her arms. "Really?"

"Well, of course." She kissed him. "You don't think I'd risk yet another rejection, fling myself at you like this, and give a damn about your mistress if I weren't madly in love with you, do you?"

"Well, frankly, Delia," he muttered, "when it comes to you, I never know what to think. You seem to adore throwing me off my trolley."

"It has become one of my greatest delights, I confess. Speaking of delights," she added, leaning closer, her hips pressing his hard arousal, "are we going to make love?" She paused, her hips moving against his in a slow, tormenting tease. "Or am I going to have to beg?"

He groaned, a groan of agonized pleasure that made her smile, the little devil, and with that, all his willpower slipped irretrievably away.

He never could manage to resist her. "I suspect I'll be the one begging before it's all over," he muttered. "You are such a tease."

"Tease?" she cried, having the nerve to sound indignant. "What an abominable thing to say."

Even as she said it, she was untying the sash of her robe, and then she pulled the edges apart just enough for him to see the shadowy outline of one luscious breast beneath her chiffon nightdress, and she laughed again.

"I rest my case," he said, wrapped an arm around her waist, pulled her close, and stopped her merriment with a long, hard, searing kiss. Only when she tore her lips from his with a shuddering gasp did he relent. Pulling back, he untied the sash of her robe. "Now, I think I've earned the right to look my fill."

He slid the garment off her shoulders, revealing filmy layers of cream-colored chiffon and the voluptuous outline of her silhouette beneath. Unfortunately, the nightgown also had a long, tedious row of very tiny buttons.

He was fully, flagrantly aroused, and he was tempted to just tear the delicate chiffon fabric apart, but he pushed aside this base masculine desire at once.

Given what he knew that she did not, making love with her now was morally questionable—at best. He ought to wait, as he'd planned, but God help him, he just didn't have the strength. Still, he wasn't about to compound his sin by rushing the moment and taking her in a grasping rush. It might assuage his present agony, but it would leave her profoundly unsatisfied, and that was not a price he was willing to pay.

So he took a deep, steadying breath and lifted his hands to the base of her throat, his fingers undoing the first button under her chin.

"Simon?"

His hands stilled and he looked up to find her smiling.

"You don't need to unfasten any buttons," she told him. "There are ribbon ties in the back."

"Thank God," he said with such heartfelt relief that she laughed.

"I was tempted to let you undo them all," she told him and laughed again. "But I decided that would take too long."

"Did you now?" His resolve renewed, he turned her around. "Then I shall definitely be taking my time."

She groaned, and it was his turn to laugh.

He suited the action to the word, beginning with her hair. Untying the ribbon, he unraveled the braid, and as he did, he caught the scent of her perfume in the raven-black locks. As always, the erotic fragrance sent his arousal flaring higher. Grasping a handful of the waist-length strands in his fist, he lifted them, inhaling deeply of the luscious scent before he wrapped them around his fist and tilted her head to the side.

He pressed kisses along the side of her throat as he lifted his free hand to her breast. He cupped it in his palm, relishing the full, round shape, his body supporting her weight as she leaned back against him with a soft moan.

"Ah, that's what I like to hear," he murmured, toying with her nipple through the thin silk, rolling it between his thumb and forefinger until her breath was quick and shallow and her body was moving agitatedly in his embrace.

Only then did he relent, and only long enough to turn them both around so that her abdomen was pressed against the footboard of the bed. Then he let her go, shoved the long tresses of her hair over her shoulder, and untied the bow at the back of her neck.

He pulled the edges of her nightgown apart and continued untying ribbons as he sank to his knees behind her, kissing his way along her spine until he reached the small of her back. Then he pulled the nightgown down her arms, over her tummy and hips, where it fell in a pool of filmy silk at her ankles, exposing her entire backside to his gaze—her slim, straight back, the deep curve of her waist, her shapely bum.

He pressed one last kiss to the dent in the small of her back; then, praying for fortitude, he grasped her hips and turned her around.

She was stunning. No other word for it. Her pale skin, luminous in the lamplight, her hair falling in black waves around her shoulders. Her breasts, round and full, with their erect nipples as rosy and tempting as ripe berries. His throat went dry, and he felt a sudden, uncharacteristic pang of uncertainty. He was no virgin, of course, but having had three husbands, her sexual experience far outweighed his, and he could only hope he could give her the pleasure she deserved.

"Simon? Is something wrong?"

He looked up, laughing a little. "I'm feeling a bit out of my depth, Delia, to be honest. You see, I've only been with two women in my life."

"Two?"

"The first," he hurried on, "I was eighteen, and on leave in the army, so it was a prostitute in Cape Town. The whole thing was a rushed, sweaty, rather disappointing encounter."

"The first time usually is," she assured him. "Mine was."

"It was?"

"Oh, yes. It was quick, and painful, and I was quite disillusioned. Things got a little better, but not much. Cocaine, I can only assume, was what made him so unpredictable and moody. And when the mood struck Roger to visit my room, things were always far too rushed. Who was the second woman?"

"As I said, I was in the army. Most of the time, I was at some fort in the middle of nowhere, receiving dismally low pay, so I couldn't keep a mistress, and after my first disillusioning experience, prostitutes held no appeal for me. After I left the army, I acquired a mistress, which was better, but we were never love's young dream. I didn't much care for the shallowness of that sort of arrangement. But this—" He paused, drawing a profound, shaky breath. "This is altogether different. I love you, Delia. I want tonight to be right for you."

She stared down at him, taking in every detail of his countenance. His hair—burnished gold in the lamplight. His thick brown lashes—gilded at the tips. His face so stunningly handsome—filled with a combination of love and desire.

Looking down at him, his words echoing in her ears, she felt things she'd never felt in her life before. This, she thought, was love—not the calf love she'd felt as a girl infatuated with a moody poet; not the frantic, snatching love she'd felt while rebounding from grief; and not the warm, bland affection she'd felt for an older man. No, this was something new and altogether different. Because Simon was a man she could rely on, a man she knew she could absolutely trust, and that knowledge humbled her and awed her and made her—just a little—afraid. If she ever lost him—

She cut off that unbearable possibility before it could take hold. "It will be totally right, Simon," she told him. "Just do what you feel."

He leaned forward, wrapping an arm around her hips, cupping one of her breasts in his free hand, his thumb caressing her nipple. He played with her breasts, shaping them, toying with them. He suckled them, softly at first, and then harder, wringing sensation from her until she was moaning low in her throat and her hands were raking through his hair.

His arm was tight around her hips, anchoring her in place as his hand left her breast, and she shivered as his fingertips danced lightly over her ribs and stomach. As he moved his hand lower and lower, she could feel her tension rising higher and higher, but when he reached the apex of her thighs, he pulled back and she gave a moan of protest, arching her hips toward his hand in a desperate plea for more.

But he didn't give it. Instead, his arm moved up around her waist, and he leaned his weight into her, settling the curve of her hip into the dent of his shoulder as he slid the tip of his finger into the crease of her sex. He touched her, his fingertip moving up and down in a light caress filled with promise.

She was close to climax, she knew, but it seemed to hover tantalizingly out of reach. She could get there, if only she could move. She tried again to wriggle her hips, more insistently this time, but his superior weight kept her still, and all she could do was stand there, helpless to move as he mercilessly lashed her with this teasing caress.

Suspended here, hovering on the edge of climax, was an unbearable torture. She wanted to tell him that, but she couldn't seem to catch her breath, and the only sound she could make was a cry of frustration and need.

He seemed to understand what she was asking for, but instead of complying, he only teased her more. "Is there something you want?" he murmured. "Tell me."

"More," she managed, the only word she could say, but he merely laughed.

"Bastard," she panted.

"Delia, Delia," he chided, his breath warm against her dampness, making her shiver. "What an unladylike thing to say."

"Damn it, Simon," she ground out. "Stop torturing me!"

He laughed again. "Open your legs," he ordered, easing back enough for her to comply.

She did it gladly, eagerly, expecting him to stand up and take her straightaway, but he didn't. Instead, he nuzzled her intimate feminine place. He kissed her there, sending keen, sharp sensation through every cell and nerve ending in her body.

He stroked the crease of her sex with his tongue as his hand caressed her stomach. Free at last, she moved against the footboard, and her panting breaths mingled with the faint squeak of the bed-frame as her hips worked against his mouth. His tongue lashed her with these carnal kisses until she was trembling all over and every breath she exhaled was a sob.

She came at last, a powerful wave of pleasure that flooded every part of her body with glorious sensation. Even before it could ebb, it came again, then again, and yet again, over and over, each wave more powerful than the last, until she finally collapsed.

His arm tightened to keep her upright, and she looked down, panting and wordless, as he pressed a last, tender kiss to her stomach. When he lifted his head, she could only stare at him in amazement, still rocked by the most powerful series of orgasms she'd ever experienced.

A puzzled frown creased his brow as he looked up at her. "Delia, are you all right?"

"Heavens," she gasped. "For a man who's only been with two women, you learned a lot."

He laughed, his breath blowing warm air against her stomach.

"I'm a quick study."

He pressed one last kiss to her navel and moved to rise. As he stood up, she saw the outline of his penis against the aubergine velvet of his dressing robe, and she realized just how much of an asset her own prior experience could be. Kicking her tangled nightgown sideways from beneath her feet, she stepped out from between him and the bed, grasped his arm, and came around, turning them both until their positions were reversed. "Two," she said as she pushed him gently back a step, "can play this game, my love."

He frowned a little as he hit the footboard behind him. "I sense trouble ahead."

"Oh, you have no idea, you tease."

With a quick tug, she pulled the sash of his robe, then she sank to her knees, and before he had the chance to realize just what she was doing, his penis, hot, engorged, and rock hard, was in her hand, and her mouth was opening around the tip.

His groan, an agonized rumble from deep in his chest, filled her with joy. She took him as far into her mouth as she could, pulled back, then came forward again. She moved her tongue in a teasing swirl around the tip, relishing that she could now do to him what he had done to her; but her delight, sadly, was far too short-lived.

"Enough, Delia," he ground out, his hand entangling in her hair, pulling her head back. "That's enough."

His hand left her hair and he pulled her to her feet. "This night isn't going to end like that, with you on your knees."

"No?"

"No." He grabbed her hand and pulled her around the side of the bed, then he eased her down onto the bed and pulled off his robe.

Delia fell back with a sigh, drinking in the sight of him with unabashed admiration. His body was magnificent. No other word for it—wide shoulders tapering to powerful arms, a lean torso of rippled abdominal muscles and narrow hips. And his desire for her on full display.

"My God," she breathed, "you're splendid."

He laughed. "You're a bit of all right yourself, Countess."

"Only a bit?" she echoed, pretending indignance, but the pretense ended as he came over her, bracing his weight on his arms, making the mattress dip, as he leaned down and kissed her.

"More than a bit. Move over."

She complied, turning to stretch out on the bed, settling back against the pillows as he followed, easing his body on top of hers.

"Come," she said, and spread her legs apart. "Come inside me now."

"Your wish is my command," he said and entered her.

The feel of him inside her was glorious, but then he went still, his weight on his elbows, nuzzling her neck, and she stirred beneath him. Despite the powerful orgasms of a few moments ago, arousal was still pulsing through her, and his breathing, hard and labored, told her he felt the same, but he still didn't move. "Simon, c'mon," she urged, pushing her hips upward, desperate for completion. "Do it."

He kissed her neck, her throat, her mouth. "Do what?" he asked.

"Simon, please."

"Why, Delia," he murmured, nibbling her lower lip as his arms slid beneath her shoulder blades, "are you begging?"

"Yes, you impossible man," she cried, unashamed, laughing. "Yes. Please. Do it now. Please, please."

Her plea ended in a groan of relief and satisfaction as he began to move, and her arousal rose higher, her desperation growing more urgent, more frantic, with each powerful thrust of his hips.

She met him thrust for thrust, relished each groan she tore from his lips, until at last, she climaxed again, her muscles clenching hard around his cock. He followed her, and she gloried even more in his climax than her own.

He thrust into her one last time and went still, his body heavy on top of hers, his face buried against her neck. She turned her head and kissed him, overcome by a tenderness she'd never felt for a man before. She lay there beneath him, caressing his broad, strong back, smiling, replete, happy.

She felt as if she'd finally come completely out of the darkness and into the light, and she was glad she had managed to endure those dark days five years ago, glad to be in love, glad to be alive. So very glad.

17

When he woke, the dim gray light of morning was peeking around the edges of the window draperies, and Delia was gone. He might have thought what had happened only a few hours ago was a dream, but the fragrance of her hair was on the pillow beside him, along with a note written on Savoy stationery.

> My darling Simon, I would have loved to watch you awaken, but since we both work for the Savoy and I came to you last night in nothing but my nightgown, I thought it best to return to my own room while there would be no staff or hotel guests to see me. I may not care much what people think, but even I am not so scandalous as to go parading about the hotel in a state of undress! Perhaps we can have luncheon together?
>
> –Delia
>
> PS—have I told you I love you madly?

He smiled a little, his happiness at her reiteration of love dimmed only by her words about the hotel, for those words were a reminder of what would be happening today and the pain it would surely cause her. Folding the note, he kissed it, inhaling the scent of her perfume one more time, then he got out of bed.

He tucked her note into his card case, then picked up his dressing robe from the floor and put it on. He stretched out one hand toward the bell, but before he could press it to summon Morgan, the valet walked in with a cart containing early tea.

"Ah," the valet said, "I was coming to wake you, my lord, as you instructed, but I see you're already awake."

"It must be eight o'clock, then?"

Morgan nodded as he poured tea for him. "Would you care for breakfast?"

He shook his head at once. "No, I've no time. I have a meeting at nine. I'll eat afterward, if I can."

As his valet shaved his face and helped him dress, Simon considered how the timing of today's events might play out.

The board was meeting at the Adelphi Terrace residence of the Cartes for the formal vote, but given the evidence, it was a foregone conclusion that Ritz, Escoffier, Echenard, Agostini, DuPont, and Mrs. Henderson would be fired. Delia's fate was much less certain.

Like DuPont, Agostini, and Mrs. Henderson, Delia was not officially part of management, and therefore had no legal employment contract with the hotel. Unlike the other three, however, there was no evidence against her. If the board voted to keep her in her present position, all well and good. But if the worst happened, if despite all his efforts of the past two days the board voted to terminate her job, he would resign in protest.

After the vote, Ritz, Escoffier, and Echenard, who did have employment contracts, would be summoned immediately to Adelphi Terrace to be given their official termination—a process that would take probably no more than fifteen minutes—then they would walk the few short blocks back to the Savoy to clean out their desks before exiting the premises for good, which gave Simon perhaps twenty minutes to break the news to Delia before all hell broke loose.

He could only hope those twenty minutes gave him enough time to explain the situation to her properly before Ritz arrived to give her lies and excuses.

Simon was shaved and dressed by half past eight. Stopping by his office, he called for Delia's maid. While waiting for the girl, he dashed off a note to Delia requesting breakfast rather than lunch, stressing that he had something vitally important to discuss with her as soon as possible, and suggesting a time of ten o'clock in the restaurant. When Molly arrived, he instructed her to awaken Lady Stratham at half past nine and give her the note, stressing that it was urgent; then he departed the hotel.

He arrived at the Carte residence fifteen minutes early, but being a familiar acquaintance at Adelphi Terrace, he knew neither Richard nor Helen would be offended. When he entered their drawing room, however, he saw that he was not the only one to arrive early. In fact, as he glanced around, he realized he was the last board member to arrive. And when he looked at Helen, he realized that she'd planned things just that way.

The vote, therefore, when it came, was no surprise. What did come as a shock to him was the sadness that mingled with his anger as he looked from Helen to Richard and back again. His vote came last, and he was glad of it, for it gave him the blessed opportunity not only to be the one dissenting voice, but also to have the last word.

"I cannot associate myself with those who would punish the innocent along with the guilty," he said. "I resign my position and relinquish my stock in the Savoy. My attorneys will provide written confirmation of it by the end of the week. As for all of you..."

He paused, glancing around the room, registering only a few expressions in the sea of faces—Richard, staring listlessly back at him...the smirking Lord Astonby...the disapproving Lord Melville...stoic Sir Charles...and Helen, her dark eyes unhappy rather than triumphant. "As for all of you," he said, staring straight back at her, "every single one of you can rot in hell."

He turned and walked out, but to his surprise, he was halfway down to the foyer when he heard Helen call his name from the top of the stairs.

"Simon, wait."

He turned on the landing and kept going, but she caught up with him as the footman was handing him his coat and hat.

"Simon, please," she said, putting a hand on his arm. "Wait one moment. There's something I need to tell you before you go."

Voices were heard at the top of the stairs, indicating that the other members were coming down to depart, and she pulled him into the nearby study. "First," she said as she shut the door behind them, "I want you to know I bear you no ill will. And—"

His sound of disdain interrupted her. "That's big of you," he ground out.

"And," she continued as if he hadn't spoken, "I hope that one day you will feel the same."

"I won't."

She sighed, having the gall to look unhappy. "I did what I felt was right."

"Right?" he echoed, giving a humorless laugh. "There is nothing right about what you did. Condemning an innocent woman, and to some of the people in her very own circle? Firing her when she's done nothing wrong because of your own jealousy and spite—"

"That's not why I did it!" she cried. "I did it for the good of the hotel. And besides," she added, looking away as he made a scoffing sound of utter contempt, "it's not as if I were alone in my opinion. Everyone but you agreed with me that she has to go."

"Persuaded by you, no doubt."

She didn't deny it. "Lady Stratham may or may not be innocent of any wrongdoing herself," she said, meeting his gaze again, "but either way, she simply cannot be trusted. Ritz," she added as he opened his mouth to reply, "will open a London hotel one day, and we cannot risk that she remains at the Savoy, when she could be his spy within the gates. Everyone here today understood that. Everyone except you."

"Which is why you went behind my back."

"Given your obvious feelings for her, I felt you could not be trusted, either."

"Then we have nothing more to say, do we?"

He moved to depart, but her voice stopped him. "There is one other thing."

"Yes?"

"I am obliged to remind you of the confidentiality agreement you signed upon becoming a member of the Savoy board."

"Of course." He gave a humorless laugh, somehow not surprised that she would have the temerity to bring that up now. Helen was first, last, and always a hardheaded woman of business. "So like you to remind me."

"You are legally pledged to silence regarding all board activities," she went on doggedly. "Your resignation does not change that."

"I fully understand the contracts I signed, Helen. There is no need to remind me of them. And since trust has now been broken on both sides, I suggest Richard make me an offer to buy my shares in the Bainbridge, for I see no way that a partnership between us can remain viable. Goodbye, Helen."

He jerked open the door and left the study, stalking by the other gentlemen putting on their coats and exiting the house without a backward glance.

The spring air was crisp and cold, but as he walked back to the Savoy, it did nothing to cool his blood. And when he heard the voice of the odious Lord Astonby behind him, his temper once again began ratcheting upward.

"Hard lines, Calderon."

Simon glanced over his shoulder to find the other man behind him, along with Lord Melville. Reminding himself it was pointless to engage in a quarrel now, he merely shrugged and kept walking.

"We would have liked to vote with you, old chap," Astonby said, raising his voice to be sure his words carried to Simon's ear over the clatter of London traffic. "Fellow peer and all that. But we just couldn't see our way clear."

"No woman," Melville added, "should work for a living. Particularly a lady. Highly inappropriate."

Simon could have pointed out that down below the ivory tower these two lived in, plenty of women worked, some because they had to, and some because they found it enjoyable. But the other two were clearly itching for a quarrel, and he had far more important things to do than accommodate them. He set his jaw and kept walking.

"Still," Astonby continued, "Lady Stratham will appreciate your efforts on her behalf. It seems she has a knight in shining armor. But, really, Calderon, is she worth it?"

"Might be," Melville put in. "Lady Stratham's a bit long in the tooth at thirty-three, but still a beautiful woman."

"Dangerous, though," Astonby added. "Deadly, in fact, if her poor husbands are anything to go by."

Goaded beyond bearing, Simon decided he could spare a minute to put this spoiled brat in his place. He stopped and turned around, causing the other two to halt as well. "Is there a point to all this commentary?" he asked.

"Concern," Astonby replied, belying that answer with a grin. "Are you sure you know what you're doing?"

Simon smiled back at him. "More than you do, I imagine."

This little jab was ignored. "You're a brave man, Calderon," the earl told him, snickering like a schoolboy. "I'll give you that."

"I'm not sure what has inspired this compliment," Simon replied, though he knew precisely. "But whatever it is, it seems to amuse you. Care to let me in on the joke?"

"Don't be coy. Plain as day you want to be husband number four. Most of us suspected something like that was in the wind, of course, when we saw you in her box at the opera, but last night when you called on me, suspicion became fact. Personally, I wouldn't choose to begin my courtship of a woman by trying to salvage her employment, but to each his own. I suppose to a man barely elevated out of the gutter, a wife with a career isn't so revolutionary."

That was, he supposed, meant to be an insult. What Astonby didn't seem to realize was that he didn't give a damn what anyone thought of him. Delia, however, was a different matter entirely.

Before he could reply, however, Astonby spoke again. "After you left, I immediately went to White's and placed a bet on it. I daresay we all did."

Lord Melville nodded in assent, and though Simon found it rather galling to think his efforts on Delia's behalf had brought about no better result than a flurry of bets about his life expectancy, even that wasn't what was causing his blood to boil at this moment.

"I gave you a year and a half after the vows." Astonby clapped him on the arm as if they were old friends. "Do be careful. I'd hate to see anything happen to you."

"Right now, Astonby," he said pleasantly, "I'm not the one in danger."

2

At this unmistakable warning, the earl's grin faltered a bit, but unfortunately, he didn't take heed. "Before you walk down the aisle, old chap, might I suggest life insurance? She is the black widow, after all."

Before Simon even realized what he was doing, his fist had connected with Astonby's jaw in a painful but thoroughly satisfying thwack that wiped that loathsome grin from the earl's face and sent him to the pavement. Simon had no time to savor his victory before Lord Melville retaliated on his friend's behalf, landing a hard, smashing uppercut to Simon's jaw.

Stars exploded in his head, and the last thing he remembered was the shrill sound of a constable's whistle before everything went black.

When he woke up, he was in jail.

Rising early had never been Delia's strong suit. And having had almost no sleep the past few nights, she was in no frame of mind to be shaken awake by a maid for the second time in three days. "Oh, leave off, Molly, for heaven's sake," she mumbled, shrugging away the hand on her shoulder and burying her face in the pillow. "Go away."

"Begging your pardon, my lady, but I've been ordered to wake you at half past nine."

"Ordered by whom?" she asked, even as she began drifting back into sleep. "Whoever it is needs to die."

"It was Lord Calderon, my lady. He ordered me to wake you and give you this. It was urgent, he said."

Delia opened one eye to find the maid holding out a note, and her sleep-fogged senses began to clear. She loved Simon, she really did, but if he was going to expect the same sort of strenuous demonstrations of her affection in the future as he had enjoyed last night, he was going to have to give her time to recover.

She smiled at the thought, gave up on sleep, and pulled the note from Molly's fingers. Still smiling, she sat up and began to read. Three seconds later, however, her smile vanished, and she gave an exclamation of dismay.

"Breakfast at ten?" she cried. "And it's—what?" She looked up at the maid. "Half past nine?"

"A few minutes after, my lady. It's taken me a bit of time to wake you."

"The man's mad," Delia declared, glanced at the penned lines again, noted that the word urgent was underlined three times, and capitulated with a sigh.

"Men!" she muttered, tossing aside the note and the sheets and moving to get out of bed. "Don't they know a woman can't be ready to go anywhere in half an hour? Pull the slate-blue wool dress out of the armoire, Molly, and fetch some hot water. Quickly, now. I've got to be downstairs by ten o'clock, it seems."

By some miracle, she arrived in the restaurant breathless, a bit untidy, and only five minutes late.

Lord Calderon, she was told as she was led to a table, had not arrived yet. Euphoric, excited, and also a bit aggrieved that he'd rushed her down here only to be late himself, Delia ordered a pot of hot coffee, but she'd barely taken her first sip before a man appeared beside her table.

It was not Simon, however. Much to her surprise, it was Sir Charles Russell, the Savoy's solicitor.

"Sir Charles," she greeted. "What brings you here today?"

"I came to see you, actually." He put his hand on the chair opposite hers. "May I join you for a few moments?"

"Any other time, I'd happily allow it, but I'm expecting someone, I'm afraid."

"Yes, I know, but Lord Calderon will not be joining you this morning. He's been...detained, I understand."

Delia felt a stab of disappointment. "He said he had something important to discuss with me."

"Does he?" The solicitor reached into his breast pocket and pulled out a folded sheet of paper. "It may have something to do with this."

As the solicitor slid the folded sheet to her across the white table-cloth, Delia's disappointment shifted and deepened, transforming into the same odd sense of foreboding that had hung over her all day yesterday. "What's this?" she asked, taking the sheet.

"Your official letter of termination."

She froze in the act of unfolding the slip of paper. "What?"

"I regret to inform you, Lady Stratham, that you have been fired."

18

Better late than never might be true in most instances, but Simon doubted that trite little phrase applied in his case. Not today, anyway.

It was three o'clock in the afternoon before he was released from the local police station. Lord Astonby, the constable told him, was willing to let the matter drop, and he was free to go. He supposed he ought to be grateful for that fact, but given that Delia had surely been fired by now, he couldn't summon up much gratitude. The news, no doubt, had hit her like a ton of bricks.

He arrived at the Savoy to find things in chaos. There were journalists loitering in the lobby. The concierge was familiar to him only because the man had been the concierge at Claridge's. A glance in the restaurant showed rushed, unhappy waiters, even more unhappy customers, and a harassed-looking maître d'hôtel who'd also been brought over from Claridge's, causing Simon to wonder in grim amusement how many Savoy employees had quit or been fired today. When he walked down the corridor to his office, he found a pair of policemen by the door, and Ross and Morgan inside waiting for him, surrounded by crates, trunks, and suitcases.

"My lord," the two men said in unison as they stood up, clearly relieved by his arrival.

He glanced into the office next door as he came in, and his mood became even darker as he saw that it was empty. No papers untidily strewn across the desk, no piles of letters waiting to be opened, and no Delia.

"Gentlemen," he greeted, returning his attention to the other two men as he set his dispatch case beside the packed boxes on top of his desk. "Things seemed to have changed a bit since I left this morning."

The two other men murmured a hearty assent to that assessment of the situation.

"It's clear we need a new place to live. The question is where."

"Ivywild, my lord?" Ross suggested.

"Too far. I need to remain in London for now."

"I could reserve us rooms at another hotel."

He made a face. "I'm rather soured on living in hotels, to be honest. Find a house to lease here in town. It shouldn't be too difficult, since it's only March. In the meantime, put most of these things into storage and reserve us rooms at the Clarendon. Morgan, you'll help him."

"Of course, my lord."

"Good. Now," he said with a sigh, "I need to find Lady Stratham. I don't suppose she's still in the hotel?"

"I doubt it, my lord," Ross replied. "I heard that Ritz has gone to the Charing Cross Hotel. Escoffier and Echenard, too. But I don't know about Lady Stratham."

Morgan gave a cough. "Begging your pardon, my lord, but I saw Molly, the maid who's been looking after the countess, earlier. She was in the lobby with her ladyship, helping sort the piles of luggage for the bellboys. The girl may know where the countess has gone."

Molly, he soon discovered, did know Lady Stratham's whereabouts, for she'd helped the Savoy footmen load the luggage into a cab, and she'd overheard the countess tell the driver to take her to the Bristol.

Twenty minutes later, he was at the Bristol, giving his card to the concierge, and asking if Lady Stratham would be willing to see him. He had no idea what he'd do if she refused, but to his relief, the concierge returned with her consent.

That relief, however, evaporated the moment the door opened and he saw her face.

"You fired me," she said. Her voice was as flat and cold as a frozen lake, her blue eyes like a northern glacier. "Me, and Ritz, and Escoffier, and Echenard."

"I didn't fire you, Delia. May I come in, or shall you make me explain while standing in the corridor?"

For a moment, he thought she would make him do that very thing, but after a moment, she stepped back and allowed him to enter her suite.

"I didn't fire you," he said again once she had closed the door behind him.

If he'd hoped to mitigate the damage done to her by repeating that little fact, the look on her face told him he'd failed. "We were dismissed for...hmm...how did the board put it?" She paused, tapping her fingertip against her chin, as if striving to remember. "For 'forgetting we were servants, rather than masters.' Yes, that was what they told Ritz this morning. I, however, didn't merit Richard's personal consideration, sadly. I got the hotel solicitor instead. Such an honor."

"Delia," he began.

"And what else did the board say? Oh, yes, our arrogance led us to the belief that we could 'use the Savoy as the place from which to carry out our corrupt schemes of fraud, theft, and chicanery.'"

He grimaced. In firing Ritz this morning, Richard had apparently not minced words.

"Well?" she said when he didn't reply. "Did I get that right?"

"Ritz told you all this, I suppose."

"He did." She folded her arms. "I'm curious why you were not the one to do so."

"I was not aware of what Richard told Ritz when he dismissed him," he said, stalling, trying to gauge from her icy demeanor how best to soften her enough so that he could explain his side. "I wasn't there."

"But those were the reasons discussed at the board meeting?"

"If it's any consolation, I voted against your termination. Unfortunately, the other board members outvoted me."

"A piece of news I had to hear about from the Savoy's solicitor, not from you. Even though you already knew."

He gave a sigh, helpless to refute that. "Unfortunately, I could not tell you anything, at least not in detail. I am bound by confidentiality agreements not to reveal any discussions of the board. Once the board voted against you, I started back here at once, hoping to arrive before Sir Charles, so that I could be with you when he brought you the news, but I was..." He paused, cursing—not for the first time today—his loss of temper this morning and its devastating results. "I was unavoidably delayed. Be that as it may," he rushed on, not wanting to get into the weeds with irrelevant details about how he'd ended up in jail, "though Ritz, Escoffier, and Echenard clearly committed fraud, we all know you did not. There was no evidence against you."

"Well, that's comforting!" she cried, her face twisting with pain. "Since I was fired just the same."

"I'm sorry, Delia. You were fired—wrongly, in my opinion—merely because of your close friendship with Ritz. But if you're afraid any of this will become public knowledge, it won't. It's best if the reasons for Ritz's termination are never known."

"Best for whom? The Savoy?"

"Best for everyone, including you."

She scoffed at that. "No one who knows me would ever think I'd steal anything from anyone. It's absurd. And the idea of Ritz stealing is equally so. Nonetheless, he doesn't have the luxury of an aristocratic title to protect him, as I do. If the press ever hears of this, his reputation could be ruined by these scurrilous lies before he ever has the chance to prove his innocence."

"They are not lies, and he is not innocent. And because of that," he added as she shook her head in vehement disbelief, "you'll have to forgive me if I don't cry about the risks to his reputation."

"You've always been against him."

"Yes," he shot back. "Yes, I have. Because he's a thief."

"Why?" she scoffed. "Because he didn't pay for some wine?"

"So he told you he's been taking wine and not paying for it?"

"He said that was the reason for his termination, but it's absurd. The Savoy has always dispensed wine to favored guests at no charge."

"There's a lot more to it than that."

"Like what?"

He set his jaw, frustrated by the legal and moral constraints that bound him. "I cannot say."

"I suppose you mean Escoffier's commissions."

He blinked, taken aback. "You know about that?"

"Of course I do. I've always known."

He felt a lurch of dismay, but he quelled it, telling himself she didn't know the whole story. "What do you know, exactly?"

"Escoffier's reputation is worldwide. The suppliers receive a great deal of gravitas with other hotels because he does business with them, and they are grateful."

"I see that you share Ritz's view of things," he said dryly. "What else do you know? What else did he tell you about today's events?"

Her eyes narrowed on him accusingly. "Enough to understand that he is being unfairly maligned by his enemies."

"By enemies, you mean me?"

"I was thinking of Helen," she said. "But now that you mention it…"

"Does it matter who his enemies are? It doesn't alter the fact that he and Escoffier have been stealing the Ritz blind, Delia. Given that you know this, I'm amazed you can justify it."

"It's not theft!" she cried. "It's for the good of the hotel. It's part of the ambience," she went on as he laughed in disbelief. "Having aristocrats and dignitaries come to the Savoy enhances the hotel's image and brings in more business. I explained this to you the first day we met."

"Ah, yes, all part of aristocratic privilege," he said contemptuously.

"Sneer if you like, but the wine, credit in the restaurant, leeway in payment, have all enabled Ritz to build the Savoy into the greatest hotel in the world. Why should Ritz have to pay for things himself that promote the hotel?"

"And extending credit to his friends who never pay?" he shot back. "Is that promotional, too?"

"They are not friends. They are investors, possible business contacts. How do you think the Savoy got the investors for their new hotel in Rome? Ritz brought them!"

"There's far more to it than that."

"Like what?"

He drew a deep breath, knowing he'd already said too much, and the reticence forced upon him felt like more of a stranglehold than ever. "As I explained, I cannot go into details. Suffice it to say that the investigation provided ample evidence that Ritz was abusing his position."

"Investigation?" She glared at him, the steel in her eyes he knew so well. "You mean the investigation that has been going on for months while you were acting as a front to cover it up? The audits, the cost-cutting measures, the calls for efficiency—that was all just a hum, wasn't it, to conceal the real purpose, which was to find a way— any way—for Helen to rid the hotel of Ritz, Escoffier, Echenard, and me. She's always resented us. There were private detectives following us, spying on us. Did you know about that, too?"

"Not you, Delia. No detectives were following you. In fact, they hadn't even started investigating you."

"But you knew they would."

"Yes," he admitted quietly. "I knew that."

"And you never told me. And why would you? You thought I was a thief."

"I thought there was cause for investigation, if that's what you mean. But I was keeping an open mind."

"Is that what you call it?" She gave a laugh tinged with unmistakable scorn. "That business in the laundry makes perfect sense now. Did you really believe I would steal wine and free meals and laundry services?"

"I didn't know for certain. Others were doing it, and I knew it was possible you could be doing it, too. But I finally concluded you were innocent—"

"Well, that was jolly decent of you. Did you come to this conclusion before or after we made love?"

That question hit him like a blow to the chest. "Before, but—"

"Well, it's good to know that when you declared your love for me, when you held me in your arms and made love to me, you knew I wasn't a common little thief. It might have been nice, though, if you had told me that I was about to be fired anyway."

"I didn't know if that would happen. Nothing was officially decided until the board voted this morning. I tried to mitigate—"

"You know, there was a time after we met when I thought my job might be in jeopardy, but eventually, I dismissed it. You were so moral, I thought. So honest, so upright and honorable, you'd never be so duplicitous. I *trusted* you, Simon, damn it. And today, I learned how misplaced that trust was."

He stared at her, wondering how the hell he was ever going to win her back when he could not explain. When he could not give her proof that Ritz, not him, was the villain here.

"I told you things," she went on. "Intimate things about myself I've never told anyone else, not even my own family. I did that because I was sure I could trust you. You could never be, I thought, the sort of man who would keep secrets from a woman, who could lie to her and make love to her at the same time. How wrong I was." She gave a laugh. "For the fourth time in my life, I've been blind to the fact that I'm falling in love with a man who cannot be honest with me. When will I ever learn?"

"Ritz is the one who's been deceiving you, not me."

"Ritz isn't the one who held me in his arms!" she cried. "Ritz isn't the one who kissed me, made love to me, knowing I was suspected of fraud, knowing I might be fired for it, knowing detectives would soon be following me. Ritz never declared love for me. Ritz never—" She stopped, her lip trembling. "Ritz never broke my heart."

Her voice wobbled on the last word, a vulnerability that tore him into pieces. "Delia, I couldn't tell you what was going on. I still can't. I was a member of the board, and though I've since resigned, I am still legally bound to silence." He could see her face hardening even more against him as he spoke, but he persevered. "I made promises—"

"I don't give a damn about legal agreements and promises you've made to other people. I care about the things you promised *me*. I came to you last night; I gave myself to you. I declared my love, and you declared yours. Is that not a promise? You lay with me. Is that not a promise? Through it all, I thought I could trust you. I had to learn from someone else how wrong I was."

"Someone else? Ritz, you mean. It's plain as day that he has filled your ears with lies about his activities, lies I am not allowed to contradict with proof."

"Ritz may have lied to me. I don't know. But you certainly have."

"I did not lie," he cut in, glad that on that score, at least, he could defend himself. "I was very careful not to tell you a single thing that was untrue."

"Lies of omission are still lies!"

"Keeping a secret that is not mine to tell isn't a lie. I was constrained by promises made before I ever met you."

"For a man who doesn't lie, you're awfully good at deception. How many other secrets are you keeping? And how can I ever know? How can I ever believe you trustworthy?"

"So, if I had broken promises made before I met you, *that* would make me trustworthy in your eyes?"

"Yes!"

He gave a laugh of disbelief at what he was hearing, but then her eyes narrowed, her pointed chin went up in that way he knew so well, and he appreciated that with every moment that passed, he was digging himself into a deeper hole. Her next words confirmed it.

"I want you to leave."

"Like hell I will." He took a step toward her, but her next words stopped him cold.

"Ritz is taking Marie-Louise and the children and moving to Paris next month. Escoffier and Echenard are going with him, and he wants me to come, too. He's offered me the same post at his hotel there that I've had here."

Cold fear closed around his heart like a fist. Bad enough that he couldn't offer her the evidence to prove his side. But now, he'd also have the breadth of the English Channel between them to deal with?

He swallowed hard, trying to think past the sick knot in his gut. "Are you taking up his offer?"

Even as he asked the question, he was wondering how Cassie would feel about moving to Paris, and he was wishing, not for the first time, that he'd worked harder on learning proper French as a boy. It was beginning to look as if he might need it.

"Are you taking him up on his offer?" he asked again. "Please, at least tell me that."

It seemed an eternity before she answered.

"I haven't decided," she said at last, and his relief was so great, he felt weak in the knees. "Many details have yet to be worked out. But either way," she added before he could savor this minor victory, "it has nothing to do with you, since once you leave here, you and I will not be seeing each other again."

If she had really decided against him, she'd have taken the job, pesky details about it notwithstanding. She was, whether she realized it herself or not, giving him a chance to regain her trust. But he also knew there was only one way to do it.

"If you think I'm giving up, Delia, you couldn't be more wrong," he said gently.

She walked to the door and opened it. "Goodbye, Simon."

He followed her, pausing in the doorway to look at her one more time, to inhale again the luscious scent of her. "This isn't goodbye," he told her. "Because you love me, and I love you. And I refuse to believe that this one issue shall divide us forever. I want to marry you, and—"

"Marry?" she cut in with such vehement scorn it made him wince. "I see no reason to marry again, and if I did, it certainly wouldn't be you. Why should I?"

He met her hostile gaze steadily. "Because I am the right man for you, Delia. I know it, and in proving it, I won't let anything get in my way, not Ritz, not your god-awful late husbands, not even the damned English Channel."

With that, he walked out, realizing exactly what he had to do, bracing himself to risk everything he'd spent his life working for, everything he'd fought to prove and protect, including his honor. He just hoped it would be enough.

19

Delia propped her elbow on the arm of the settee in her suite at the Bristol and rested her chin in her hand, staring disinterestedly through the doorway at her new maid, who was packing her trunks for Paris. Normally, a trip to Paris would fill her with delight, but not this time. Turning away, she leaned her head back and closed her eyes. Only midmorning, she thought with a sigh, and she already felt tired.

"What do you think of these, my lady?"

Delia opened her eyes and turned her head toward the bedroom where Bartlett was holding up two evening gowns.

"Leave the ciel-blue satin," Delia told her. "I'm not going to any balls in Paris, so I won't need a ball gown."

"You might be invited to a ball, my lady. One never knows."

"There won't be time for such things. Ritz will have me working most of that time, if I know that man at all. No, put the satin back in the armoire. But pack the tangerine silk. I might have need of that. Marie-Louise may drag us off to some dinner party somewhere."

The maid returned to the bedroom, and Delia once again leaned back and closed her eyes, overwhelmed by a weariness of spirit that was all too familiar.

The past few days had been utter hell. Stories about Ritz's departure—and hers—from the Savoy had been the stuff of lurid speculation in every London paper. Interestingly enough, nothing about those absurd accusations of fraud had leaked out. Simon had assured her that would be the case, but given his duplicity during the past two months, she was hardly feeling inclined to be grateful.

During the past three days, her emotions had run the gamut— pain, love, and betrayal had all come and gone, leaving her now both spent and weary. She'd been here so many times before, and she was once again baffled at her own willful blindness when it came to men she loved.

Not surprisingly, such self-recrimination hadn't helped boost her spirits. Nor had blaming Simon done much good, either. Her mood remained as bleak as a winter's day.

For the second time, Ritz had come to her rescue. He'd told her he was taking his wife, Marie-Louise, and the children to Paris, and he thought she might like to come, too. Not only would she have the chance to see the progress made on the Paris hotel, she could pick which of the staff offices she preferred, hire a secretary, and start looking for an apartment. And, Ritz had added with his uncanny knack for knowing just what she needed, she might like to be away from London and the wild stories that were circulating in the press.

With happy relief, she had agreed. She'd hired a maid, notified her family, and written a carefully worded letter to Cassandra Hayden, explaining that something had come up and that she would not be able to launch her for her London debut, but promising to find some-one willing to chaperone the girl in her stead.

It was, she knew, a rather craven thing to do, but she couldn't bear the idea of seeing Simon, being near him, deceiving herself into thinking she could trust him. And anyway, she was moving to Paris when Ritz opened the new hotel in June. Wasn't she?

Feeling the need to move, she stood up and walked to the window. From here, she could see the tip of the spire decorating the roof of the Savoy. There would be no hothouse banquet room up there now, she realized.

Stupid tears stung her eyes, and Delia squeezed her eyes shut, trying to keep them at bay.

"Everything's packed, my lady."

With relief, Delia turned from the window. "Excellent. Thank you, Bartlett."

"Of course, my lady. If you'd just look things over, and make sure I've got everything you'll need, I'll go down to fetch a footman and order a cab. We've got only an hour before we catch the train for Dover."

The maid went out, and Delia went to the bedroom, where trunks, valises, and hatboxes lay open on the floor. She glanced through them, noting that Bartlett was proving to be an excellent lady's maid. Not a thing had been forgotten.

She straightened, staring down at the clothes and hats without a speck of enthusiasm. Her heart felt like a ten-ton weight in her chest, and the idea that she might soon be leaving England for good was like a hard, tight knot in her stomach.

She didn't want to go. But would staying in London be better? Cassie would be coming out, which meant even if she didn't launch the girl herself, she'd surely see Simon if she remained here. How could she bear that?

A knock on the door of her suite roused Delia from these depressing contemplations. Relieved by the distraction, she returned to the sitting room and opened the door to find a boy of perhaps twelve standing in the corridor.

"Delivery for Lady Stratham," the boy said.

"I'm Lady Stratham."

"Here you are, my lady." The boy held out a large envelope containing a thick sheaf of papers. "From Lord Calderon."

At the mention of Simon, Delia's heart gave a leap, but she quelled any foolish excitement. Why should she want to read a letter from him?

She took the packet anyway. "Thank you. What's your name?" she asked as she tucked the envelope under her arm and reached for her handbag from the table by the door.

"Joseph, my lady."

"And do you work for the hotel, Joseph?" she asked as she opened her bag and extracted a half crown from the coin pocket.

"What, the Bristol? No, my lady. I'm at the Clarendon."

The Clarendon. So that was where Simon was staying. Not that she cared, of course. She was going to Paris. And it wasn't likely she'd care when she got back, either, she reminded herself firmly.

The boy tipped his cap and started to turn away, making her remember her manners. "Thank you, Joseph," she said, holding out the coin.

The boy took it, tipped his cap again, and departed. Shutting the door behind him, Delia stared at the envelope in her hands, studying the direction written in Simon's precise copperplate script. She had no idea what had inspired him to write her pages and pages, but she couldn't bear to read justifications and explanations and declarations of love. Not now. The pain was still too fresh.

She tossed the envelope onto the table, but then, on impulse, she picked it up. She returned to the bedroom and shoved the letter into the side pocket of her valise. She'd read it later. Maybe.

"Well, gentlemen?" Simon leaned back on the settee of his hotel sitting room, lifting his glass of whisky as he glanced back and forth between the other two men in his suite at the Clarendon. "Shall I have my solicitors draw up a partnership agreement? Or do you wish to take more time to consider?"

"No need for more time as far as I'm concerned," the Duke of Westbourne said at once and lifted his whisky glass. "I'm in."

Simon turned to the man seated beside him. "Well, Devlin?"

His best friend frowned, gesturing to the man across from him with his whisky glass. "I'd feel better about this whole venture if I had more shares than he does."

"There are other investors," Simon reminded. "Wilson Rycroft, Lord Hever... And anyway, I own the controlling interest, so I have final say when you two get quarrelsome."

"You'll have no quarrels from me," the duke assured him. "As long as he doesn't spirit another underage friend of my sisters off to Gretna Green in the dead of night."

"If you're implying," Devlin began, but Simon cut him off.

"Gentlemen, enough," he said, his incisive voice making it clear to both men there would be no quarrels, at least not today. "Well, Devlin, are you in or out?"

Devlin heaved a sigh. "Of course I'm in. You know I can never turn down a good business deal."

"Excellent," Simon replied with profound relief. "Perhaps one day you two could even become friends."

"Don't count on it," the other two said in unison, making him grin.

"To new beginnings," he said and held up his glass.

The other two put aside their animosity enough to echo this optimistic sentiment, and the three men clinked glasses, swallowed the last of their whisky, and stood up.

After handshakes all around and an agreement to meet three days hence to sign the papers, Simon escorted the other two men downstairs to the hotel lobby. As Devlin went to see the doorman about a hansom cab, Simon took advantage of this private moment with the duke.

"Have you heard from Delia?" he asked.

Westbourne nodded. "I got a letter from her just before I came down. She's in Paris."

"Paris?" Dismay knotted his guts like a fist. "She's decided to take up Ritz's job offer then?"

But to his profound relief, the duke shook his head. "She's only gone to have a look at things there. She'll make a decision when she gets back, she said."

Simon drew a deep, steadying breath. "And when will that be?" he asked, striving to sound as casual as possible.

"She didn't say. Ah," he added, glancing past Simon's shoulder. "I believe the hansom has arrived."

Simon walked out with him, said farewell to both men, and noted with amused chagrin that Devlin had ordered two hansoms. Despite having just formed a business partnership that included the duke, and despite the fact that both men were going to the West End, Devlin's opinion of Westbourne hadn't softened enough to share a cab. Ah, well. Perhaps with time, Simon could effect a more amiable truce there. After all, Devlin was his best friend, and if his hopes ever came to fruition, Westbourne would become his cousin-in-law.

But the latter would only happen, he thought, his smile fading, if he could persuade Delia to marry him. And at this point, that prospect wasn't looking too promising.

Defying the confidentiality agreements he'd signed, he'd sent her the investigators' reports, thinking that reading the actual documented proof would show her the extent of Ritz's guilt. Simon had also hoped subjecting himself to a civil lawsuit that could financially wreck him would demonstrate to her that he was worthy of her trust, but neither of those hopes appeared likely to come true. She'd gone to Paris anyway.

During the week ahead, Ritz would be working on her, dazzling her with his grandiose plans and schemes, but as nauseating a prospect as that was, there was nothing he could do about it. All he could do was ensure that when she returned, he was in a position to make an offer of his own that might, just might, appeal to her more. If not—

"Simon?"

The sound of a feminine voice calling his name caused his heart to give a leap. But he knew it wasn't Delia's voice, and when he turned toward the front desk, the sight of Helen standing there confirmed the fact.

She spoke before he could do so. "Forming new alliances, I see," she said, nodding to the door through which Max and Devlin had just departed.

"I didn't have much choice."

"Well, you certainly burned your bridges with the old allies," she said with a touch of wry humor he could not share. "I'm the one who persuaded Astonby not to press charges, by the way."

He met the amusement in her eyes with a hard look of his own. "Is that why you came? To show me what a Lady Bountiful you are? Then why are you here?" he asked when she shook her head.

"I regret things happened the way they did."

"But you don't regret the part you played in them?"

"No."

"Anything else?" he asked.

"You were right, you know," she said. "When you told me that my own suffering is why I dislike Lady Stratham. I know I ought to have some sympathy for her, since she's lost three husbands and I know I'm losing mine. But I couldn't feel that, because I was jealous as hell. You see, despite her pain from losing three husbands, she has never lost her zest for life, and I can feel myself slowly losing mine. When Richard dies, I think I will just dry up and wither away."

He stirred, impatient. "Is this a bid for my sympathy?"

"No, actually. I just wanted you to know that you were right. That's why I was so vehement about her guilt. I wanted her to be guilty."

"And yet, after you knew she wasn't guilty, you worked to have her dismissed anyway. And you succeeded."

"As I told you, I did what I felt was best for the Savoy. You may trust that woman completely, but I do not have that luxury. I am a woman of business, you see."

He heard the bitterness in her voice, but he was unsure what she expected him to say or how she expected him to feel. "I'm quite busy, Helen. Is there a point to this little visit or not?"

"I heard you've been visiting house agents."

"How do you know that?"

"You called on Smythe, Ellis, and Hall, the house agents Richard and I use."

"What of it?"

Instead of answering, she reached into her handbag and pulled out a card. She handed it to him without a word.

He glanced at it. "Jessop and Davis, Piccadilly," he read. "So?"

"I take it you have not seen them yet?"

"No."

"You should." She turned away. "I've already told Mr. Jessop to expect you."

He frowned at her retreating back, puzzled. "But what—"

"Good luck, Simon," she called as she walked away, but then she paused and looked at him over her shoulder. "To both of you."

With that, she walked out of the hotel, leaving a bemused Simon staring after her. He doubted Helen's wish to regain his goodwill would ever come to fruition. Her wish for him to have good luck, on the other hand, he'd gladly accept, for he feared that when it came to winning Delia over, he was going to need every scrap of luck he could get.

20

Well, *mon chéri*," Ritz said, smiling at Delia as they settled into chairs at a Parisian café in the Place Vendôme, "what do you think?"

"They've done so much," Delia exclaimed, leaning back as a waiter poured coffee for them. "Really, César, I can hardly believe it. When I was here in January, I despaired at the idea of a June opening. I didn't think we'd ever be ready. I thought surely you'd need more time."

The dapper little man across from her smiled into his mustache. "Money can always accomplish great things. I say I want to open in June, and *comme ça*." He paused to snap his fingers. "It happens."

"That's always been your way," she agreed. "And it shows in this hotel. You've done incredible things here. I just know it is going to be the finest hotel in the world."

"You have been a part of making it so, don't forget."

That was true, she supposed, and yet, as she glanced at the hotel across the square, she felt no sense of accomplishment. Curiously, she felt nothing at all.

"Now that you have toured the suites," he said, breaking into her thoughts, "have you picked which one you wish to make your own?"

She shook her head. "I haven't, actually."

"But why not? I told you that you could have your pick."

"I know, but..."

She paused, Simon's words from their first meeting echoing through her brain.

Suites are a valuable commodity to the hotel.

As she had done more times than she could count during the past two weeks, she shoved that man out of her mind. "Oh, I don't know," she answered with a laugh. "Perhaps it's because none of this seems quite real. I haven't yet accepted your offer, you know."

"But you will."

Such a complacent reply irked her a little. She was accustomed to Ritz's arrogance, of course. He wouldn't have become the most famous hotelier in the world without that particular trait. On the other hand, his arrogance had been part of the reason he'd been so ignominiously dismissed from the Savoy. Richard had said as much, according to Ritz's own account of his firing.

Either way, this quality in Ritz's character was something she'd accepted long ago. It couldn't be the reason she was hesitating, could it? And it certainly couldn't be because she harbored any romantic hopes about Simon. That was all over. So what was making her hesitate?

During the past ten days, as they had toured the hotel and surveyed the progress of carpenters, tradesmen, and decorators, she'd felt enveloped in a dreamlike haze. As usual, Ritz had asked for her opinions and solicited her advice, but not once had he asked her for her acceptance of his offer, and now she appreciated that was because he'd taken that acceptance completely for granted. She, however, was not quite so sanguine, and she did not understand why.

"Either way," she said, neatly sidestepping in case Ritz did actually press her for a formal answer, "I'm not really sure I want to live in the hotel. It was all very well before. I mean, after Hamish died, I had to leave Stratham House and I had no home of my own, so living at the Savoy was quite convenient. But after five years of living in a hotel, I've grown a bit tired of it."

"Lease an apartment, then. There are several nearby."

"I know. I looked at a few, but..." Delia paused, wriggling a little in her chair, hating to be put on the spot this way, so she took refuge in flippancy. "But they are so expensive. When the house agents told me the rent, I nearly keeled over."

"My dear!" Ritz stared at her, looking stricken. "Is that what makes you hesitate? I had no idea you were strapped for cash. All the years we have known each other, and I have never known this. You should have told me."

She wasn't short of money, not in the least, but she seized on the excuse. "Oh, you know how it is with my lot," she countered lightly. "We don't talk about money."

"Of course, but it's not a problem at all. I can easily fix you up."

Delia blinked, bewildered. "Fix me up?" she echoed. "How?"

He shrugged. "The usual way, of course. The hotel will extend you credit."

"Oh," she said, relieved by that reply, though she wasn't quite sure what she'd been expecting him to say. "I know we have extended credit to hotel guests in the past, but I'm not a guest, and anyway, I do hate charging things. When the bills come due, they are always so much higher than one expects."

"But, my dear, you are my friend. For my friends, the bill never comes due!"

She stared, riveted, more of Simon's words echoing in her head.

And extending credit to his friends who never pay? Is that promotional, too?

"I wasn't sure," she said, keeping her voice carefully noncommittal, "that sort of thing was possible."

He chuckled. "I had no idea you were so naïve, my dear."

"Neither did I," she murmured with feeling. "But I'm getting a quick education. Do—" She broke off and gave a little cough. "Do very many of our friends do this?" she asked, striving to keep her voice as casual as possible. "Charge things to the hotel and not pay for it?"

"Of course! Friends, employees—"

"Employees, too?" she cut in.

"Of course. In return, they are loyal to me. They do what I want done and do not question it."

"Including me," she murmured.

"When you came to work for me, I thought you understood all this. I assumed you did not take advantage of these opportunities because you had no need to do so, but now I see that you simply didn't know how it works. Still, there is no need for you to worry about the cost of your apartment. The hotel will pay for it."

"Do your fellow investors know that?"

He waved that aside as if it didn't matter. "I decide these things. They do not need the details."

This, she realized, was what the investigation had revealed to the Savoy board and why the hotel had not been making a profit. Not just a few bottles of wine or credit to aristocratic clientele, but fraud on a massive scale. As Simon had told her.

Delia felt sick to her stomach, nauseated not only by this entire scheme, but also by her own unknowing part in it. She'd always assumed that most people were like her—that they paid their bills eventually, that their loyalty to Ritz stemmed from respect and affection, not bribery. "Is this how it's always been?"

"Of course."

Once again, she'd been a mug. How many times did that have to happen before she learned her lesson? When it came to judging the character of men, she was hopeless. Granted, her fondness for Ritz was platonic, not romantic, but still…Her only comfort was that she wasn't the only one who had been fooled. It had taken Richard and Helen eight years to figure out what was going on. "The Savoy board didn't seem to understand that this is how it works," she murmured. "That was why we all got fired."

"Bah!" he said contemptuously. "They have no imagination, no vision, no idea what is needed to run a great hotel. But here—" He broke off and leaned back, spreading his arms in an expansive gesture that included the nearby Ritz hotel. "Here we will show them how it is done. Here…"

Ritz's voice droned on, but Delia scarcely heard. Simon had wanted to tell her about these schemes, but he'd been unable to do so. Something about legalities and confidentiality agreements.

He should have told her anyway. He should have trusted her. She had trusted him.

But had she, really? The moment her trust had been tested, she'd turned him away. If he had broken his promise of silence, would she have listened?

She rubbed a hand across her forehead, her thoughts spinning in circles. How could she ever again know who to believe about anything? Who to trust?

So, if I had broken promises made before I met you, that would make me trustworthy in your eyes?

She'd answered yes, because if he'd told her, they could have faced it together, decided what to do together. If only he had trusted her, if he had explained—

Perhaps he had. Delia stiffened, remembering the letter he'd sent her, a thick enclosure of multiple sheets. She'd thought it merely a reiteration of what he'd already said, with perhaps a plea for her to understand, but what if it was exactly what she'd asked for: a gesture of trust?

Delia lurched to her feet. "Pardon me, César, but I'm not feeling well. I have to go."

César stood up. "Of course, my dear. Shall Marie-Louise and I see you for dinner? Or is it serious enough that you need a doctor?"

"No doctor," she said and reached for her handbag. "And no dinner. And," she added, meeting his gaze across the table, "no job. I'm not taking it. I appreciate the offer," she rushed on before he could reply, "but I don't want to live in Paris, César. I want to stay in England. My life is there. Good luck to you."

She turned away from his astonished face and ran across the square toward the hotel, sending the pigeons into startled flight, feeling a bit like them.

For the past ten days, she'd felt like a bird who'd crashed into a window—dazed and numb, paralyzed by pain and indecision, mired in self-doubt because of all her past mistakes—but now she knew it was time to fly again. To try again.

Darting between workmen, she sped through the lobby of the hotel, up the only working lift, down a corridor, and into her room that still smelled of fresh paint. She earned herself a startled look from Bartlett as she ran past her, unstrapped her travel valise, and yanked out the envelope. With shaking hands, she broke the seal, opened the envelope, and pulled out the papers Simon had sent her.

One glance at the top page told her this was not a letter at all. And the first typewritten lines told her that Simon had given her exactly what she'd asked for. Exhilarated, relieved, and suddenly gloriously happy, she laughed out loud.

"My lady?"

She looked up to find Bartlett staring at her askance. "Is something wrong?"

"No, Bartlett," she cried, waving the thick sheaf of papers in the air. "Everything is absolutely right. Start packing my things, please. We're returning to London."

Simon leaned over the desk of his new office, studying the plans of the hotel in which he stood. Old and yellowed with faded ink, they were difficult to read. "So, in your opinion, the kitchens will need a complete gutting?"

"*Évidemment.*" The Frenchman opposite him gave a shrug. "The ovens, the ranges…they are ancient. And the plumbing." He gave a shudder. "*Mon Dieu.*"

Simon nodded, not the least bit surprised. During his first tour of the place with Mr. Jessop, he'd only needed one glance at the kitchens to know everything would need to be redone there. And the kitchens were not the only problem. According to Jessop and Davis, the Mayfair hadn't had any renovation in nearly forty years. Draperies, mattresses, and bedding were all below the way things ought to be…

Surely you wouldn't want the guests to sleep on lumpy mattresses with yellowing sheets and rotting drapes, would you?

As Delia's words from their very first meeting went through his head, he smiled. How they had butted heads that first day, and many more times since then, too. They were still doing that, obviously, or she'd be here with him now. They could be looking over hotel plans together, battling over the budget, perhaps even planning their own wedding. If only…

Two weeks she'd been in Paris. Two weeks for Ritz to harden her more against him and justify himself. And against that, what did he have? A thirty-page report from the Savoy's private investigators.

Would it be enough?

Given that two weeks had passed with no word from her, he feared it wasn't. Surely she'd read it by now. Perhaps he ought to have followed her to Paris. He'd thought it best not to push her too hard. Better, he'd thought, to give her breathing space; but that choice had come with its own set of risks. It had given Ritz an unfettered opportunity to work on her. A Hobson's choice, if ever there was one. He was banking on the fact that she hadn't agreed to Ritz's job offer straightaway, hoping with all his heart that he was the reason she was hesitating. Would that hope prove true, or would it be the most colossal mistake he'd ever made?

"*Vicomte?*"

Roused from these agonized contemplations, Simon returned his attention to his newly hired chef de cuisine and their plans for renovating the kitchens of the hotel he'd just bought. "And the electricity, Monsieur Frossard? I assume you will want that as—"

A cough interrupted him, and he looked past Monsieur Frossard to find Ross in the doorway of his office.

"Begging your pardon, my lord, but you have a delivery in the lobby."

"The lobby? Well, bring it in here, then."

He started to return his attention to the architectural drawings spread across his desk, but then Ross spoke again.

"Begging your pardon, my lord, but bringing it here will be... difficult. Impossible, I should say. Might I suggest you come and see for yourself?"

Simon capitulated with a sigh. "Monsieur Frossard, if you will pardon me for a moment?"

"But of course."

Given this assent, Simon stepped around the piles of not-yet-unpacked crates and boxes that had been brought here from the

Clarendon this morning, started down the dimly lit corridor, and entered the main lobby, where he came to a startled, stunned stop.

All he saw was color—every possible shade of pink and purple nature had ever invented seemed spread out before him. Flowers, he realized—masses of them. But not just any flowers.

Hyacinths.

Vases and pots of them covered the desks and the tables. Gigantic sculptures of them in the shapes of cones, balls, squares, and animals stood on the floor. Baskets of them stood on chairs. In the middle of it all was an arbor covered with them. And under it, in a dress of buttercup yellow that was like a burst of pure sunshine, stood Delia.

"What the devil?" he muttered, staring at her, too stunned to move. "Delia?"

From beneath the brim of an enormous hat of white straw, yellow ribbons, and purple hyacinths, she studied him, biting her lip. "I'm hoping," she said after a moment, "we might call a truce?"

Joy rumbled within his chest—joy, relief, and exhilaration—and he began to laugh.

As if galvanized by the sound, she moved, running toward him, zigzagging her way among the flowers like a gazelle.

He moved as well, meeting her halfway, catching her up in his arms and hauling her against his chest. He ducked his head beneath her hat, kissing her mouth, her cheeks, her chin, her nose. "My God," he said and kissed her again just to be sure she was real. "My God."

"I suppose that's a yes?" she said, laughing.

"How could I not say yes to an offer of truce like this?" he countered, sliding her down to set her on her feet again. "But are you really here? When did you get back, and what in blazes took you so long, and how did you know where to find me?"

These questions, fired in such rapid succession, made her laugh. "I arrived three days ago. The Clarendon told me you were at the Mayfair now, and they were forwarding your mail here, but I don't see how you could be living here, since the sign outside says the place is closed for renovations."

"And so it is. I'm the only one living here at the moment. Well, me and Ross. I bought the place."

"What?"

"Not only me. I formed a new investment group with Devlin and your cousin Westbourne."

"Max? And Devlin Sharpe? In a company together? Heavens."

"You're not the only one who can forge truces, my love."

"Obviously not, but Devlin Sharpe?" She made a face. "Did it have to be him?"

"Don't start," he admonished. "Devlin's top-drawer. You'll just have to trust me on that. But," he added as she groaned, "I haven't told you the most surprising part of it all. Helen is the one who told me the Mayfair Hotel was for sale. She sent me to the house agents Jessop and Davis so they could show me this property before it officially went up for sale."

"She did?" Delia sniffed, clearly skeptical. "Then there's something wrong with it. Drains or boilers or something. Helen," she added as he laughed, "would never pass off a good business deal to someone else, especially someone she now sees as an enemy."

"There's nothing wrong with the drains," he assured her, "or the boilers. I had everything inspected by experts. No, I actually think it was her way of offering a truce. Like hyacinths, you know. Speaking of which…"

He paused, glanced around, and laughed again. "You really are the most unexpected woman I've ever known. How on earth did you manage this?"

"I cut my decorating teeth at the Savoy, my darling. Ritz taught me you can do anything with enough imagination and money. And no," she added, pressing her gloved fingers over his mouth as he started to reply, "I'm not telling you how much it cost, so don't even ask."

"I won't," he assured her. "The expense didn't even occur to me."

"A miracle." She cupped his cheek. "I must be rubbing off on you."

He reproved her with another kiss, this one into her palm. "Don't get used to it," he said, then glanced around, shaking his head. "You must have bought every hyacinth in London."

"I really think I did. The flower sellers won't have any available for the local churches in time for Easter, I fear."

He grinned. "Their loss, then. Does this mean—" He paused, taking a deep breath, not wanting to make assumptions. With Delia, that always got him into trouble. "Does this mean you aren't moving to Paris and taking up Ritz's offer?"

"It does." She slid her arms up, wrapping them around his neck. "I came back to see if that other offer was still open."

"So my letter convinced you? Well then, damn it, woman," he added before she could reply, "what took you so long to come back? It doesn't take two weeks to read a letter."

"What you sent me wasn't a letter, it was a tome. And anyway, I didn't even read it."

He blinked. "You didn't? But then…" He paused, pulling back so he could look fully into her face. "I sent it to show you that I trust you and that you can trust me."

"Yes, I know."

"But you didn't read it?"

"No."

He must have looked as disconcerted as he felt, because she laughed. "I didn't have to read it, Simon. I knew what you'd done and why the second I saw the letterhead at the top." She sobered, her laughter fading. "I know it took me a while to open it, but I was so hurt. I thought it was just some long-winded explanation from you, justifying what you did, and I was in no mood for that. I thought you were just my latest romantic mistake. I mean, falling in love with the wrong man seems to be my special gift, you know. But then, when I was with Ritz talking about the new hotel, some of the things he said made me see *him* in a whole other light. He was my mentor, my friend. I worshiped him."

"Yes, I know," he said with feeling.

"I thought he could do no wrong, but then, suddenly, I realized that you and the board were right about him."

He stared at her, hardly able to believe it. "How did that happen if you didn't even read the report?"

"He offered to let the hotel pay for my apartment."

"That scoundrel. He hasn't learned a thing."

"That's when I realized he and the others had been skimming off the Savoy profits for years in ways that went far beyond the trivial things I knew about, and I couldn't look the other way about it. I knew at that moment that I had picked yet another wrong man in whom to place my trust, but that it wasn't you. It was him. And I caught the next train for home."

"A miracle," he said, having no idea what else to say but to repeat her own words back to her. "I must be rubbing off on you."

"You are. I really think you must be, because when Ritz was showing me the new hotel, I was adding up what everything cost, and even I was a bit staggered. Don't misunderstand me. I still believe Ritz is a wonderful hotelier. He is," she added as he scoffed. "And the Paris Ritz is going to be the most famous, amazing hotel in the world."

"If it stays afloat."

"If it stays afloat," she agreed. "And it might not, the way he's spending money like water."

"My Delia becoming frugal," he said and kissed her nose. "Definitely a miracle."

"That's not even the biggest miracle of all, though."

"No?" He smiled, sliding his arms around her waist. "What is?"

"I've finally fallen in love with a man I really can trust. And who trusts me, trusts me enough that he risked everything he's worked for to prove it to me. And that's you."

"I'm glad you know that, my darling. So you'll marry me? Are you sure? If you're not, and you want to think it over, I'll wait however long it takes."

Her black brows came together in a little frown, but her mouth was a teasing curve. "For someone who was so sure he was the right man for me a few days ago, you're not sounding very sure now."

"It wasn't a few days ago," he grumbled. "It was fourteen days, one hour, and about seventeen minutes ago."

"Been counting the hours, have you?" She smiled, the little devil, clearly pleased that he'd been suffering in an agony of suspense.

"Don't tease. Are you going to marry me or not?"

"Yes, Simon," she said so meekly that he was instantly suspicious, and then she looked around and added, "but only if you promise to let me be the one to do up this place. It could certainly use a decorator."

"Decorator?" He shook his head. "I'm afraid that's not possible, darling. I've already hired someone to handle that."

"Oh." Her face fell, making her look like a little girl who'd been told there wasn't going to be a Christmas. "I see."

"I have a different job in mind for you."

"Wife, I suppose. Viscountess. Mother to our children. If—" She broke off and cleared her throat. "If we have any," she whispered.

"Either way," he said, kissing the tip of her nose, "there's another role for you as well, if you want it."

"What's that?"

"This hotel needs a general manager."

She pulled back, staring at him, looking so stunned that he laughed.

"I believe I've rendered you speechless," he said. "Wonders never cease."

"Well..." She paused, clearly confounded. "Me as general manager of the Mayfair? But don't you want to do it?"

"I've already got four other hotels under my purview. And Jessop and Davis have two hotels by the sea they want me to consider as well. If I'm going to take on all that, I'll need help."

"And you want it to be me? But, Simon, you know how I am. I'm extravagant and over-the-top, and I'm horrible at keeping track of expenses, and—"

"That," he interrupted tenderly, "is why you have me. I'll keep you in line."

One of her eyebrows rose, warning him he might have some trouble with that notion. "Oh, really?"

"Yes, really," he said firmly, cupped her face in his hands, and kissed her.

EPILOGUE

London, 1900

*D*elia stared in disbelief at the budget estimates spread out across her office desk. "How?" she murmured, shaking her head. "How can flowers possibly cost so much? This can't be right."

"Delia, look."

She lifted her gaze from the columns of figures she'd been studying and watched as Simon rose on his knees, their son's fists wrapped around his index fingers. "Look. He's walking."

Any budget projections for the Mayfair's coming year were forgotten as she watched Oliver slide one chubby foot forward on the carpet. It was a tentative move that only the proudest of proud parents would define as walking, but that didn't stop a bubble of happiness from rising inside her, pressing against her heart, and making it hard to breathe. Was there ever a woman so lucky as she?

She pressed her fist to her mouth, choking back a sob, but it was too late.

His attention diverted by the faint sound, Simon looked up to find her watching them, and at once, she tried to dissemble.

"Oh, stop," she said with a sniff, striving to sound no-nonsense and stiff-upper-lip about it all. "He's only nine months old. You're imagining things."

"Did you hear that, my son?" Simon disentangled himself from Oliver's grip, wrapped his hands around the baby's midsection, and lifted him into his arms as he rose from the floor of her office. "Your mama doesn't believe me," he murmured as he propped the boy's bottom on his forearm and crossed the office toward her. "Let's show her what you can do, hmm?"

He paused in front of her desk, set Oliver atop the papers on her blotter, and then he let go, his hands cupped on either side of the wobbly baby, ready to catch him if he started to fall.

Delia smiled, holding out her hands. "Come to your mama, then, and prove your father right."

She had no expectations of her son's success, but to her astonishment, the baby took a step toward her, a real step, and the bubble pressing against her heart burst into a thousand shards of pure joy that made her feel as if she'd swallowed a box of fireworks. Oliver started to sway, pitching forward, and she caught him up before Simon could do so, pulling him to her breast. "My boy," she whispered fiercely, holding him tight as a tear she could not contain slid down her cheek. "My darling boy."

"Delia, are you all right?" At once, Simon straightened and circled her desk, halting beside her. "My love, why are you crying?"

She swallowed hard, struggling to find a way to explain what she felt, but words seemed so inadequate.

"My lady?"

She and Simon both turned as Mrs. Barton entered Delia's office. "It's time for Master Oliver's bath, my lady," the stout, red-haired nanny told her as she came toward Delia's desk.

"Of course." She kissed the baby's blond head and handed him to the woman on the other side of her desk. "Go with Nanny, now. And mind you," she added, trying to sound stern, "don't make a fuss this time when she cuts your nails, young man."

She watched as Nanny took the baby and departed, then turned to her husband, who was watching her closely.

"Two years ago," she said softly as he pulled her into his arms, "I had come to accept that I didn't need a child to complete my life. But now, I can't imagine my life without him." She looked up, blinking hard. "Or without you."

He lifted a hand to her cheek. "I'm not going anywhere," he said, his beautiful gray-green eyes so steady and sure. "I hope you know that."

She nodded. "I do know."

"Do you?" Simon's hand fell away, and his arms slid around her waist, pulling her close. "There was a time when you were rather afraid you were fated for perpetual widowhood. I hope you've gotten over that."

"I have. Truly."

His eyes crinkled at the corners as he smiled. "Good. After all," he added, his voice light as he pressed a kiss to her damp cheek, "it's a moot point, since I fully intend to defy the expectations of the bettors at White's for fifty years at least. So no more crying, my darling."

"It's happiness making me blubber," she assured him.

"Are you happy? Have I made you happy?"

"More than you could ever know, and in ways I never could have imagined. I won't say I don't still worry sometimes about what the future might bring. I do. I probably always will, now, at least a little. After all, grief and loss have changed me, and there's no denying it. They've made me more wary, more circumspect than I was as a girl. But when we met, I'd taken it much too far, holding myself apart, hiding behind a facade of glib words and flirtation—"

"Don't I know it," he interrupted with a groan, earning himself a gentle kick in the shin.

"The point is," she went on, "I was convinced I could never fall in love again. But the truth was that I didn't want to. I'd become afraid of love, sure it could only bring me another round of pain and loss. I'd become afraid to trust myself, or to trust any man that got too close. I was resigned to a life alone. But then you came along, barreling past all my defenses, bullying me into changing my ways—"

"Bullying?" he interrupted. "Well, I like that."

"You should, because it worked."

"Did it?" His brows lifted in obvious skepticism.

"Yes." She did her best to look ho-hum and wise. "I'm not afraid of love, or new ways of doing things, or—"

"Budgets, too?" he asked hopefully, nodding to the papers spread across her desk. "I hope this means you won't be ordering thousands of pounds' worth of flowers this year like you did last year?"

"Don't bet on it, my darling." She rose on her toes and kissed him before he could give her a lecture on the wisdom of proper budgeting. "Don't bet on it."

DON'T MISS THE NEXT
SCANDAL AT THE SAVOY
NOVEL COMING SUMMER
2025!

Author's Note

Although most of the characters in this story are fictional, some are actual figures from history. César Ritz, Auguste Escoffier, and Louis Echenard did exist, and their departure from the Savoy Hotel occurred exactly as I have shown it here, including the anonymous letter that led to their downfall.

The reasons they were fired, however, remained largely unknown until the mid-1980s, when the signed confessions of these men and other evidence that detailed the reasons for their mysterious dismissal from the hotel were uncovered, including the scope of the fraud and embezzlement they committed.

In the end, however, Ritz and Escoffier may have had the last laugh. After their departure from the Savoy Hotel, Echenard's name was lost to history, but the other two men became even more famous.

Ritz went on to not only create the Ritz Paris Hotel mentioned in my story, but also London's Ritz and Carlton hotels, launching what would become one of the most successful empires in the hotel industry: Ritz-Carlton. Ritz's name became so famous, in fact, that it led to the coining of a new word in the dictionary: ritzy, and a new saying: putting on the ritz. Ritz's name has become synonymous with extravagant taste, flamboyant style, and unparalleled luxury.

Escoffier revolutionized the world of haute cuisine, banishing forever the methods of all previous famous chefs, including the great Carême, and replacing those methods with his own. Escoffier's way of arranging the restaurant kitchen and dividing the labor within it became the industry standard and is used in virtually every restaurant in the world today.

As to the famous anonymous letter, the identity of the writer has never been discovered.

ABOUT THE AUTHOR

New York Times bestselling author **Laura Lee Guhrke** spent seven years in advertising, had a successful catering business, and managed a construction company before she decided writing novels was more fun. The author of twenty-seven historical romances and a two-time winner of the Romance Writers of America RITA® Award, Laura lives in the Northwest US with her husband and two diva cats. Laura loves hearing from readers, and you can contact her at:

LauraLeeGuhrke.com
Facebook/LauraLeeGuhrkeAuthor
Instagram @Laura_Lee_Guhrke
X @LauraLeeGuhrke